# No Way to Live

## A Chuck McCain Novel

Book Six

David Spell

This is a work of fiction. Any similarities to events or persons, living, dead, or fictitious are purely coincidental. Some actual locations are used in a fictitious way and the descriptions included here are not meant to be accurate. No part of this publication can be reproduced or transmitted in any form or by any means, electronic or mechanical, without permission in writing from the author.



DavidSpell.com



ISBN: 9798325345609

Imprint: Independently published

Back cover image courtesy of azerbaijan_stockers on Freepik

For the Victims

# Author's Note

This is a work of fiction. It's a story, a novel, written to entertain. However, it is important to note that all good fiction also carries a message or lesson within its pages. *No Way to Live* is no exception. I've written about the Mexican Cartels in several of my novels because they are real, powerful, and do control so much of the criminal activity in America, as well as their own turf of Mexico. Shockingly, law enforcement estimates suggest that a staggering 90% of cocaine entering the U.S. does so through the Southern Border, utilizing one of the many cartels' pipelines.

In *No Way to Live*, the focus shifts to one of the other primary revenue streams of these cartels— human trafficking. Drawing from personal experience as a former police officer in the Metro-Atlanta area, I have witnessed firsthand the horrors of trafficking operations orchestrated by various criminal groups, including both Asian and Mexican gangs. The women we rescued from these locations were trapped in a cycle of debt bondage, mirroring the harrowing tales depicted in this novel. They were slaves to the gangsters and would remain so until their debt was paid off. Many of the details portrayed in these pages are rooted in reality, shedding light on uncomfortable truths that society often shies away from discussing.

As a father, and now a grandfather, recounting the plight of children caught in the web of human trafficking was particularly challenging. The alarming rise in the trafficking of minors, exacerbated by the open border policy of our government, underscores the urgency of addressing this issue. The influx of thousands of, "unaccompanied minors" into the country, as portrayed in the media, is a stark reminder of the exploitation and abuse faced by vulnerable children, teenagers, and adults.

Through *No Way to Live*, my intention is not only to captivate and entertain readers, but also to illuminate the darkness that shrouds these heinous crimes. It is my fervent hope and prayer that this novel serves as a catalyst for awareness and action against the evils that lurk in the shadows.

David Spell

"Rescue the weak and the needy; deliver them from the hand of the wicked."

Psalm 82:4

"If slavery is not wrong, then nothing is wrong." Abraham Lincoln

"We tend to think of human trafficking as a foreign issue, not something that could happen here in our own back yards. But it's a fast-growing problem in the United States, in every area, with no real defined demographic." Lori Foster

"What we do see is that the trafficking of children is becoming an income revenue stream for organized crime, for gangs. So where they would typically be selling guns and drugs, they're now turning to the selling of children."

Dalia Racine

"Human trafficking is a multi-billion dollar growth industry because, unlike drugs, which are gone as soon as they are used, humans can be recycled. Because they can continue to be exploited, they're a better investment for traffickers." Terry Coonan

# Chapter One

**Sterling, Virginia, Monday, 0425 hours**

The lights on the white box truck went off as it turned onto Potomac Hill Square from Rock Hill Road and slowed to a stop in the dark parking area, several of the street lights in need of replacement. Potomac Hill formed a horseshoe, encircling the lower-income townhome community. The target building was just a hundred feet away, around the curve. One of the heavily armed men in the rear slowly pulled the sliding door open for the tactical team to quietly let themselves out. Five blacked-out unmarked police vehicles joined them, parking nearby and disgorging a squad of Loudon County narcotics investigators.

Chuck McCain nodded at the new arrivals as everyone circled around him.

"We'll let you get in place," he said softly, addressing Detective Sergeant Dwayne Thomas and his team. "Everyone knows where they need to be. Scotty will smash the door at 0445. Make sure you've got someone covering the backdoor, just in case one of them tries to slip out. I'll let you know as soon as we have it locked down so you guys can come start your search."

Thomas gave a slight smile. "We'll be ready."

Dwayne and his team had been working this case for months and the detectives all felt the tingle of excitement that their hard work and long hours were about to pay off. McCain pointed to Gabriella Vargas and Century's newest employee, Walker "Tex" Davis. Walker had driven the truck and both he and Vargas were kitted out like the rest of Chuck's entry team.

"You two are our backup. Set up across from the target and if we get in trouble, I'll call you to come running."

Gabby grinned. "Got it."

Tex nodded as he stuffed a pouch of Skoal between his cheek and gum. "Sounds like a plan."

Chuck glanced at Thomas. "And if the shit really hits the fan, Sarge, y'all are the next level of backup."

The sergeant gave the big man a thumbs up and the eight narcotics detectives moved into the shadows. The wore their normal casual attire with the addition of heavy body armor, tactical thigh holsters, ballistic helmets and AR-15 rifles. Their armor had "Deputy Sheriff" displayed in yellow letters on the front and back. These five men and three women would provide a perimeter around the townhome while Chuck and his tactical team made entry. Vargas and Davis followed them to get into position, as well.

Another police car whipped into the complex, this one a marked cruiser containing the shift commander, Lieutenant Jake Donaldson.

"Sorry I'm late," he said, stepping into the circle of Chuck's entry team. "Do y'all need anything?"

"I think we're good, LT," McCain answered. "Dwayne's team just left to set up. We will need a couple of marked units for transport in a little while."

"I'll take care of that. Y'all be careful."

While McCain's team executed a search warrant at their location, the actual Loudon County Sheriff's Department SWAT team would be hitting another address in nearby Dulles. Both locations were connected to the Jalisco New Generation Cartel out of Mexico. After more than three months of digging and putting the puzzle pieces together, the narcotics detectives finally had enough evidence to obtain search warrants. They expected to find narcotics, weapons and, if they were lucky, the NG gang leader for Northern Virginia and beyond, Ramon "Asesino" Contreras.

Killer Contreras had earned his moniker during his rise through the ranks of the New Generation, both in Mexico and the US, as one of their most ruthless sicarios. Now in his mid-forties, he was making the move into more of a management position in the crime family. At the same time, all of his colleagues understood that el Asesino was never afraid to use violence to exert his will. The detectives had multiple arrest warrants for Contreras whenever they located him. The search warrants at the two locales needed to be executed simultaneously to prevent the criminals from notifying their comrades that the police were on the way.

Between Thomas' two squads of investigators, the one in Sterling and the one in Dulles, they were hoping to arrest Contreras tonight and put the NG Cartel out of business in Northern Virginia. Loudon County Sheriff Jerry Schaefer had personally asked for Chuck's assistance in serving these warrants. McCain and his team held reserve deputy status within the agency in exchange for providing ongoing firearms training for the entire department, SWAT training, and yearly qualifications for the sheriff's department through Century Tactical Solutions where Chuck served as the vice-president, along with his team members, who served as instructors.

Like every other law enforcement agency in America, Loudon County was struggling to keep its ranks full. They were receiving fewer and fewer qualified applicants to replace the many deputies who were retiring or leaving for the private sector. The "Defund the Police" movement had sent thousands of good police officers around the nation in search of a new career. Loudon County was almost two hundred deputies short and the SWAT team was one of the casualties, with a number of the experienced tactical officers moving on to federal law enforcement or the private security sector.

A few years earlier, Loudon County's SWAT team could have easily handled simultaneous operations. Now, they only had the manpower to hit one target at a time. Normally, the sheriff would've hesitated at having reserve deputies involved in serving a high-risk search warrant. McCain and his team, however, had years of real-world experience in both the law-enforcement and military special operations arenas. While having no rank within the SO, Chuck had retired as a lieutenant from a large metro-Atlanta police agency after twenty years of service, most of those as a member and team leader on the SWAT team.

After retiring, McCain had taken two one-year contracts in Afghanistan as a law-enforcement advisor to an Army Special Forces A-Team. There, he had honed his tactical skills as he learned from some of the best operators in the world in a hostile environment. After returning to the United States,

Chuck had been recruited as one of the first CDC Enforcement Officers just before the Iranians had launched the bio-terror weapon known as the zombie virus. Chuck and his team of warriors had tracked down and arrested or eliminated many of the terrorists responsible, as well as killing hundreds of the infected.

Now, he and his friends were training SWAT and small military units all over America in the CQB tactics that they had perfected during the zombie crisis. Sheriff Schaefer and retired Major General Wallace Perkins, the president and CEO of Century, were close friends. By providing reserve deputy credentials in exchange for the tactical expertise that Century provided, it was a win-win situation for everyone.

What only a select few knew, however, was that McCain and his squad also frequently took contract jobs for the CIA when the Agency needed deniability. In most of those assignments, taking prisoners was not always a priority. Tonight, they were operating as cops again and would have to abide by not only state and federal law, but also the sheriff's departmental policy.

Former Army Ranger sniper Scotty Smith led the entry team through the parking lot, using parked cars for cover until they were in front of the target location. He glanced around, picking out Gabby and Tex standing behind a parked van, opposite of the NG's stash house. Smith carried the thirty-pound metal ram and was followed by former MARSOC Marine and McCain's assistant team leader, Andy Fleming, who carried the ballistic shield. Chuck was next, armed with his suppressed H&K 416 rifle. Rafael "Hollywood" Estrada followed McCain, also carrying an H&K. Hollywood would be the team's translator and had another former Marine, Jimmy Jones, following him with a Mossberg .12 gauge Taser X12 LLS shotgun. Chloe Wilkerson would be bringing up the rear, armed with her 9mm Glock 17 pistol. Each of the team members wore olive green BDUs with heavy body armor and ballistic helmets containing their night-vision devices.

The former Ranger made eye contact with McCain who motioned towards the front door, where the team quickly lined up to the right of the entrance. They could hear the television playing inside with what sounded like a porn movie. At the end of the stack, Wilkerson visually confirmed that her teammates were in place. She then reached up and gave Jones a squeeze on the shoulder. Jimmy repeated the movement on Hollywood, who squeezed Chuck's deltoid. McCain kept it going, letting Fleming know it was time. Instead of stretching to reach Smith's shoulder, Andy squeezed the back of Scotty's right thigh.

"Stand by," Chuck whispered to his team. He pushed the transmit button on his radio. "Tac 2 to all units, we're executing now," he quietly told the dispatcher and the detectives manning the perimeter.

At that, the tall, muscular bearded man stepped out of line and up to the door, slamming the ram near the handle and deadbolt. Rather than bursting open under Smith's legendary strength, the door buckled but remained closed. Without hesitation, Scotty brought the heavy metal ram back and drove it into the door again. This time, the frame shattered and the metal door flew inward.

Andy darted into the room, the ballistic shield up, his 9mm Glock 17 aimed around the right edge, the rest of the team following him inside, with Scotty now bringing up the rear, the ram left behind and his H&K 416 up and ready.

"Sheriff's Department! Search warrant! Everyone get down on the floor!" Hollywood yelled in both English and Spanish.

They had studied the floorplan of the condominiums in the complex and understood the layout. Normally, they would have tossed in a flash bang grenade or two before rushing in. As McCain and the tactical team developed their entry and movement plan earlier, the non-lethal grenades were ruled out. With this being a known drug house, they didn't know if the suspects were storing chemicals for cooking meth or crack at the location. The last thing the deputies wanted to do was to blow themselves up, along with the entire block.

A staircase was to the right of the front door, with a living room just inside to the left, and a kitchen and dining area on back side of residence. A New Generation gang member had fallen asleep on the couch with the Playboy Channel showing on the television. The disoriented thug rolled off the couch, trying to fasten his jeans. Chloe quickly moved in, dropping a knee into the gangster's back, jerking his arms behind him and securing his hands with flex cuffs as Scotty covered her. A 9mm Beretta 92 pistol lay on the end table where the perp had just been lying.

Andy, Chuck, Hollywood, and Jimmy moved up the stairs with Fleming leading them towards the second level, the heavy shield up and ready if needed. The three bedrooms were all to their left when they reached the top of the landing. McCain reached around Fleming and tried the first door they came to.

Locked. Without hesitation, he kicked the flimsy door, smashing it open.

A long-haired, shirtless and heavily tatted figure stood at an open window on the other side of the bedroom. He glanced over his shoulder at the deputies and then swung a leg through the opening, trying to make his escape. Chuck charged across the room as Andy covered him. The team leader grabbed a handful of the suspect's hair and jerked him backwards, slamming the suspect facedown on the floor. The Mexican reacted quickly, pushing himself to his knees before McCain could secure him. As the reserve deputy moved to take the thug's back, the suspect reached for Chuck's holstered Glock, trying to rip it from the holster.

During his first law enforcement career in Atlanta, McCain had also enjoyed a part-time career as a professional MMA fighter, compiling a 10-4 record around the Southeast. Even now in his late-forties, he still trained regularly and was able to shift his gun side away as he controlled the perp's head. He quickly transitioned to a standing guillotine choke, rendering the thug unconscious in seconds and ending the fight. Chuck lowered him to the floor and handcuffed and searched the suspect, instinctively reaching for his own right cargo pocket before stopping himself.

While working with the Special Forces in Afghanistan and in many of the missions he had conducted on behalf of the CIA, suspects' heads were normally covered with a hood after they were secured. This was to keep them disoriented and to prevent them from identifying those who had snatched them. Hooding suspects, even violent cartel members, however, would be frowned upon in American courtrooms.

Down the hallway, a voice yelled out profanities in English and Spanish as Hollywood told a gang member to get his hands up. He had somehow slept through the tactical team's tumultuous entry, a television in his room showing a soccer match.

"You gonna to shoot me, pig?"

"If you insist," Jimmy said calmly.

The pop of his Taser shotgun was followed by a scream as the projectile struck the perp in the abdomen and the electrical charge briefly incapacitated him. Chuck turned his attention back to his own prisoner, taking the time to glance around the room. An AK-47 stood against the wall, next to the bed the perp had been sleeping in. A .40 caliber Smith & Wesson M&P pistol lay on the bedside table. I wonder why he didn't grab a weapon? He was definitely much more concerned about escaping.

McCain rolled the suspect over to get a good look at his face as he started to come around. Wow! We hit the jackpot, he realized, recognizing Ramon Contreras from the photos they had studied. The two tactical teams had both hoped they would be the ones to capture the cartel lieutenant. We get bragging rights tonight, he thought.

He left the perp on the floor and motioned to Andy, who was still covering him. Chuck pointed at the closet even as he heard Hollywood and Jimmy advising that the rest of the upstairs was clear. Chuck carefully opened the closet door, careful not to silhouette himself in the doorway. He activated the rail mounted flashlight on his rifle, noting the kilo packages stacked inside. Several AR-15s, AKs, and shotguns stood in the corner next to the drugs. The only question was what kind of drugs? That would be for the narcotics detectives to determine when they conducted their search.

"Holy shit!" Jimmy Jones voiced carried from further down the short corridor. "We're still clear up here but there's a whole lot of dope and guns in this back room."

"We still need to go clear downstairs," Andy reminded everyone. "Jimmy, can you watch the bad guys for a couple?"

"10-4," he answered, dragging his own restrained suspect to where Contreras was starting to stir after having been out for a little while.

Scotty and Chloe were still in place at the bottom of the stairs, covering the short walkway that led to the rear of the condo, the first perp still facedown where the powerfully built African-American woman had left him. With McCain and Fleming providing security, Smith and Wilkerson quickly checked the rest of the home, declaring it secure.

"Tac 2 to dispatch, residence is secure. We've got three in custody."

"10-4, Tac 2," the Loudon County dispatcher acknowledged.

Across the parking lot, Davis and Vargas both visibly relaxed after hearing McCain's radio traffic.

"I've got a question for you," Gabby said, glancing at her partner.

"Shoot," Tex replied, a heavy drawl in his voice. He spat off to the side.

"What made you leave APD? Chuck said Atlanta has a really good SWAT team. Weren't you in charge?"

Davis was an athletic five feet, eleven inches tall. His face had the weathered look of a man who spent a lot of time outdoors. Vargas thought he would've looked right at home on the back of a horse, herding cattle. Walker had only been with Century Tactical Solutions for a couple of months.

"Chuck would know," he answered. "Century came down and ran the team through a week of advanced training a couple of years ago. Chuck, Andy, and Jimmy taught the class. That was a great course. I became SWAT Commander not long after that. The first time I met Chuck, though, was back when the Zs took over Atlanta. Him and that retired FBI agent who does some work for Century..."

"Thomas Burns?"

"Yeah, him. He was in charge of trying to stop the Zs but he was smart enough to know he was in over his head. He asked McCain to come up with a way to slow the zombies down as they moved up I-75. Chuck was over the Atlanta CDC Enforcement Unit at the time and he put together a good plan, but there was no way we were going to stop them. There were just too many of those nasty things, but we at least thinned them out and slowed them down a little.

"While we were fighting the Zs coming north on I-75, three terrorists hit the command post— two suicide bombers and another asshole shooting at us with an AK." Davis shook his head as he remembered that day. "McCain took out one of the suicide bombers and one of his agents was killed taking out the other. Atlanta lost over half of their SWAT team and it was a miracle that any of us got out of there alive. I lost a lot of friends that day."

He paused and Gabby wondered if Tex was going to say anymore. After a moment, he spit again and looked over at her.

"Were you a cop or military?"

She smiled. "No, my thing has always been computers."

Davis raised an eyebrow in surprise. "Computers, huh? Sounds like there's a story there. I've seen you in the shoot house and I would've thought you'd been a hardcore operator for years. You're really good. But back to your question, there's a lot of politics in law enforcement. I got asked to lie about something and I said, 'No.' Once a man violates his own code of honor, what does he really have left? Anyway, once I told the major and the assistant chief to go...well, never mind what I told them, but my career was over. I had to leave after that and thankfully Century was hiring."

Gabby nodded, glowing inwardly at Tex's kind words about her tactical skills. She decided not to probe any deeper into what was clearly a sensitive area. From what she had seen, he was a great fit with the rest of the Century team.

"So, what part of Texas are you from?"

This elicited a laugh. "I'm not. I'm from Greenville, South Carolina. People started calling me 'Tex' in the 90's after that TV show, 'Walker, Texas Ranger.'"

Chuck exited the condominium, followed by the rest of the team. Gabby and Tex started towards them.

The young woman grinned. "I've never met anyone from South Carolina named Tex. Welcome aboard."

Sergeant Thomas and Lieutenant Donaldson both cleared on the radio traffic and joined McCain in front of the town home, other residents now peering out their windows at the police activity. Tex and Gabby walked up as Chuck gave a quick breakdown on what had happened and what they had seen inside. As the narc detectives entered the residence to start their search, the tactical officers hustled the three suspects outside and into three marked SO vehicles. Andy escorted Contreras, who slowed as he passed Chuck, recognition in his eyes. He spat in McCain's direction.

"You assault me, cop! You hit me with your rifle. I need doctor. I sue you, pig!"

Fleming held the perp's right arm with his left hand. He reached behind the cartel leader and grabbed one of his little fingers and applied slight pressure causing the gangster to grunt in pain and come up on his toes.

"Keep walking," the former Marine growled. "He didn't need to hit you with his rifle. He choked you out and put you to sleep."

Ramon winced as he glanced over his shoulder towards McCain.

"Next time I see you, pig, things are gonna to be different. Asshole!"

Andy increased the pressure on the suspect's finger, steering him towards the cruiser.

"Nice guy," the lieutenant commented.

Chuck shrugged. "The sarge told me he's got no bond on any of his warrants, plus they'll tack on more charges for all the drugs and guns in the townhouse. I doubt Killer Contreras will ever walk the streets again as a free man."

**Century Tactical Solutions, Leesburg, Virginia, Monday, 1125 hours**

The detectives at the Sterling raid had recovered a hundred kilos of narcotics— fifty of meth and fifty of crack, along with ten stolen National Guard M4 rifles, six AK-47s, and an assortment of shotguns and pistols. The SWAT team's raid in Dulles turned up twenty-five kilos of heroin and twenty-five of meth, gallon-sized ziplock bags of pills, a few more stolen weapons, and two surprised cartel members entrusted with guarding the stash house. McCain finished up his after-action report for their part in the service of the search warrants and emailed it to Lieutenant Jake Donaldson and Sergeant Thomas.

This was a big blow to the Jalisco New Generation Cartel. Taking a hundred and fifty kilos out of their pipeline was a lot of money. Of course, they would continue to funnel drugs across the border but this would slow them down a little. A few years earlier, Chuck and his team had staged an unauthorized over-the-border raid into Matamoros, Mexico against the NG gang. The leader of the crime family at that time was Vincente Villarreal and the cartel had been contracted to send a team of sicarios into the United States to assassinate the CIA's director of operations, Sandra Dunning.

The attack had left Sandra paralyzed from the waist down and forced her out of the Agency. Dunning was now the VP of Intelligence and Investigations for Century. She brought with her a lifetime of experience from the Agency and had created a highly sought-after team who conducted private investigations, intelligence gathering and even training.

Retired FBI agent Thomas Burns was one of the key players in Century's I & I section.

McCain's incursion into Mexico had gone better than they had hoped for. The team had killed a number of NG soldiers, blown up a drug operation in the middle of the city, captured Villarreal, burned his house down, and smuggled the gangster back across the border into America. The FBI had taken custody of the cartel leader and he was currently serving a life without parole sentence in a maximum-security prison in the United States. It had taken the New Generation almost a year to get back on track. They were now as powerful as ever.

The NG's main competitors in Mexico and in the US are the Sinaloa Cartel. The NG had actually been a break-off faction from the Sinaloas and there was plenty of bad blood between the two groups. Less than a year earlier, Chuck's squad had been a part of a joint mission with the Mexican National Guard to serve American federal arrest warrants on Sinaloa leader, Javier Guillén, and the Iranian terrorist who was working to recreate the zombie virus. Both men were killed by the task force, along with many other cartel soldiers.

In Northern Virginia, as in many other parts of America, both cartels had established footholds, controlling the drugs and most of the sex trafficking business. The Sinaloa group was the largest and most established in the US and was still functioning, even after Guillén's death. This was due to the strong leadership of Eduardo Sanchez, the Sinaloa lieutenant in charge of the region. Like Contreras, the Sinaloa lieutenant had a list of outstanding warrants, but for the moment, he was doing a good job of staying off of federal and local law enforcement's radar. At least el Asesino was no longer going to be a problem, Chuck thought. The best that the NG lieutenant could hope for was a plea bargain that might send him away for just thirty years as opposed to life without parole.

Getting any kind of a deal would involve some type of cooperation from Contreras and McCain didn't figure Ramon as a snitch. Even if he did cut a deal, the cartel's reach was long and the gangster would die a violent death inside the prison. Chuck's thoughts were interrupted by a rap on his open door.

General Perkins stuck his head in. "Hi Chuck, great job this morning. Sheriff Schaefer is here in the conference room bragging on you and your team."

"The sheriff's here?" McCain queried. "What's up?"

"Could you join us? He has a situation that he's looking for help with."

When they got to the conference room, Sandra Dunning and Chloe Wilkerson were already there, chatting with Schaefer. Two Hispanic men and a frail-looking woman were also seated at the table. One of the strangers had a protective arm around the woman who had obviously been crying. He spoke softly to her in Spanish.

The sheriff grinned as he stood and extended his hand as McCain entered. "Congratulations on this morning, Chuck. The lieutenant told me that was a textbook operation: no one got hurt, bad guys went to jail and we recovered a lot of drugs and stolen guns."

"Thanks, Sheriff. Century's been doing y'all's firearms training for the last few years. At least the deputies can see that we know how to execute in the real world."

Schaefer nodded in agreement. "That's true. Let me introduce Pastor Luis Miranda of the Iglesia Cristiana Transformando Vidas over near Dulles. Pastor, would you introduce your friends?"

"Of course," Miranda stood, answering in excellent English. "Thank you, Sheriff Schaefer, General Perkins and the rest of you for giving us a few minutes of your time." He pointed at the couple. "This is Henrique and Ivonne Sagarra. They are members of my church and have a very serious problem."

The pastor said something in Spanish and the woman pulled a manila folder from her lap, withdrawing an 8x10 photo of a beautiful teenage girl.

"That's their fifteen-year old daughter, Lara," Miranda sighed, making eye contact with each person in the room. "She's in big trouble. She stole money from the cartel and has now disappeared."

Chuck felt his stomach drop. If she ripped off one of the crime families, she had likely been brutalized by a group of the gangsters and her mutilated body dumped in a remote area of rural Virginia.

"Which cartel are we talking about?" Chloe asked. "And why would she think that she could get away with stealing from them?"

Pastor Luis translated the questions for the Sagarras. The woman started crying again, burying her face in her hands.

"Ivonne has a rare blood disease," Miranda replied to Wilkerson. "It's treatable but the medicine is very expensive.

They're not here legally and don't have insurance. Lara started dating a drug dealer at her high school who is connected with the Sinaloa Cartel. Her parents found out about it and were very angry so Lara ran away for a week. When she came home, she gave her mother ten thousand dollars. That was enough for almost a year's worth of the special medicine."

Sandra spoke up for the first time. "Did Henrique and Ivonne know where the money came from?"

The pastor sighed. "Where's a fifteen-year old girl going to get that much money? She told them she'd been saving all her earnings from her job at McDonald's. Of course, they suspected she had stolen it but the medicine was working and Ivonne was finally on the road to recovery."

"Until the Sinaloas come to collect," Chuck commented. "They won't just be happy with punishing the girl. They'll also kill mom and dad to make a point. How did Lara disappear?"

"Maybe two days after she gave her parents the money, they found a note on her bed, telling them the truth. She apologized for putting them in danger but said she just wanted to see her mother get better. The note said she was running away to protect them but didn't give a destination."

Sheriff Schaefer cleared his throat. "This was where the SO got involved. The Sagarras did a walk-in three weeks ago to report Lara as a runaway. The deputy entered her on NCIC but we don't have the manpower to investigate these kinds of cases, especially when it does look like a legit runaway. She's been gone for over a month now.

"Pastor Miranda went with the Sagarras to the phone store where they bought their cell phones. Since they had a copy of the runaway report, the cellular company pinged Lara's phone.

It showed that it was in Atlantic City, but they wouldn't give any more specific of a location than that."

"Did they contact the Atlantic City Police?" Chloe asked.

"I had one of our investigators contact them," Schaefer replied. "Like most other police departments, they're struggling to keep cops on the street. Their chief has been putting detectives back in uniform and they just don't have the resources to devote to a runaway teenager. That's why I came to see the general. He told me a while back that Century had an intelligence and investigations section now. I was hoping that maybe y'all could take a look and see what you can turn up."

Silence hung over the room as the Century employees contemplated what the sheriff was asking. After a few moments, General Perkins spoke to the sheriff, pastor, and the Sagarras.

"Can we have a couple of minutes to talk about this? Why don't you all go grab a cup of coffee down the hall in our break room?"

When it was just him and his fellow Century employees, Perkins spoke up.

"I'd love to hear everyone's thoughts on this."

Sandra Dunning had been in the intelligence business for decades, starting with the CIA towards the end of the Cold War, and working her way up through the ranks. She had been the ops director at the time the New Generation Cartel had launched their attack on her. Two of Sandra's bodyguards had been killed defending her. Dunning was grateful for the opportunity the general had given her as the VP of Intelligence and Investigations at Century Tactical.

"We can take a look," the middle-aged woman spoke up. "We don't have much to work with but that's never stopped us before. If it was one of my girls, I'd want to know something."

Chloe nodded. "I agree. Is she still alive? Dead? I can't even imagine what the Sagarras are going through but maybe we'll get lucky. We know that Atlantic City is a known sex-trafficking hub. If this Lara Sagarra is still alive and in Atlantic City, the Sinaloas may have her working that debt off."

Perkins nodded thoughtfully. "I hadn't even thought of that angle, Chloe."

Chuck was glad he hadn't spoken first. He had been about to say there were several upcoming SWAT and other courses over the next few months and that they really didn't have time to be looking for a wayward teenager who had made some really poor life choices. After his two colleagues had spoken up, though, he realized they were right. He was a father himself and tried to imagine the anguish these people were feeling.

The big man sighed. "Sure. Let's give it a shot. General, how do you want us to handle this?"

Perkins steepled his fingers as he stared at a spot on the wall.

"I don't think they're going to be able to pay us and we do have a full calendar. How about if Sandra, you and your team, work on this for the rest of the week to see what you can come up with? If nothing, we at least gave it our best shot. But, if you turn up anything on this young woman, we'll bring more resources into play with Chuck and the operations side."

"If we can uncover some of the cartel's dirty secrets in Atlantic City," Chuck added, "let's package it and give it to the local cops. We might even be able to get the feds involved if it's big enough. That would keep us off the radar."

"That sounds like a good plan," the general agreed. "Chuck, would you go get our guests?"

McCain went to the break room and brought the sheriff, the pastor and his friends back into the conference room. As the general told them what Century would do, the Sagarras both started crying in appreciation, even after Perkins told them there were no guarantees. Sandra told the couple what type of information that her team would need for them to get started. After lunch, Dunning, Wilkerson and Vargas would start digging.

**Atlantic City, New Jersey, Tuesday, 1310 hours**

Lara Sagarra hurriedly touched up her makeup as the skinny construction worker put his clothes on. Acne covered his face and torso. The young Mexican laborer hadn't said a word. He just gave Ernesto his money, followed Lara into her room, taken off his clothes, done the deed, and was on his way out. The teenage girl forced a smile.

"See you next time, handsome," she purred in Spanish.

The young man paused at the bedroom door, a shy grin on his face.

"Hasta luego," he said quietly as he left.

After hearing the front door open and close, Lara peeked out into the living room. It was empty, except for Ernesto, who was staring at his phone while the television blasted Spanish music videos. Ernesto was in charge of her and Bella Suarez, the other prostitute. The pimp glanced at her, a sneer on his face.

"He left happy and said he'd be back in a couple of days."

Lara didn't answer the man, heading to the kitchen to get something to eat before her next client showed up. So far, Ernesto left the girls alone as long as they did their jobs. Bella's door was closed, indicating that she had a customer. At nineteen, she was a few years older than Lara, having come to the United States via one of the Sinaloa's human smuggling routes.

Like so many women wanting to get a fresh start in America, the gang had promised her free passage and then a menial job inside of the US, telling her she could repay the cartel from her earnings. After making it all the way to New Jersey, Bella was horrified to find that instead of cleaning homes or working with a landscaping crew, she would be forced to sell her body, turning up to twenty tricks a day to pay off her debt to the Sinaloa crime family. If she tried to escape, the cartel would kill her and her family back in Mexico.

Sagarra heated up a plate of beans, rice, and corn tortillas from the refrigerator. As she sat at the small table in the kitchen, she thought of her parents, guilt and shame sweeping over her at what she had done and what she was doing now. Tears sprung up in her eyes and she quickly dabbed at them with a napkin.

At least her mother had the medicine. Did the end justify the means? The young woman felt so dirty, but now her mom would live for many years. Of course, Ivonne had no idea what had happened to her only child. The conflicting emotions left Lara depressed and exhausted.

Bella had given Lara some pills to deaden her pain. They definitely made it easier to endure the hell that her days had become. Both teenagers serviced fifteen to twenty clients a day, each used condom saved and layered between paper towels for Ernesto to count and add to their ledgers at the end of their shift. How many used condoms would it take for Lara to pay off her debt? As her depression lingered, Sagarra knew she needed one of those pills before she saw another client.

She wondered what had happened to the baby-faced Roman. The seventeen-year old boy had fallen in love with her and she had used and manipulated him to steal the money he earned in two weeks, selling drugs at school and at his part-time job at the car wash. The teenage boy looked much younger than his age and no one would have ever suspected him of being the top drug dealer at Loudon County High School.

Roman had been so easy to take advantage of. He bragged to Lara that he met his Sinaloa boss every other Friday night to turn in his earnings and pick up another supply of weed, crack, meth, powder cocaine, and pills. After a romantic rendezvous in the young man's room one Friday after school while his parents were at work, the young woman transferred the bundle of cash from his gym bag into her backpack while Roman was in the bathroom.

She had only kept enough money for a bus ticket to New York. Her dad's sister lived there and Lara planned to go stay with Aunt Alma for a few months until things blew over. Lara had given the rest of the cash to her parents, telling them it had come from her McDonald's earnings. She knew that her parents knew she was lying. At the same time, her dad was able to purchase the medicine for Ivonne and seeing how quickly her mom's energy levels went back up was worth everything to the teenager.

Lara understood that the Sinaloa gang would come for her. If she stayed in Leesburg, she was as good as dead. Sagarra did not think that the gang would come after her parents. They might have in Mexico, but the Sinaloa Cartel had become one of the most powerful criminal organizations in America by staying off the nightly news.

She never made it to New York. Roman called her the next night, after she had gone to bed and told her that he was coming by to pick her up. His boss Eduardo wanted to talk with her. If she tried to flee, her parents would die, Roman warned her. The teenager had left a note on the bed, apologizing to her mom and dad for lying to them, packed a few things in a backpack to make it look like she was running away, and climbed out her window. The terrified young woman didn't expect to live through the night.

Roman ignored Lara's nervous attempts at conversation as he drove her to a split-level home in Fairfax and walked her inside. Two thugs sat watching a soccer match on television, but at the sight of the teenage girl, their eyes hungrily worked their way up and down her lithe frame. Lara shuddered, thinking she might throw up.

"Up the stairs, first door on the right," Roman said coldly, joining the other two men on the couch.

Lara started to ask Roman to go with her but he had pointedly turned his back to her. He knows I was just using him to get the money, she realized. He must hate me now. What have I done?

The young woman slowly managed to put one foot in front of the other and found herself standing in front of the closed door. She knocked timidly before it was snatched open. The regional director for the Sinaloa Cartel, Eduardo Sanchez, glared at her. He wore a white wife-beater, jeans, and several gold chains. The gangster was heavily muscled, with tattoos covering much of his exposed skin. After a minute, he stepped out of the way and motioned with his head for Lara to enter and then closed the door behind her.

Sagarra glanced around the room, looking for a way of escape. A king-sized bed was against the wall to the right. On the left side of the room, Sanchez had a work space set up with a desk and computer. The gangster seated himself in a leather office chair and rested his arms on the armrests. A big black pistol lay on the desk, just inches from Eduardo's right hand.

"You stole from me."

The thug made the statement quietly, without any emotion but his eyes bore through her.

"I...I'm sorry. My mother's sick and needed medicine."

Lara hung her head as tears began to stream down her cheeks. She was never going to see her parents again.

"I don't give a shit about your mother. You took my money and now you're going to pay me back."

"Please, I'll pay you. Just give..."

"Take your clothes off."

"No, please, I'll get you the money," Lara sobbed, wrapping her arms around herself.

Eduardo stared at her. "I was planning to have you and your parents killed. I have to set an example. I can't have people thinking they can steal from the Sinaloa family and get away with it. Your boyfriend talked me out of killing you."

"Roman?"

The sobs continued to come but she fought to control her emotions.

The thug laughed. "He loved you but you used him. Even now, though, he asked me not to kill you or your parents. Take off your clothes."

Realization dawned on Lara what the gangster wanted. She was shaking, her fingers struggling with her buttons but eventually she stood nude before the man, attempting to cover up as best she could. Eduardo's eyes never left her, watching every move.

"Roman is right. Very beautiful. You're going to work for me and pay off your debt of one hundred thousand dollars."

"I only took ten!" Lara gasped.

"You forgot about the interest, little girl," Sanchez replied with a cruel smile, standing and unfastening his jeans. "Go get in the bed and let's see what you know."

How long had that been? A few weeks? A month? More? When she first arrived in New Jersey, she had hidden her phone at the bottom of her backpack, planning on letting her mom and dad know where she was but Ernesto had found it. The house guard had slapped her a few times and then punched her in the stomach dropping her to the living room floor, gasping for breath.

"No phones! You try to contact anybody, I'll kill you and then go visit your mother and father. I saw a photo of your mom on your Facebook page. She still looks pretty good. I'll have some fun with her before I cut her throat."

"I'm sorry," Lara had gasped, tears pouring down her face. "I forgot it was in my backpack. It won't happen again."

Ernesto had pulled her close, putting his face right up against hers. "You do your job and your madre y padre will be fine. You make the men happy. Give them their money's worth and your parents will live a long life. Comprende?"

The sound of the doorbell startled her out of her reverie.

"Lara!" Ernesto called. "Back to work."

**Loudoun County Circuit Court, Leesburg, Virginia, Wednesday, 1050 hours**

"Ramon Contreras," Superior Court Judge Randolph White said from his bench, "your 'not guilty' plea to the charges against you is entered into the record and you are hereby freed on a bond of one hundred thousand dollars. Your attorney, Mr. Hernandez, will communicate with you in regards to the next hearing."

"Thank you, your honor," Hernandez smiled, before leaning over to whisper into the orange jumpsuit-clad suspect's ear. He then looked back at the judge and the Loudon County Deputy standing to the side of the bench. "I have some clothes for Mr. Contreras to change into."

The deputy nodded and took the bag, leading the gangster back into the holding area for him to put his fresh outfit on. The New Generation lieutenant stopped, pausing at the door and slowly turned to make eye contact with Sergeant Dwayne Thomas. A wicked grin spread across the gangster's face and he winked at the detective as the deputy nudged Contreras and told him to keep moving.

The silver-haired judge rapped his gavel and stood, "We'll take a fifteen-minute recess before our next case."

Thomas waited until the judge left before approaching the prosecutor, sitting silently at her table. Several other Loudon County investigators sat in the courtroom in stunned silence at what they had just witnessed.

"See you at the discovery hearing, Deputy," the attorney said with a smirk, picking up his leather briefcase and heading out to wait on his client.

"I don't know what happened, Dwayne," Linda Hurst said, continuing to stare straight ahead. "I've never seen bond given on those kinds of charges. Never. Contreras' attorney filed a motion for bond late yesterday afternoon, but I just assumed the judge would deny it. Another superior court judge issued the original warrants so Judge White will have to show cause for why he modified them. He could be censured by the bar for this."

Hurst was one of the Assistant Commonwealth Attorneys that Thomas had worked with many times before. The Commonwealth Attorney's Office functions like the District Attorney in other states. She had graduated from the George Washington University Law School seven years earlier and had shown herself to be an excellent prosecutor.

"We recovered a hundred and fifty keys of meth, crack, and heroin, bags of pills and a bunch of stolen guns. Contreras was already wanted for conspiracy, trafficking, possession with intent, and aggravated assault for stabbing some guy in a bar last year. Our homicide detectives say that he's the prime suspect in at least two murders. He's running a large chapter of the Jalisco New Generation Cartel here in Virginia. You know he's going to jump bond."

The prosecutor shrugged. "I don't know what to say, but I'll ask the judge about it. Commonwealth Attorney Franklin is going to be pissed, as well."

Back in his chambers, Judge White sat at his desk, holding his head in his hands. The plain white envelope lay in front of him. It had been dropped off at the information desk at the courthouse early that morning by courier with his name printed on the outside.

Inside the envelope was a photo of his five-year old granddaughter, Lucy, swinging at her pre-k playground, a joyous smile on her face. A three-by-five index card accompanied the photo. A single sentence had been written in block letters. "RELEASE CONTRERAS ON $100,000 BOND."

The motion requesting bail had come in at closing time the previous day but the judge had stayed late to study it, fully intending to deny it. The charges against Ramon Contreras were serious and there was no legal reason to set him free on bail. The snapshot of Lucy and the cryptic note that morning had changed everything. White understood that his decision would be questioned and he knew he would face serious consequences for his actions. At the same time, he kept up with the news and had read story after story of the cartels killing judges, prosecutors, police officers, and their families in Mexico.

If the Jalisco New Generation Cartel in Virginia had already tracked down where his granddaughter went to school, they surely knew where he and his entire family lived. The judge had considered calling Sheriff Schaefer and reporting the incident. The sheriff's department was responsible for security at the courthouse and investigating any threats against the judiciary. White had just as quickly decided against involving the authorities. Would they really be able to protect him and his loved ones?

No, I'm going to have to face the consequences of my decision. He still had two years left in his four-year term. I could always step down early and retire, he thought. A knock at the door startled the judge, his right hand reaching for the drawer where he kept the 9mm Sig Sauer P365. No one was supposed to have a firearm inside the courthouse except the Loudon County Deputies who worked there. As a superior court judge, however, he was exempt from passing through the metal detector every morning.

"Yes?" he said, his hand wrapping around the pistol inside the drawer.

The door opened and prosecutor Linda Hurst stuck her head in.

"Hi Judge, can I have a minute before we get started again?"

White sighed with relief and closed the drawer, motioning the Assistant Commonwealth Attorney in.

"Sure, Linda, have a seat. What can I do for you?"

"Well, Sergeant Thomas and his detectives were pretty upset about you giving Ramon Contreras bail, especially since Judge Cowart had specified that he was a flight and public safety risk and specified no bond."

The prosecutor watched White closely as he removed his glasses and rubbed his eyes. He was clearly troubled and didn't answer her immediately. Something caught his attention on the desk and he slid a manila folder over what looked like a white envelope and a photograph.

"I have no doubt that Judge Cowart had good reasons for not setting bail but after reviewing the charges and the police report, I felt that justice was better served releasing the defendant on a large cash bond. His attorney assured me that Mr. Contreras is not going anywhere. Now, if you'll excuse me..."

"Sergeant Thomas said that Mr. Contreras is the prime suspect in two on-going murder investigations and their intel says that he's the regional lieutenant for the New Generation Cartel..."

"Ms. Hurst, there are other cases on today's calendar and we need to get back to work. When, and if, Mr. Contreras is charged with additional crimes, we'll take those under consideration to discuss revoking the bond that I set this morning. He is still presumed innocent until proven guilty."

With that, Judge White stood and walked over to the small lavatory attached to his chambers, went inside and shut the door. Linda sat for a moment before standing to leave. She glanced over at the restroom door confirming that it was closed and then reached across the judge's desk, sliding the folder to the side, revealing a photo of White's granddaughter at a playground and an index card with "RELEASE CONTRERAS ON $100,000 BOND," printed on it. A toilet flushed and the prosecutor quickly rearranged things as she found them before hurrying out of the judge's office and closing the door behind her.

### West of Haymarket, Virginia, Wednesday, 1615 hours

Chuck wheeled his Chevrolet Silverado onto the gravel driveway and followed it around to where construction crews were hard at work building five homes, each on its own three-acre lot. The entire fifty-acre tract of land had belonged to Josh Matthews. He and Chuck had been close friends, having served together on the same Metro-Atlanta SWAT team before McCain took early retirement to serve as a contractor with a Special Forces team in Afghanistan.

The two men had reconnected during the zombie crisis when Chuck's CDC tactical unit was called in after the bio-terror weapon had been released in one of suburban Atlanta's biggest high schools. Josh's SWAT team had been overrun and he had been one of the few survivors in their attempt to rescue students, teachers, and even parents as the walking dead walked the halls of the school.

A couple of years later, as the zombie crisis was finally being brought under control, McCain had gone to work for the CIA in the operations directorate as an assistant director while the Agency attempted to rebuild after the devastation wrought by the bio-terror attack. Matthews joined his mentor at the Agency and eventually followed him to Century Tactical Solutions as an adjunct SWAT instructor.

Sadly, Josh had died during a terrorist attack in Trenton, New Jersey. He and Hollywood Estrada were there to conduct a week-long tactical course but when suicide bombers launched themselves at the courthouse, the two warriors threw themselves into the fray eliminating three of the remaining terrorists before they could kill even more innocent people. Matthews was murdered when the last suicide bomber was able to detonate his vest after Josh shot and wounded him.

The rural piece of land had been in the Matthews' family for years but before his death, he had divided it up and sold three-acre lots to five of his friends so that they could all live near each other. The plan was to leave over half of the property undeveloped so that they would have a place to hunt close to home. The Bull Run Mountains Natural Area Preserve backed up to the property and Josh had hunted the area for years.

A couple of years after his death, Josh's friends had finally started to build their homes. They had found a builder who had been willing to take on the project for them and the houses were starting to take shape. Chuck, Andy, and Scotty, along with Tu Trang Donaldson, and Eric Gray were stopping by regularly to check the progress. Donaldson and Gray both worked full-time for the CIA— Tu as a team leader in the operations directorate and Eric as one of Ops Director Colonel Kevin Clark's protection detail.

The McCain's four-year old son, Ray, had chatted almost non-stop for the entire drive from Reston, finally falling asleep as his dad got off of I-66 for the last few miles. Chuck left the windows down as he and Beth exited quietly to stare at their dream home. The exterior of the single-story house was the classic, all-American red brick. The construction crew had just finished painting the interior and left early to allow the paint to dry.

As the big man strolled towards the front door, he realized Elizabeth was still standing by the truck staring at the front of their new home. He walked back over to where she was, thinking she had spotted something wrong.

"What's the matter?" he asked, his trained eyes scanning the exterior of the structure.

It was then that he realized his wife was crying. He quickly put an arm around her shoulders.

"What's wrong? Did they mess something up?"

Beth laughed, wiping the tears from her eyes. "Nothing's wrong. It's perfect. Never in a million years did I think we'd get to build our own home out in the country, near our best friends."

Chuck breathed a sigh of relief, always hating it when his wife was sad.

"Come on. Let's take a look inside and see how much they've done. Be careful not to touch anything because the paint is still drying."

After seeing the progress in their own house, they drove around the property to check the others. The homes all had similar floor plans, but also had their own differences according to each family's preferences. One of the features that all the men had insisted on, however, was a safe room. Several years earlier, the Tijuana Cartel had sent sicarios into the United States, specifically targeting McCain, Fleming, and Smith.

Chuck had been slightly wounded but had managed to kill all his attackers. Andy had not been home when his family was attacked. Both his wife and son had taken bullets while managing to kill three of their assailants. Amy and Tyler Fleming had lived but their recoveries had been long and slow. The Smiths had also not been present when their residence was attacked, but the cartel soldiers had burned the row of townhomes to the ground, killing one of their neighbors.

Each of the new houses would be equipped with a well-stocked safe room that would be impervious to all but a direct tornado strike or a rocket propelled grenade. This would provide peace of mind for the warriors that while they were away, their families would be protected while the authorities were enroute.

"It won't be long now," McCain said, as they started to drive away. "I guess we need to start picking out furniture?"

"I already have," Beth smiled. "I've got a pretty good idea of what I want. I'll pull it up on the computer and show it to you when we get home."

Chuck nodded, thrilled that he wouldn't have to go furniture shopping.

"Sounds good to me."

**Outside of Leesburg, Virginia, Thursday, 0235 hours**

Ramon "Asesino" Contreras climbed out of the passenger seat of the silver Nissan Altima. The other two carloads of New Generation soldiers were waiting for him at the end of a deserted gravel road off Highway 662, west of the city. The eight gangsters were thrilled to see the Assassin, shaking his hand, hugging, and patting him on the back.

Contreras pointed at one of the men, a tall Mexican with short hair.

"Good work, Andres, getting that photo of the judge's grandkid. He looked like he had seen a ghost when he came into the courtroom."

Andres grinned. "I also found his house and his daughter and son-in-law's. If he changes his mind, we can go pay them a visit. What about the other guys? Will they be released, too?"

"Maybe, but I don't think so. The lawyer filed a motion for them, too, but they were all on probation and that automatically means no bond."

"So, we gonna have some fun tonight, Ramon?" Victor asked.

Victor had driven Contreras to meet up with the others. He and Andres were known throughout the NG gang as two of the most ruthless sicarios in the entire cartel.

"Sí! We're gonna take out the pig who's been investigating us," Ramon said, pulling several sheets of paper from his back pocket and spreading them on hood of the Altima and turning on a small flashlight to illuminate the Google map pages.

"They live two miles from here. There are no neighbors close by so we'll park on the street and sneak in. Kill the cop but keep his wife alive. I saw pictures of her and she's hot. We can take her with us and enjoy her for a while. Whoever kills the pig gets to bang his woman first. This asshole took a lot of things from me, from us. He took over a million dollars worth of drugs and thousands of dollars worth of guns."

El Asesino paused and looked around at his men. "Tonight, we take everything he has."

This elicited nods of approval from the other nine gangsters. They liked the odds. Ten against two.

"We get in fast and don't give them a chance to fight back," Ramon added. "He's a cop but he's just a piece of shit dope detective so he won't be a problem. If we had time, we could kill him slow and let him watch us do his wife. But most Americans have alarms and maybe someone will call in the gunfire. Since this is a pig's house, they'll send a lot of other cops to the alarm so let's make it fast."

"Where are we taking her, Ramon?" one of the gangsters asked.

"The farm. We can stay out of sight for a few days while the cops chase their tails. Then, we bury the bitch and lay low for a while. Vamos!"

# Chapter Two

**Outside of Leesburg, Virginia, Thursday, 0725 hours**

Chuck parked at the end of the long line of marked and unmarked police cars and located the command post in front of Sergeant Dwayne Thomas' house. Lieutenant Jake Donaldson was speaking with Sheriff Schaefer, along with two of his lieutenant colonels and three majors. The house was hidden behind a small patch of woods but uniformed officers, detectives, and CSI personnel were moving purposefully up and down the driveway, their faces grim. Two black hearses were parked just beyond the CP, the drivers clad in dark suits, speaking quietly next to their vehicles until they would be called upon to perform their grisly task.

The sheriff motioned Chuck over as the command staff moved off to check on their respective teams. The big man noticed that Schaefer's eyes were red as if he had been crying.

"Are your people on the way, Chuck?"

"Yes, sir. They should start arriving any time. What happened?"

The sheriff started to speak but lost his voice as he tried to keep from sobbing. "You tell him, Jake."

Donaldson took a deep breath to compose himself. "We got an alarm here at Dwayne and Shelly's house at 0303 hours. The first deputy arrived at 0315. They were dead, both of them."

The lieutenant had to pause a moment to get his own emotions under control.

"The perps kicked in the rear doors from the back deck. It was like a war zone inside. Jake engaged them from the doorway of their bedroom and managed to drop two of the gunmen in the hallway. They look Hispanic but we're waiting to get their fingerprints back. These bastards were heavily armed, Chuck. We found 5.56, .12 gauge, 9mil, and .40 cal casings from the bad guys. They shot the shit out of Jake."

"What about Shelly?" McCain asked, not wanting to hear the answer.

"They killed her, too, but it looks like she also put up one hell of a fight. Her Glock 42 was locked open and there was a lot of blood on the floor of their bedroom. She took a shotgun blast to the face and then it looks like the bastards just emptied their guns into both of them."

"I'm so sorry," Chuck managed to say, feeling as if he'd been punched in the stomach. "Any witnesses or suspects?"

"No witnesses," the lieutenant answered. "The assholes that Jake killed should point the investigators in the right direction. CSI thinks that Shelly shot and wounded at least two others, but forensics will let us know after they test the blood splatter. The detectives are already speculating that this was a New Generation Cartel hit. This sounds exactly like something Ramon Contreras would do."

Sheriff Schaefer cleared his throat. "Chuck, the general told me that you have a lot of experience investigating the cartels. He was a little vague about the circumstances but I was wondering if I can utilize that expertise? We'll be launching a task force today to track these murderers down and bring them to justice. The state police are already here and the FBI even has people on the way to assist. Would you add your team to the mix? I know it's a lot to ask of reserve deputies, but we're going to need all the help we can get."

Chuck took a deep breath. He couldn't tell the two law enforcement officers about his forays into Mexico. He also knew that his group of reserve deputies would not hesitate to do whatever they could to catch Dwayne and Shelly Thomas' murderers.

"Just tell us what you need, Sheriff."

McCain alerted his team and rerouted them to meet at the Loudon County SO's headquarters where he could brief them on the situation and they could develop a strategy. The first task force briefing was scheduled for 1300 hours. His phone vibrated as he climbed back into his truck. He glanced at the screen. News travels fast, he thought.

"Hey, Kevin."

"I just saw the news. I'm sorry, buddy," Colonel Kevin Clark told his friend.

Clark was a retired Army Ranger and currently the director of the Operations Directorate for the CIA.

"Thanks. I didn't know him real well, but he was a good cop. We were with him the other night when we served warrants on a New Generation lieutenant. The guy we arrested is the prime suspect at the moment."

Clark sighed. "Damn cartels. The other reason I called is that I just got an interesting packet of intel on the Sinaloa Cartel's operations in the US."

"Where'd you get that?"

"Your good friend, the Spartan, sent it to Tu on a thumb drive. This is evidently the compilation of all the stuff you guys turned up the last time you were in the neighborhood."

The Spartan was Inspector Sebastian Sandoval of the Guardia Nacional. Because of the rampant corruption in the Mexican Federal Police, they had been disbanded several years earlier with the Mexican National Guard taking over their duties. Sandoval reported directly to the Guard's commander, Comisario General Reyes Luna. The Spartan led a team of hand-selected warriors who took the fight to the cartels inside of Mexico. Earlier in the year, McCain's and Tu Donaldson's teams had linked up with Sandoval to take down the previous leader of the Sinaloa gang, Javier Guillén, along with the inventor of the zombie virus, Iranian terrorist Dr. Ramin Shahriari.

"After you guys left," Clark continued, "General Reyes had his Guard units raid several of Guillén's other properties while the cartel was still reeling. I guess it's taken a while to sift through all of it. This is like a phone book for Sinaloa operations in the US. You've got a good relationship with that senior FBI agent, what's his name?"

"Joe O'Reilly?"

"Yeah, him. You know how the Bureau is when we try to give them intel. Could you and Tu meet with O'Reilly and let him know this is solid information? I was even thinking about having that DEA supervisor you met before the last op in Mexico at the meeting, as well."

"The sheriff just assigned my team to a task force to find these cop killers," McCain replied. "I'm gonna be tied up for a while."

Chuck and Kevin were close friends and McCain knew that the CIA ops director wouldn't ask him for a favor like this unless it was really important.

"Tell you what," Chuck continued. "Have Tu contact me and I'll put a meeting together. If we can get the Bureau and the DEA to thin out these Sinaloa bastards that would be great."

"Thanks, Chuck," Clark replied. "And I know it's not exactly national security related, but if we can help track down your New Generation pukes, let me know."

**Lovettsville, Virginia, Thursday, 1315 hours**

The "farm" that Ramon Contreras had directed his surviving sicarios to was a remote double-wide trailer that sat on five acres of land at the northernmost point of Virginia, with the Potomac River just a hundred yards from the back door. Maryland was on the opposite bank and West Virginia was just nine miles to the west. The location had served as a safe house, as well as a stash house, for the NG cartel for the last year. With access to the river, the gang was able to transport drugs, weapons, and people across into Maryland or both north and south along the waterway, with minimal risk of being caught. The strategic location allowed them easy access into Maryland, West Virginia, and even Pennsylvania.

While he would never admit it to his soldiers, the Assassin regretted his hasty decision to go after that deputy. Yes, they left the pig and his woman shot to pieces but the cost had been very high. They had also left behind the bodies of Victor and Chico. The narcotics sergeant was not the pushover that Ramon had anticipated and his accurate gunfire had killed two of el Asesino's best men. The rest of the sicarios had pumped bullet after bullet into the gringo cop and he finally collapsed to the floor in the doorway of his bedroom.

The pig's wife had not been a helpless victim, either, shooting and wounding Andres and Hector as they stepped over her dead husband into the bedroom where she waited, kneeling on the opposite side of the bed. Even after being wounded, Hector managed to unleash a load of .12 gauge buckshot into the bitch's face. The other sicarios kept shooting until their weapons were empty, the dead couple now full of cartel lead.

Both of the wounded men needed immediate medical attention. Andres was hit in the left forearm and was in a lot of pain. Hector, however, had taken a round to the abdomen and probably wasn't going to make it. He might survive if they could take him to a hospital, but that wasn't an option. One of the woman's bullets had even grazed Ramon's calf but the cartel lieutenant had not even felt it in the heat of combat.

The gangsters did not have much in the way of first-aid supplies at the farm and a couple of Hector's friends sat with him as he lay moaning softly on the living room couch, holding a bath towel over the wound just above his belt line and offering him sips of tequila. Contreras checked on his soldier a few times as they waited for the cartel doctor to arrive. The Assassin noticed that the small hole wasn't bleeding very much. He knew enough to understand that Hector was probably slowly bleeding to death internally.

Andres' arm continued to bleed, the .380 bullet having struck him at about the mid-way point on the outside of his left forearm. The sicario was a tough hombre, though, and had wrapped the appendage with an old white t-shirt and sat at the kitchen table drinking beer and smoking the joint his friends were passing around.

Since a hospital emergency room was out of the question, Ramon texted Miguel, one of his trusted associates in Arlington, to gather some reinforcements and join them. Miguel was also instructed to bring along Dr. Perez. The doctor served at an inner-city clinic in a predominantly Hispanic area of Washington, D.C., but was on retainer for the NG Cartel. Perez had removed bullets from the gangsters and sewn them up on numerous occasions.

It had taken Miguel some time to gather the troops and the doctor at that early hour and even after getting them all together, it took over two hours for them to drive to the farm in the heavy Metro-DC traffic. Dr. Perez and the seven NG soldiers arrived in an extended cab Ford pickup and a Toyota Corolla. The doctor immediately examined Hector, who lay unmoving on the couch, his breathing becoming shallower.

"You assholes gave him tequila?" the doctor exploded, looking around at the gangsters taking care of Hector. "He's been shot in the gut. The worst thing you can do is give him something to drink, especially booze!"

Perez pulled on a pair of latex gloves and spent fifteen minutes probing the hole in Hector's abdomen as the wounded man moaned in pain. The doctor finally sighed and reached into his bag, withdrawing a loaded syringe, and sticking it into the arm of his patient. Within seconds, Hector stopped groaning and lay still.

"Is he dead?" Contreras asked quietly.

"He will be soon. That's a bad wound. I don't know if they could have saved him at a hospital. He's bleeding out internally. I just gave him a shot of morphine that'll let him go quietly."

The gangster nodded. "He was a good soldier. You check Andres now?"

Perez picked up his bag and joined the other wounded man at the table. Andres declined anything to numb the arm, choosing instead to hold onto a bottle of Don Julio tequila, taking a big swallow every few minutes as the doctor probed his forearm in an attempt to remove the projectile. Several of the gangsters held Andres' arm in position so that the doctor could work.

Ten minutes later, Perez dropped a bloody, deformed .380 caliber bullet onto the table. Andres picked it up with his good hand and examined it before passing it around and sucking down more tequila.

"That bitch! I'm glad Hector shot her in the face!"

Perez gave the wound a thorough cleaning before pumping in a healthy dose of antibiotics, sewing it up, bandaging it, and applying a splint.

"The bullet was up against your forearm bone," the doctor said. "It's broken but there's no way to tell how bad without an

X-ray. The splint will help it to heal but there's no guarantee that you're not going to have problems with it. It's a good thing you're right-handed."

The doctor then examined the slash on Contreras' left calf. It wasn't deep and in just a few minutes, Perez had cleaned and bandaged the wound.

"Hey, Ramon! Somebody's coming!" Miguel shouted, staring out the front window and drawing a pistol from under his shirt.

The gang members all grabbed their weapons and moved to where they could peer outside, expecting to see police cars. Instead, a white full size GMC van, followed by a black Nissan Frontier quad-cab pickup rolled down the driveway, stopping behind the other vehicles parked outside. Two men warily exited the van, followed by the four in the pickup, each of them armed with a handgun.

"What the hell?" Ramon muttered as he peeked outside, pointing at the obese man who had been riding in the passenger seat of the van. "That's Chilo."

Alberto "Chilo" Barajas was the New Generation lieutenant responsible for Maryland, New Jersey, and Pennsylvania. The nickname came from the large lips that protruded from his puffy face. His fat frame had caused more than one opposing cartel member to let their guard down. The hefty man moved surprisingly well for someone tipping the scales at over three-hundred pounds. He was known for his blade skills, but was also not afraid to pull the trigger on the FN Five-Seven pistol he held in his beefy hand.

The new arrivals hovered near their vehicles assessing the situation. They had clearly not expected anyone to be at the safe house. Ramon certainly wasn't expecting Alberto to show up. Contreras carefully pulled the front door open a few inches, placing his mouth near the opening.

"Chilo! It's me, Asesino."

The gangsters outside visibly relaxed, but kept their weapons out.

"Hey, Chilo, I'm coming out. Don't shoot, OK?"

With that, Contreras opened the door and stepped out, his hands empty. He had picked up the murdered police officer's 9mm Sig Sauer P-320 but it was now safely tucked into his waistband. Chilo Barajas broke into a grin at the sight of the other NG lieutenant. He put away his own pistol and moved forward to embrace his friend. The two groups were quickly mingling, talking, laughing, and reconnecting.

"I wasn't expecting anyone to be here," Chilo commented, noticing Asesino's limp.

"We just needed a place to hide out for little while."

A knowing smile broke out across the obese man's face. "I heard the news while we were driving. I wondered who the bad ass was who took out that pig and his bitch."

Ramon shrugged. "He was running an investigation on us and had me and a few of the hombres arrested but I got out on bond. Those pigs confiscated a hundred and fifty kilos of our product and a bunch of guns. I decided to pay him a little visit in the middle of the night, but the asshole killed Victor and Chico when we broke into his house. Hector was hit bad. He's inside, probably dead by now. Andres got shot, too, but he's gonna be OK. What are you doing here?"

"It looks like you were also wounded?" Chilo commented, pointing at Asesino's leg.

"Just another scar for the collection," the gangster answered with a smile.

Barajas nodded and pointed at the cargo vehicle. "We've got almost half a million dollars in product heading across the river. You want to see? Come here."

He led the way to the rear of the windowless van. Instead of kilos of meth, cocaine, and heroin stacked inside, however, seven pairs of frightened young eyes blinked in the bright light. Contreras appraised the children with a knowledgeable gaze. Four girls, no older than ten years, two others who were probably in the twelve to thirteen range, and a boy who was about eight. Fast food wrappers were scattered around them. A covered plastic five-gallon bucket sat against the wall, their "toilet" during the road trip. The children's faces showed fear, resignation, and fatigue.

"It won't be long now, my little friends," Chilo smiled broadly at his cargo. "We'll be at your new home in America in a few hours. We'll even get you some more Happy Meals before we get there."

"Por favor, Señor," one of the older girls spoke up, "can we get out?"

"Not yet, chica. You've all done so well on this long trip. Just a little longer."

A tall, thin man wearing a black tank top and slicked back hair appeared at the fat man's side.

"You want me to sit with the kids and keep them company?" he asked, looking into the van and licking his lips.

"Stay away from them, Rodrigo," Barajas growled, looking the man in the eye, as he slammed the door closed.

Rodrigo glared at Chilo before wandering off.

"Very nice, amigo," Ramon commented. "Those girls are hot. Where'd they come from?"

"I think one or two are Mexican, but the rest are from Guatemala. Damn parents sold them to us for a few hundred bucks."

"Where you taking them?"

Alberto laughed. "We've got a couple of houses in a nice area, south of Frederick, near the interstate. Amigo, these rich gringos from DC, Baltimore and other places come to bang one of these kids. The sick bastards pay up to two thousand dollars a visit. I think there's even some politicians in the mix, but I don't care who they are, as long as they bring cash.

"We have to keep rotating the merchandise out to keep them fresh, so we just got back from picking these up at the border in Texas. You ought to think about adding some kids to your brothels, Ramon. I'm telling you, man, these crazy gringos can't get enough!"

"Thanks, amigo. I'll think about it."

"Listen, I may need your help, Asesino. The Sinaloa pricks think they control Maryland but we're taking over. We may end up having to flex our muscles."

"Is that asshole Eduardo Sanchez still in charge?"

Chilo nodded. "Virginia, DC, Maryland, New Jersey. They've got some other hombre they call El Guapo who has the rest of the Northeast."

"El Guapo?" Contreras parroted, a hint of disgust in his voice.

"Yeah, he likes his silk suits and thinks he's a model or something."

"Sure, let me know what you need. The only thing better than killing a cop would be killing some Sinaloa bastards. I may need your help, too."

"Of course, amigo. Are you planning on taking out some more pigs?"

"At least one— a SWAT cop and maybe some of his team. He and his people were the ones who arrested me the other night. I don't know his name yet. He's a big son of a bitch who beat me up after they handcuffed me. I'm waiting on one of my contacts at the sheriff's department to give me his information."

"Ha! This cop took you down by himself?"

"No way! It took five of them to get me handcuffed, but the big one hit me in the head with his rifle and knocked me out. Then the rest of them took turns punching and kicking me, but they're cops so they know how not to leave any marks. The big asshole was in charge and I need to show him what happens when you cross el Asesino and the Jalisco New Generation family."

The obese man held out a fist for a bump from his fellow lieutenant. "Sounds like a good time, Asesino."

"When are you taking your cargo across?"

Chilo glanced at his watch. "After it gets dark. I've got someone meeting us on the other side. I heard from one of my sources inside the Virginia State Police that they just went through some special training on human trafficking and they're looking for any excuse to stop Mexicans on the interstate. It's a longer trip using the back roads, but much safer. Crossing the river here will shave hours off of our trip.

"I'll send out one of my guys to get them some food later. I can't have them showing up looking malnourished," he said with a laugh. "And tell your hombres to keep their hands off the merchandise!"

"If we bundle up Hector in a tarp with some heavy stones, can you dump him in the middle of the river?" Ramon asked.

"Sí, amigo. You get him wrapped up and we'll take care of it."

**Starbucks, Reston, Virginia, Saturday, 0820 hours**

Chuck and Tu Trang Donaldson had arrived twenty minutes earlier to discuss their meeting with the two federal agents. Donaldson had risen to the rank of master sergeant in the Army Special Forces, wearing the coveted green beret. After retiring, he spent several years as a Secret Service Agent before being recruited for the CDC Enforcement Unit, working out of the office in Washington D.C., during the zombie crisis. Tu was now a team leader in the ops directorate for the CIA.

"Have you looked at that intel?" Chuck asked. "Kevin told me that it contains information on most of the Sinaloa's operations in the US."

"It's a lot. I went through some of it," the Vietnamese-American answered, sipping from his coffee. "If the Bureau and DEA will work it, they could put a big dent in that cartel."

A burly man in a rumpled suit, minus the tie, accompanied by a younger, clean-cut Hispanic man wearing glasses approached their table. Chuck and Tu stood to shake Supervisory Special Agent Joe O'Reilly's hand. The G-Man had a perpetual scowl on his face, compounded by a frown as he took a swallow of his coffee.

"Damn," he muttered. "Do people really like this stuff?"

Chuck laughed. "You're drinking it, Joe."

"Yeah, but I'm a cop. I'm supposed to drink shitty coffee."

He nodded to his companion. "Special Agent Carlos Hernandez, meet Tu Donaldson and Chuck McCain. Donaldson works for an Agency that we can't mention and McCain has been around the block a few times, but now spends most of his time training SWAT teams. These are two very dangerous men who love nothing better than dragging our beloved Bureau into their drama."

As they shook hands, Chuck put the young agent in his late-twenties. Hernandez gave McCain and Donaldson a slight smile, but still had not said anything.

"Agent Hernandez is one of our experts on the various cartels," O'Reilly added, glancing at McCain and Donaldson. "Since you said you had some intel related to the gangs, I figured I'd bring him along. Plus, I always feel like I need backup when I'm around you guys. So, what do you have for us?"

"We're waiting on one more," Tu replied.

O'Reilly grunted something close to a chuckle. "You spooks and your secrets."

"Weren't you talking about retiring?" McCain asked.

Joe waved his hand dismissively. "I think about it every time I get mixed up on something with you. I just hope I get the chance to retire before I get fired from covertly helping you or one of your underlings. Is the job offer at Century still open?"

"It is," Chuck smiled, "if you can pass the background check."

A man sporting a shaved head and a runner's physique entered the coffee shop and made his way to where the four men were sitting. Frank Simpson was the assistant special agent in charge at the Drug Enforcement Agency office in Arlington. He wore a black windbreaker over a navy blue polo shirt tucked into a pair of khaki cargo pants.

After the introductions were made, the senior FBI agent looked at the DEA agent and motioned to Chuck and Tu.

"I'm getting a bad first impression here, Simpson, if you're friends with these troublemakers."

Frank stared at the older man, not sure if he was being serious or not.

"You'll have to excuse Joe," Chuck said. "He's still bitter he couldn't get on with the DEA. He wasn't able to pass the physical so he had to settle for joining the Bureau."

O'Reilly laughed at this and Simpson seemed to relax.

"Good to see you again, Agent Simpson," Tu commented.

"Thanks. I haven't really gotten a chance to thank you, Chuck, for your help in uncovering that dirty agent in El Paso."

Using their cover as Homeland Security Agents, Chuck, Tu, and Chris Norris' squads had temporarily been assigned to a DEA task force earlier in the year in an effort to stop the influx of the new street drug, the Devil's Dust. McCain's team had worked out of the DEA office in El Paso, Texas for a few weeks. A raid on a confirmed cartel drug house had come up empty, leading Chuck to suspect that the gangsters had been tipped off.

McCain's squad did a bit of digging on their own and found out that Supervisory Special Agent José Marín was a long-term informant for the Sinaloa gang. While they conducted a surveillance of Marín's home, a team of cartel sicarios attempted to assassinate the dirty federal agent. Chuck and Scotty Smith managed to take out the hit-squad but Marín suffered fatal gunshot wounds, passing away during surgery.

Joe chuckled again, glancing at his partner. "That's another thing about these guys, McCain especially. They always seem to wind up in the middle of the shit. I read about the thing in El Paso. McCain and one of his guys took out an entire team of sicarios."

The younger FBI agent's eyes widened in surprise. Since it was cartel related, he had read the report on that shootout, as well. The four assassins had been one of the most experienced Sinaloa hit teams in the United States. Three of them had died at the scene, while the fourth survived his wounds to be sentenced to a long prison sentence in a maximum-security federal penitentiary.

"Agent Hernandez and I are actually off today," O'Reilly continued, "so we'd love to find out why you wanted to meet this morning."

Tu withdrew two thumb drives and laid one each in front of O'Reilly and Simpson.

"After we spent some time working on that taskforce," the CIA agent explained, "Chuck and I got sent to Mexico to coordinate with their National Guard in an attempt to serve warrants on Javier Guillén and Ramin Shahriari."

"But they decided to go out in a blaze of glory?" Simpson asked.

"Pretty much," McCain confirmed. "Two of the most wanted terrorists in the world, along with a bunch of their soldiers won't be causing any more problems. Those thumb drives evidently contain everything the Mexicans recovered after searching Guillén's multiple homes. You've got a treasure trove of intel on the Sinaloa's operations in the US."

The federal agents looked up in surprise. Frank picked up the thumb drive.

"How reliable is the information on here?"

"Chuck and I both trust the source. There are a lot of dirty cops, politicians, judges, etc, south of the border, but the federales that we were working with were the cream of the crop. The scope of what's on those disks is huge. I hope you guys can use it to put a dent in the Sinaloa's operations in America."

"The cartel is still in disarray in Mexico from Guillén's death," Hernandez said, speaking for the first time. "In the US, it's a different story. The Sinaloas are so well-organized here that the leader's death doesn't change how they do business."

"What about the other cartels in America?" McCain asked. "Would you say the same thing about the New Generation gang?"

The FBI agent pushed his glasses up his nose. "The NG leadership philosophy is different from the Sinaloas. The NG gang is much more about controlling their operation through violence. The Sinaloa family is more like the Italian Mafia in the US. They'd rather do business with their competition than to get into a shooting war. They've built some large networks and alliances with other, non-Mexican gangs.

"They're still incredibly dangerous, but most of the violent cartel crimes we hear about in the US are committed by the NG gang. I just read a report of a local police officer and his wife being murdered in their home. The suspects are allegedly members of the New Generation Cartel. It's not that the Sinaloas are above that kind of violence, but they've been moving more towards the mafia model. Why attract attention to yourself if you can conduct business instead? Everyone makes a lot of money and the Sinaloas continue to expand their control of the drug and sex markets in America."

"Thanks for the insight," Chuck replied.

Joe picked up his disk and stared at it with the hint of a smile before handing it to Hernandez. "Here I am trying to retire and you guys just keep giving me work."

**Atlantic City, New Jersey, Saturday, 10:05am**

Lara Sagarra sat around the kitchen table with her parents, laughing and talking as they enjoyed a leisurely Saturday breakfast. Oh, she had missed them so much! How had she even gotten back to Virginia? Ernesto's angry shouts suddenly interrupted their conversation, turning her mom and dad's smiles into frowns, rousing the young woman from her dream. Sadness and disappointment left an empty feeling where just moments before had been joy and contentment.

As Ernesto continued to yell, it sounded like he was directing his anger towards Bella Suarez. What had Bella done to deserve that kind of a wakeup call? Lara hurriedly pulled on a pair of sweatpants and a hoodie before sticking her head out the bedroom door. The gangster stood on the far side of the living room, now speaking quietly into his cell phone. The other prostitute's bedroom was directly adjacent to hers, just off the living room in the small frame home. Ernesto had the third bedroom on the backside of the residence.

Lara glanced over to see Bella's door standing open. Had she fled? Maybe Ernesto was angry because the sex slave had escaped during the night? Sagarra had certainly fantasized about running away and going home. She slowly peered into her friend's room and gasped in surprise. Bella lay unmoving on the floor next to the bed. Lara instinctively knew that she was dead. She didn't see any injuries but her skin was a ghastly gray and her sad eyes stared unblinking at the ceiling.

"Bueno," Ernesto said as he disconnected the phone call, making eye contact with Lara. "I need your help."

"Qué pasó?" Lara asked, as a wave of sadness washed over her.

The cartel soldier shrugged. "No sé. A plastic bag of pills is on the table next to her bed. Did she ever talk about killing herself?"

The teenager wiped her eyes with the sleeve of the hoodie as tears started to flow.

"No. She just talked about wanting to bring her family to America one day."

Ernesto shrugged again. "We've got to get her wrapped up in the bedsheets. They're sending a couple of guys over to get rid of her. I hope you're feeling good, Chiquita, because you're gonna be extra busy until we can get a replacement."

The next hour was a blur as Lara helped Ernesto roll her friend's body in a sheet and a heavy comforter and drag her to the back door. She then had to box up Bella's meager possessions, change the covers on the bed, and give the room a thorough cleaning. The depression that had become her constant companion was now joined by a numbness on the inside, making Lara want to give up.

Maybe I'll take a handful of Bella's pills, she thought, holding up the zip-lock bag for a closer look. That would make the pain go away. I could just go to sleep and never wake up. Another thought suddenly brought her back to reality. Or maybe I would wake up and have to give an account to God?

The doorbell rang, causing her to jump. No, no, no. How much longer can I do this? As long as it takes to protect Madre y Padre, she thought, answering her own question.

"You've got a customer, Lara," Ernesto called from the living room. "Back to work, Chiquita."

**Century Tactical Solutions, Leesburg, Virginia, Saturday, 1315 hours**

Sandra Dunning, Gabby Vargas, and Chloe Wilkerson had set up a command center in the conference room. Sandra arranged for lunch to be delivered and they continued working as they enjoyed soup, sandwiches, and salads from Panera Bread. The staff at Century normally took Saturdays off but they were all interested in locating Lara Sagarra. No one had verbalized it, but the three women all suspected that the teenager was dead, buried in a shallow, unmarked grave or wrapped up in plastic, weighted down, and resting at the bottom of a lake, river or even the Atlantic Ocean. The least they could do was to give her parents a sense of closure.

Having daughters of her own, Sandra especially wanted to help the Sagarras. As the VP of Intelligence and Investigations at Century Tactical, she could easily delegate others to come in on Saturday. The fact that she was there, working alongside two of her key players was one of the many reasons that they loved her so much.

For almost a week now, they had been searching through police reports, news articles, hospital admission records, and book-in information for jails and detention centers in the areas surrounding Northern Virginia up to Atlantic City. Gabby was a world-class computer hacker and was in her element, even breaking into the databases of the largest morgues on the East Coast. A number of unidentified murder victims or homeless corpses had turned up in the larger cities but up to now, the sex, race or age hadn't matched up with Lara Sagarra.

While Vargas was the computer expert, Dunning and Wilkerson had backgrounds in intelligence and investigations. When not sifting through reports that Gabby had forwarded them, they had spent hours on the phone calling police department after police department, speaking with bored detectives who weren't particularly interested in a missing Mexican teenager.

The three women felt the deadline closing in on them. That past Monday, General Perkins had given them the rest of the week to work on the case and the women had volunteered to keep going over the weekend. By Monday morning, however, Perkins expected everyone to be back on their regular tasks. That is, unless they generated a concrete lead of where Lara might be.

It had taken them a few days, but Chloe and Sandra had finally gotten used to Gabby muttering to herself as she worked, staring at her computer screen.

"Oh, really? You sick bastard, I may have to track you down after this is over."

Wilkerson glanced at her friend. "That sounds personal."

"The dark web is so nasty," Vargas said, with a frown, "but I think I found something."

"That would be nice," Chloe said, "because I think I'll scream if I hear one more police detective ask, 'What do you expect me to do?'"

"What'd you find, Gabby?" Sandra asked.

"I found a hobby-board that rates houses of prostitution or individual escorts in different cities— kind of like Yelp for hookers."

"What's a hobby board?" Wilkerson asked.

"It looks like an innocent place to discuss hobbies. This one is about vintage cars. When you go below the surface, though, the moderator, Shane, and his friends give in-depth reviews of call girls they've used and where they're located. One of the pricks on the board mentions a 'very young Hispanic teen' that he visited in Atlantic City. He said her name was Lara and if anyone DM'ed him he'd provide a way to get in touch with her."

"Wow! How did you know to look there?" Dunning queried.

"It's kind of hit or miss," Vargas explained. "Even on the deep web, a lot of people try to cover their tracks. In the US, the Bureau and even some police departments are getting better about cracking their code language and have busted up some big pedophile and trafficking operations. Now, a lot of these perverts run a hobby board. They'll talk about their vintage cars or antiques or whatever, but if you dig in a bit, sometimes you'll find their dirty laundry."

"Did he give any more details?" Chloe asked.

"He gave a lot of details but nothing I want to repeat," Gabby answered, shaking her head. "This may be nothing, but her phone pinged in Atlantic City before it went dark. The comments on the board were from two weeks ago. I don't know what kind of presence the Sinaloas have there but AC is known for prostitution and sex trafficking around the casinos."

"Do you think you can get some more info out of this guy?" Sandra asked, excited at finally having something to work with, even if it was a long shot.

"I've got to tread carefully. There's only a couple of hundred members on that message board and I don't want them to think I'm a cop."

"Hello, ladies," a loud voice startled them all as retired FBI agent Thomas Burns strolled into the conference room.

"Thomas!" Sandra exclaimed. "We thought we were the only ones here. Don't scare us like that."

The ruddy-faced man laughed. "Sorry about that. I've seen all of you shoot so it's probably not a good idea to startle you. I just got in last night from teaching an interviews and interrogations course for new FBI recruits at Quantico. When I checked in with Chuck, he said you guys were burning the midnight oil and might could use some help? Something about a missing girl and the cartels? That sounds like a good time."

Sandra flashed the retired G-Man her biggest smile. "We could definitely use your help. Let's go to my office and I'll brief you and bring you up-to-speed. I'll be back in a little while," she told Gabby and Chloe.

The two younger women giggled to each other after their boss allowed Thomas to roll her out of the room.

"She really likes him, huh?" Vargas asked

"Oh yeah," Wilkerson nodded. "He seems like a really good guy. Ms. Dunning said Mr. Burns was there for her after she got shot and paralyzed. They became good friends during her recovery. She told me they try to have dinner at least once a week when they're both in town."

"That's nice. She's been through hell so it's always nice to see her smile."

Gabby turned her attention back to the hobby board that she had located on the dark web. By the end of the day, the computer hacker had gotten a feel for how the members interacted with each other and created a persona that she hoped would fit in. Using a nome de guerre of "Calvin," she sent a direct message asking for more information about Lara. Calvin said he was going to be attending a week-long trade show in Atlantic City in a few weeks and would love to enjoy spending time in bed with a cute teenager. Now, all Gabby could do was wait. There was no guarantee that this was even the Lara that they were looking for, but for now, it was the only lead that they had.

# Chapter Three

**Atlantic City, New Jersey, Monday, 2035 hours**

Eduardo Sanchez accompanied Nayara Palacios and two of his soldiers from Maryland. Nayara had been a popular prostitute at one of the Sinaloa's brothels in Baltimore for the past three months, another woman who had thought she would be working as a maid, cleaning rich people's homes. Instead, the twenty-year old was having sex with multiple men a day to pay off her debt.

Sanchez was furious to hear of Bella Sanchez's death. Not that he cared anything about Bella, but dead whores attracted attention. It sounded like his soldiers in Atlantic City had disposed of her body without incident but it was important to keep their operation in AC off the radar of the local police. Nayara would replace Bella at the small house in the Venice Park community. She and Lara would continue to service customers there, hoping that one day they would be allowed to walk away from the cartel and go back to their former lives.

The Sinaloa gang had a second sex operation south of the Boardwalk at the Seaside Club Condominiums. The cartel rented two condos at the beachfront location, paying the property manager an extra thousand dollars a month not to ask any questions. A soldier named Enrique was in charge of this part of the operation and seemed to be doing a great job.

For big spenders visiting the resort city, the gangsters also provided escorts who would spend one or more hours or even days with their customers. The drug business was also flourishing in Atlantic City as the Sinaloas worked with, and through the local street gangs, their drug pipeline allowing them to operate as wholesalers to the Bloods, the Crips, and MS-13.

When they arrived at the white frame house, Sanchez escorted Palacios inside, followed by Reynaldo and Salvador. The young woman clutched her small duffel bag, nervously looking around at the new surroundings. Lara poked her head out her bedroom door at the sound of people in the living room. Eduardo made eye contact with her and pointed to Nayara.

"Show her which room is hers," he ordered.

Ernesto reluctantly walked over to the cartel lieutenant, nodding at the two soldiers who flanked him. "Hola, Eduardo. ¿Cómo estás? You want something to drink?"

Lara hurried to obey Eduardo, not wanting to incur his wrath. She motioned for Nayara to follow her, but made the mistake of glancing back at the gangsters. Eduardo's right hand flashed, punching Ernesto in the face, dropping him to the floor. The Sinaloa regional leader stepped in and drove the toe of his shoe into the downed man's body. Over and over, she heard Ernesto grunt in pain as the kicks connected with his exposed midsection.

Sagarra quickly turned away and focused on guiding the new girl into her quarters. From the living room, Eduardo's voice thundered.

"This was your fault! You're supposed to take care of these girls! You failed me, Ernesto! You failed me!"

The sounds of the beating continued for a few more minutes, Ernesto pleading with his attacker to stop. Finally, Sanchez spoke again, this time sounding out of breath.

"This was just a warning, Ernesto. If you fail me again, I'll kill you. ¿Lo entiendes?"

"Sí, lo siento, Eduardo. Lo lamento."

"You better be more than sorry, amigo. These girls are too valuable to allow them to commit suicide or overdose on drugs. It better not happen again."

"No, Eduardo," the bloody man whimpered. "Never again."

"Get out of my sight," the cartel lieutenant said. "And clean that blood off of the floor. Our customers don't need to see that."

Ernesto painfully pulled himself to his feet, blood dripping from his split bottom lip. He made his way to the kitchen to follow his boss' orders.

Sanchez spoke to his two soldiers. "We leave in five minutes. Since we're here, I want to stop by the condos on the beach and see how Enrique's whore houses are going."

The gangster walked across the living room to the bedroom where the two young women sat talking on Nayara's bed. He stood in the doorway, staring at them. Lara was fifteen, Nayara was twenty. They were both fresh-faced and still had an innocence about them. An idea came to him that would make him and the cartel even more money. They sat in silence, fear evident in their eyes, wondering if Eduardo was going to hurt them, as well.

"You both keep working hard and I'll have a better job for you," he said, softening his tone. "I've got more girls coming into los Estados very soon. Don't cause any problems until then and I'll promote you."

"What kind of a promotion, Señor?" Nayara timidly asked.

"No questions," he answered, tapping his chest. "Never forget: you belong to me. Don't take any drugs. Work hard, make all the men happy, and I'll give you a better job."

With that, the gangster gathered his two soldiers and left.

**Headquarters, Loudon County Sheriff's Department, Leesburg, Virginia, Tuesday, 1605 hours**

The task force to track down Dwayne and Shelly Thomas' murderers had struck a brick wall. The detectives were following up lead after lead, while Chuck, Andy, Scotty, Jimmy, and Hollywood had been out in the field, knocking on doors and surveilling known and suspected gang locations. Even the FBI, with their vast resources, was coming up empty. While everything pointed towards Ramon "Asesino" Contreras and the Jalisco New Generation's involvement, the lead investigators didn't feel that they had enough evidence to obtain warrants and they had no idea where Contreras was hiding. So, they all continued to work.

As reserve deputies, Chuck's team had to follow all state and federal laws, as well as departmental policy. This meant that their tactics and approach was much softer than when they were on a contract job for the CIA. On the plus side, while conducting "knock and talks," they had arrested three NG soldiers and two Caucasian meth dealers working with the cartel. McCain had learned early on in his law enforcement career the value of knocking on a suspect's door. On more than one occasion he had talked himself inside of a drug dealer's house. Once inside, anything in plain view was fair game.

The arrests had come from going to home addresses listed on booking records from previous arrests of the gang members. The three cartel gangsters all had active probation violation warrants and the two meth dealers had made the mistake of answering the door with drugs in their pockets. With these five now in custody, the Loudon County detectives could interview them, offering a plea-deal in exchange for information on Ramon Contreras' whereabouts. They probably wouldn't want to shorten their lives by snitching on the cartel lieutenant but it never hurt to try.

As the big man settled into his borrowed cubicle to type up a synopsis of their activity for the day, Lieutenant Jake Donaldson and Major Joon Kim suddenly appeared. Kim was the Commander of the Criminal Investigations Division. Chuck smiled a greeting at the men. He didn't know the major well but he seemed like a competent administrator to oversee all the detectives and support staff.

"Lieutenant, do you ever sleep? Don't you work the 1800 to 0600 hours shift?"

Neither Donaldson nor Kim returned McCain's smile.

"Hey, Chuck, we got something going on that you need to know about. Can you grab your guys and meet in my office?" Major Kim asked.

"Yeah, sure, Major. I'll round them up and we'll be right there," Chuck replied, not liking the expression on the two men's faces.

Five minutes later McCain, Fleming, Smith, Jones, and Estrada were seated in front of Kim's desk in his second-floor office. To their surprise, Sheriff Schaefer was there, as well.

"I'll get right to the point," the major said. "Internal Affairs arrested one of our records clerks earlier today. A while back, one of her co-workers found where she had been accessing some gang-related reports. Not long after that, her supervisor caught her making a copy of several Sinaloa arrest reports. When questioned, she played it off saying she just found it interesting and wanted something to read in her spare time.

"The supervisor had a chat with IA and they opened an investigation. It looks like the clerk was passing the documents to someone in the New Generation Cartel. While IA was still putting their case together, this woman accessed all of your teams' personal data and passed it off to her gang contact before we knew what she was doing."

The sheriff spoke up. "Before we go any further, why don't you guys go call your wives or significant others to make sure they're OK? We can send marked units to your homes if that would make you feel better. We'll chat some more after you check in with them."

McCain and his men all stepped into the hallway, pulling out their phones. Chuck dialed Beth's number, knowing she was probably picking up Ray from daycare. The dial tone rang and rang, but there was no answer. Across the corridor, Andy was speaking softly with his wife, Amy, who was an ER Supervisory Nurse at the Inova Fairfax Hospital. A moment later, Scotty had connected with his wife, Emily, who had just given birth to their first child a couple of months earlier.

McCain disconnected and dialed his wife's phone again, panic starting to settle in. Chuck quickly computed the distance in his head as his mind went to dark places he hadn't visited in years. This time of day, it was around a forty-five minute drive back to Reston. Jimmy's relieved voice broke through his anxious thoughts as he managed to get ahold of his fiancée, Grace Cunningham, who worked for the CDC Enforcement Unit in Atlanta.

"Hey, sweetheart, how you doing?" Jones asked. "Are you at work?"

As the dial tone continued to mock him, McCain started for the door.

"Beth's not answering," he called over his shoulder, now sprinting down the stairs.

As he burst outside, he heard steps behind him, glancing to see his teammates following him. He dialed her phone again as he dove into the Silverado, started the engine and jerked the transmission into "Drive."

"Hey, babe," Elizabeth answered cheerfully. "I saw you called. I was inside talking with Ray's teacher."

Beth heard her husband's loud sigh of relief and it took him a minute to compose himself before he could speak.

"What's wrong, Chuck?"

"I'm just glad you're OK," he finally answered, climbing out of his truck and waving to his teammates in their own vehicles, waiting to follow him back to Reston. "We've got a situation going on and I'm not sure it's safe for you to go home."

"A situation? What kind of situation?"

McCain heard the fear in her voice. She knew some of the things that he was involved in and had seen him in action on several occasions.

"Listen to me, Beth. Do you have your pistol with you?"

"I do, but what's this about?"

"Why don't you come meet me at Century? We'll eat somewhere in Leesburg and I'll fill you in."

After all they had been through, Elizabeth knew that this was not the time to argue.

"Okay. Ray and I are on the way."

"I love you and I'll see you soon."

After disconnecting, Chuck and his relieved friends made their way back to the major's office. Estrada hadn't moved, his family all living in California. The SO did not have any of their contact information so he knew that his people had not been compromised. He was concerned about his companions, though, having been through hell with all of them on many occasions and they were like family to him. He looked up from a copy of the IA report the major had let him read.

"Everybody OK?" Hollywood asked.

After being reassured that everyone's families were safe, at least for the moment, Major Kim resumed the briefing.

"We're very sorry we didn't catch this. It's been a little hectic since the murder of the Thomas' but that's no excuse. The ex-records clerk is being interviewed as we speak. At this point, she hasn't lawyered up and has been spilling her guts. The NG member that she's been providing info for has dropped off the grid. We've got investigators sitting on his apartment, but I doubt he'll return."

"What was her connection to this Julio Perez?" Hollywood asked, motioning at the report.

"She's admitted that he paid her for the information, but there was also a romantic element. She thought he loved her."

"You said that she also provided intel on the Sinaloa gang?" Andy queried. "Was that so the NG guys could target them?"

The major nodded. "We've got two unsolved gang-related homicides from last year. I'm sure Julio Perez will be charged with those homicides and our ex-records clerk will be charged as an accomplice. It'll be the same with Dwayne and Shelly's murder."

"For now," the sheriff spoke up, "you guys take as much time as you need to make sure your loved ones are safe. Like I said, I'll be happy to park a deputy twenty-four/seven in front of your homes if it'll make you feel better."

Chuck glanced around at his teammates. "Let us talk about it, Sheriff, and I'll let you know. We're going to head out, but I'll check in with you gentlemen in the next couple of days. Please keep us updated if any other pertinent information comes in."

The team huddled briefly outside around McCain's pickup.

"Beth is meeting me at Century and I'll let her know what's going on. I'm planning on driving her to Hendersonville tonight. She can stay on the farm with Melanie and Brian and their family."

He nodded at Andy and Scotty. "Amy and Emily are welcome to go with us. They have plenty of room and they'll be safe there."

Fleming laughed. "I'd like that but my wife isn't going anywhere. Tyler still has another couple of years left at Virginia Tech so it's just me and her at home. After getting shot the last time those sicarios tried to kill us, she's tougher than ever. Plus, they're running short-handed at the hospital. She's won't leave them hanging."

Scotty looked more subdued than usual. "I'll check with Emily, Chuck. I'd feel better knowing that she and Macey are somewhere safe, especially while we're focused on tracking down these assholes."

"Grace is OK in the ATL," Jimmy grinned. "She told me that after all the zombies we had to fight, she's not worried about some Mexican gangsters."

"That sounds like Grace," Hollywood chuckled. "Plus, she's got Eddie Marshall as a boss. He's another dangerous hombre. Amigos, I didn't put any of my families' details on our applications, so I'm free to help wherever you need me."

An hour later, Chuck, Beth, and Ray were eating takeout food from the Hunan Garden in the break room at Century Tactical Solutions, a couple of miles from the sheriff's department. Chuck also asked Hollywood, Jimmy, Chloe, Gabby, and Tex Davis to join them, having ordered enough entrees for everyone.

"Was this records clerk the one who provided the Thomas' address to the cartel?" Tex asked, anger in his voice.

Hollywood nodded. "Yeah, the detectives found where she accessed Sgt. Thomas' personal file the day that Contreras was released on bond. They're planning on charging her as an accessory to their murder. They've already taken out warrants for Julio Perez for four counts of murder and a bunch of other stuff. He was the banger she gave the info to. The other two murders are for a couple of Sinaloa members who got capped last year."

"I know I'm the new guy," Davis said, looking at McCain, "but let me know how I can help. I'm single so I don't have a family to protect."

The former Atlanta police officer had been married, but his wife had been an early casualty when the zombie virus was released in the city. His pain was still not far below the surface.

Chuck smiled. "Thanks, Tex. I'll take you up on that. Some of us are going to take a road trip tonight and I'd feel better if you and Gabby checked in with Andy. Those Marines hate asking for help, but don't take 'no' for an answer."

"No problem, Chuck," Gabby answered. "I think we'll just drive over to the Fleming's house and call from the driveway. I haven't seen Amy in a while and I'm sure she'll be happy to have some extra security around."

Davis nodded. "I'll let you do the talking, Gabby. You know them better than I do."

After hearing of the potential threat to all of their families, Elizabeth was quick to agree to a trip to Hendersonville, North Carolina, where Chuck's adult daughter and her family lived. The big man had been divorced for years when he and Beth had gotten married and she and Melanie had become close friends.

Chuck had told Scotty that his wife and baby were welcome to come with them. Emily Smith had immediately said "yes" to the invitation and Scotty went home to help her pack. Elizabeth and Emily were close friends and this would give Beth a chance to help her friend with the new baby.

McCain outlined his plan for the trip, getting input from the others. It was around an eight-hour drive to the farm where Chuck's daughter and husband lived and everyone knew that it was going to be a long night. By 2100 hours, Chuck, Elizabeth and Ray were on the road to their home in Reston to pick up some clothes and baby items. As Chuck and Beth went up to their apartment to pack, Jimmy, Hollywood and Chloe kept watch.

The sentries were taking no chances, wearing their body armor with their H&K 416 rifles slung over their chests. Their badges hung from their necks, hopefully reassuring any of the neighbors who happened to look out their windows.

A gray Dodge Ram pulled into the parking lot of the McCains' apartment complex. Scotty Smith exited, nodding at his friends. Emily stayed in the truck, reaching around from the passenger seat to check on the sleeping baby.

"I appreciate you guys going with us," Scotty said, more serious than they had ever seen him. "What's the plan?"

"The boss, his family and Chloe will be in Beth's Mercedes GLB," Jimmy answered. "You and Emily will be behind them. Hollywood and I will bring up the rear in Chuck's Silverado."

"You got your radio?" Estrada asked.

Smith nodded and tapped his earpiece. "I stopped and filled up with gas on the way over."

"Chuck and Beth did the same so we're good to drive for a while," Jones said. "He'll call the stops. Hollywood and I'll stay back a bit and change lanes to see if we can pick up any tails."

Scotty took a deep breath before climbing back into his Ram. It was one thing going into combat with these world-class warriors. The former Ranger sniper knew that they all were as good of operators as there were on the planet. This was different from any situation that he had ever encountered before, though. Before he could go after the bad guys, he had to make sure his wife and infant were safe. Once that was done, he could focus on bringing judgment to those who had threatened them and it wasn't going to be pretty.

**Reston Town Square Park, Reston, Virginia, Tuesday, 2220 hours**

Less than a hundred feet away, Julio Perez crouched behind a row of shrubs in a dark corner of the park. He stared through his binoculars across the street to the well-lit parking lot of the upscale apartment homes where the pig named Chuck McCain lived. Julio's job was to alert el Asesino as to when McCain got home.

The NG soldier knew that he was a wanted man. With that stupid, fat records clerk getting herself arrested, it was inevitable that she would talk. Contreras owed him a bonus for working that ugly bitch. He had to act like he enjoyed it every time he slept with her. She had provided the goods, though, getting a pair of Sinaloa gang members' info the previous year. He and Chico had gotten the drop on them in the driveway of their house, filling their bodies with 9mm bullets.

And now Chico, Victor, and Hector were dead. All the more reason to kill this piece of shit cop, McCain, and use his wife as a plaything until they got tired of her, the gangster thought. He watched closely as the SWAT cop pulled into the complex followed by a dark-colored Mercedes SUV. A good-looking woman, probably McCain's wife, exited the German vehicle. Julio felt a stirring in his loins as he stared at her. A powerfully-built man climbed out of the Silverado. Julio recognized him as Chuck McCain from the Loudon County ID photos his snitch bitch had provided. The gangster shifted his gaze back to McCain's wife. She's really hot, the gang member realized, a smile spreading across his face.

Julio was about to send a text to Contreras, already imagining what he was going to do to Mrs. McCain, when two additional men and a woman appeared from inside the vehicles. They were armed with long guns and they were clearly on alert, scanning the surrounding area for any threats. One of the guards was a black guy, while the other male looked Hispanic. A black female with short hair carried herself with the same confidence as her male counterparts.

A few minutes later, a full-size Dodge pickup pulled in, stopping adjacent to the guards. A massive bearded men got out, a pistol visible on his side. Perez had seen each of the others on their ID photos, as well. He had heard they were all part of McCain's team of reserve deputies. They chatted for several minutes before McCain and his sexy woman exited the building carrying a large suitcase, a backpack, and a small black bag. After a quick huddle, everyone loaded up and the three vehicles turned out of the parking lot, heading west towards Highway 267.

Perez sprinted for his gray Nissan Sentra parked half a block away. As he pulled away from the curb to catch up with his prey, he called Ramon to alert him to the situation.

"Where's he going?" Contreras demanded.

"No lo sé, Señor. I'll follow them and let you know."

"I want him dead, Julio. I'll get some more hombres headed your way as soon as you know where you're going. There's a bonus for whoever kills this pig. Don't fail me, Julio."

"Gracias, Señor. I'll be happy to collect it after I take care of him for you. He has security traveling with him— at least three men and a woman. I saw badges and they're all armed with rifles and pistols. You send me a few more soldiers, el Jefe, and we'll take them all out."

After turning south onto Sully Road, Perez figured they were heading for the interstate, but he waited until the caravan was westbound on I-66 before recontacting Contreras.

"Bueno," el Asesino acknowledged. "I'm sending you four more soldiers. Do you have Miguel's number?"

"Sí, Señor. Miguel is good sicario."

"He's already on the road with three of his men. Keep him posted and you guys take care of this cop and his friends. Kill them all!"

Julio planned on doing just that, except he also planned on kidnapping Mrs. McCain as part of his reward for solving Ramon's problem. Her life expectancy was also short, but she was going to get banged by him and his crew before they put a bullet into her head or cut her throat.

The gangster had sped to catch up to his targets, but now he was trying to stay around the speed limit. The fugitive was on a mission and did not need any encounters with the state police. McCain and his friends were driving ten to fifteen miles an hour over the speed limit, making Perez nervous. The .40 caliber Smith & Wesson M&P pistol tucked into his waistband would take care of any cop who tried to stop him for speeding but he didn't want to lose his target. El Asesino would not be happy if Julio failed. Even with no traffic, Miguel and his crew were at least thirty to forty minutes behind him. Hopefully, the sicario and his hombres would catch up soon.

"What do you think?" Jimmy asked Hollywood.

Jones had the first shift driving while Estrada kept an eye behind them. Traffic was still moderate, even this time of night as many of DC's late workers hurried home for a few hours sleep, just so they could repeat the process tomorrow.

"He's definitely following us. He's been back there for at least five miles. I'll let the others know."

Hollywood pushed transmit on his radio. "Charlie Two to other units. We've got a tail. It looks like a mid-size passenger car and he's been following for a while. I can't tell how many passengers he's got. For now, it's just the one car. We'll keep you posted."

Chuck and Scotty both acknowledged the transmission, trusting their friends to cover their backs.

"Thankfully, this clown is an amateur," Estrada commented, continuing to monitor their follower.

"We can thank him later."

"Man, I've never seen Scotty so serious." Hollywood commented. "Usually, he's got a joke for everything."

"Yeah, I guess getting married and having a baby has a way of sobering you up especially when you find out some really bad men want to do them harm. Maybe me and you'll find out one day."

"You're getting close, amigo. When you going to pop the question to Grace?"

"Alpha One to Charlie One," McCain's voice came over their earpieces.

"Go ahead," Hollywood answered.

"We're coming up on I-81. Let me know if our friend goes south with us or heads north."

"10-4. How well do you know 81?"

"The exits are spread out and there won't be a lot traffic," Chuck answered. "There will be plenty of places to get acquainted with these idiots. Maybe we can even get some information from them. I've got Chloe checking the map now."

"Sounds good, amigo."

"Bravo One to other units," Scotty's voice transmitted. "For what it's worth, I'll be happy to ask the questions. These assholes have pissed me off and I'm about ready to leave the reservation."

A few minutes later, they were southbound on I-81. During the day, this was a scenic drive through the Shenandoah Valley. At night, however, it was a dark and remote two-lane interstate. Their tail was still there and although he had dropped a little further back, he continued to pace them.

"Charlie One to other units, he's still back there."

"Alpha One's clear," Chuck answered. "Keep watching him and I'll advise in a few."

Chuck's mind raced through all the possible variables, trying to decide the best course of action.

"What are you going to do?" Beth asked from behind Chuck, next to the sleeping Ray's car seat, a slight tremor in her voice.

"We could call the state or local police to come stop these people," Chloe suggested from the passenger seat, studying the map on her tablet.

"We could," Chuck answered, "but the problem is we don't know who's following us. It could very well be a cartel member or members who are in the US legally and have never been arrested. They haven't broken any laws tonight by being on the same interstate with us. Plus, I hate the idea of putting some state trooper into a situation where they're in over their head. We don't know if there's one perp or five in that car."

"I hadn't thought of that," Elizabeth commented.

"I think the best option is for us to have a heart-to-heart chat with them. We'll find a way to do it where you, Ray, Emily, and Macey will be safe."

Chuck heard his wife take a deep breath. "I don't like it but I trust you. It's been a while since we've had an adventure like this."

"What do you have, Chloe?" McCain asked.

She used her fingers to enlarge the image on the iPad.

"Get off at the New Market exit and turn right. I think I've got just the place."

Wilkerson had led an intelligence unit in the Army, resigning her commission as a captain to work as an analyst for the CIA. She was eventually recruited to the operations directorate when Sandra Dunning had been over that division. After Dunning left, Chloe followed her mentor to Century Tactical.

The former analyst quickly briefed her team leader on what she had found studying the satellite map. He finally nodded.

"Sounds good. I've been to both of those museums. I'll let the others know," McCain said, taking a deep breath. "Alpha One to all units, here's what we're going to do."

**Interstate 81 Southbound, North of New Market, Virginia, Wednesday, 0010 hours**

Julio disconnected the phone call. Miguel's crew sounded like they were making good time but were still twenty minutes behind him. No problemo. McCain and his friends didn't give any indication that they were leaving the interstate any time soon. He wondered where they were going?

The Mercedes and the Dodge Ram were currently in the fast lane, with the Chevrolet pickup hanging back a bit in the slow lane. Perez had maneuvered his Nissan Sentra behind the rear vehicle, maintaining several car lengths distance and changing lanes periodically to hopefully confuse the gringos. An eighteen-wheeler passed the gangster on the left and changed lanes, putting itself between him and the Silverado.

Perez quickly moved to the outside lane, the Ram and the Mercedes still in the same lane, ten car lengths ahead.

Suddenly, the vehicles veered to the right in front of the tractor-trailer, off of the interstate and onto an exit ramp. The long truck had blocked his view of the exit sign and Julio had no idea where he was. He cut back into the slow lane as the eighteen-wheeler lumbered into the fast lane, just in time to see the Silverado following the other two vehicles down the ramp.

The cartel member jerked the steering wheel to the right, tapping his brakes, and almost missing the exit. Several hundred feet ahead of him, he watched the three vehicles he was tailing turn right at the bottom of the ramp without even slowing down. Julio touched his brakes again, not wanting to get too close, but also not wanting to lose them in unfamiliar territory.

Julio grabbed at his phone to let Miguel know they had exited the interstate but he wasn't sure what the exit number was. He dropped the phone onto the passenger seat as he reached the bottom of the ramp, looking for a street name. Before he could locate one, however, the Mercedes, Dodge, and Chevrolet made another right turn, heading north on an access road.

Perez hesitated. There weren't a lot of cars out and about. Back to the left appeared to be a small town. A lone convenience store was the only thing he could see to his right. Other than the 7-Eleven's lights, the surrounding area was bathed in darkness. He turned and continued after his targets, picking out taillights now a quarter of a mile away on the narrow two-lane road. They must have friends who live out here, he thought. Maybe that's where they're going, the gangster told himself, a sense of unease settling on him. I wished I knew where I was at.

"It's almost a mile on your left. We pass the New Market Battlefield Military Museum and then we'll come to the Virginia Museum of the Civil War. You can let us out as you're turning in. The driveway curves sharply around to the left and you can park out of sight. We'll intercept near the entrance."

"Right, now I remember it. Good job, Chloe. You guys are going to have to work fast but be careful! We still aren't sure what we're dealing with. As soon as I park around the curve, I'll come join you."

"All good, Boss," the young woman smiled. "It'll be me and Hollywood. This car load of gangbangers doesn't have a chance. Let me give them the latest."

The young woman spoke quickly to the rest of the team, letting them know what has happening.

While she was doing that, Chuck glanced over his shoulder, "Hey, Beth, can you hand Chloe that black bag?"

"Sure. I hope you guys know what you're doing."

The cartel soldier reached for his phone again, but what would he tell Miguel? He still hadn't seen a street sign. Whenever they stopped, he could pull up the location on his phone but the cop and his companions kept going north on the dark, deserted country road, now accelerating away from him. Julio shoved the gas pedal to the floor, anxious not to let them out of his sight.

After a mile, they disappeared from sight as the road curved to the left. Julio took his foot off of the accelerator as he followed them around the bend, spotting another street veering off to the right in a fork. Did they turn or stay on the curvy road? he wondered, craning his neck to the right, attempting to spot taillights. Suddenly, his Sentra shuddered as he ran over something in the roadway. He instinctively steered towards the shoulder, but his controls were sluggish and it took a moment for him to realize that all four of his tires were flat. Perez rolled to a stop with his foot on the brake.

As he tried to process what had happened to his car and discern which way the caravan went, his driver's door window was shattered as the muzzle of a rifle thrust through it, slamming into the side of his head. A flashlight attached to the rifle momentarily blinded him and illuminated the passenger compartment of his Nissan sedan.

"Hands on the steering wheel," a voice ordered him in guttural Mexican Spanish.

Julio complied without hesitation, feeling blood trickling down the side of his head.

"Very slowly, put it in park. If you try anything, I'll kill you," the voice said, matter-of-factly.

The cartel soldier again did what he was told, his mind racing as he tried to grasp what was happening to him. His door was jerked open and someone yanked him out of the vehicle and slammed him facedown on the asphalt. His hands were roughly secured behind his back with what felt like heavy tape. He was searched, disarmed, and a black hood was pulled over his head. As he was dragged off the road, he heard the flat tires flapping as his car was driven slowly away.

"Where are you taking me?" Julio asked as he was pulled across the asphalt and then for at least fifty feet through the grass and undergrowth.

The gang member was scared now. He hadn't paid much attention to his dark surroundings as he had followed McCain. He just remembered seeing a lot of trees going by. They finally quit dragging him, dropping him roughly to the ground. He could hear the movement and low voices of several people.

"You picked on the wrong man, amigos," he grunted, raising his hooded head and trying to sound confident. "You don't know who you're messing with. You let me go now and maybe my friends will kill you before they hack your families into little pieces."

A humorless laugh came from near his ear as a hand slammed his face back to the ground. "No, amigo," the Mexican voice said again. "You don't know who you're dealing with."

A hand pressed the back of his neck, holding him in place as the hood was removed. Perez attempted to turn to get a look at his attackers but the pressure increased on his neck holding him down. A red flashlight shone around him but he wasn't able to see who he was dealing with, just several pairs of legs.

Without warning, a plastic bag was drawn over the thug's head and face before being pulled tight under his chin so that he couldn't breathe. Julio tried to inhale so he could scream but the plastic adhered to his nose and mouth, blocking any sound. He attempted to roll onto his back but the strong hands held him securely in place. Just as he thought he was going to die, the bag was removed. The NG soldier greedily sucked in the cool air.

"Maybe we have an understanding now, sí? I need some information. You tell me what I want to know and you might see another sunrise."

Perez coughed and told the man behind the voice what he could do to himself.

"No problem," the voice said with a laugh. "I've got all night."

The plastic bag came back down over Julio's head as the hands kept him immobile. He had no idea how many people were holding him, but he thrashed in effort to get free, burning what little oxygen he had left. This was it, he realized. They're going to kill me if I don't talk! As Julio started to black out, the plastic was loosened and adjusted to allow some air in. The thug's heart rate was racing as he tried to bring his breathing under control.

"What...what do you want to know?" he gasped, stalling for time.

"I thought you were a smart man," the voice said. "Just a few questions. Let's start with an easy one: what's your name? I already know the answer so if you lie..."

The plastic bag started to come down again over his nose and mouth.

"No! Julio Perez! Mi nombre es Julio Perez."

More air was allowed in, allowing him to inhale deeply.

"See? Easy. Next question: why were you following those people?"

"What people? I wasn't following anyone. I was just...no!"

His air supply was abruptly cut off again. Perez had never felt so hopeless in his life. He was usually the one in control, the one bringing the pain and the torture to his victims. He was the one who caused people to piss themselves because of the fear and agony he inflicted on them. Julio must have blacked out because he woke up as smelling salts were shoved under his nose. He felt a wetness around his groin, realizing he had lost control of his own bladder.

"Ready to try again?" The voice chuckled. "I thought you New Generation hombres were tough, amigo, but you pissed yourself. I think we need to take this to the next level."

The sicario felt his jeans being unfastened and ripped off of him.

"¿Qué estás haciendo? You assholes, I'm going to kill you!"

In an instant, he was again unable to breathe while he felt himself being relieved of his pants and underwear. Just before the darkness settled in, the bag was loosened, the oxygen again reviving the career criminal. He was still facedown on the cold ground and felt hands spread his legs apart, a new terror filling the gangster's heart. What are they going to do to me?

"I'm tired of dealing with you, Julio. I'm going to start cutting until you answer my questions. I'll start with your nuts and I'll move on from there."

A slight prick brought a sharp pain and was followed by the cold steel of a blade, now nestled near the thug's privates. Perez started crying, the bully now a broken man.

"No, por favor, no," he sobbed. "I'll tell you anything."

As the voice asked him a series of questions, the gangster answered each one truthfully, hoping that telling the truth might allow him to live. He hesitated once or twice but a slight jab with the tip of the blade to a testicle got him chatting again. After twenty minutes of interrogation, Julio sensed that it was over and he began to worry again that he was going to die.

The Mexican suddenly spoke again near his ear. "When you talk to your people, Julio, you tell them that the people they were following belong to the Sinaloas. We own those cops and the detective that the NG killed. Now, we're going to punish all you New Generation pieces of shit."

The voice made him repeat the message several times before Perez felt a jab in the arm. A minute later, he was unconscious.

After Scotty injected Julio with a strong cocktail of Midazolam and several other sedatives, Chuck helped him and Hollywood drag the nude man through the wooded area to where Chloe had parked his car around the curve. The road was the entrance to the Virginia Museum of the Civil War. Jimmy stood by their vehicles, holding his rifle, guarding Elizabeth, Emily and their children. The naked gang member's hands were freed as he was dumped behind the steering wheel of the Sentra, with his clothes and car keys tossed into the trunk. Estrada unloaded the thug's pistol and laid it on top of the man's clothes.

After checking on Beth, McCain gathered his team for a quick debrief.

"That was a great takedown, Chloe and Hollywood," the big man said. "That spike strip did exactly what it was supposed to do."

He made eye contact with both of them. "I'm sorry you had to torture him, but I appreciate it."

"Don't worry about it," Estrada grunted. "That piece of shit deserved worse. He needs a bullet in the head, but I do see a long prison sentence in his future."

Wilkerson nodded in agreement, even though the emotional strain was evident on her face. "After what he said they planned on doing to you and your family, I don't have any sympathy for him."

McCain nodded, anger evident on his face, remembering what the gangster said they intended for his wife.

"Chloe, as soon as we get going, call 911 and get the local cops on this. I'll check in with Andy and make sure he's OK. If they were coming after us, he's probably next."

A few minutes later, the convoy had retraced their steps and were heading south again on I-81. Wilkerson gave the 911 operator a crazy story of a nude man standing in the middle of the road near the Virginia Museum of the Civil War, trying to wave down traffic.

"That'll have them racing to the scene," Chuck smiled.

"What did y'all do to that man?" Beth asked quietly.

Wilkerson glanced at her team leader wondering how he would answer his wife.

"We asked him some questions and he eventually gave us the answers," he said, looking at her in the rearview mirror. "You really don't want to know what he told us. Scotty gave him a shot to knock him out for a while. The local cops will find him and once they verify who he is, Loudon County will extradite him. He's wanted for the murder of Dwayne and Shelly, and a stack of other charges."

Elizabeth accepted Chuck's answer, knowing that her husband would do whatever it took to protect her, Ray, and his team. She had hoped that his job with Century Tactical would take him off of the front lines. As a contractor for the Agency, though, he was still involved in the war on terror and in confronting the cartels who continued to spread their tentacles deeper and deeper into America. Beth understood the arrangement that Century had with the Loudon County SO, but up until recently, Chuck and his friends had only provided firearms instruction and qualifications for the department.

After making sure that they weren't being followed, Chuck called Andy and told him what had happened. The former MARSOC Marine listened in silence.

"Thanks for sending Gabby and Tex over," Fleming finally responded. "I'm glad you guys are OK. I wonder if those assholes are already on the way to pay us a visit? The sheriff sent a marked cruiser to sit in front of the house but I have a feeling that won't deter the NG if they're serious about coming after me."

"Who's the deputy?"

"Some young kid who just hit the street. I think his name is Jenkins? I brought him inside the house and made a pot of coffee. I don't want his blood on my conscience. A sicario wouldn't think twice about slipping up behind him and putting a couple of rounds into his head."

"Good call. I'll be glad when we get our homes finished out in Haymarket," McCain commented. "We'll all be close together and have a much better setup for defense."

"You got that right. Let me go update everyone on what you found out."

**Herndon, Virginia, Wednesday, 0320 hours**

The black Honda Passport and the red Ford F-150 stopped in front of an empty lot just inside the quiet neighborhood. Miguel turned the headlights off and studied the map on his phone.

"It's up there," he said, pointing ahead of them, "the eighth house on the right. It looks like the one with the car parked in front of it."

The sicarios in his vehicle stirred, checking their weapons. What could be easier than taking out a pig and his wife in their own home in the middle of the night? Miguel had killed federales, judges, prosecutors and their families in Mexico. In Los Estados, though, his killing had been confined to rival gang members or NG members who tried to steal from the family. He and his men knew of el Asesino's recent murder of a Loudon County deputy and his wife. Tonight, it would be Miguel's turn to show the cops that they couldn't screw with the Jalisco New Generation Cartel and get away with it.

He climbed out to speak with the additional soldiers in the F-150 that Contreras had sent to assist him. There were four additional gunmen, all of them grinning in anticipation as they passed a thick joint around. Miguel told them what he needed them to do before getting back into the Passport.

"Remember, we're going in to kill them. We don't have time to mess around with this cop or his wife. We get in and get out before the other pigs show up."

Squad leader Javier nodded and turned the Ford to the left, down a side street to approach from the opposite end of the block. It was almost time, Miguel thought, feeling the tingle of adrenaline. They were going to bring some terror into this upper-middle class community. All the homes were dark with an occasional light visible. The street lights were spread out and would not be a problem.

Miguel suspected that something bad had happened to Julio. Neither he, nor Ramon, had heard from the man in over three hours. Miguel and his three soldiers had checked several of the exits off of I-81, hoping to find the missing man. There had been no sign of the gangster and he wasn't responding to calls or texts. He had simply vanished.

After getting off at the New Market exit, two police cars shot by them with their blue lights flashing and their sirens wailing. They disappeared down a dark street that paralleled the interstate. Miguel steered his Honda SUV back onto I-81 and reported in with el Asesino. After looking for Perez for an hour, Contreras had finally called back and given Miguel a new assignment: assassinate another Loudon County deputy before daybreak. This one was named Andy Fleming and the sicarios were to make a statement, murdering him and his wife in their Herndon home. El Asesino wanted to send a message to all the pigs in Northern Virginia— mess with the NG Cartel at your peril. By killing another deputy in the sanctity of his home, along with his wife, Contreras wanted every cop to feel that there was no place that the New Generation soldiers couldn't reach them.

Miguel's phone vibrated with a text from Javier. They were in position on the opposite side of Fleming's residence. He texted a quick reply.

*"Vamos."*

The sicario left the lights off as he accelerated towards the house. As Miguel braked to a stop just before reaching the target location, he realized that the car in front of the house was a marked police cruiser. He could just make out the shape of the deputy sitting inside the vehicle. Bueno, we can kill two pigs for the price of one, he thought, as he and his men jumped out of the Passport.

The Ford F-150 came from the other direction, stopping a hundred feet away, disgorging the NG soldiers it was carrying. The sicarios carried a combination of AR-15s, AK-47s, and shotguns. How could that cop not see Javier's squad directly in front of him? Miguel wondered, leading the way, his Bushmaster AR locked into his shoulder. Maybe he's taking a nap, the sicario concluded, pushing the safety off on his rifle.

Andy really hoped the thugs would take the rest of the night off. He had no qualms about violence and relished the idea of thinning out the NG cartel. At the same time, though, he didn't want to see his peaceful neighborhood turned into a war zone. The Flemings had become close friends with a few of their neighbors and the former Marine certainly did not want to see any innocents hurt. He had positioned Tex and Gabby in strategic locations as he waited in the shrubbery near the right front corner of his house.

Amy Fleming had to be at work at 0600 hours. She had placed her .357 magnum Ruger SP-101 revolver on the bedside table, kissed her husband, hugged his teammates, and gone to bed at 2330 hours. Andy had been outside for almost two hours, but planned on remaining in his hiding spot for the rest of the night. If the cartel did show up, they would be leaving in body bags, Fleming thought.

Tex's voice broke the silence, speaking softly in Andy's and Gabby's earpieces.

"Here they come," he announced from his perch in Tyler's bedroom. The room overlooked the street and Davis had removed the screen from the window, providing excellent high cover. "We've got an SUV coming from the west and a pickup from the east, both with the lights off. They've each stopped a house down."

"10-4," Fleming acknowledged softly "Just remember fire discipline. I like most of my neighbors and I don't want to see any of them hurt."

"I've got four armed tangos from each vehicle for a total of eight," Tex announced, as he pushed the selector on his H&K 416 to semiautomatic.

Fleming took a deep breath to control the adrenaline he felt coursing through his system. The four thugs from the SUV would be in his line-of-sight in seconds. The former MARSOC Marine knew that his position in the waist-high shrubs was great concealment, but the bushes would not stop bullets when the thugs started shooting back. That just means I'll have to work fast, he thought, smiling grimly to himself.

"I'll initiate the ambush," Andy whispered to his teammates.

Gabby waited in the garage on the opposite end of the house from Andy. An open window allowed her to focus on the squad coming from the pickup. She raised her H&K rifle and sighted through the window, looking for a target.

Miguel led his squad up the sidewalk, stopping just before the cop's house. The streetlights cast a pale glow over the area and the Mexican killers clung to the shadows. The police car was just a few feet away, the lone deputy sitting motionless behind the steering wheel. This cop picked a bad time to take a nap, the sicario thought. Miguel glanced up and saw Javier's squad making their approach from the other end of the street. They had just reached the short driveway which led to the Fleming's garage. The plan wasn't sophisticated— they were all heading for the front door. The eight assassins would kick or shoot their way inside, kill the Flemings and then flee.

"I'll take out the pig in the car and then we hit the house," Miguel whispered to his soldiers.

The gunman crept up to the passenger side window and raised his AR-15. Something didn't look right, he realized. Suddenly, the horn started blaring and the lights on the cruiser started flashing. Startled, Miguel pulled the trigger, sending a 5.56mm bullet through the side window. The muzzle flash illuminated the interior of the police car. The "deputy" was the rubber torso of a punching dummy, a ball cap perched on his head. As Miguel spun around to order his men forward, two bullets slammed into his chest, knocking him back against the police car. The gangster was unable to catch his breath or speak but tried to raise his rifle when a third round punched a hole between his eyes, sending him into eternal darkness.

Gabby placed the red dot from her EOTech optic over the head of the tall thug she assumed was the team leader. He had been the one driving the pickup and was now leading his squad towards the house, all of them armed with long guns. The young woman knew that the car alarm on the police car was coming, but it still made her jump. The four gangsters were bunched together on the driveway and the lights and sound of the horn froze them in place, indecision plastered on their faces. After Andy's first shot, Gabby squeezed the trigger, her 5.56mm round destroying the cartel member's face and splattering his teammates with his brains and blood.

The thugs were just thirty yards away making it easy for Vargas to transition to the next perp. Her next three pulls of the trigger sent soft point bullets into a stocky sicario's chest, his multiple gold chains glinting in the ambient light. The gunman staggered but managed to fire his .12 gauge Remington 870 shotgun towards Gabby's muzzle flash. The buckshot ripped into the side of the house next to her window. Vargas shot him again, this time in the nose, before swinging the red dot towards one of his companions.

Tex couldn't believe what he was seeing. Eight heavily-armed men were converging on Andy Fleming's house and it was up to their small team to stop them. This was a first for the former Atlanta Police SWAT officer. He had been in plenty of dicey situations over the years and had three officer-involved shootings to his credit. This, however, was a military-style ambush and they were about to kill some NG cartel soldiers.

The car alarm was the former MARSOC operator's idea and the shock of the loud horn and flashing lights had given the auxiliary deputies the advantage. As Andy's first target collapsed after shooting into the police car, Tex picked out a gangster with an AK and pumped three rounds into his sternum, sending him facedown on the sidewalk. Tex swung his EOTech optic over the scene, but realized that the other two gangsters coming from the SUV were already down and not moving. He quickly slid his aim over to where Gabby was engaging her four sicarios.

Only two of the Mexicans were still standing and they were backing towards the street, returning fire. One of them blasted his AK towards Vargas, while his AR-armed partner squeezed off two rounds towards Fleming's position. Davis brought the red dot over AR Man's face and sent a bullet into the thug's skull. He moved his muzzle to take out AK Man but that gang member was now sprawled on his back with several holes pumping blood out of his torso. The cartel soldier cried out in pain as his life drained into the street. Twenty seconds later, the man had gone silent. Tex swept his optics over the scene, looking for any additional threats, but just seeing unmoving gangsters lying in Fleming's front yard, driveway, or in the street in front of his house.

"Cease fire! Cease fire!" Andy's voice came over their radios. "I think that's all of them. Status check?"

"This is Vargas, I'm code four in the garage."

"Tex is good upstairs. It looks like we've got eight suspects down."

"Deputy Jenkins is code four; the back of the property is clear."

"Fleming's clear. Deputy Jenkins, I'm sure a neighbor or two has called 911 but go ahead and notify dispatch to request a supervisor, additional deputies, and ambulances. Then, we need to go secure those cars and the suspects before EMS arrives. It's gonna be a long night."

Andy changed magazines in his rifle as he watched lights come on in his neighbors' houses. He and Amy had enjoyed living here, but Chuck was right. It was going to be better living further out in the country, surrounded by his teammates and their families. Hopefully, these eight dead assholes would make an impression on the NG leadership that attacking the police from here on out was a quick way to die. In reality, he knew the cartel would keep doing what they did and he and his friends would keep doing what they did— sending the gangsters to Hell.

**I-81 Southbound, Southern Virginia, Wednesday, 0356 hours**

"Thanks for the update," Chuck said into his phone. "Good job, buddy. I'm glad you guys are OK."

After disconnecting, he related to Beth and Chloe what Andy had told him.

"Oh, my God!" Elizabeth exclaimed. "I can't believe they attacked his house! Thank God they're alright."

Wilkerson just shook her head in disbelief as the big man transmitted a sit-rep to the others in the caravan.

"Andy representing for the Corps," Jimmy's voice came over their earpieces.

"And that's eight less of the assholes that we'll have to kill later," Scotty added.

The caravan soon transitioned onto I-26, continuing south.

"How long do you think we'll need to stay at the farm?" Beth asked.

"I'd plan on at least a week," Chuck answered. "As soon as the team gets back, we're going hunting. We'll see how many of these guys we can take down. I'm also going to call our builder and ask him to hurry things up. I'll feel so much better when we're in our new house."

"But you guys are so isolated out there in the country," Chloe commented. "It'll take forever for help to arrive."

"Help for us or the bad guys?" Chuck smiled. "It is a bit of a drive, but we all paid extra for some enhanced safety features for everyone's home. There are also going to be plenty of security measures in place around the property. You'll have to come spend the weekend with us when we get moved in and we'll show you around."

"That would be fun, Chloe," Beth agreed. "We don't get to hang out enough. Chuck's always taking you and the others away on some kind of an adventure."

Wilkerson laughed. "I guess that's one way to look at what we do."

# Chapter Four

**Herndon, Virginia, Wednesday, 0535 hours**

Sheriff Jerry Schaefer and Major Joon Kim stood outside the yellow crime scene tape and watched the detectives and CSI officers work. The area around the Flemings' home was now illuminated by several large lights provided by the fire department. The Virginia State Police Department's shoot team were enroute to assist the local investigators with the officer-involved-shooting. Neighbors huddled in several front yards, trying to get a better picture of what had happened at their neighbor's home in their quiet subdivision. From all accounts, Amy and Andy Fleming were unharmed, but the gun battle had awakened the entire street.

News trucks from the local networks had been sequestered to the parking lot of the subdivision's recreation area two streets over. The public information officer had already briefed them once, giving them just the basics of the incident, with a press conference scheduled for 0800 at the sheriff's department. Schaefer had just arrived twenty minutes earlier and waited until the major had a good handle on the situation before pulling him aside.

"Okay, Joon, what do we have?"

The Asian-American motioned towards the white-sheet covered bodies scattered around the front of the Fleming home.

"Thankfully, not a repeat of last week. Andy, Tex, and Gabby were waiting for them. They killed all eight of the suspects before they could break into the house. The dead perps are all Hispanic males, so it's a safe bet they're going to be identified as NG soldiers. At Fleming's request, Deputy Jenkins was already inside, watching the rear of the home. They'd set up a rubber punching dummy in the driver's seat of Jenkins' patrol car and one of the gunmen fired into the side window thinking the deputy was in there. The rifle bullet ripped through the dummy's neck."

Schaefer nodded in appreciation. "That was slick. None of our people hurt?"

"No, sir. Those auxiliary deputies are good, Sheriff. Each of the suspects was carrying a rifle or shotgun and a few of them had pistols, as well. Andy, Tex, and Gabby took them out before they were able to do much of anything. The bad guys only managed to get a few shots off, with two of them striking the front of Andy's house. The next door neighbor's home took an AK round but the brick siding kept it from penetrating. No civilians were injured. All the deputies are at HQ giving their statements."

"Do you foresee any problems with this when it gets forwarded to the Commonwealth Attorney?"

"I don't. I've already got a call into their office, asking if they want to send one of their investigators over. I like having them involved at the beginning of an investigation like this.

This looks like a clear-cut case of self-defense, especially after the murder of the Thomas'."

"How's Deputy Jenkins? Was he involved in the shootout at all? This is one of those things that will have you wondering if you made the right career choice or not."

Kim hesitated before answering. "He wasn't directly involved. Just between you and me, sir, I think Fleming knew exactly what he was doing. If Jenkins had been sitting in his car, he would be dead. Andy brought him inside and positioned him to keep an eye on the backyard in case the perps came from that direction. Fleming was outside, waiting in the bushes in front of his house, Davis was covering the front from an upstairs window, and Vargas was watching from a garage window that allowed her a great vantage point of the street, as well."

"It's almost like they were expecting the cartel to show up," Schaefer concluded.

The major shrugged. "The report will indicate that they were just being safe after their personal data was given to a Jalisco New Generation Cartel member."

"Sounds good to me," the sheriff smiled. "How's Mrs. Fleming? I imagine she was pretty shook up?"

"She left for work just before you got here. She's a supervisory nurse in the ER at Inova over in Fairfax. We tried to interview her but she said she didn't see anything and had nothing to say other than, I quote, 'good riddance to the assholes who wanted to kill my husband and I.' I did send a deputy to follow her to work but she wasn't even happy about that."

"Those ER nurses are tough," Schaefer grinned. "Well, Major, let me know if you need anything. I told our public information officer that I'd join them for the news conference. This is a pretty high-profile incident."

After the sheriff left, the major slowly looked at the chaos around him. More neighbors were outside, some of them holding up their phones to take photos or video of the carnage just outside their own front doors. CSI was now in the evidence gathering part of the investigation after photographing the scene from every angle. Shell casings and other pieces of evidence were marked with plastic yellow numbers. The two suspect vehicles would soon be loaded onto tow trucks. They would be thoroughly processed back at HQ. There were so many things that went into an investigation of this size. The good news today was that the only casualties were the suspects, the major thought, moving around to check on his people.

**Caesars Atlantic City, New Jersey, Saturday, 2315 hours**

Once again, Lara Sagarra suppressed a shudder at where her choices in life had taken her. The overweight, gray-haired, middle-aged man patted her nude bottom and climbed out of the bed, pausing to survey the teenager.

"That was nice," he grinned at her. "Real nice. You can go, but I'll be back in town in a couple of weeks for another convention. I'd love to see you again."

Lara forced a smile onto her face. "Oh, yeah. I'd love that," she purred. "You know how to get in touch with me."

A minute later, she could hear the shower running in the bathroom and she quickly got dressed, wishing she could shower, as well. It would take more than hot water and soap to cleanse her soul, she thought, praying a silent prayer for forgiveness. She paused as she slid her heels on, glancing at the phone on the bedside table. Maybe she could call her parents? Would the call go through a switchboard? What if Ernesto or Eduardo found out? They would kill me and my parents, she realized, tears suddenly filling her eyes, a feeling of helplessness sweeping over the young woman.

The water in the bathroom cut off and she didn't want to be there when Gerald, if that was his real name, returned. She grabbed her small bag and hurried out of the room. Ernesto was waiting for her in the lobby. He wordlessly guided her out of the massive building and around the corner to the parking deck where he had left his silver Hyundai Elantra. A few minutes later, Lara was relieved to see that the gangster was heading off of the strip. No more customers tonight.

Since her "promotion," there had only been three dates that day at three different casino hotels. Three was better than the ten or fifteen or even twenty tricks a day she had been turning. The men were all old enough to be her dad or even her grandfather but at least they hadn't hurt her. Lara suspected that they must be paying a lot of money to the cartel to have sex with a fifteen-year-old girl.

The previous day had been the start of her new job as an escort. In the morning, Ernesto had taken her and Nayara shopping to buy them some "sexy" clothes and underwear. The thug explained to them that Eduardo was going to utilize them as escorts catering to the city's many conferences and trade shows. She had no idea how much the gang was making off of her body or how the money changed hands.

For her first date on Friday afternoon, Ernesto had simply introduced her to an older black man in one of the bars at the Tropicana. George's eyes had lit up when he saw the pretty teen and he casually threw an arm over her shoulders and led her up to his room. Lara knew her role and spent a couple of hours with him before he told her to leave.

Like so many teenagers, Lara had thought she knew everything there was to know about the world and life in general. Her current situation was a reminder of how ignorant she really was. Occasionally, Ernesto would answer her questions, while most of the time he just ignored her.

"Don't the police ever arrest prostitutes?" she asked him on the ride home. "I'm just asking in case I get arrested. What do I do?"

Her escort glanced over at her. "Sometimes they do prostitution stings around the strip but our contact with the police department said they are so short-handed, they've put a lot of the vice cops back on patrol. Plus, we have a couple of ways to verify our customers."

"Entiendo. Gracias."

"You think that if you get arrested, you can escape us?"

That was exactly what she was thinking. "No! I've just never been arrested before and I don't want to get tossed in a cell with murderers and drug addicts."

"If you did get locked up, we have a lawyer who works for us and he would come get you out. No problemo."

"That's good to know," Lara replied quietly.

As the lights of the strip now faded behind her, Lara wondered if this was going to be her new normal for years to come. How many other girls were trapped like she was, paying back debts to the Sinaloa or one of the other cartels?

"Mañana, we leave after lunch," Ernesto told her. "You'll have tres o cuatro dates. Enrique will drive you."

The young woman nodded in resignation. Enrique was one of the new gang members that Eduardo had sent to help run the sex trafficking operation in Atlantic City. She had overheard conversations between the two men and it sounded like there were a number of cartel brothels around the city. He and Ernesto would take turns driving Lara and Nayara to whichever hotel they would be working at. Another Sinaloa soldier, Tiago, had also been added to the mix to watch over the girls who had taken Lara and Nayara's jobs at the house now that the two young women were meeting their clients off-site.

All of the gang members scared her, but being alone in the car with Enrique tomorrow was terrifying. He had touched her a few times and made her show him her boobs. Enrique had told her what he wanted to do to her whenever Ernesto wasn't around. It was just a matter of time, she thought, before the thug forces himself on me.

Sagarra noticed that Ernesto was taking a different route than normal. Where was he taking her? Fear suddenly filled her mind, wondering if Ernesto had orders to kill her. Maybe one of her dates had complained on her?

"Where are we going?" she asked nervously.

"Una casa nueva," the gangster answered. "The other house is too small so Eduardo rented another one."

Lara's panic slowly subsided as Ernesto guided the Elantra through another low-income neighborhood in the same general area where she had been living. He parked in front of another small white, single-story residence.

"The new girls packed up your stuff and moved it over here earlier."

Inside, Ernesto pointed out Lara's room. Nayara was still out on her own "date." Sagarra found her backpack on the bed, breathing a sigh of relief when she unzipped one of the interior pockets. The small photo of Lara and her parents from the previous Christmas was where she had hidden it. She stared at the smiling faces for several minutes, the tears leaving streaks in the heavy makeup she was wearing. She carefully replaced the snapshot, took a long, hot shower, and went to bed, praying as she fell asleep that God would somehow deliver her from the hell in which she was currently living.

**S Street, SE, Washington, D.C., Saturday, 2345 hours**

Ramon Contreras sat across from his attorney, Sebastian Hernandez, at the kitchen table of one of the NG's inner-city locations. The brick structure contained three apartments, all of which were rented by the cartel. El Asesino occupied the middle residence which served as a safe house for him and his soldiers. One of the end apartments was used as a brothel, while the one on the opposite side stored drugs, weapons, and provided additional housing for the gangsters. The cartel lieutenant and his team of sicarios had only stayed at the

Lovettsville safe house for a few days, preferring the congested city to the rural isolation. The low-income neighborhood was known for its crime and violence. No one, however, dared to bother any of the cartel members.

Now that the police had located and raided both of the New Generation's stash houses in Sterling and Dulles, Contreras felt safer inside the crowded inner-city of DC. The NG also had a pair of other locations just two miles away that Ramon occasionally frequented. He seldom saw the pigs in any of the high-crime areas. They were just like the scared Mexican cops, he often thought, preferring to hide in the rich neighborhoods where they felt safe. For the moment, Contreras had decided against fleeing to Mexico. He wanted revenge for the losses that he had suffered.

It had been a rough week for the cartel. The same night that Julio was arrested, Miguel, Javier, and their teams had been gunned down by Deputy Andy Fleming and a couple of his friends. That wasn't the ending that el Asesino had pictured. The eight NG soldiers should've had no trouble with a single reserve deputy and his wife. Instead, the pig had reinforcements and they had easily eliminated the sicarios.

"That's bullshit!" Contreras exclaimed, finishing off his fifth Corona of the evening. "What was Julio talking about?"

Hernandez had already repeated everything that Julio Perez had told him that morning when the lawyer had met him at the Loudon County Jail. He had been arrested on a variety of charges by the New Market Police Department, but once his fingerprints came back, they contacted Loudon County who sent two deputies to take custody of the fugitive. He was being held without bond as an accessory to the murders of

Dwayne and Shelly Thomas and would also be charged with the two open homicide investigations involving rival Sinaloa gang members. The fact that he was on parole for a previous arrest for aggravated assault ensured that the gangster wasn't going anywhere until his trial.

"Like I said, Señor, he claims Sinaloa soldiers flattened his tires and captured him while he was following Chuck McCain and his friends. They dragged him into the woods and tortured him. He didn't tell them anything but they told him to leave McCain and the others alone because they were on the Sinaloa's payroll."

"That's impossible!" Ramon roared, tapping his own chest with his index finger. "I would've heard about it if those pigs were working for another gang."

"Maybe, maybe not, Señor," Sebastian shrugged. "The Sinaloas have a big operation in los Estados."

The lawyer didn't add that the Sinaloa presence in the US was much larger than the NG's.

"How did the police arrest Julio? You must've read the report."

"Sí, it's right here in my briefcase," the attorney said, pointing at the leather bag. "The police found him naked and passed out in his car. His clothes and his pistol were in the trunk. They arrested him for DUI, but won't have the results of a blood test back for another couple of weeks."

"So, Julio got drunk while he was supposed to be following McCain?" Contreras was livid. "I'll have him killed in jail!"

Hernandez frowned. "Julio has always done a good job, Señor. He swears to me that he wasn't drinking at all that night. He says the Sinaloa hombres who tortured him gave him a shot in the arm that knocked him out."

"And you believe him?" Contreras asked, an accusing tone to his voice.

"I do," the lawyer answered with a shrug. "It seems like a crazy story about the Sinaloas being involved, but Julio certainly believes that's what happened. I'm an attorney, Señor. I listen to crazy stories for a living. Unless we get more evidence to the contrary, I'll trust Julio's account of what happened to him."

El Asesino got himself another beer from the refrigerator and took a long swallow. He wanted to lash out in anger at Julio or someone else, but he trusted the lawyer's judgment and would try to keep his temper in check, for the moment as least.

"Can you get him out on bond? I'm sure Judge White would be happy to help us again," Contreras said with a grin.

"Not this time. Judge White has taken a leave of absence for 'unknown personal reasons.' Plus, with Julio being on parole, he'll be in jail for a while."

"That Judge White sounds like he needs another dose of reality," el Asesino commented. "Maybe I need to send some men to pay him and his family a visit."

The lawyer frowned. "I wouldn't recommend it, Señor. In Los Estados, the gringos care more about their judges than they do their cops. You kill a police officer and that will eventually blow over. You assassinate a judge, they'll bring in the FBI and it will never blow over. It's not like Mexico. The gangs kill judges and prosecutors all the time down there and no one seems to care."

Ramon drank some more beer, pondering what Sebastian was telling him. The attorney understood the American criminal justice system and had never steered him wrong. That was why he kept the man on a retainer. He was one of the few people that Contreras listened to.

"What about Miguel and Javier?" Ramon asked, changing the subject. "It sounds like that pig Fleming was waiting on them. What have your sources at the sheriff's department told you about that?"

The lawyer sighed. "Nothing, Señor. I have to tread very carefully. The police already suspect that I'm more involved with the NG than just representing you and the others when they get arrested."

Ramon waved his hand dismissively. "Don't worry about it. The Americans have too many laws that protect a criminal's rights. They're not going to bother you."

Sebastian knew better but wasn't going to argue with the senior gangster. "I'll keep asking, Señor," he said, standing to leave. "If I learn anything, I'll let you know. Julio has his first hearing on Monday so I'll be preparing for that tomorrow."

After the attorney left, Contreras stared at his beer. Had the cop he had murdered really been on the Sinaloa payroll? He wasn't worried about the larger cartel, but he knew they would want revenge for the detective's death. It all made sense now. The rival cartel must have passed information on the NG's operation to the narcotics sergeant, which had led to Ramon and his men's arrests when the SWAT teams raided their other locations.

The two criminal organizations had had their share of violent confrontations, but those were mostly in Mexico. In the

US, however, they tended to ignore each other, focusing on creating their own criminal empires. That would be just like those assholes, el Asesino thought. Maybe we need to get some revenge of our own.

**Lovettsville, Virginia, Sunday, 0310 hours**

After making sure their families were safe, Chuck, Scotty, and their teammates returned to work on Saturday, anxious to track down the gang members responsible for assassinating Sergeant Thomas and his wife, as well as those who were behind the assault on the Flemings. No one believed that the gunmen were operating on their own orders. Had el Asesino sent them? The thug that Hollywood had interrogated provided the location for the rural safe house and McCain passed the information on to Major Joon Kim. When questioned as to the origin of the intel, Chuck told him it came from a confidential informant.

Two members of the SO's SWAT team infiltrated the property Saturday night to observe the activity at the double-wide. To obtain a search warrant, they would need specific intel about what was happening there. A white van and a black pickup were parked in front of the residence. There were lights on inside and occasionally voices would carry outside to where Sergeant Brandon Cobb and Corporal Norman Stephens lay concealed a hundred feet away, inside the tree line.

The Virginia Marine Police had dropped the two snipers a mile upstream, around a bend in the river, after dark on Saturday night. They had worked their way through the forest to set up an observation post for the suspect location. In the darkness, they had created a hide in the thick underbrush, their ghillie suits blending in perfectly. Four additional SWAT officers sat in an unmarked Chevrolet Tahoe a mile away, just off the remote country road, on a narrow dirt trail. They were in place as backup if the snipers were discovered by the gang members.

Cobb and Stephens had gotten this assignment because they were more than just SWAT marksmen. Both deputies had completed the rigorous Marine Scout Sniper Course and had served as snipers, Brandon in Iraq and Norman in Afghanistan. After leaving the Marines and getting hired by the Loudon County Sheriff's Department, the next logical choice was for them to apply their skills on the department's tactical team.

Their mission tonight was to watch the cartel location and see what they could learn. The best-case scenario would be to find Ramon Contreras hiding there. Even though the SWAT officers were armed with their MK 12 Special Purpose Rifles, sidearms, and plenty of ammo, their goal was to gather intelligence and not be seen. Corporal Stephens was also armed with a night-vision equipped camera with a long telephoto lens.

On the whole, the thugs had stayed inside the modular home. Around 2300, a gangster came out to retrieve something from the van. Later, another NG soldier stepped out the back door to urinate. Norman had gotten several phots of each man. Around 0130 hours, most of the lights inside went out and the only noise the deputies could hear sounded like a television.

Alberto "Chilo" Barajas' stomach growled as he steered the eighteen-foot metal boat across the Potomac River. Rodrigo and Danny kept watch, scanning up and down the waterway. With their cargo finally handed over to their NG contacts in Maryland, they could relax a little.

Earlier in the evening, just as they were removing the tarp from the boat where it lay hidden in a bamboo thicket, a Virginia Marine Police craft had slowly made its way downstream. The hefty cartel lieutenant watched from the shadows until the cops had gone around the bend to the east. Rodrigo and Danny had pulled the four little girls deeper into the forest and ordered them to keep quiet, their eyes wide with fear. Two of them clutched small toys, their only possessions. They would be given some new clothes when they arrived at their final destination.

After waiting thirty minutes to make sure the cops didn't double back, they had loaded their young cargo into the boat, forcing them to lay flat on the deck. Chilo covered them with a dark blanket as his two companions shoved the craft into the water.

"Not much longer, chiquitas," the heavy man whispered to the terrified girls. "You're going to love it in America."

A whimper could be heard from underneath the blanket. The engine started on the first try and ten minutes later, Rodrigo jumped into the shallow water on the Maryland side of the Potomac and pulled the metal boat onto the bank and out of sight behind a bamboo patch.

They hustled the children onto the shore, where Danny took the lead with a red-lensed flashlight on a well-used trail. The girls were instructed to follow him, don't talk, and don't stop, with Rodrigo bringing up the rear. The oldest of the little girls paused, looking at the obese man. She was maybe eight or nine, Alberto speculated.

"Señor Chilo?" she whispered.

"What is it?" he answered gruffly.

"Gracias por la cajita feliz." *Thank you for the Happy Meal.*

"De nada," he said quietly, watching as his men lead them away.

Barajas was too big to go stomping through the woods at night on a half mile jaunt to where his associates would pick up the human cargo in their gray Nissan Rogue for the trip to their new home in Frederick, Maryland. Having a couple pick them up attracted less attention than when he transported them in his van. Agnes and Arturo had not been at the rendezvous, however, and Rodrigo texted Alberto of the situation.

The couple had always been reliable in the past and Chilo informed the soldier to wait. For the obese man, though, sitting alone in the boat was torture. The metal bench was uncomfortable, he was starving, and the mosquitoes were feasting on his large frame. Rodrigo texted him every fifteen minutes, wanting to know what they were supposed to do. Barajas' message was the same every time— "Wait."

Arturo and Agnes finally showed up over an hour late. They told the soldiers that the State Police had two DUI checkpoints set up that they had to detour around. Neither of them had been drinking, but as illegals neither of them had a valid driver's license, either. Chilo sighed with relief after Rodrigo's text that he and Danny were on their way back to the boat.

Barajas thought back to the child who had thanked him for the Happy Meal. If that little girl knew what awaited her, she wouldn't be thanking me for anything, he thought. She and one of the others were from a poor village in Guatemala. The cartel had bought her from her parents for a hundred dollars. It had probably been the first time she had ever enjoyed fast food and, hopefully, it wouldn't be her last.

Maybe in an unspoken way, she was also thanking him for protecting her from Rodrigo. He had caught his colleague in the back of the van with the children during one of their rest stop breaks. Chilo had ordered him to ride in the front of the van for the remainder of the trip. It wasn't that Barajas was soft-hearted, but he didn't want Rodrigo damaging the merchandise.

The other two girls had been snatched off the street in Southern Mexico. None of them had spoken much on the long trip from the Mexican Border to Virginia. They seemed resigned to their fate, having no idea of the hell that awaited them. The children seemed to become friends during the journey and were heading to the same house in Maryland. At least they would have each other.

The cartel lieutenant caught himself. What's the matter with you, Chilo? What do you care about these chiquitas? It's all about supply and demand. The Jalisco New Generation Cartel is providing a service and is being well paid for it. He enjoyed his girls young, too. Maybe not that young, but sampling the merchandise was one of the perks of his job. The hefty man sighed, trying to get comfortable in the boat.

After Rodrigo and Danny returned, they made sure that the river was clear before shoving the boat back into the water and motoring across. After securing the craft in its hiding place and covering it with the tarp, they made their way up the well-traveled pathway to the house. Chilo's stomach continued to let him, and everyone around him, know that he was starving and he needed to eat before going to bed.

The sergeant and the corporal heard voices coming up the trail from the river before ever seeing who they belonged to. Moments later, three bright flashlight beams forced the SWAT officers to push their night vision goggles up so that they wouldn't be blinded. Stephens quietly maneuvered the camera so that he could snap them all before they disappeared inside. An incredibly obese man with fat lips trailed his two smaller companions, the exertion causing him to huff and puff with each step. A few minutes later, the sound of pots and pans could be heard from inside.

The deputies had accepted the assignment without hesitation, knowing they were operating in a gray legal area. They had no right to be on the property without a warrant, but it would be impossible to get a search warrant without their surveillance. They had checked the property lines through the tax office and discovered that the lot went several hundred feet further to the east. Technically, anything that they learned or discovered might be ruled inadmissible in court later because they were trespassing. At the same time, they were willing to take the risk and argue that they thought they were beyond the property line when they snapped all their photos.

Around 0400 hours, the lights inside had all been extinguished. Brandon and Norman had two more tasks to take care of before they could exfiltrate. First of all, they needed the license plates on the two vehicles at the safe house. They moved slowly through the woods to a point where the corporal would only have a short crawl to get the tags. The sergeant was positioned behind a large pine tree, his rifle aimed at the front of the doublewide to provide cover for his partner.

Norman slithered across the open space, leaving his camera behind. It would be easier to do it the old-fashioned way. At the rear of the GMC van, the corporal was able to read the plate using his NVGs and write the number in his palm. He then withdrew a small, black square device from his pocket. The deputy reached underneath the van and attached the metallic GPS tracker to the vehicle.

As he started to slide over to the Nissan pickup, a light suddenly came on inside the house. He flattened himself on the ground between the two vehicles, caught out in the open. He slowly slid his own rifle around so that he could use it if needed. After what seemed like an eternity, a flushing toilet was heard and the light was extinguished. Stephens let out the breath he had been holding and crawled to the pickup, jotting that tag on his hand, as well. Another tracker was attached to the Nissan.

A few minutes later, he rejoined Sergeant Cobb and the former snipers made their way back into the safety of the forest. Cobb leaned over and whispered into his partner's ear.

"Let's follow that trail down towards the river and see what they were doing down there."

Before they started, he notified their backup team of their status and let them know they would soon be wrapping up their mission. They cautiously made their way through the trees to where the three figures had emerged earlier and found a worn footpath. The sergeant took the lead, his rifle locked into his shoulder, just in case they ran into any surprises. They could hear the Potomac ahead of them and scanned the area as they moved, looking for any reason that the three gangsters might have been walking through the dark forest in the middle of the night.

A hundred yards later, they reached the river. It was a dark night and they could barely make out the Maryland shore a thousand feet away. Stephens pointed to an area near where they were standing. Fresh footprints in the soft soil were adjacent to where something had been dragged to the water.

"They must have a boat around here somewhere," Cobb whispered. "Let's find it."

He led the way back up the trail, moving more slowly this time. After fifty feet he pointed off the trail to his left. A large object lay hidden behind thick underbrush, covered with a tarp. Stephens carefully pulled back the covering to find a silver, metal-hulled motorboat. He shone a red-lensed flashlight into the craft, looking for anything that would give them a clue as to what the NG soldiers were up to. It was empty and the corporal started to replace the tarp, but something caught his attention.

"What the...?"

He reached inside and pulled out a small plastic mermaid figurine, attached to what looked like an ocean wave.

"What's that?" Cobb asked quietly, continuing to watch the area.

"This is out of a McDonald's Happy Meal. It's from the Little Mermaid. My daughter's been trying to collect the whole set."

"A Happy Meal? I find it hard to believe these assholes are collecting toys."

Both deputies arrived at the same conclusion at the same time. They had heard rumors that the cartels were transporting children into America to be used in their many brothels. The narcotics unit at the SO had been focused primarily on the large quantities of illegal drugs the gangs were importing and selling. Up to this point, there had been no evidence of the NG trafficking children. Maybe the Little Mermaid toy didn't mean anything. Or, maybe it was a clue to something much more sinister.

Norman stuffed the toy into a cargo pocket, took a last look through the boat and the surrounding area before pulling the tarp back into place. Brandon knelt beside the path staring at something, shining his own tactical light on the ground. He turned and motioned to his partner, pointing to the trail. Several sets of very small footprints lined the muddy path with the adult-sized tracks.

"I didn't see these before," the sergeant whispered. "Snap some photos of those prints and let's get out of here."

Twenty minutes later, they were a half mile from the cartel location and Cobb radioed the Virginia Marine Police to request a pickup.

**Headquarters, Loudon County Sheriff's Department, Leesburg, Virginia, Sunday, 1005 hours**

McCain hated to miss church. He and Beth were a part of the Word of Life Christian Center in Reston, but he had been in law enforcement in one form or another long enough to understand that working on Sundays came with the job. And even though he and his team were just reserve deputies, they had all accepted the mission to track down Ramon "Asesino" Contreras and his sicarios responsible for murdering Dwayne and Shelly.

Sergeant Cobb and Corporal Stephens briefed Major Joon Kim, several key investigators, SWAT commander Lieutenant Tony Adams, and Chuck about their surveillance of the New Generation safe house. Norman projected the photos that he had taken onto the wall.

"That's Chilo Barajas," Detective Sergeant Julia Lopez spoke up. "I think he's got an active parole violation warrant."

Nicknamed "J-Lo" by her friends for her name and her resemblance to a younger version of the singer and actress, Lopez had been investigating the cartels and gangs for several years and was considered the SO's leading authority on the criminal groups.

"What's his role in the cartel?" Major Kim asked.

"We're not really sure," the investigator answered. "He's probably a lieutenant like Contreras. As best we can tell, he controls a piece of the NG's operation on the East Coast. His name has come up a lot on the sex trafficking front. He's on parole for a kidnapping and rape charge. He claimed that it was consensual and that she liked it kinky but the jury believed the victim. If Chilo is at that location, I think we can get a search warrant to attempt to locate him. Can SWAT serve it for us?"

"You get the warrant and we'll go get him," Lieutenant Adams replied.

"What about the other two guys with Chilo?" Chuck asked. "Any idea who they are?"

Lopez shook her head. "None of my people recognized the short one, but the tall one with slicked back hair is wanted on multiple counts of aggravated child molestation. Rodrigo Valdez is one sick bastard. Three different agencies have open child abuse investigations on him. A fingerprint check might turn something up on the other guy, but at least we know Barajas and Valdez are wanted and that'll make it easy for us to get our foot in the door."

McCain's phone vibrated with an incoming text. He glanced at it and replaced the phone in one of his cargo pockets.

"There's one more thing," Sergeant Cobb said. "Corporal Stephens found something at the location."

The corporal held up the Little Mermaid figurine. "This was in a boat they've got hidden down by the river. It's a McDonald's Happy Meal toy."

He pushed a button on the clicker showing a photo of several child-sized footprints with the adult tracks on the path near the Potomac River.

"Those are fresh prints," the sergeant added. "I think they're transporting kids across the river into Maryland."

After the briefing, Chuck waited for the two snipers to finish their own paperwork. He made eye contact with them and they followed the big man out into the parking lot.

"Good job, guys," he said, when they were out of earshot of the others.

"Thanks," Sergeant Cobb replied. "Any action on those GPS trackers?"

"That's what I wanted to tell you," McCain replied. "I got a text a few minutes ago. The van is on the move, but the pickup is still at that location."

"Is the van still in the area?" Corporal Stephens asked. "Maybe they're just going to the store."

"Let's check," Chuck said, withdrawing his smartphone and accessing the app that allowed him to follow the tracker. He enlarged the screen with his index finger and thumb. "Heading west on Highway 7, approaching Interstate 81."

"I wonder where they're going?" Brandon wondered aloud.

Norman shrugged. "Sounds like we'll be hitting that safe house later today or tonight. Hopefully, there will be still be some bad guys there. Chuck, are you gonna pass that information on the van up the chain-of-command?"

"We all know it's a bit of a gray area," Chuck answered, "but I'll have Gabby track it to see where it goes. In a perfect world, I'd get the FBI involved but they'd figure out a way to screw things up. I've got some contacts in the DEA. That might be the way to go."

**Lovettsville, Virginia, Sunday, 2310 hours**

A Superior Court judged signed the search warrant earlier that afternoon. Alberto "Chilo" Barajas and Rodrigo Valdez were named on the search warrant, as was Ramon "Asesino" Contreras, along with any evidence related to Dwayne and Shelly Thomas' deaths. The SWAT team staged on a deserted side street, a mile from the target location. One of the support members deployed a small drone equipped with night vision and FLIR capabilities and within minutes SWAT commander Lieutenant Tony Adams, his assault team leader, Sergeant Billy Myers, and Chuck were staring at a computer screen in the tactical command truck. Several other support officers sat in the vehicle with them, monitoring radios and watching the drone video on their computers. More sets of eyes were always better, especially at night.

"Looks quiet," commented Myers, sipping coffee from a Washington Nationals tumbler.

"Cobb and Stephens should be in place in the next half hour," Adams said. "Once we hear from them, I'll send you guys in."

Billy nodded. "I'll go let the team know. Chuck, it's good to have you guys here, just in case."

McCain smiled. "We're glad to help out. Hopefully, y'all will be able to get that second assault team up and running again soon."

"That would be nice," Tony agreed. "It just seems like fewer and fewer people want to be cops anymore."

"Can you blame them?" McCain asked.

A few minutes later, drone footage showed the two snipers slowly working their way through the forest before crawling into place. Sergeant Cobb would position himself sixty yards off the front right corner of the modular home. Corporal Stephens circled around the house to set up forty yards back from the left rear corner. The marksmen would be able to cover the entire residence, functioning as both observers and snipers for the assault team.

Cobb's whispered voice finally came over the air. "Sniper One in place. There are still lights on throughout the house and it sounds like they're watching TV. The pickup truck is the only vehicle I see."

"Command is clear," Lieutenant Adams responded.

"Sniper Two to Command," Stephens transmitted a few minutes later, "I'm in position. All clear on my side."

After acknowledging both snipers, the lieutenant watched the drone footage for another minute before pushing the transmit button on his radio.

"Command to Assault Leader, you're clear to execute."

"10-4," Sergeant Myers replied. "We'll be pulling out in five."

Alberto Barajas belched loudly as he downed his fourth Budweiser of the evening. Rodrigo had driven to town earlier for a pizza and beer run. The pizza was gone and there were only a few beers left. Mexico and Argentina were battling in a 1–1 soccer match with just three minutes left in regulation. While the USA was Mexico's biggest soccer rival, playing Argentina was always a big game, as well.

Chilo had sent Danny and two more of his hombres on a trip to Brownsville, Texas, to pick up a fresh group of merchandise. Their clients were loving the access to children that the NG gang was providing. The cartel lieutenant had been on the last three road trips to Texas and had decided to sit this one out. Barajas normally bounced around the different cartel locations in his region, spending most of his time in Fredericksburg or Philadelphia.

His three soldiers had left Sunday morning and would be back by Wednesday night, so the hefty gangster decided to stay in place at the safe house in Lovettsville. It was in a remote corner of Loudon County and its river access made it easy to move the little girls into Maryland. He also anticipated a load of drugs accompanying their human cargo. The gringos loved both the drugs and the flesh he provided.

There wasn't much to do at the double-wide, but at least there was a television with satellite programming. He could watch all the soccer, porn, and action movies that he wanted. He would send Rodrigo back out to the store tomorrow for some more groceries and beer. Chilo knew that he had an active parole violation warrant so he tried to stay out of sight, as much as possible. I'm a pretty hard hombre to hide, though, he smiled to himself, as the referee blew his whistle and waved his hands over his head signaling the end of the match. A tie is better than a loss, he thought.

In reality, Rodrigo was also a wanted man but it was easier for him to blend in and not attract any attention, unless he saw a little chiquita that he liked. The sound of gravel crunching came through the open front window, interrupting his thoughts. His companion snored quietly in a recliner as Barajas lumbered to his feet to peer outside.

"Rodrigo! Wake up!"

The multiple beers had taken their toll and the other gangster did not budge. Chilo kicked the side of the chair.

"¿Qué pasó?" Rodrigo exclaimed, rubbing his eyes.

"There's someone coming," Barajas answered, flipping off the television and the lights in the living room and peering through the curtains.

A diesel engine was quickly coming their way. A rival gang or the cops? The fat man was betting that it was the pigs. They didn't have any current issues with the other gangs. He reached over and grabbed his FN Five-Seven pistol off of the coffee table. Rodrigo retrieved an AR-15 from the bedroom to go along with his Taurus 9mm pistol that he had stuffed into his waistband.

"Can you see them, Chilo?"

"No, I think they're driving with their lights off."

The big engine was getting closer.

"Let's take the boat, Chilo. We can get away!"

Barajas thought about it for a moment before shaking his head, a resigned expression on his puffy face.

"No, amigo, I'm too fat. If you want to go, take off, but I think I'll stay here."

"I can't leave you, Chilo."

"Rodrigo, if you get arrested, the gringos will find out that you're wanted for murder in Mexico, plus you've got those warrants for you in Los Estados. After you serve time here, they'll send you home. With all the crackdowns in Mexico, you'll get sent to the worst prison in the country. You better go, amigo. All they have on me is a parole violation warrant. I'll be out in six months or less."

The gangster stared at his NG leader, nodded, and started for the back door.

Corporal Norman Stephens saw the lights go off inside the modular home as he watched the back door. Sergeant Cobb had a view of the front entrance and windows. The sound of the SWAT truck coming down the long, gravel driveway broke the silence of the quiet night. The rear door suddenly flew open and a lean man carrying a rifle sprinted into the darkness. The corporal had to make the instant decision to radio in that he had a runner or confront the man before he disappeared into the forest.

In a flash, the escaping man was out of sight, sprinting towards the river. Stephens jumped to his feet and started after him.

"Sniper Two to all units," he whispered into his radio, "I've got a suspect fleeing out the rear door, armed with a rifle. He's moving towards the river. Does the drone have a visual?"

"Tech One to Sniper Two, that's a 10-4. The suspect is fifty yards ahead of you. I confirm he's armed with a long gun."

At that moment, shouts erupted from behind the corporal as the assault team deployed in front of the safe house. Norman slowed down now that he knew the drone was tracking his suspect. He didn't want to get ambushed. The thug had run straight down the trail but the sniper moved into the trees paralleling the path.

"Assault Team is Code Four," Sergeant Myers' voice came over his earpiece three minutes later. "Location is secure and we've got one in custody. Sniper Two, be advised, I've got two SWAT officers heading your way."

Stephens clicked a response, not wanting to give away his position. The NVGs gave everything a greenish tint but the cartel soldier had not been wearing any so he would be struggling in the dark. Up ahead, a flashlight flicked on and off and the corporal sensed he was getting closer.

"Tech One to Sniper Two, he's just twenty-five yards in front of you. It looks like he's trying to push a boat towards the river."

The former Marine sniper had seen combat on multiple deployments and was no stranger to violence. The sudden memory of the Little Mermaid toy and the small footprints popped up in his mind. He pushed the selector on his MK 12 SPR to "Auto." He was close enough now that he could follow the sound of the boat being dragged through the brush.

He could hear the suspect just ahead of him now on the pathway and Stephens' mind went onto autopilot. He stepped out on the trail, sprinting footsteps coming up behind him. He needed to handle this before his reinforcements got there. The cartel soldier still wasn't aware of the deputy's presence as the NVGs gave the sniper the advantage. Rodrigo Valdez had the metal-hulled boat at the edge of the water and was about to shove it in.

"Where you going?" Norman asked quietly from twenty-five feet away.

He got exactly the reaction he was hoping for as the child molester swung around, startled by the voice, trying to bring his AR-15 into play. Stephens' rifle was already locked into his shoulder as he squeezed off a ten-round burst, all of the 5.56mm bullets finding a home in the gangster's abdomen, sternum, and throat. The AR fell to the ground as he stumbled backwards into the boat, his feet hanging over the edge.

"Sniper Two to Command," he said, consciously adding a little excitement to his voice, "shots fired next to the river. One suspect down. Request an ambulance and a supervisor."

"Command is clear," Lieutenant Adams responded. "I was watching. Confirming you're C-4?"

"10-4, Command. I'll wait until the other units get here before checking the suspect."

# Chapter Five

**Headquarters, Loudon County Sheriff's Department, Leesburg, Virginia, Monday, 0225 hours**

Alberto Barajas sat handcuffed to a chair in one of the interview rooms, waiting for a pig to come talk with him. He knew they were watching him through the one-way glass or through the camera that hung on the wall. He looked up at the camera and then spat on the floor. The orange jumpsuit he was wearing was stretched to the bursting point, straining to contain his obese frame.

Chilo yawned, wondering what time it was. He hadn't heard anything about Rodrigo, hoping his friend had escaped but not really believing it. At the same time, if the cops had arrested the other cartel soldier, he should have seen him at the jail. Barajas had not even tried to resist when the SWAT team burst inside the safe house. When the assholes had dragged him outside, he noticed several other pigs running around the double-wide, in the direction of the Potomac.

He wondered why he was even in this interview room? Barajas had nothing to say, just like every other time that he had been arrested. The NG lieutenant knew how the system worked in America. They would revoke his parole and he would serve out the last year of his prison sentence. His reputation as a high-level cartel member meant that no one would bother him inside the maximum-security penitentiary. With good behavior, Chilo could be out in six to eight months. Easy.

Finally, the door opened and a hot Latino woman with dark, curly hair and glasses strolled in, accompanied by a muscular white man. The lady cop carried a folder and sat at the table, opposite of the thug. The big man stood by the door, his arms crossed.

"How you doin', Alberto? I'm Detective Sergeant Lopez."

"No English," Chilo answered, bringing a slight smile to the woman's face.

"No problemo," she replied. "El español fue mi primer idioma."

Lopez slid a sheet of paper across the table, continuing in Spanish. "Here are your rights in both English and español. I'd like speak with you about..."

"I don't have anything to say to you, Sergeant Puta! You can take your big boyfriend and get the hell out of here!"

Chilo didn't know if the man knew Spanish or not, but the expression on his face clearly conveyed that he wasn't happy with the gangster. Maybe I can get him to beat me up, he thought. Then I can sue them and enjoy a nice payday.

Sergeant Lopez kept talking as if she hadn't even heard the prisoner's outburst.

"I need two things from you. First, we want Ramon Contreras. You give him to us and we can offer you..."

The Mexican laughed loudly. "Oh, you want el Asesino? Why didn't you say so? You stupid puta, what makes you think I even know where el Asesino is?"

"Second," J-Lo continued, "give us the locations where you're taking the children. I know you act like a heartless thug, but here's an opportunity to do the right thing and let us go free those little girls and boys."

Chilo masked his surprise. He had no idea he was on the radar for human trafficking. How did that happen?

"What children? I don't know what you're talking about. I've got a heart, though. It's right down here between my legs. You want to come find it?"

Barajas leered at the woman who stared at him impassively. After a moment, the investigator stood, nodded at her partner and they started to leave the room. Lopez opened the door but paused, speaking over her shoulder.

"They found the pistol you hid under the couch. It's got your fingerprints all over it. A convicted felon in possession of a firearm is going to be good for at least five more years in prison."

The gangster did not answer, glaring at the two deputies.

"Also, that's too bad about Rodrigo."

Chilo's eyes locked with hers, clearly interested but not about to ask the pig for information.

"He's in the morgue, full of holes," the detective continued. "That's one more predator off the streets. Your hearing is not for a few days so I'll give you a chance to think about what we talked about."

With that, they were gone. The thug screamed out several profanities as the door slammed shut. Four deputies entered the interview room, two of them holding tasers. Chilo didn't resist as they escorted him to his cell.

McCain followed Lopez back to the conference room where a number of investigators were hard at work. Major Kim had again requested the state police to conduct the investigation of the officer-involved-shooting. His own detectives would work alongside them to make sure all departmental policies were followed.

"How'd it go?" Lieutenant Jake Donaldson asked.

J-Lo shook her head. "What an asshole!"

Chuck nodded. "You tried and hopefully you planted the seed. Let me work my informants and see what I can come up with. I'm hoping to give you something good in the next day or two."

"Where did you get these 'informants?'" Julia asked, tilting her head to side. "I do this full-time and struggle to find good snitches and you're an auxiliary deputy with another job."

McCain shrugged. "Yeah, just lucky, I guess. How's Norm?"

"I think he's got ice water in his veins," the lieutenant replied. "Did you see the footage from the drone?"

"Yeah, I was in the command truck at the time."

"There shouldn't be any issues with the shooting and the taxpayers won't have to foot the bill for that perp for the next thirty years."

Sergeant Cobb walked over to join the group as Sergeant Lopez retreated to write a short synopsis of her attempted interview of Barajas.

"That sounded like a good op, Brandon," Donaldson said.

"For sure. Norm took care of business and that fat asshole is in jail."

"Well, gentlemen, I'm going to call it a night," McCain yawned. "I'll be back in after lunch."

Cobb walked with McCain out to the parking lot and offered his hand. Chuck shook it, taking the GPS tracker that had been on the Nissan Frontier pickup.

"Any trouble getting it back?" the big man asked.

"No one was paying any attention to me after Norm capped that guy."

"I appreciate y'all doing that. We're still tracking the van. It looks like they're heading to Texas. I'll let you know how it goes but any leverage we can get against the cartel, the better the chances we have of rescuing some children and putting these animals away."

Both men knew that a judge-issued warrant was required to use a GPS tracker on a suspect's vehicle. There hadn't been time for that and there was no guarantee that a judge would have given it to them. Thankfully, the two snipers had been willing to bend a rule so that McCain's team could see where Chilo's van was going.

**Century Tactical Solutions, Leesburg, Virginia, Monday, 0740 hours**

Gabby Vargas watched the blinking red dot on her left computer monitor as Chilo's GMC van continued to move southwest on I-59. They would eventually pick up either I-20 or I-12 in Mississippi if they were heading to the border like she thought. She shuddered to think of the fate that awaited the human cargo the gangsters we're probably going to pick up.

The computer hacker had been the first one in the office that morning, anxious to get started. Gabby, Andy, and Tex were technically on administrative leave from the sheriff's department while the shooting at Fleming's house was investigated. We're reserve deputies, she pondered, so I wonder if admin leave really applies to us?

She had given the investigators a statement two hours after they had taken out the eight sicarios. The young woman had replayed the shootout over and over in her mind, pleased with how she'd performed. Gabby had dropped three of the four perps on her end of the house, while Tex had taken out the other. As a career computer hacker, she had only picked up a gun for the first time a few years earlier. What she lacked in experience, however, she made up for in determination and consistent training. Scotty had also taken her under his wing and was turning her into a sniper.

At the moment, however, it was her high-level IT skills that she was drawing from. On the other computer screen, Gabby was reading through the vintage car hobby board she had been monitoring for information about the escort scene in Atlantic City. An avatar with the name of "Gerald" had posted a glowing review of a young woman named "Lara."

*"I don't know if she's legal or not but she looks real young with that sweet, innocent look,"* he had written before going into more detail about the services Lara had provided. *"I definitely plan on seeing her again the next time I'm in AC!"*

Was he talking about Lara Sagarra? That was what Vargas was determined to find out. Gerald had not given the name of the casino in which he had hooked up with the girl but implied that it was on the strip in the New Jersey resort city. Maybe we could go stake out a few of them and see what we see? A quick Google search revealed that there were only nine casinos in the city. That was still a lot, even if we took the entire team, Gabby thought.

At this point, the computer whiz didn't have any fresh ideas. There had been no answer to the DM inquiry she had sent in the name of "Calvin." These group members were very cautious, probably using the hobby board to share general information about the escorts. She was beginning to wonder if maybe they used something like WhatsApp or Discord to communicate more directly.

Vargas was so caught up in pondering a next step, she never noticed Sandra Dunning wheel herself into the conference room.

"Good morning, Gabby. You're up early."

The computer hacker almost came out of her seat.

"Sorry! I didn't mean to startle you."

"It's OK, Ms. Dunning, I was just thinking about how we can find Lara Sagarra. I think I've got an idea but I'll need your approval."

The VP of intelligence and investigations smiled at the young woman. "We haven't had much to go on so far. Tell me what you're thinking."

After hearing what Vargas had to say, Dunning stared at her thoughtfully. After a moment, she nodded.

"Let me run it by the general and Chuck. I think it's worth a shot if they can spare a few of you for a trip to New Jersey."

**Hard Rock Hotel & Casino, Atlantic City, New Jersey, Wednesday, 2035 hours**

Chloe and Jimmy checked in at the Hard Rock where they would be based for the next week and dropped their bags in their room. After freshening up, it was time for dinner and they enjoyed a sumptuous meal at the Council Oak Steaks & Seafood inside the iconic resort. It wasn't cheap, but Century was footing the bill, plus it was possible that Lara Sagarra might meet a client there. After a delicious dinner of steak and lobster, it was time to get to work.

They moved to the Lobby Bar and took a table that allowed each of them to cover a one-hundred-and-eighty degrees around the bustling nightlife hotspot. The bar provided views of the casino and the lobby of the hotel, along with a steady flow of guests moving from one location to the other inside the popular resort. Wilkerson nursed a glass of white wine while Jones slowly sipped a Blue Moon Belgian White Beer.

The plan was to stay in place for a couple of hours, occasionally taking turns making a lap around the gambling area and other bars and restaurants, hoping to catch a glimpse of Lara. Gabby and Hollywood were at Harrah's, about two miles away, following the same pattern. The two couples would each visit two casinos every night and meet for lunch the following day to compare notes.

"Anything?" Chloe asked as Jimmy placed another glass of wine in front of her and seated himself at their table after strolling around the vibrant night spot.

The former Marine shook his head, taking a swallow of his fresh beer.

"Just a bunch of grannies in there, gambling away their Social Security checks. We've been watching for almost two hours now. Why don't we finish our drinks and head over to the Ocean?"

"Sounds good."

They sat for a few minutes, carefully studying the customers as they moved through the lobby, bar, and gambling area, the laughter, voices and music mingling into a numbing background noise. Chloe scanned every face, hoping to spot the missing teenage girl.

"You haven't had much to say. Everything OK?" Wilkerson asked her partner.

Jones glanced around the area, his trained eyes taking in everything.

"Yeah," he sighed, "this just isn't our normal kind of mission. I'm all for helping people, but I feel like here, we're trying to save this girl from her own dumb choices. She's lucky the cartel didn't kill her and her parents as soon as they'd discovered she'd stolen from them. And, for all we know, she might already be dead, dismembered, and discarded somewhere."

Chloe nodded, taking a sip of wine.

"I sure hope not. I'm praying we get the chance to at least help one girl get away from these animals. We've seen first-hand how evil they are."

"That's a fact and I'm always happy to do my part to rid the world of a few of them. We just have to remember that we're not in Mexico this time. Corpses seem to attract more attention here than they do south of the border."

"This place is so big!" Gabby exclaimed after meeting back up with Hollywood at the Eden Lounge, frustration etched across her face. "There's no way we'll ever find her."

Rafael sipped from a bottle of Dos Equis, the music pulsating around them as the dance floor started to heat up. They had each taken a slow walk around Harrah's massive casino and multiple restaurants and bars. The former soldier sensed his friend's frustration, agreeing with her in his mind. There was no way they were going to find the lost girl.

"We might get lucky," he smiled. "This was a good plan you came up with. Let's let it play out for the week and see what happens. With the four of us combing these resorts, we're bound to see her if she shows up."

"I'm not so sure," Vargas replied with a frown, taking a swallow of her Corona, "but thanks for the encouragement."

"Isn't there any way you can hack into the security cameras of these resorts?"

"I'm working on it, but the IT infrastructure at most casinos is almost as good as the Agency's."

"But didn't you get caught hacking into the CIA's systems?"

Gabby waved her hand dismissively and grinned. "Yeah, after the fifth or sixth time. I got a little over confident. I've haven't said anything because I didn't want to get our hopes up, but I've already hacked into four of the casinos and have a program running."

"You do? What kind of program?"

"All the major casinos have a sophisticated facial recognition software to catch known cheats. The systems are actually all connected, at least in the sense that they can share information. If a guy is counting cards here and gets kicked out, security will upload his pic and if he shows up at Bally's, their system will trigger their security officers as soon as he walks through the door.

"What's less known," the computer expert continued, "is that they also upload photos of known prostitutes. Everyone knows what happens at these resorts but none of them want a reputation for allowing sex trafficking on their property."

"So you added Lara Sagarra to the list?" Estrada asked, finishing his beer.

"I did. It's another long shot," she shrugged, "but it's worth a try."

"I don't know how you do it," Hollywood said, shaking his head. "I get aggravated every time I have to change my banking password and here you are hacking into some of the best computer systems on the planet."

**Loudon County, Virginia, Wednesday, 1530 hours**

Between keeping up with Jimmy's team in Atlantic City, trying to locate Ramon Contreras, and monitoring the GPS tracker on Chilo Barajas' van, Chuck also attempted to get the DEA involved in the case. He couldn't tell them about the tracking device on the vehicle so he wasn't able to answer all the federal agency's questions about where he was getting his intel. They didn't care that he was promising them a van full of drugs, exploited women and children, and a few bad guys. Even Virginia based senior Special Agent Frank Simpson was unable to pull any strings for McCain for a scenario that developed in America's Southwest. The big man finally gave up as the beeping red light continued to inch its way along his computer screen, ever closer to Virginia.

He finally decided to call Lieutenant Jake Donaldson on Wednesday afternoon, asking if he and Scotty could ride along that night on the 1800-0600hrs shift. This was not an unusual request as Chuck required his teammates to ride periodically with some of the Loudon County deputies to stay sharp and in tune with what the uniformed cops had to deal with on a day-to-day basis. McCain knew Donaldson always got to work early and he and Scotty Smith joined the shift supervisor in his office at 1730hrs.

"Hey, Chuck, Scotty glad to have you guys with us tonight."

"Thanks, LT. Can I run something by you before roll call?"

"Sure, whatcha got?"

Smith pushed the door closed as McCain pulled out his phone and laid it in front of the lieutenant. A red dot was moving north on Interstate 81.

"What am I looking at?"

"That's Chilo Barajas' van. The reason it wasn't at that safe house in Lovettsville a few nights ago, was because he had sent a few of his boys back to Texas to pick up some drugs and maybe even some children and girls that they'll assign to one of the New Generation's sex trafficking operations."

"Is there a tracker on that van? I don't remember seeing where that was authorized."

"There is a tracker on the van and no, it's not authorized."

Jake stared across the desk at his friend. He had come to trust and respect Chuck and his team. They were as good as anybody he'd ever worked with. At the same time, they couldn't break the law to enforce it.

"That van full of human cargo and drugs should be in the area in the next couple of hours," Chuck continued. "I've got a plan for stopping it and the GPS tracker won't even need to be mentioned in the report."

"I'm listening," Jake answered, praying that what Chuck proposed didn't get both of them in serious trouble.

"I spoke with Sergeant Lopez earlier today. One of Chilo's men—he's identified as Danny in Barajas' phone— has been trying to get in touch with the fat man. Danny's tried to call and has texted both Chilo and the thug that Norm capped. He asked Barajas if he was still supposed to bring the cargo to the farm. That's the location on the river in Lovettsville. She texted him back as Chilo and said he would see him there. She also texted that he (Barajas) suspected the police were listening in on his calls and told Danny not to call him. It sounds like they'll be driving right through Loudon County. Here's what I was thinking we could do."

McCain outlined what he had in mind for the next ten minutes. Donaldson nodded as he glanced at the time.

"I'm in. If there are kids in that van, I'm willing to take a chance. Scotty, I'll let you ride with Sergeant Miller. He'll want in on this, too. I just hope you guys know what you're doing. Let's go have roll call and then we can finalize a few things afterwards."

After roll call, Chuck, Scotty, Sergeant Brad Miller and Jake pulled up a map of the county and worked out the final details. They hit the road with McCain riding shotgun in the lieutenant's marked Chevrolet Impala. The only thing that set Donaldson's car apart from his troops' was the absence of a light bar on top. The blue lights were all located in the grill. Smith and Miller would be in the area to assist. Scotty would also be tracking the van on his phone.

By 2030 hours, Donaldson and McCain were parked in the center of the county, watching the red light on Chuck's phone. The van exited I-66 and started north on Highway 15. Chuck breathed a sigh of relief.

"Here they come. ETA of twenty."

Jake nodded. "Remember. This is my traffic stop. You cover the passenger side."

Chuck had tried to convince his friend to let him make contact with the driver. The lieutenant wouldn't hear of it.

"If this goes to court later, the first thing a defense attorney will ask me is why did I let a reserve deputy take charge? You're my cover officer. And, don't forget everything is on camera now."

McCain nodded reluctantly, knowing Donaldson was correct.

"Right. Bodycams were just starting to become a thing when I retired. Our traffic units had dash cams to get video evidence for DUI cases, but none of the rest of us had them."

"We're all equipped now, but I don't mind. The camera has saved my ass more than once when some citizen has called to complain, hoping to get out of a ticket, accusing me of saying something improper."

"For sure," Chuck commented. "I carried a voice-activated digital recorder in my shirt pocket for that same reason."

"Why'd you take early retirement from your PD in Georgia?" Jake asked as they waited in the parking lot of the Church of Our Savior Anglican Church. "You were a lieutenant and are a sharp guy. I'm guessing you would've been a shoo-in to get promoted to captain."

"I was bored out of my mind as a lieutenant," Chuck answered. "You know how it is. Sergeant is the best job in any police department, but then I got promoted. That first year, I was a road LT like you. That was great. Then, I got tapped to take over a few special operations units. I was confined to my office instead of being able to go out and play. Plus, they didn't let lieutenants serve on SWAT so I was off the team and staring at my four walls, answering emails and returning phone calls. When I found out I was eligible to retire, it was a no-brainer.

"When I announced I was leaving, I had a couple of assistant chiefs rush over to my office and try to talk me out of it. I was unofficially promised that I would be promoted in the next year if I stuck around. It was nice to realize I was appreciated, but I was done.

"I had a couple of friends who had done the military LE contractor thing so I put my resume out there and got a call from a recruiter. I ended up serving with an SF A Team on two one-year contracts. That was a blast. I knew after my first firefight in Afghanistan that I had made the right decision. I learned more working with those Green Berets than in my previous twenty years as a cop."

Donaldson laughed. "A firefight let you know you'd made the right career decision, huh?"

"I know it doesn't sound normal but those two years were exactly what I needed at the time. And, it got me ready for the zombie apocalypse. I got recruited for the CDC Enforcement Unit right after I finished up the second contract and came home."

"That was a crazy time for everybody," Jake commented, pointing at Chuck's phone. "How we looking?"

"They should pass us in about five minutes."

"Well, it sounds like things are about to get interesting."

Danny Lopez was tired. He, Carlos, and Ricardo had rested for almost a day at one of their safe houses in Brownsville. The children were already at the location after being smuggled into Los Estados by one of the New Generation's best mules. This load contained four little girls, from eight to twelve years old, along with sixteen and a nineteen-year old, plus twenty kilos of meth, twenty of crack, and several thousand fentanyl tablets packaged in gallon-sized ziplock bags.

Danny had been doing this long enough to know that the children would get restless on the long drive. He told the two teenagers to look after the younger ones and he would put in a good word for them when they got to their final destination. Not that it would matter. They were all going to be sex slaves; it was just a matter of where they were would be working.

Lopez and his two companions had also picked up two additional sicarios. Ramon Contreras had requested some additional men after losing soldiers in the assassination of the gringo pig and his woman. After they arrived at the safe house in Lovettsville, the new gangsters could get in touch with el Asesino and arrange a ride to wherever he was currently staying.

Danny and his two friends had taken turns driving over the long road trip. The sicarios had refused to help out, preferring to remain in the back with their cargo. When Danny exited off of I-66 onto James Monroe Highway, he finally felt himself relax. The state highway would take them most of the way to Lovettsville and he knew it wouldn't be long before he could stretch out for a good night's sleep.

Lopez had been a little surprised by Barajas' lack of communication. At the same time, Danny had worked with Chilo long enough to know that he preferred face-to-face conversation rather than using a cell phone. If something had come up, his lieutenant would have let him know. The text about the cops listening in on their phone calls made sense. The gringo pigs still hadn't realized that they couldn't stop the Jalisco New Generation crime family. They were in America to stay, no matter how hard the police tried to stop them.

"And there they go," Chuck said, watching the full-size cargo vehicle pass the entrance to the church.

Jake waited thirty seconds before switching on his headlights and turning north onto James Monroe Highway. The van was almost a quarter mile ahead of them and the police cruiser quickly closed the distance. A pickup truck was between them and the van but Jake and Chuck were still able to watch the suspect vehicle as they maintained the speed limit. Two miles later, the pickup truck turned off into an Exxon station. Donaldson backed off a few car lengths as they continued to follow the gangsters, looking for a good excuse to stop them.

The van drifted to the left, weaving across the center-line and then back into its lane. Less than a minute later, the vehicle bumped the center-line again.

"That'll work," Donaldson said. "Failure to maintain lane."

Jake quickly radioed the dispatcher, giving their location, the tag, a vehicle description, and letting her know it was a possible impaired driver.

The lieutenant glanced over at the reserve deputy. "Let's see what they've got in that van," he said, activating his blue lights.

Lopez felt his eyes getting heavy as he sensed the van drifting into the oncoming lane. He quickly pulled the steering wheel to the right, fighting to stay awake.

"Is that the pigs behind us?" Carlos asked from the passenger seat, staring at the mirror on his side of the vehicle.

Danny couldn't tell what kind of car was behind the bright headlights in his mirrors, but cursed loudly as the van weaved again. He made the correction, but swerved too far to the right.

Carlos' question was answered as flashing blue lights lit up the dark stretch of highway.

The van slowed, coming to a stop on the shoulder of the road. Donaldson stopped over a car length back, activating his high-beams and the spotlight mounted just in front of the driver's door. He aimed it into the driver's side mirror, grabbed his flashlight and exited the cruiser. Chuck was already out, watching the rear and passenger sides of the vehicle. The cargo area of the van was windowless but that didn't mean the back door couldn't come flying open.

Lieutenant Donaldson slowly made his way down the side of the van, stopping behind the driver's door. He reached forward and lightly tapped on the glass with his flashlight, causing the driver to bring the window down. The deputy moved just far enough forward to where he could see the driver and illuminate him with his flashlight, but where the suspect would have to turn around in his seat to see the police officer.

"Good evening! I'm Lieutenant Donaldson with the Loudon County Sherriff's Department. The reason I stopped you tonight was because you were weaving across the center-line and onto the shoulder. Have you got your driver's license and registration with you?"

"No English," was the reply.

"No problemo," Jake said, switching to his limited Spanish. "Déjame ver tus manos." *Let me see your hands.*

The driver instantly complied, raising both hands.

"Tienes una licencia*?"* Donaldson asked.

"No," the driver answered with a shake of the head.

The deputy pulled open the driver's door. "OK. Let me have the car keys and then step out and talk with me."

Reluctantly, the driver turned off the van, handed him the keys and climbed out of the vehicle.

As Danny pulled the van onto the shoulder, he had alerted the men in the back to what was happening. Outrunning the police in a cargo van was out of the question. For now, their only chance was stopping and looking for an opportunity to kill the pig. All of the gangsters and sicarios were armed and would wait for the right moment to act. After they stopped, however, Carlos informed them of a second officer watching the passenger side of the van.

Lopez's own 9mm Ruger pistol was wedged between his seat and the console. He felt confident that he could drop the cop before the pig knew what hit him. The presence of another officer changed the scenario. When the first deputy appeared at his window, Danny realized that this pig would not be so easy to kill. He carried himself with confidence and conveyed the sense that he was in control. Lopez certainly didn't expect the cop to speak español.

Before he knew what was happening, Danny was complying with the pig's orders, getting out of the van with his hands raised and being escorted back to the police car. The cartel soldier glanced unconsciously back at the van, wondering what his companions were going to do. Lopez suddenly found himself being pushed facedown on the hood of the cruiser, his hands being cuffed behind him. The police officer searched him and seated him in the back of the squad car, on the passenger side.

"You're under arrest for not having a driver's license and for weaving. Have you been drinking tonight?"

"No drinking," Danny answered nervously.

A second police car materialized, pulling in behind them, the extra blue strobes adding to the intensity of the light show. This cop had not given Danny any opportunity to resist, the thug realized too late, looking around for a way of escape. The backup officer was standing beside the passenger door of the cruiser, continuing to watch the van. The arrival of more pigs let the gangster know that his night was probably not going to end like he had envisioned it.

The deputy who had stopped him withdrew a small notebook and a pen.

"¿Cómo te llamas?"

Lopez hung his head in disappointment as the two other officers strolled up. He had failed Chilo. He had failed his brothers and he had failed the NG family. He wasn't about to tell this cop anything.

"Who's in the van with you?"

When it was obvious that the suspect wasn't going to answer, the deputy shut the door.

"He's not talking," Donaldson advised Chuck, Sergeant Brad Miller and Scotty Smith.

Smith slung his H&K 416 over his chest as the lieutenant updated the newcomers.

"Let's get the passenger out next?" McCain suggested.

"And we'll put him in Brad's car," Jake agreed.

The lieutenant and sergeant slowly made their way up the passenger side of cargo vehicle. Chuck covered the deputies from the open passenger door of the cruiser as Scotty moved to the left rear corner of the LT's vehicle. From this position, he could watch the driver's door and the rear of the van. Jake stopped behind the passenger door and rapped on the window. The second occupant reluctantly opened his door.

"Stick your hands out!" Donaldson ordered in Spanish.

The Mexican climbed out slowly, making sure to keep his hands in plain view, glancing over his shoulder back inside the cargo vehicle. Carlos considered trying to kill these cops, but they gave him no chance. The gangster left his .40 caliber Glock in the van, hoping the sicarios would be able to turn this situation around in the cartel's favor. The two deputies led him to the rear of Jake's cruiser. The thug saw his friend in the backseat of the police car.

"¿Cómo te llamas?"

"Mi nombre es Carlos."

"Do you have any ID, Carlos?"

"No ID."

Before he knew what had happened, Carlos found himself handcuffed, searched and placed in the sergeant's Ford Interceptor SUV. Smith and McCain continued to watch the van. With no rear windows, it was a tactical nightmare. There was no safe way to approach the cargo compartment. Chuck backed up and the four men stood behind the LT's cruiser.

"Any ideas?" Jake asked his companions.

"How about if we issue a challenge," Chuck suggested, "and tell them to come out slowly or we'll send in the K9?"

"Good idea except we don't have a K9," Brad commented.

"I can do a pretty good imitation of a German Shepherd," Scotty quipped.

A child's scream suddenly came from inside the van. Before the deputies could react, the rear doors burst open and an AK-47 started chattering from within, the 7.62x39 rounds slamming into Donaldson's cruiser. The lieutenant and sergeant both dove to the ground behind the police car, drawing their pistols. Smith and McCain had trained and fought together for years and their reactions had been rehearsed in both shoot houses and actual gunfights. With no traffic coming on the rural stretch of highway, Scotty moved left, further out into the roadway while Chuck took a couple of big steps to the right.

Thankfully the sergeant had offset his police car giving Smith a safe lane from which to work. The muzzle of his H&K rifle came up as the AK's bullets continued to track across the hood and windshield towards McCain, the gangster moving towards the open doors to get a better angle. Both reserve deputies fired in tandem, the former Ranger sniper quickly pumping two 5.56mm soft point rounds into the sicarios chest, as the former SWAT officer squeezed off a single shot from his Glock 17, sending a 9mm hollow point into the gangster's forehead. The AK-47 fell from the dead man's grasp, his heart, lungs, and brain destroyed. The gunman's momentum carried him forward and he dropped face first onto the asphalt, landing with a sickening thud.

The police car's headlights now illuminated the interior of the van where a second Mexican held a hysterical young girl in his arms as a human shield, a pistol jammed against the side of her head.

"Drop your guns, pigs!" the sicario ordered in Spanish. "Now, or I shoot the little girl!"

The child was no more than eight or ten years old, her loud screams suddenly stifled as the sicario brought a rough hand over her mouth.

"You've got this, Scotty," Chuck said quietly.

"Easy," the bearded man answered.

"No problemo!" Chuck called out, lowering the pistol to his side and raising his other hand with a waving palm towards the gangster. "Just don't hurt the girl."

As soon as the gangster's eyes flitted towards McCain's moving hand, Smith snapped up the H&K's muzzle and fired a single shot, the bullet punching into the thug's right eye, and disconnecting his brain. His gun dropped to the floor of the vehicle and the child, now covered with her attacker's blood, pushed free of him, her eyes wide with terror, as she started to scream again.

"There are more kids in the van," Smith announced, his optic picking up the small figures huddling on the floor. "And another bad guy."

The sniper's finger was already taking up the slack on the trigger as he sighted in on the other Mexican's head. This one wanted no part of what he had just witnessed. He threw his hands into the air. Ricardo had already discarded his pistol under his seat in the van, not wanting to give the police any reason to kill him.

"No shoot! No shoot!" Ricardo yelled in English.

After getting the live thug out of the van, the sergeant and lieutenant quickly handcuffed him and the two dead gangsters. Once the scene was finally secure, Smith transitioned into his role as a medic.

"Hey, Chuck, can you grab my backpack out of the sarge's car? My med kit is in it."

Scotty checked each of the girls in the van, trying to calm them down and ease their fears. As soon as Chuck brought his bag, the paramedic began cleaning the blood and gore off of the girls who had been sprayed. Thankfully, they were unharmed physically, but the emotional trauma they had suffered was another matter entirely. At least now, they were free from the evil designs of the cartel.

Sergeant Miller glanced at his lieutenant's cruiser, now full of bullet holes. Something didn't look right in the rear compartment and Brad pulled open the door to check on the prisoner. He was slumped over in the seat, not moving. The sergeant pulled him upright and saw the wound to his torso. An AK round from the gangster's friend had found him.

"Hey, the driver's wounded!" Miller announced, reaching in to press his fingers against the man's neck. "I'm not feeling a pulse!"

Smith grabbed his pack and hurried over, pulling the wounded man out of the car so he could work on him. As he was doing that, the lieutenant called in the shooting and requested detectives, CSI, and an ambulance. The bearded man stood, shaking his head, and pulled off his rubber gloves.

"He's dead."

"Are those girls OK?" Jake asked.

"Yes, sir. Shook up and traumatized, but they're safe now."

The lieutenant nodded. "That's good news. I've got a couple of female deputies enroute. That'll probably make those young ladies feel a little more at ease. They've still got a tough time ahead of them while the system tries to figure out what to do with them."

**Headquarters, Loudon County Sheriff's Department, Leesburg, Virginia, Thursday, 1105 hours**

Loudon County Sheriff Jerry Schaefer strolled into the small auditorium, pausing at the lectern to stare out at the assembled reporters. The dramatic deputy-involved shooting and the rescue of four children and two teenagers from being sex-trafficked had gotten the attention of the national media. This was Loudon County's third officer-involved shooting in less than a week, to go along with the homicide one of their deputies and his wife. The media outlets quickly picked up on this unusual trend in the normally quiet county.

The sheriff started the press conference by reading a prepared statement about the incident. It highlighted that the two suspects in custody and the three dead ones were connected with the Jalisco New Generation Cartel. Two of the children told the Loudon County investigators that they had been kidnapped off the street in Mexico City walking home from school. The other two were sisters, one eight and the other nine years of age, and they related the heartbreaking story that their parents in Guatemala had sold them to some men who had promised to take them to America where they would be adopted by rich families.

The teenage girls in the van had already suspected what was in store for them after they started the long trip across America. The teens told the investigators that two of the dead suspects had made them perform sex acts on the men during the drive. The two living perps were being held without bond on a laundry list of charges, multiplied by the six victims. The cargo van had also contained large quantities of illegal drugs, along with additional weapons.

After reading the statement, Schaefer looked around the room at all the cameras.

"I'll take questions now but please understand that this is an ongoing investigation and I won't be able to get too specific into the details of the case."

A short, stocky Hispanic man quickly stood. "I'm Marcos Salazar from CNN. Sheriff, your department has killed eleven Mexican men in the last week. Is there a crackdown on Latinos in Loudon County?"

Schaefer stared down at the man for a moment before he answered.

"CNN, huh? Didn't you used to work for MSNBC?"

"That's right," the surprised reporter responded. "I've been with CNN for over a year now, but back to my question..."

"It's a ridiculous question, but considering your work history I can understand why you would ask such a thing."

"That's not fair, Sheriff," Salazar stammered. "The Latino community of Loudon County have a right..."

The sheriff cut him off. "How many Hispanic or Latino people have you spoken with in Loudon County, Mr. Salazar? The Hispanics, African-Americans, Asians, white people, and any other group I might have missed who live in Loudon County, all have a right to live in a community in which law and order are respected. I was elected by people of every ethnicity because they trusted me and my deputies to keep them safe. Just a few weeks ago one of my deputies and his wife were murdered in their home in the middle of the night by the New Generation Cartel and..."

A middle-aged white man seated next to the CNN reporter jumped to his feet.

"Sheriff Schaefer, from what I've seen of that case, you don't really have any clear suspects for that murder of your employee, do you? So, aren't you speculating on who the suspects might be?"

"Who are you?"

"Oh, sorry. I'm Ronald Meadows with MSNBC."

"I'm not sure what you've been reading, Mr. Meadows, but our investigators had enough evidence to obtain murder warrants on the local lieutenant for the NG gang, Ramon Contreras. He calls himself, "the Assassin" or "the Killer." We already have one of his men in custody as an accomplice to those murders. So, as I was saying, the citizens of Loudon County want to know that their sheriff's department is doing everything they can to keep them and their families safe."

Schaefer ignored the upraised hands of several other national media representatives and called on Alice Crenshaw with the Loudon Times.

"Sheriff Schaefer, how are the children that your deputies rescued and what can you tell us about what will happen to them? Also, has your department located where these children and teens were heading? Have you identified a specific house or apartment where they were going to be held?"

"As you can imagine, Alice, they were incredibly traumatized by what they had been through. They are currently being looked after by our local social services. The two teenagers who said they'd been sexually assaulted have been checked and treated at our local sexual assault center.

Our investigators will try to have their interviews completed in the next couple of days. We've been in contact with the United States State Department about having all these young ladies returned home. Of course, that presents a different set of challenges for the state department as two of the children were allegedly sold to the cartel by their own parents.

"For the second part of your question, Alice, no, we haven't located where the victims were going to be taken. We have evidence that they were enroute to a safe house when they were stopped, but we don't believe that was the final location. We're still working on that."

"Yeah, Wayne, did you have a question?" Schaefer asked, pointing at Wayne Waters, a representative for one of the local news channels.

"Thanks, Sheriff. What do you think is the reason for this latest upsurge in gang violence? Can you point to anything that might have triggered it?"

"Well, Sergeant Dwayne Thomas and his wife Shelly were murdered just a few days after we raided two New Generation safe houses. Sergeant Thomas was in charge of that investigation. We recovered a large quantity of drugs and weapons, and made several arrests, including Ramon Contreras. For reasons we're still trying to unravel, he was released from jail on 'no bond' warrants. Those homicides appear to be in retaliation for that investigation into Contreras and the NG Cartel. Maybe when we locate Contreras, we'll get some more answers."

The sheriff held up his hands and spoke to the reporters. "Now, if you'll excuse me, I need to get back to work."

He turned to leave, but Marcos Salazar called out another question, "Sheriff Schaefer, how many more Mexicans does your department plan on killing?"

The senior deputy slowly turned and locked eyes with the reporter.

"Only the ones who need killing, Mr. Salazar. We didn't declare war on the cartel but they seemed to have declared it on us and we'll do whatever we have to do to protect the citizens of Loudon Country from these animals. As the sheriff, I'll also do everything that I can to protect my deputies."

With that, Schaefer turned and left the room.

**Atlantic City, New Jersey, Sunday, 10:20am**

Lara was startled out of a restless sleep by a knock at her bedroom door.

"Wake up!" Ernesto ordered. "You've got an early date today."

"Sí," she answered groggily. "I'm awake."

"Be ready to leave at 11:00."

The young woman glanced at the clock on her bedside table and pulled herself out of the warm bed. She'd turned a late trick the evening before at the Golden Nugget, not getting back to the house until after midnight. The Nugget was the smallest gambling house and hotel in Atlantic City and Lara had met a number of men there since she'd been working as an escort, suspecting some of their employees were on the cartel payroll.

After showering, dressing in a short, tight black dress, and putting on her makeup, she found Ernesto in the kitchen.

"Do I have time to eat?"

"No," the gangster answered, standing and motioning at the door, "but this hombre is paying for you to have lunch with him before he takes you to his room."

"¿Qué?"

Ernesto shrugged, giving the hint of a smile. "Some of our clients want it to feel like a real date before he bangs you. Don't talk too much, laugh at his jokes, and enjoy your lunch. He's paying."

A few minutes before noon, Ernesto led Lara into the Tropicana Shopping Mall. He pointed out the Firewaters Saloon, where they would meet after her date. A trim, middle-aged man with salt and pepper hair was waiting inside A Dam Good Sports Bar & Grill. The two men shook hands and the cartel pimp nodded at the client and backed away as Sagarra approached the man.

"Hi, I'm Thomas," he smiled nervously, motioning to a booth.

Thomas wore a powder blue polo shirt tucked into his khakis.

"I'm Lara," she said quietly, forcing a shy smile onto her face.

"I hope this place is OK? I heard the burgers were great here."

"Sure, this is fine," she replied, trying not to let her surprise show.

Even though Eduardo had told her that she was now an escort, all of her other clients had just escorted her upstairs to get their money's worth.

A server appeared, handing them menus and placing glasses of ice water in front of them. Lara noted the wedding ring on Thomas' hand before turning her attention to the menu.

"Please, order whatever you want," he encouraged her.

A few minutes later, Lara was ravenously working on a bacon cheeseburger and a stack of fries while Thomas munched a steak sandwich. Her date told her he was from Nashville but had been in Atlantic City for a Realtor Convention. He chatted non-stop about the real estate market, seminars he had attended during the week, and his own success in the hot Nashville housing market.

For her part, Lara smiled, nodded, and laughed at the appropriate times as she devoured the burger. She had surprised herself by finishing the entire thing.

"Wow! You were hungry," Thomas noted with approval, as he motioned for the check. "I'm glad you liked it. Can we go to my room now?"

"Of course. I thought you'd never ask," Lara replied in the low voice that most of her clients seemed too like.

Thomas took her hand and guided her across the street into the resort, through the lobby, and onto the elevator to his fifth-floor executive suite. The curtains were open revealing a magnificent view of the Atlantic Ocean. Lara excused herself to use the restroom. As she finished up, she could hear Thomas talking to someone on the phone.

"I'm sorry, honey. I had to meet a client for a late breakfast and the first available flight is at 7:00pm. I know, I miss you, too, but I'll be home tonight."

A sudden queasiness stirred in Lara's stomach as another layer of guilt dropped onto her shoulders. She forced herself to take a deep breath and thought of her parents. If she didn't do what the cartel wanted, her mom and dad would die a horrible death and she knew that she would be forced to watch it before the animals killed her, too. Let's just get this over with, she resigned herself.

Forcing her emotions down into the basement of her soul, she opened the bathroom door and heard the man's voice drop to where she couldn't hear the rest of what he was saying. His back was to her, staring out the large windows, the phone to his ear. He ended the conversation and turned towards her. The momentary guilt that she saw in his eyes was quickly replaced by lust. He tossed the phone onto a table and started to undress.

"You are one of the most beautiful girls I've ever met and I think it's time you got out of those clothes."

**Ocean Casino Resort, Atlantic City, New Jersey, Sunday, 1155 hours**

Gabby, Hollywood, Chloe, and Jimmy met at Harper's for brunch to compare notes. Sadly, neither couple had anything to report and after almost four days, the group was clearly discouraged. Chuck had designated Jimmy as the team leader and the former Marine officer understood the importance of keeping his people motivated. The plan was to keep working the casinos until Wednesday. After that, the investigation would be closed and Sandra would have to break the sad news to the Sagarras that they had found no trace of their lost daughter.

"On the plus side," Jones said, "we're eatin' good and I've made almost a hundred bucks on the slot machines."

This elicited a strained laugh from the others. No one wanted to give up or go home empty-handed, but they all knew that the odds of finding the wayward teen were stacked against them, especially in the gambling Mecca of Atlantic City.

Gabby's phone vibrated as she finished her orange juice. A glance at the screen almost caused her to drop the empty glass.

"We need to get to the Tropicana!" she said excitedly, using her fingers to enlarge the security camera photos of Lara Sagarra. "She's there!"

Gabby quickly passed the phone around and hurriedly told her friends how she had managed to penetrate the casino's firewall and upload her program, along with a photo of the young woman. The current picture showed Lara wearing a short black dress and high heels accompanied by a stocky Hispanic man with greasy, shoulder length hair and a scruffy beard.

"I'll go get our car and meet you out front, Chloe," Jones said, standing moving quickly away.

"Good call. I'll get ours, too," Hollywood commented, following their team leader.

Chloe withdrew enough cash to cover their meal, along a generous tip, dropping it on the table as she and Gabby hurried to meet their partners.

"We probably need some kind of a plan," Vargas said, as they rushed outside.

Wilkerson nodded. "Yes, we do. Let's huddle up outside before we drive over there.

They still didn't have much of a plan as they approached the resort. A block from the Tropicana, Gabby got another automated alert from another of the casino's CCTV cameras. This photo showed Lara getting onto an elevator with a fiftyish, clean-cut white male. Vargas sent the photos to her teammates' phones. The two women were let out in front of the hotel entrance and the men parked in the public lot two blocks away. Everyone pushed their earpieces inside their ear canals. Jones and Estrada each grabbed a small backpack from the trunk that would provide some extra tools that might be needed before the day was out.

Jimmy instructed everyone to split up and locate the Mexican who had accompanied Lara into the resort. They stood a much better choice of finding him than of locating the missing girl among the two thousand plus hotel rooms.

"If you spot him, let's just hang back and see what he does," the former Marine officer ordered. "We're gonna have to make this up as we go but if nothing else develops, I'd love to follow them home."

It took thirty-five minutes, but Hollywood's voice came through everyone's earpieces.

"I've got him. He's in the Firewaters Saloon, all the way at the back of this place, right off the Boardwalk. He's at the bar, trying to charm the bartender."

"I figured him more of a Casa Taco & Tequila Bar kind of guy," Jones transmitted. "Gabby, why don't you go have a drink?"

"10-4, I'm on the way," Vargas answered.

Ernesto figured he had at least another hour to wait, already halfway through his second Budweiser. The gringo businessman had paid two-thousand dollars up front to enjoy the petite teenager. Twenty one-hundred dollar bills had slid into the gangsters palm during their handshake. Ernesto had ducked into a restroom to count the money but it was all there. He had already instructed Lara where she was to meet him after her date.

Now, he was trying to figure out how to get into the heavily tattooed bartender's pants at the Firewaters Saloon. The thug knew he could easily bang Lara, Nayara, or one of the girls at the whorehouse. That was too easy, though. He wanted a woman to go to bed with him because she was attracted to him, not out of fear. Plus, he had a reputation for enjoying rough sex and Eduardo had warned that if he hurt one of the whores again, it would not end well for him.

Ernesto wasn't afraid of much but he had watched Eduardo use his knife to slowly slice another cartel member to death. That soldier had been caught skimming money and drugs for his own use. And after the beating Eduardo had given him as a result of Bella's drug overdose, he didn't want to get on his lieutenant's bad side again.

The saloon had a country & western theme, all the way up to the barstools featuring actual saddles where the customer could rest his or her ass. Behind the bar, Jill wore a white cowboy hat, a tight black t-shirt with "Firewaters Saloon" emblazoned on it, denim shorts, and red cowboy boots. She had been pleasant, even a little flirty, as she served him his cervezas. There was no one else at the bar, but several of the booths and tables were occupied and the bartender assisted the other server in taking care of the lunch crowd.

During a lull, Ernesto motioned for another beer. As Jill put it in front of him, the gangster smiled broadly at the woman.

"What you doing after work tonight?"

She laughed pleasantly. "Well, I'm working twelve hours today and won't be off until midnight."

"Eh, that's a long day. Maybe you go out with me your next off day?"

"That's sweet of you to ask, but I'm pretty serious with my boyfriend."

"You go out with me, I make you forget all about him!"

The bartender smiled again, shaking her head as she went to check on her other customers. Ernesto sighed in frustration. What was wrong with these American women? They didn't know what they were missing, he thought, taking a long pull from the Budweiser. Out of the corner of his eye, he noticed a shapely, curly-haired Latino girl take a seat on the far end of the bar. She was wearing black tights, a New York Giants ball cap, and a Yankees hoodie that did nothing to hide her lovely curves.

Jill made her way back behind the bar and spoke with the newcomer, asking her what she was drinking. Ernesto couldn't hear the conversation, but motioned at Jill.

"Put her drink on my tab."

A few minutes later, the bartender set a glass of red wine in front of the woman and said something to her, pointing at Ernesto. The gangster held up his beer in a salute and gave the young lady his best smile. She raised her glass of wine towards the man and nodded at him.

Now what do I do? Gabby wondered. She didn't expect the thug to take any interest in her, especially today. Vargas had not washed her hair that morning, pulling on the ball cap to cover the unruly curls. She wasn't wearing any makeup and was dressed casually for her brunch meeting with her teammates. The plan was to dress up later for a night of scouring the casinos, but now they had photo evidence that Lara Sagarra had recently entered the Tropicana. The man at the other end of the bar was definitely the one who the cameras captured accompanying Lara.

Gabby had just planned on sitting at the bar until the cartel pimp left or met up with Lara so that the rest of her team could pick up the surveillance. Instead, the gangster had bought her a drink and the lustful smile on his face showed that he didn't care how she was dressed. The computer hacker pretended to check messages on her phone, purposefully ignoring the Mexican while she drank her wine. Just as her glass went empty, however, she saw him slide onto the saddle barstool next to her.

"You want another one? My treat," he said in passable English.

Vargas gave him a slight smile and spoke in Spanish. "Gracias. Uno más, por favor."

The man snapped his fingers at Jill, no longer interested in wooing her. He motioned at his empty beer and the young woman's wine glass. The bartender nodded, waiting until she turned away to roll her eyes. As the man was momentarily distracted, Vargas activated an app on her phone that allowed her teammates to listen in on the conversation. She then turned the device face down to give the appearance that she was focusing on her new companion.

"¿Cómo te llamas?" the gangster asked.

"Sophie. ¿Y tú?"

"Ernesto. Where you from? Your Spanish is very beautiful."

"I was born in Puerto Rico but grew up in New York. And, let me guess," she said, pausing for a long moment. "Your English is pretty good so I'm guessing you're from Texas?"

Ernesto laughed loudly, clearly pleased by the woman's approval of his English. "No, I'm Mexicano, but I live here now. So, what brings you to Atlantic City? Maybe you looking for a little excitement? Maybe some gambling?

Now it was Gabby's turn to chuckle. "No, just work. I'm attending an IT convention starting tomorrow over at the convention center."

The beers had slowed down Ernesto's processing time. After a moment, his eyes widened.

"So, today you are free?"

"I hadn't really thought about it," Gabby said, "but I guess I am. I was wondering how I was going to spend my afternoon."

Oh, shit, Vargas thought. Now what do I do?

"What the hell is she doing?" Jones asked Estrada and Wilkerson.

The three were parked at a booth in the Caesars Sportsbook Tropicana, just around the corner from the Firewaters Saloon.

"Sounds like she's trying to bait him," Chloe said, shaking her head, "but where's she going to take him?"

Hollywood shrugged. "Gabby's pretty smart. I'm sure she's got a plan."

"Have you got a room here?" Ernesto asked.

"I haven't checked in yet. I needed a glass of wine to relax after the drive. Traffic was terrible, even on a Sunday."

Gabby had only taken a sip from her second glass of cabernet sauvignon, knowing she needed to keep her mind clear. This was getting complicated fast. She hoped the transmitter app was working and her team was listening in. She looked at the thug and licked her lips suggestively.

"What about you? Do you have a room here?"

"Oh, no, I was just...uh, having a drink in the bar."

There was a long silence before Gabby spoke again, glancing at her watch.

"Well, I've got about an hour to spare before my friend, Carol, gets here. She and I work together and will be sharing a room. I might be looking for a little excitement."

Ernesto couldn't believe his luck. He buys this bitch two drinks and she's ready to invite him to her room. He pulled a roll of cash out of his pocket, leaving more than enough to cover the drinks. As Jill came over to see if he needed change, the Mexican handed her another twenty.

"My niece is supposed to meet me here later," he told the bartender. "She works in the casino and I'm giving her a ride home. Her name is Lara and she's wearing a black dress. If I'm not back, take care of her and I'll cover her bill when I come get her."

Jill shrugged, glancing at Gabby, suspecting that she was one of the hookers who worked the various casinos along the Boardwalk. She certainly wasn't dressed like a prostitute, but Atlantic City was a strange place. Vargas started for the door with Ernesto stumbling after her. When they got into the hallway, she took the pimp's right arm, keeping her concealed

9mm Glock 43 away from him. She let her hands begin to wander over the thug's body, exciting him but also letting Vargas know that he wasn't armed.

Gabby still wasn't sure how this was going to play out, but now that they were this close to locating Lara Sagarra, she wasn't going to let her only link to the missing woman get away.

"We're following you," Jimmy's voice came through her earpiece, concealed by her hair. "I hope you know what you're doing."

Me, too, she thought, relieved to know her friends were keeping an eye on her.

When they got to the spacious lobby, she told Ernesto to have a seat on one of the leather couches while she checked in, praying that there was a vacancy. While it was unusual for someone to walk up and book a room without pre-registering, it wasn't uncommon in Atlantic City. She was able to get a first-floor room near one of the exits onto Pacific Avenue, a plan starting to form in her mind. She asked for two room keys, and then gave the second one back to the clerk.

"My friend Chloe should be here anytime now and we'll be sharing a room," she said for her listening team's benefit. "Would you please give this to her? I'll probably be napping when she arrives."

A few minutes later, Gabby was leading the pimp to her room, trying not to let her nerves show. She knew what was on his mind and hoped she could make it through the next few minutes without getting hurt.

"Where's your suitcase?" he slurred.

"I left everything in the car," she replied. "I'll get it out later. I really needed that drink first."

The thug accepted her answer, still not believing his luck.

"I'm really glad I met you, Ernesto. I wasn't looking forward to spending the afternoon by myself. I'm just sad my friend won't be here until later. Carol's a little kinky and loves Mexican guys, too."

"Oh, wow!" he grinned broadly. "I'm sorry to miss her!"

"Give me your number and I'll call you the next time we're in town. Look, here's my room, number 110," she said, swiping her key over the lock and pushing open the door.

"See if you can figure out how to put some music on and help yourself to the minibar," Gabby said, quickly stepping into the restroom. "Let me freshen up and I'll see you in a few minutes."

After shutting and locking the door and turning on the shower, the young woman sat on the closed toilet and took several deep breaths to get her nerves under control.

"I got him into room 110," she whispered into her phone. "I'm in the restroom. They're expecting Chloe at the front desk to check in soon. I heard him telling the bartender about Laura. She's supposed to meet him at that bar later. I'm not sure what to do next. He's not armed but he wants to get physical with me real soon."

There was no answer in her earpiece so she repeated the message, being careful that her voice couldn't be heard over the running water. Again, there was no response from her friends. A sudden sense of panic started to overtake her. The pimp clearly had sex on his mind and was much bigger than her.

Gabby knew she wasn't nearly as strong as her powerlifting friend, Chloe. They both had been training regularly with Chuck in mixed martial arts but Vargas didn't want to go one-on-one with Ernesto. She had her gun but really hoped she wouldn't have to kill him inside an Atlantic City hotel room. That would be complicated. So, what was she going to do? And why wasn't Jimmy or the others answering her?

She stood, washed her face in the sink, dried off, removed the belly band that contained her Glock, and then pulled off the hoodie, revealing a pink tank top underneath it. She wrapped the pistol in her hoodie and turned off the shower. Her phone was still set on transmit mode and she prayed that her friends were receiving. She took another deep breath and reached for the door. It was time for Act Two.

Ernesto wasn't sure what kind of music Sophie liked, selecting a Latino hip-hop playlist. The minibar was well stocked and he transitioned from beer to Tequila, pouring two mini-bottles into a tumbler and enjoying the burn as the clear liquor went down his throat. He was already turned on and was ready to get the little Puerto Rican bitch into bed.

The bathroom door opened and Sophie exited, the tight pink tank top drawing the thug's eyes to her chest. She laid her hoodie and phone on a shelf and smiled shyly at the man.

"Me gusta el rosa," he grinned, taking step towards her.

She swiftly slid around him with a laugh, reaching for the minibar. "Gracias. I need a drink, too. Is there any red wine in here?"

"Oh, now you want to play hard to get?" Ernesto asked, the friendly demeanor now replaced by an angry tone of voice.

"No, I just need some more wine," she replied, forcing the smile back onto her face.

I'm really not very good at this, she thought, after realizing he was now between her and the hotel room door. The gangster set his glass down and removed his shirt, exposing a hairy chest, gold chains, and a panorama of ink. He closed the distance between them and put his right hand on her shoulder.

Gabby found a small bottle of cabernet sauvignon and poured it into a glass.

"Your turn. You take your shirt off, too," he growled.

She took a step backwards and forced a laugh. "Hang on. Let me have a drink first."

Ernesto moved in close again, his eyes full of lust and grabbed the front of her shirt, ripping it downwards. The fabric of the garment and her bra were no match for his strength.

"You asshole!" she screamed, dropping the empty bottle to cover herself.

The pimp shoved her backwards onto one of the beds with a laugh, the red wine spilling onto the comforter

"I knew you liked it rough. My kind of girl," he grinned, unfastening his pants.

Suddenly, a switched was flipped inside of Gabby and she went into fight mode. She drew her legs up to her chest as the Mexican bent slightly to pull his pants and underwear down. Vargas then drove both feet forward, one catching him in the shoulder and the other in the side of the head. Ernesto stumbled awkwardly, falling face-first into the large, flat-screen TV. With his jeans around his knees, the gangster's mobility was now limited.

Gabby was quickly off the bed and smashed the heavy glass tumbler against the side of Ernesto's skull, opening a large gash along his temple. The Mexican grunted in pain as he tried to pull up his pants with his left, but managed to lash out with his right in a punch, catching Vargas full in the face. The blow staggered the young woman, knocking her backwards onto the edge of the bed and then to the floor.

Ernesto dove on top of her, blood dripping from his face onto hers, as he wrapped his hands around her throat and started squeezing.

"You going to pay for that, bitch!"

Vargas scratched at her attacker's face as her oxygen supply was being cut off. The gangster kept choking her with his left hand as he attempted to pull her stretch pants down with the other. Gabby was fighting as hard as she could, but he outweighed her by at least a hundred pounds. Even though he was only choking her with one hand now, she knew it was just a matter of moments before she blacked out. With a panic-fueled burst of energy, she grabbed the pinky finger of the hand around her neck and bent it backwards until it snapped.

The pimp screamed in pain and momentarily quit trying to get her pants down. He slammed another vicious right fist into Gabby's face that slammed her skull against the floor and knocked her out cold.

"You like that, you little whore? I've got something else you're gonna like."

He went back to work undressing her but a sound to his rear made Ernesto turn just in time to see three figures rush into the room. Before the would-be rapist could get his hands up to protect himself, the point of a boot caught him under the jaw, viciously snapping his head back and knocking him off of his victim. The gangster was tough but before he could recover from the kick, a thudding fist to the temple dropped him unconscious onto his face next to Gabby.

Jimmy and the others had been able to hear most of Gabby's conversation as she checked in and secured a room. Chloe waited until Gabby and the pimp were out of sight before approaching the front desk and giving her name.

"I think my friend checked in a little while ago."

The clerk smiled. "She said you'd be here soon, but that was fast."

Wilkerson shrugged. "Traffic was light."

Jones and Estrada followed Vargas and her companion from a distance while Wilkerson got the key. When Gabby turned right at the end of a long corridor, her two teammates hurried to see where she had gone. The hallway was empty. The two continued down the corridor to where it dead ended at a T-intersection. There was no sign of their teammate, nor the dangerous man with her. They had heard bits and pieces of the conversation between the gangster and Gabby through their earpieces, but reception inside the massive resort was poor.

Once inside her hotel room, however, Vargas' transmissions weren't coming through, just two long bursts of static. Jimmy and Hollywood retraced their steps to find Chloe, rushing down the corridor with a key. By the time they located room 110 at the end of a long hallway, the sounds of a struggle could be heard from inside. Wilkerson swiped the key and Jimmy led the way inside, his Glock 19 extended in front of him.

The half-dressed cartel soldier was on top of Vargas' unmoving form, having just managed to get her tights down. As the thug turned to see the intruders, Jones snapped a front kick that sent Ernesto reeling. Not wanting to get left out of the action, Estrada stepped past his team leader and slammed a powerful punch into the thug's head. They both dove on top of the gangster, securing his hands and feet with zip ties and duct tape from their backpacks. A piece of tape also went over his mouth to keep him quiet.

Chloe grabbed Gabby by the legs and pulled her to safety, fearing the worst when the she saw how much blood was on her friend. A quick check revealed that she was breathing and had a strong pulse. Wilkerson grabbed Ernesto's discarded t-shirt and placed it over Gabby's torn shirt. After a moment, the unconscious woman stirred.

"Grab a pillow case," Jimmy said, holding the gangster in place as he also began to wake up. Jones checked his jeans and confirmed that he was unarmed.

Hollywood pulled the covering off of one of the pillows and covered Ernesto's head. They weren't sure what they were going to do with him and the less he knew about them, the better. Now that the prisoner was secured, Jimmy turned his attention to Gabby, kneeling beside her as Chloe checked to see where she was bleeding.

"I think most of it is his blood," Vargas mumbled, still dazed from the beating she had taken.

"I think you're right," Wilkerson nodded, helping her friend pull her pants up. "Your bottom lip is busted and you've got some swelling around your left eye. You also might have a concussion. Jimmy, help me stand her up and get her into the bathroom. Gabby, the first thing we're going to do is get you cleaned up. Then, we'll get some ice for your face. You're going to be fine."

The team leader helped Chloe walk their injured teammate into the restroom. Vargas grabbed her hoodie along the way. Jimmy left them and shut the door behind him. Hollywood came over where they could speak quietly.

"What now?"

"After they finish, let's drag him into the restroom out of the way. Then I'll call Chuck and see what he suggests."

Ten minutes later, the two women rejoined them. Vargas seemed to have her legs back under her and her eyes were clear. She had scrubbed off Ernesto's blood and was wearing her Yankees hoodie, but her face still bore testimony to the fight she had been through. Gabby put her hand on Hollywood's arm.

"I need my laptop," she said. "Why don't you go back to Harrah's and pack up our stuff and check us out? When I've got my computer, I'll see what I can do about erasing as much of our footprint here as I can. Also, I'll download Ernesto's phone. There's no telling what kind of good stuff we'll find on there."

Estrada nodded. "Will do. What else?"

Chloe spoke up. "Before you go, please get Gabby some ice. I need to go back to that bar where she picked up Ernesto. That's where Laura was supposed to meet up with him. I'll go make contact and bring her back here."

"Sounds like a plan," Jimmy commented. "We're gonna drag Señor Asshole into the bathroom and then I'll call Chuck to see if we can get some help here."

Estrada and Jones grabbed the injured cartel soldier by the feet and deposited him onto the cold marble bathroom floor. They hadn't bothered to redress him, not caring about his modesty. The white pillowcase was now soaked with the thug's blood and he left a trail across the carpet. Before leaving for his errands, Hollywood pulled on a black balaclava to check Ernesto's wounds. They didn't need a corpse on their hands.

The Sinaloa thug stared at Estrada with unconcealed hatred, unable to say anything because of the tape on his mouth and unable to move because of the flex cuffs and multiple layers of gray tape. Hollywood pulled on a pair of rubber gloves and examined the gash from the glass tumbler. That's gonna leave a mark, Estrada thought, and would definitely need a few stitches, but it wasn't going to kill him. Jimmy's kick to the head had probably broken the criminal's jaw and maybe a few teeth, but again, it wasn't a fatal wound.

Estrada taped a thick gauze bandage over the open wound on Ernesto's head and pulled a fresh pillow case back on to keep him disoriented. Before leaving the gangster, Hollywood turned on the faucet to prevent him from hearing any of their conversations, turned off the light, and shut the door.

**Firewaters Saloon, Tropicana Resort, Atlantic City, Sunday, 1445 hours**

Lara had been sitting in the booth at the back of the saloon for over twenty minutes, wondering where Ernesto was. She told the waitress who seated her that she was meeting someone. Lara had never had to wait on the gangster before. For a fleeting moment, she considered trying to escape. But where would she go? She had no money, no identification, and no transportation. And even if she did somehow get away, Ernesto and Eduardo had both assured her that they would torture and kill her mom and dad. Lara shuddered, remembering what Ernesto had threatened to do to her mother.

No, I'll wait for him, she thought, resigned to her fate. I have no choice. Maybe one day, I'll have my debt paid off and they'll let me go. For now, though, these bad men own me. Thomas had used her twice before telling her she could leave. He said he had a plane to catch that afternoon. A plane back to his wife and kids, Lara realized, as that sense of guilt and shame washed over her again.

A different waitress, this one with a lot of tattoos, approached her table.

"Hi, are you Lara?"

Startled, the teen didn't respond.

"Your uncle was here earlier and he said you'd be coming in and that you should wait for him. Can I get you anything? Are you sure you're old enough to work in the casino?"

"My uncle? Work in the casino?" Lara asked nervously, not sure what she should say.

Ernesto had warned her repeatedly against speaking to strangers when they were out in public. Maybe the pimp was hiding somewhere close by to see how she would respond. Would he hurt her for speaking with the waitress?

"Your uncle said you worked there."

"Oh...yeah. That's right. Where did he go?"

"He picked up some girl at the bar and was heading back to her room. He said to tell you to wait and order whatever you want."

"I'll just take a Coke."

The bartender stared at her for another moment before turning to go.

Before Lara knew what was happening, another woman slid into the booth opposite of her. The black woman was built like an athlete and her hair was cut short.

"Hi, Lara. I'm here to help you."

"Who...who are you?" Sagarra asked, her eyes wide and darting around the bar.

If Ernesto saw her talking with this woman, he'd be furious. He would beat her or even worse. Lara felt her breath coming in short gasps now. She needed to get away from there. She had no idea who this person was, but the muscular lady knew her name. Maybe she was married to one of the many men the escort had serviced and wanted to cause some problems. As the teenager moved to slide out of the booth and flee, the newcomer slid a photo across the table.

"Your parents asked us to find you, Lara."

It was the same photo that the teenager had managed to hide in her backpack— her mom, her dad, and Lara laughing in front of their small Christmas tree a year earlier. She paused and stared at the happy image, tears filling her eyes.

"You talked with them?" Her question came out as a whisper, a tear running down her cheek.

"We did. We've been trying to find you for a while, but now we're here to take you home."

"I can't," the young woman said, taking a deep breath and sitting back in the booth, her eyes continuing to scan the area, waiting for Ernesto to come storming into the bar. "He'll kill me. He'll kill my mom and dad. Please just leave."

"Who? Ernesto?"

At the mention of the pimp's name, Lara visibly flinched as if she had been slapped.

The woman shook her head and smiled. "Ernesto's not going to be hurting anyone. He's got his own set of problems right now. I've also got some friends who will protect your parents."

"Who...who are you? Are you a cop?"

"It's complicated but my name's Chloe and my friends and I help people like you. I promise you that you're safe now. We're going to get you out of here and take you home. We've still got to tie up a couple of loose ends here, but we should have you home with your parents tonight."

"Tonight?"

It was too much to hope for and Laura buried her face in her hands as she cried. Jill returned with the Coca Cola and a straw, puzzled by the powerfully-built black woman who was now at the table and wondering why the young girl was sobbing.

"What's going on? Do I need to call security?"

Chloe locked eyes with the bartender, trying to get a feel for what kind of person she was.

"You can do that, but I wouldn't recommend it. This young woman is being exploited by the man you met earlier. He's a really bad man."

"Somehow, that doesn't surprise me," Jill said. "Lara, is that true? Do you feel comfortable with this lady?"

Sagarra managed to pull herself together and took a deep breath.

"I...I think so," she replied, looking into Chloe's eyes. "Where's Ernesto now?"

"He's being detained near here, but I promise you, he won't bother you anymore."

Lara nodded slowly, wiping her eyes with a napkin, looking at Jill and then Chloe.

"Can you take me home now?"

A few minutes later, Chloe knocked on the hotel room door. She had prepped Lara on the walk over about her teammates and their encounter with Ernesto.

"But what if he sees me?" the teenager had asked with a tremor in her voice.

"I promise, he's not gonna to see you. You can trust me, Lara. My friends and I are very good at what we do. We'll kill Ernesto before we allow him to hurt you or your family."

Sagarra stared at her guardian, surprised by how nonchalantly she had spoken of killing someone. Of course, she had often wished that Ernesto, Eduardo, and all the other cartel members she had met were dead. In reality, though, she figured that she would be the one in an unmarked grave before any of the gang members met their fate.

A clean-cut, African-American man opened the door to admit them, a cellphone pressed to his ear. He nodded at Chloe and gave a polite smile to Lara.

"They just got back to the room," he said into the phone, relief evident in his voice. "Yeah, I think that'll work. Hollywood's on his way back over here with Gabby's computer and she's gonna to work some magic."

A Latino looking girl was lying on one of the beds, a plastic bag of ice pressed against her face. She burst into a grin when she saw Lara.

"Ouch! It hurts to smile, but I'm so glad to see you. I'm Gabby," she said, standing to embrace the young woman.

"Chloe told me what happened. Are you OK?"

"I'll be fine," Gabby answered dismissively. "I'm better than Ernesto."

Lara's eyes widened in terror. "Where is he?"

"Relax, he's tied up in the bathroom. We're trying to figure out what to do with him when we leave."

Jimmy disconnected his call. "That was the boss. He got me the info we needed on Ernesto. After we leave later, one of us will call the Atlantic City PD from a payphone to make an anonymous report about a fugitive hiding in room 110 of the Tropicana. He's wanted out of Texas on a parole violation charge.

"Lara, our boss in Virginia is already working on getting in touch with your parents and also providing security for them in case the Sinaloa thugs try something."

Sagarra was momentarily overwhelmed with emotion again, wiping the tears from her eyes.

"Thank you all so much."

"We're getting you out of here today," Jimmy told her, "but I was wondering— what do you know about the cartel's operation here in the city? I'm guessing there are other girls in the same situation that you're in?"

"Oh, yes! I can give you two addresses, if that'll help. One is where I used to live. The girls stay there and the men come to the house. When I moved, there were two new women there. They moved me and Nayara to another place in the same area. That was when Ernesto and Eduardo started using us as escorts and having us meet the men in the casinos and hotels."

"Any information you can give me will help. I'll pull up a map on my tablet and you can show me. I want to pass all that on to the police."

"Hang on a minute," Chloe interjected, putting an arm around the teenager's shoulders and pulling her to the other side of the room.

"Would you like to take a shower and have some fresh clothes?"

Lara looked down at her 'hooker dress.' She wanted to get rid of the low-cut, revealing garment but all of her meager belongings were on the other side of town.

"Yeah, but I don't have any other clothes with me."

A knock startled Lara. She was even more shocked as Jimmy drew a pistol and approached the door, peering through the peephole. He slid his gun back into a holster and let a handsome, solidly-built Hispanic man in. He was carrying a small suitcase and a leather computer bag. At the sight of Lara, he paused to greet her.

"Mucho gusto. I'm Hollywood.

"Hollywood? Are you an actor or something?"

"Sometimes," he laughed.

Chloe spoke up, taking charge. "Lara, would you go wait on the other side of the room with Gabby? Hollywood, I need you and Jimmy to drag Ernesto out of the bathroom and put him somewhere out of the way. Lara needs a shower and Gabby is going to loan her some clothes. We'll need to make a stop after we leave and get her a few more things."

"Yes, ma'am!" The two men replied, each delivering a crisp military salute.

# Chapter Six

**Century Tactical Solutions, Leesburg, Virginia, Monday, 0010 hours**

Chuck had called Andy, Scotty, and Tex into the office late Sunday evening. When he told them why he needed them to report, there was no mention of the late hour or the inconvenience. They had simply thrown on their kit and broke every speed limit between their homes and Leesburg. Lara Sagarra was coming home and would be meeting her parents at the Century office. His team had performed magnificently in locating the young woman, but now they needed a strategy to protect her and her family from the cartel when they inevitably came for revenge.

Henrique and Ivonne, along with Pastor Luis Miranda, waited in the break room. They had rushed over after McCain's phone call two hours earlier. Lara's parents could hardly contain themselves, pacing the small room, waiting to be reunited with their lost daughter.

The big man also called Sheriff Jerry Schaefer, who originally asked General Wallace Perkins, the president and CEO for Century, to help locate the missing teenager. Schaefer asked Chuck to convey his congratulations to the team and offered whatever resources McCain thought they might need for short-term protection of the Sagarras.

Now, just after midnight on Monday morning, Elizabeth joined her husband in the conference room with the others as they waited. She had put Ray down in Chuck's office, the toddler fast asleep on a pallet on the floor. The men were all throwing out ideas on how they could best keep Lara and her parents safe. Beth sipped from a mug of tea, tuning out the conversation and letting her mind wander.

Chuck and Scotty had driven down Saturday afternoon to pick up her and Ray, along with Emily and baby Macy, from the farm in Hendersonville. They had left midday Sunday to drive back to Reston. The search for Ramon "Asesino" Contreras was still underway, but Chuck felt comfortable in bringing his family home. The New Generation Cartel had become very quiet since the raid on the safe house in Lovettsville and the arrest of Alberto "Chilo" Barajas. The death of eight gangsters at the Flemings' house to go along with the three NG soldiers at the hands of Chuck, Scotty, and the help of a stray bullet, plus the arrest of two human traffickers had left the cartel short-handed.

During the drive from the mountains of North Carolina back to Northern Virginia, Chuck had received a phone call from Jimmy, letting McCain know that the missing teen had been located. The situation was complicated by the capture of Ernesto Salazar. Even though she could only hear her husband's side of the conversation, she picked up pretty quickly that the team in Atlantic City had been successful.

After disconnecting and letting Beth know the good news, Chuck had made a couple of other phone calls, getting the information that Jimmy requested, even having Beth write some things down for him as he drove and talked on the phone. He then called Jimmy back.

"Here's what I found out about your friend, Ernesto Salazar. There's an active parole violation warrant on him out of Texas. He served three years of a ten-year sentence on an aggravated sexual assault charge and was then paroled. It looks like he skipped the state without letting anyone know where he was going. His criminal history is full of rapes and other assaults so good job on capturing this guy. Just do what we talked about earlier and Ernesto will be heading back to prison in Texas."

Beth was always amazed at the kinds of cases and situations that Chuck and his people were involved in. She only knew a little of what he did with the CIA as a contractor, but understood the inherent risks of dealing with some of the world's most dangerous terrorists and criminals. She was thrilled to hear how Jimmy, Chloe, Hollywood, and Gabby had found the young woman who was being exploited and trafficked by the largest of the Mexican crime syndicates.

"I want to be there when Lara meets her parents," she told her husband, as the Silverado brought them closer to home.

"It'll probably really late tonight when they get in."

"I know, but this is going to be too good to miss."

Chuck smiled at his wife. "I think you're right about that."

A knock on the front door of Century brought her out of her revery. Tex went to check and returned with Loudon County SWAT officers Sergeant Brandon Cobb and Corporal

Norman Stephens. After greeting everyone, they took a seat with the others around the conference table.

The sergeant nodded at McCain. "The sheriff said that we're to consider ourselves on a special assignment to you until further notice."

Chuck smiled. "That's great. Here's what we're dealing with."

Just as he started to brief the deputies, his phone vibrated with a text.

"Sorry, but we'll continue this in a few minutes," he said, glancing around at the others. "That was from Jimmy. They're about to pull in with Lara. After they hug and cry for a while, I'll bring them in here. They'll need to be a part of the security briefing."

There was a lot of hugging and crying. In fact, even Chuck and his hardened warriors found themselves dabbing at their eyes as they watched the Sagarra reunion. For Henrique and Ivonne, it was like getting their daughter back from the dead. They had prayed and hoped for the best, but as the weeks had gone by, they both had feared the worst. Lara, herself, had come to terms with the fact that she would never see her parents again, expecting her life to end in a nondescript hotel room at the hands of someone like Ernesto.

McCain let the happy family have a few minutes of privacy in the break room. Handshakes, hugs, and back slaps were exchanged among team members.

"Jimmy, I don't know what to say," Chuck started, as they all took a seat around the big table. "I don't think any of us thought you guys were going to find her."

Jones laughed and pointed at Vargas. "It was Gabby. She did her voodoo-computer-magic and poof— a picture of Lara and her pimp popped up at the Tropicana. But then Gabby has to go and be an overachiever and instead of just observing the bad guy, she seduces him into coming back to the room with her."

"The room she didn't even have booked yet," Chloe added with a grin.

Gabby smiled shyly, her black eye, swollen lip, and bruised throat evidence of her near-death encounter with the cartel soldier.

"Yeah, not my best idea."

"No, it was a great idea, other than the fact that he almost killed you," Hollywood added.

"She definitely gave Ernesto something to remember her by," Jimmy laughed. "I'm guessing he'll need at least fifteen stitches on the side of his head and he has a broken finger. Of course, Hollywood and I had to use a minimal amount of force to bring the suspect under control."

Chuck gave an understanding nod. "I'm glad all that time on the mats paid off, Gabby. I'm so proud of you guys. Getting Lara back was the mission. Taking down Ernesto Salazar was icing on the cake. Do you think Atlantic City PD has him by now?"

"Well," Jones cleared his throat, "I know the original plan was to wait until we were about an hour down the road to call them, but I got to thinking about it. Leaving him zipcuffed in a dark bathroom for a few hours was a better idea. I figured the longer he's out of contact with the rest of the cartel the better.

Anyway, I just called the police a few minutes before we got here."

"Ha!" Scotty laughed. "Good call. And I'm guessing you haven't heard what me and the boss got into the other night?"

The incoming team stared at Chuck.

"That wasn't you guys that capped those two gangsters, recovered a bunch of drugs, and rescued some girls on a traffic stop, was it?" Hollywood asked. "I saw it on the news but they were a little sketchy on the details."

McCain grinned. "Yeah, Scotty and I are on admin leave at the moment. We dropped two of the bad guys. We would've had three in custody but one of the thugs killed his buddy with a stray round in the back of Lieutenant Donaldson's cruiser, before we put him down."

"That's crazy!" Gabby exclaimed.

"From the little they said on the news, that sounded like some pretty good shooting," Jimmy commented, pointing at his two friends. "Not that I'm surprised."

Chuck and Scotty shared a brief synopsis of how things had transpired, leaving their teammates shaking their heads in amazement. Tex, especially, had never been a part of such a group of talented operators. One squad managed to locate a missing girl in one of the largest sex-trafficking cities in America and two more of his colleagues rescued six young women on their way towards a life of slavery and torment. Of the five cartel members involved, the two survivors would likely spend many years in a maximum-security prison.

"I know I'm the new guy and all," Davis commented, "but y'all don't forget me the next time you're off to have a good time."

"You stick around with Century and you'll get plenty of opportunities," Andy grinned. "But we just got off of administrative leave ourselves."

"Hey, Chloe, can you go bring our guests in?" Chuck asked.

A few minutes later the Sagarras and Pastor Miranda joined them in the conference room. After expressing their thanks to Lara's rescuers and crying some more, McCain spoke up.

"Getting Lara home was just the first part of our mission. Now, we have to keep y'all safe. One of the things that we know about the Sinaloa Cartel is that they're going to be looking for revenge. There's no way they'll let this go unanswered."

The pastor translated the big man's words to make sure that Henrique and Ivonne understood. The joy of having their daughter back was replaced on their faces by worry. Chuck pointed around the room.

"But, we're all here to talk about how we can protect you."

McCain shared his plan with the Sagarras, with help from his team, for the next forty minutes. Henrique and Ivonne nodded, as the pastor translated for them. They agreed to everything that Chuck suggested. McCain expected the cartel to make their move within the next week and he and his people would have a surprise for them.

**The Tropicana Resort, Atlantic City, New Jersey, Monday, 0105 hours**

Detective Paul Liotta was finally finished and on his way home. It was his weekend to be on call and he had just responded to a domestic stabbing. Neither of the gay men would say what prompted the fight but whatever it was, it led to the "wife" in the relationship sticking the other in the arm with a steak knife. Liotta took the victim's statement in the hospital emergency room where he was being sewn up. The victim didn't want to press charges against his lover, but it didn't matter. The investigator would still file charges against the other man for aggravated assault under the domestic violence law.

The detective heard the call at the Tropicana come in over the radio as he was pulling out of the hospital parking lot, a uniformed officer requesting that an investigator be enroute to the resort. Paul could have easily allowed dispatch to call the next detective on the list. He enjoyed his work in the criminal investigations section, however, and let the dispatcher know he would handle it. Liotta had seen too many of his friends transferred out of detectives back into the uniform division to fill vacancies on the road. He figured that if he kept his case rate up, maybe that would protect him from the next purge.

He parked his unmarked Crown Vic on the curb behind an ambulance and a marked cruiser, threw his police placard on the dash, and hurried inside. A young, African-American female patrol officer met him inside. He nodded at her as he hung his gold shield around his neck.

"Detective? I'm Officer Rogers," she said, motioning down one of the corridors, leading the investigator out of the lobby. "The paramedics are loading him up. My partner's waiting for us in the room."

"What was the call? All dispatch told me was a possible assault."

The young officer didn't answer right away, thinking about her response.

"We got it from dispatch as a wanted person located, but it's a weird one. We found a Hispanic male, restrained with duct tape and those plastic temporary handcuffs lying on the bathroom floor with a pillow case over his head and his pants down. The dispatcher said someone called it in from a payphone but disconnected before they could get the caller's location. When we got here, hotel security let us into the room where we found the guy. He's been beat up pretty good, but the paramedics said that none of the injuries are life-threatening."

"Do we know who he is?"

"He didn't have any ID on him but there was a note in the bathroom with him."

"A note? What kind of note?"

"We're almost to the room. Officer Tonelli will show it to you, and other than us and the paramedics, we've kept the room locked down. CSI is on the way."

As they turned the corner and approached the room, the EMTs were wheeling a stretcher into the hallway. The detective saw that the victim's left hand was cuffed to one of the rails. The shirtless, stocky Hispanic man glared at the detective as they rolled him away, his head wrapped in gauze.

Before Liotta could even ask the question about why a possible assault victim was being restrained, a tall, middle-aged white male officer wearing latex gloves, held up a piece of Tropicana Resort stationary.

"I'll hold it. Just read this before you say anything," Senior Patrolman Anthony Tonelli grunted.

Someone had used a black sharpie and printed in block letters:

"HELLO OFFICERS. MY NAME IS ERNESTO SALAZAR. I'M A LIEUTENANT WITH THE SINALOA CARTEL AND RUN OUR SEX TRAFFICKING OPERATION IN ATLANTIC CITY. THERE'S A PAROLE VIOLATION WARRANT ON ME OUT OF TEXAS AND I'M IN AMERICA ILLEGALLY. I HAVE A LONG HISTORY OF VIOLENT ASSAULTS AGAINST WOMEN SO PLEASE MAKE SURE YOU KEEP A CLOSE EYE ON ME SO I DON'T ESCAPE. TODAY, I TRIED TO ASSAULT THE WRONG PERSON.

HERE ARE THE ADDRESSES OF TWO OF OUR LOCATIONS IN THE CITY. WE HAVE SEVERAL WOMEN WHO ARE BEING FORCED TO WORK THERE AS PROSTITUTES AGAINST THEIR WILL. FEEL FREE TO DROP BY AND SHUT THEM DOWN."

At the bottom of the page, were two addresses in the Venice Park area of the city.

"Holy shit!" Detective Liotta exclaimed, withdrawing his phone.

Tonelli laughed and nodded at his partner. "Those were my exact words, weren't they, Rogers?"

She smiled and nodded. "Detective Liotta, do you want me to have another beat car meet the ambulance at the hospital?"

"Yeah, that's a good idea," Liotta answered, taking a photo of the note. "What kind of injuries does he have?"

"He's got a three or four inch laceration to the head, a few cracked teeth, and probably a broken jaw," Officer Tonelli replied. "The paramedics said it looks like he's got a concussion and is dehydrated. Oh, and his left pinky is broken."

"This guy's having a rough day. Did you confirm that warrant?"

The senior patrol officer grunted again. "That's legit. Of course, we won't know if this guy really is Ernesto Salazar until we take fingerprints, but the physical description from the hit is the same, including some of his tattoos."

"While we're waiting on CSI, Officer Rogers, would you go check with the front desk about who was in this room and with security to see if they'll give you access to their cameras? There's got to be footage of our perps or heroes, depending on how this pans out."

Thirty minutes later, CSI was processing the hotel room, collecting fingerprints, blood samples, or anything else that needed to be sent to the crime lab. Officer Rogers returned to the room, holding a small notebook, a confused look on her face.

"What'd you find?" Liotta asked.

"Nothing. Absolutely nothing," she answered, shaking her head.

"What's that supposed to mean?"

"The people at the front desk came on at 2300. There was no record of anyone checking into room 110 for the last twenty-four hours. My chat with security was even stranger. They pulled the camera in this hallway and ran it back for the last twelve hours. No one went into or came out of this room during that time. They're gonna go back further and let me know if they find anything."

The investigator started to speak but the young officer held up her hand.

"I did get the names and phone numbers of the two employees who had the early shift. They would've been the ones to check someone in our out of 110 if they arrived yesterday."

"What'd they say?"

Rogers sighed. "No answers. They're probably home asleep with their phones on silent. I left voicemails so I'll let you know when I hear something."

"Damn. This is getting weirder by the moment. Okay, I'm going to drive over to the hospital and see if Señor Salazar wants to talk. CSI should be done here soon. Just forward your report to me."

It was less than a ten-minute drive back to the AtlantiCare Regional Medical Center. Paul again parked behind a black and white cruiser next to the curb at the ER entrance. As the sliding doors parted, he could hear a man yelling in Spanish. Although he didn't habla español, the detective didn't need a translator to determine that someone was angry. A woman's voice answered in English, trying to calm Ernesto Salazar down. I should've gone home after that gay stabbing, Liotta sighed to himself.

Following the voices, the detective turned the corner into a triage room where a large African-American nurse, two male hospital security guards and two female police officers were struggling with the man from the hotel. They had evidently removed the handcuffs for the nurse to check his injuries. A burst of strength sent her flying across the room, knocking over the blood-pressure machine, and then falling awkwardly to the floor.

Liotta watched in disbelief as the heavily tatted Mexican attempted to come off the gurney. The security guards wrestled him to the ground as the younger of the police officers jumped onto Salazar's back, attempting to apply a rear-naked choke. For the first time, Paul recognized the other cop as a friend of his. Donna Corso's black hair was pulled up into bun. She made momentary eye-contact with the investigator, smiled, and shook her head at the absurdity of the situation.

The security guards were both on the obese side and were already huffing and puffing as they tried to gain control of the injured man's limbs. The suspect easily managed to push himself to his feet, shoving one of the security officers away with one hand and grabbing at the young female officer who was still clinging to his back with his other hand. She wasn't quite able to get her short arms around his neck as the thug grabbed a handful of her hair.

Donna shook her head again and drew her taser. "Taser! Let him go!"

Officer Corso waited until she had a clear shot with the non-lethal weapon. The second security guard immediately backed away from the Mexican as the cop let go, falling hard to the tile floor, some of her hair still in the suspect's hand. Corso squeezed the trigger and Salazar immediately squealed in pain, stiffening up as the two prongs struck him in the chest and sent fifty-thousand volts through his body, causing him to land face-first on the hard surface. One of the security guards waited until the five-second burst was over and then moved in to secure Ernesto's hands behind his back with handcuffs before he could recover. The fall had busted open the gangster's nose, blood streaming onto the white floor.

The nurse quickly regained her feet and prepped a syringe. As soon as the thug was secured, she moved in and jabbed him in the arm, depressing the plunger.

"Asshole," she muttered. "That'll knock his ass out for a while. Can you guys put him back on the gurney?"

"That's why I told you to leave him handcuffed to the gurney," Officer Corso told the nurse.

"Protocol is that we have to check them without the cuffs," the woman snapped at the police officer.

"Yeah, and how'd that work out for you?"

The nurse started to reply but thought better of it and stomped out of the triage room.

"I guess having a talk with this clown is out of the question?" Liotta asked.

Officer Corso shook her head. "He told us he didn't speak English. Whenever he comes around, you're going to need a translator. What did he do? The paramedics made it sound like he was the victim of a crime but the cops at the scene told them to leave him cuffed until they had more info."

The detective shrugged. "That's about the sum of it. CSI is on its way over to fingerprint him for me. If those come back to who I think he is, you guys can transport him to the jail as soon as the hospital releases him. It sounds like this is a really bad guy."

The big nurse came back into the room and confirmed that the shot had knocked the patient out. She cleaned his busted nose and scribbled furiously on his chart before leaving again.

"Listen to this," the investigator said.

Liotta pulled his phone out and read the note recovered with the mystery man to everyone in the room. Corso laughed and shook her head.

"I've missed working adjoining beats with you, Paul. One of us was always stirring something up. If this guy really is running the Sinaloa's sex-trafficking ops here in AC, I'd love to help you take them down."

"Works for me. Let's get him fingerprinted so we can confirm his identity and then I can really get to work."

**S Street, SE, Washington, D.C., Tuesday, 1220 hours**

Ramon "Asesino" Contreras stirred as one of the two nude women in the bed with him coughed. He sat up, rubbed his eyes, and grabbed the cell phone off the bedside table to check the time. A sharp pain pierced his head and his mouth was dry. Numerous empty beer bottles were scattered around the room, testifying to the party the threesome had enjoyed the previous night. The two girls were some of his newer whores and were stilling learning the ropes of the sex industry. Ramon was only too happy to teach them.

"Hey, wake up!"

Neither of the women moved so he nudged them with his feet.

"Time to get up and go to work," he growled, as the women slowly came around, blinking at the sunshine illuminating the room. "You need to go take a shower and get ready to use those cute little asses to make me some money."

One of the prostitutes was eighteen, the other twenty-one, both from Mexico. They were just two of the many who would be paying off their debt to the New Generation Cartel for years to come. A few minutes later, they had dressed without a word and slipped out of Contreras' bedroom, walking back to their apartment next door, where they entertained clients throughout the day.

The gangster had been partying hard for the last week, binge-drinking, snorting cocaine and screwing his sex slaves. He knew he needed to get his head back in the game. He had several problems to solve. He had sent a request to Mexico asking for some more soldiers. With the loss of Miguel and Andres' teams when they tried to kill Deputy Andy Fleming, he needed some more muscle. He was still stunned at losing two complete squads. Somehow, Fleming and his wife had not been touched.

Contreras was also concerned to hear of Chilo Barajas' arrest at the safe house in Lovettsville. The pigs had also gunned down one of Chilo's soldiers. What was happening? El Asesino expected some heat after he and his men had killed that pig and his wife, but how had they found the safe house on the river?

The gangster felt relatively secure in the inner-city DC neighborhood. He had ordered his men to go out of their way to be nice to their neighbors and had even given out cash gifts from time-to-time to a few of the families that lived near him. He believed that he had created enough good will to keep his neighbors from reporting the NG location to the Metro-DC Police Department.

A knock at the door brought Ramon back to reality.

"What is it?"

"Señor, your lawyer is here."

"'I'll be out in a minute."

He got up and pulled on a pair of jeans and a white t-shirt. What was Sebastian Hernandez doing here without calling first? This must be important. The attorney was seated at the small table in the kitchen, holding a large Starbucks cup. Hernandez had a serious expression on his face, nodding when his client appeared.

"Qué pasa? I hope you've got some good news for me."

Sebastian frowned. "First of all, the reason I didn't call before I came is that one of my contacts with the Loudon County Sheriff's Department thinks they might be listening in on my phone calls and even tracking me. I left my phone in the car and parked four blocks away. I just hope my car doesn't get stolen while I'm with you."

"I didn't think the gringo pigs could do that?"

"They have to get a warrant signed by a judge first, but they can do it. My contact wasn't positive but overheard it being talked about. I also received notification from the court that you're to turn yourself in immediately. A new judge reviewed your case and found that Judge White acted improperly and revoked your bond. And, a detective from the sheriff's department contacted me that he wants to interview you about that dead cop and his wife."

Contreras laughed. "They can kiss my ass. What have you told them?"

"Nothing yet. I got the letter from the court yesterday and the detective left a voicemail this morning. My plan is to tell them that I've lost contact with you."

The gangster nodded, crossing the kitchen to retrieve a Corona from the refrigerator. He took a long swallow as he seated himself across from the lawyer.

"What about Chilo? Have you spoken with him?"

"Do you not watch the news? Loudon Country deputies stopped his van last week. He had a load of girls, including some children and a shipment of drugs."

"That's Chilo's problem," Ramon waved his hand dismissively. "The cost of doing business."

"No, Señor, it's your problem, too. Chilo's men were transporting two extra soldiers for you—the sicarios you asked for."

Contreras felt his heart sink. "Damn! Can you get them out of jail?"

"Jail? They're dead. The deputies killed the two sicarios and one of Chilo's men. You really should watch the news."

El Asesino cursed for a full in minute, in both Spanish and English, before running out of gas. They sat in silence a while longer before the attorney spoke again.

"I did speak with Chilo yesterday morning at the jail. He's not going anywhere. He has a parole hearing next week. I'll try to get it reduced but I'm sure he's going to serve the remaining fourteen months of his original sentence. The detectives also added a weapons charge so he may spend a few years in prison."

"How did the pigs know to stop that particular van?"

"Chilo doesn't know but his two men who survived are in jail with him. Carlos said the cops stopped him for weaving like he was drunk. Chilo did tell me something interesting, though."

El Asesino sucked down the last of the beer and grabbed another out of the fridge. The lawyer waited until his client was seated again.

"A Latino female detective was asking him about you. She offered to make him a deal if he gave you up. The police also seem to know all about the kids he's bringing across the border."

"That's Chilo's slice of the business," Contreras shrugged. "I stay away from kids. I know there's a demand, but my girls here screw all day long and keep the cash flowing for my part of the operation. Plus, we have other enterprises that we're involved in."

Sebastian knew these "other enterprises" were illegal narcotics, weapons, and smuggling people across the Southern border. These also kept the cash flowing for Ramon and the NG crime family.

"There's something else I found out," the lawyer said.

Ramon motioned with his beer for the man to continue.

"I know an attorney who works for the Sinaloas."

Contreras glanced up at the mention of the rival gang.

"You're friends with this man who works for our enemies?"

"I wouldn't say that we're friends, but we do talk occasionally. I spoke with him last night. He told me about some problems the Sinaloas are having that I knew you would be interested in."

"I thought you said the police had your phone tapped?"

Hernandez shrugged. "I don't know if they do or don't but when he texted me last night, we met at a club in DC for a beer. I asked him point-blank if they had anyone on the inside of the Loudon County SO. He said he didn't think so, but he would check and get back with me."

Contreras shook his head. "He'll never admit it, even if they do."

"Probably not, but he asked me if the NG was trying to move into Atlantic City."

"Atlantic City? That's Chilo's territory. He told me that he'd stayed out of that city so far but was building a network in some of the smaller New Jersey towns. Why do they think the NG is trying to move in?"

"One of Eduardo Sanchez's top lieutenants just got arrested. He ran their sex operation in the city. This lawyer told me that he picked up a Puerto Rican girl at a bar in one of the casinos. When they went back to her room, he got overpowered by several big guys. At least one of them was Hispanic. They beat him up and left him tied up in the bathroom. Several hours later, the police showed up. He had a parole violation warrant on him from Texas and will be headed back to prison."

"So, Eduardo thinks we had something to do with it? You can tell this lawyer to tell Eduardo that if it was me or Chilo, we'd have cut his man up into little pieces. There would have been nothing left for the pigs to arrest."

Sebastian smiled. "That's what I told him. It's still very strange, though. The police don't work that way because they would be the ones getting arrested for violating the suspect's rights."

"Maybe the gringo cops are forming vigilante squads like the federales used to have."

The lawyer stood to go. "No, the Americanos have a strong sense of law and order. The people would never tolerate vigilantes. After Ernesto got arrested, the police also shut down two of the Sinaloa's whore houses in the city. Eduardo told the lawyer he suspects Ernesto gave the cops the addresses to reduce his sentence."

"Sounds like this Ernesto asshole isn't going to last long in prison."

Hernandez nodded. "I think you're right. I'll let you know if I hear anything else, Señor."

**Fairfax, Virginia, Wednesday, 2255 hours**

Eduardo Sanchez paced the floor of the living room as he waited for news from his squad of sicarios. He didn't know what to believe about what had happened at the Tropicana in Atlantic City. The attorney who represented Sinaloa gang members when they were arrested shared the crazy story Ernesto had told him. Even for Ernesto, this was hard to believe.

Up to that point, the gangster had actually done a pretty good job running the whore houses and escorts in the resort city. Eduardo had kept his lieutenant on a short leash after that prostitute overdosed. The escort business and the brothels were generating big money for the cartel and Ernesto seemed like he was on track to move up the leadership ladder in the Sinaloa family.

Enrique, Ernesto's assistant, had barely escaped the raid from the Atlantic City Police Department. When the pigs hit the two houses, Enrique was taking Nayara to meet a client at Harrah's. Francisco had been the soldier in charge of the brothel when the pigs showed up and he'd been arrested along with three of the girls. The young women were taken into custody, but Eduardo's lawyer was having trouble locating them.

The attorney also told Eduardo that warrants had been issued for Enrique but there was no way he was turning himself in. After several phone calls, the lawyer had finally discovered that the women were in protective custody until they could testify against Ernesto and Enrique. According to the attorney, none of the girls had brought up Eduardo's name, fearing his reprisal, but they seemed willing to turn on the other two Sinaloa soldiers.

It didn't matter to Sanchez. The prostitutes and their families in Mexico would suffer horror and pain that they couldn't even imagine if they took the stand against anyone in the Sinaloa family. The lawyer was attempting to find out where the women were being kept. *Maybe a few of my hombres could deal with the whores before this went to court*, he thought.

In the meantime, Enrique was tasked with rebuilding the sex operation in Atlantic City, while trying to stay off the radar of the local pigs. So far, Nayara Palacios had done a great job as an escort. Eduardo was hoping to have a few new girls from Mexico within the next week or two. This was a big step up for Enrique but, for the moment, he was el jefe in AC. Thankfully, the police hadn't visited the beachfront brothel and Enrique and Nayara had moved in.

For now, Eduardo was focused on another problem, this one in Northern Virginia. Somehow, Lara Sagarra had escaped while Ernesto was thinking with the wrong head and being led into a trap. The teenager had been a popular escort, generating thousands of dollars for the crime family. When she saw her chance to flee, though, she had done just that. Without any money or ID, the girl somehow managed to get back to her parents in Leesburg, Virginia.

Eduardo sent a squad of his best hombres to watch their house, but the family had not been home in several days. The gangster guessed they had also gone into hiding, but where would they go? The cartel's resources were vast and if they tried to slip back into Mexico, the gang would find them.

Even in Los Estados, the Sinaloa reach was long and eventually Sanchez and his sicarios would track them down and make them an example. That's what I should have done after the teenager stole from us. There will be no mercy this time, he thought.

The gangster's phone vibrated with an incoming text.

*"They're here."*

*"Are you sure?"*

*"It was the father's car with three people in it. They just pulled into the garage and all the lights came on in the house."*

*"Bueno. Wait until they go to bed and then handle it."*

*"Sí, Señor."*

Pancho was one of Eduardo's most experienced sicarios. He alone had probably killed twenty people and his team was made up of hardcore soldiers who loved nothing better than permanently solving problems for the cartel. And, if they got to rape some women along the way, even better. They also got to divide up any spoils they discovered, unless it was the cartel's money or drugs. The Sagarras probably didn't have much money, but the two women would provide the killers with some fun before they died.

Eduardo had planned on being a part of the operation. The teenager had caused Sanchez a lot of grief and he personally intended to inflict some pain on the little bitch. Pancho had talked his lieutenant out of getting involved.

"You're too valuable, Señor. I don't think we're going to have any problems, but if something goes wrong, la familia can't afford to lose you. Plus, we may end up sleeping in the van for a couple of days before they show up."

Sanchez was glad that he had listened to the sicario. The squad had waited in the vehicle for over forty-eight hours, with the Sagarras just now showing up. Well, now they were home and the hit team was about to pay them a visit.

**Sterling, Virginia, Thursday, 0110 hours**

Across the street and two houses down, a white Ford work van was backed into the driveway of a vacant home with a "For Sale" in the front yard. The neighborhood was lower-middle class with plenty of other work vans and pickups with ladder racks scattered around the area. From what the hit team had seen, most of the residents were Hispanic, probably in Los Estados illegally, and not likely to call the police on them.

Pancho and his three men had sat in the cramped quarters since Monday night, waiting for the family to show up. Now, they were home and the lights in the house had gone out around midnight. Pancho waited another hour before leading his team towards the target house. The sicarios were ready to get out of the vehicle. They had been pissing and shitting into a bucket, and eating the tasteless convenience store food they had brought with them. The smell inside the van was awful and they were all tired and irritable, wanting to hurt someone. The fear of Eduardo's wrath had kept them on the stakeout, even though they would've much preferred to be in one of their safe houses, banging one of the cartel's whores.

With the arrival of the Sagarras, the men sensed the tingle of anticipation that preceded every mission. When the house finally went dark, the team leader gave the family time to go to sleep before quietly opening the rear door of the van. Thankfully, the street light was out on this end of the block and the Sagarras had not left any outside lights on.

This should be easy, the team leader thought, looking forward to having his way with that hot little teenager before they killed her. The area was quiet with just a few windows illuminated up and down the street. If things went according to plan, the sicarios would not even have to fire a shot. No gunfire meant no one calling the cops. That meant the Mexican assassins could take their time and kill the family slowly. Eduardo's instructions to Pancho were simple: "Make them an example to anyone tempted to steal from the Sinaloa family."

They slipped quietly across the street and around the left side of the house. A rear entry would prevent any of the neighbors from seeing what was happening. Each of the men wore leather work gloves and painters overalls to protect from blood splatter. They all carried a handgun and a razor-sharp machete.

There was no deck behind the house, just a concrete patio containing some cheap outdoor furniture and an old charcoal grill. A sliding glass door separated the sicarios from their victims inside. Pancho had been hoping for a conventional door with a lock he could pick. He shoved the packet of picks back into a pocket and reached for handle of the glass door.

Their other options for entry would be to pry open a window or take their chances at the front door. Before he could choose an alternate entry, the team leader realized that the door was sliding noiselessly along its track. It wasn't even locked.

"Bueno," he whispered over his shoulder. "Vamos."

In seconds, the four killers were all standing in the Sagarras' living room. Hector was the last man in. He turned on a small flashlight and pulled the door closed, locking it behind them. Suddenly, the overhead light came on, startling and blinding the Mexican assassins.

Chuck, Andy, Jimmy, and Scotty were positioned strategically inside the single-story home. To the right of the sliding door was a kitchen and small dining area. The living room opened all the way to the front door on the other side of the residence and over to the left, a hallway led to three bedrooms and two bathrooms.

Most houses are not constructed to stop bullets. The heavier appliances will do the trick, such as a refrigerator or washing machine, but sheetrock walls and cloth or leather furniture will barely slow most pistol and rifle rounds. For this reason, McCain's squad would rely on concealment and speed instead of cover to end the confrontation quickly. Fleming and Jones were on the other side of the small bar between the kitchen and the living room. McCain was just around the corner of the hallway. Smith was flat on his belly behind a recliner directly across from the sliding door, the muzzle of his H&K 416 pointing at the back entrance.

Chloe and Tex had placed several cameras on the outside of the small home on Monday morning while the Sagarras packed. Sergeant Cobb and Corporal Stephens, along with Hollywood and Gabby, drove the family over to Dulles where they were staying with one of the other Mexican families from the Iglesia Cristiana Transformando vidas. The four deputies, or some of their friends, would be providing security for the family for least a few more days. Even though Estrada and Vargas both wanted to be where the action was at, they had already built a rapport with Lara, and were bilingual. Chuck especially wanted Gabby on the security detail to look after the young woman to make her feel comfortable and give her someone she could talk with besides her parents.

The cameras allowed the team in the house to monitor the area around the house, watching the suspects as they approached. The reserve deputies were waiting when the sicarios made entry. When Jimmy flipped on the lights, before Andy could even issue a challenge in his limited Spanish, Pancho, Hector, and Leo instinctively raised their pistols.

Between their constant training, along with their many real-world missions, Chuck and his people were razor sharp, each warrior firing in semi-automatic mode at the armed cartel soldiers. Pancho cried out in pain as multiple 5.56mm rounds punctured his chest and head. Hector and Leo both jerked from the impact of bullets before their bloody corpses collapsed to the floor. Even with the suppressed H&K 416s, the two seconds of gunfire left everyone's ears ringing.

Alejandro suddenly realized he was the last sicario standing, blood and brain matter from his friends coating his face and clothes, staring into the muzzles of four rifles, his pistol still pointing at the floor. He dropped the .40 caliber Glock but still clutched the machete in his left hand, his eyes wide with fear.

"You want to bring a knife to a gunfight, asshole?" Scotty asked from across the room.

The stunned sicario let the blade fall to the carpet and raised his hands.

"Andy and Jimmy, secure him and the others," Chuck ordered. "Scotty and I'll cover you."

A minute later, the surviving sicario was zip cuffed, searched and lying away from his dead companions. A check of their pockets revealed twine and duct tape to secure their victims before raping and hacking them to pieces. Chuck checked his tablet, making sure the cameras didn't show any more perps lurking in the darkness.

After confirming that the area was clear, he stepped outside to call in the shooting. He then called Chloe who was waiting nearby with Tex. They were the backup team, staged at the Dominion View Park, a half mile away. Now that the Sinaloa assassins were down, he requested his friends to join him at the scene.

When the sicarios saw the Sagarras drive into the garage earlier that evening, what they had really seen in the low light was Andy driving, along with a disguised Jimmy and a mannequin in the vehicle. The dummy was made up to look like Lara from a distance. Jones wore a wig, playing the part of Ivonne Sagarra, and knew he would never live down the comments from Scotty earlier in the day when Jimmy was trying on the disguise.

"Hey buddy, you're looking pretty good. I'm kinda sorry I'm married or I'd ask you out."

Jones had given his friend a one-finger salute and said, "Yeah, and if we ever need somebody to dress up like Chewbacca, that'll be you, big boy."

McCain and Smith had also been at the house while the Sagarras packed but had stayed behind in case the cartel came before they were ready for them. After the arrival of the work van at the empty house across the street, Chuck and his team waited to set the trap, wanting to give the FBI time to finish their interview of Lara on how Eduardo Sanchez and others in the Sinaloa Cartel exploited her and so many other women. After the FBI was done, the Sagarras were moving away to get a fresh start in Florida. With the arrest of Ernesto Salazar in Atlantic City, the Bureau had finally taken an interest in the case and were working with the AC Police Department in putting an investigation together that would significantly hurt the Sinaloa Cartel.

Just a few minutes ahead of the responding police cars, Tex pulled up in front of the house and the two operatives hurried inside. Jimmy had each of the perp's cell phones laying on the kitchen table. Chloe pulled her laptop out of her backpack and plugged a cord into each phone, one-at-a-time, quickly downloading their contents. By the time the first Loudon

County deputy showed up, she had gotten all the data from the sicarios' devices and placed them with the perps' other property. The CSI Unit and the detectives would go through the gangsters' phones but McCain wanted the intel, as well.

After securing the prisoner in the back of a marked police car, the responding deputies began roping off the crime scene with yellow tape. Lieutenant Jake Donaldson strolled over to Chuck and his team, standing in front of the residence. The neighbors were awake now, many of them peering out their front windows, trying to figure out what was happening in their quiet corner of the world. Donaldson motioned with his head and the big man stepped off to the side where they could speak privately.

"I just took a look through the sliding door. Good job on taking out those gang bangers. Were those machetes laying next to them? Did these assholes really have machetes?"

"You've read the reports about how the cartels treat traitors," Chuck answered. "These animals are as savage as any terrorist group in the world today. That's why they're all wearing painter overalls. They planned on hacking up Lara and her family. Of course, I'm sure they were going to rape the women before they killed them—probably keeping Henrique alive and forcing him to watch."

Donaldson shook his head. "Shit! That's awful. Any reason one of them is still alive?

Chuck shrugged. "We could've killed him, too, but he never raised his gun and dropped it pretty quick after realizing he was the last man standing. Maybe the detectives can get something useful when they interview him."

The lieutenant nodded. "It wouldn't have hurt my feelings to have four dead perps, but you're right. Maybe he'll cooperate with the investigators. Another question: what is it about you and your people? Do y'all have ice water flowing through your veins? I've been in one shooting in my entire career and I was a nervous wreck for months. Everyone on your team is as cool as can be. Hell, it's only been a week or so since you and Scotty took out those other two assholes on the traffic stop."

"This isn't our first rodeo, LT. Other than Tex, Gabby, and me, every one of them was in the military. Andy, Scotty, Jimmy, Hollywood, and me were hunting down Iranian terrorists and killing zombies for the CDC just a few years ago. I hate to sound callous, but this is just another day at the office for us. The only negative part is the administrative leave. Thankfully, the sheriff has pushed to speed these investigations up so we can get back to work. All of my guys are gonna be ready to go again tomorrow, so I'll have to schedule some training to burn off that excess energy. We're also still looking for Asesino Contreras but this sidetracked us a little bit."

"You know the drill," Donaldson said. "Give your statements to the detectives and take a couple of days off. Although the beauty of being a reserve deputy is that if you guys stay under the radar, you can keep working on the Contreras case."

McCain smiled. "That's the plan."

# Chapter Seven

**Century Tactical Solutions, Leesburg, Virginia, Monday, 0815 hours**

True to his word, McCain had his warriors in the shoot house on Friday for most of the day, running drill after drill, reinforcing their already deadly tactics. Going after Ramon Contreras or Eduardo Sanchez might very well find them in the middle of the action again and Chuck and Andy had never shied away from pushing their people to get better. Fleming was the training director for Century and McCain allowed his friend to create the various scenarios the team would encounter as they ran their drills.

As SWAT instructors, Chuck required them to train regularly. He had attended different courses over the years in which he or others in the class were more qualified than those who were teaching. When Century Tactical Solutions was created, McCain vowed that his people would be the most proficient and tactical operators available. This gave them credibility, not only in the law enforcement community, but in the special operations world, as well.

The other reason that Chuck and Andy pushed their warriors so hard, was to keep them ready for whenever Kevin Clark called from the CIA with a contract mission. McCain and his elite team had taken on some of the most violent and deadly terrorists and criminals in the world and their rigorous preparation had always given them an edge. None of the operators were enjoying the current parameters that they were having to work inside as reserve deputies. At the same time, Sheriff Schaefer had asked for their help in catching Contreras and they would do everything they could to bring the murderer to justice, dead or alive.

Chuck called Kevin during one of their breaks on Friday to take him up on his offer for assistance in tracking down el Asesino. The CIA's ops director had offered the Agency's help after Dwayne and Shelly Thomas had been murdered. Of course, the CIA wasn't supposed to be operating on American soil, but the longer that Contreras roamed free, the greater the likelihood more innocent people would be hurt.

With the FBI finally involved with Lara Sagarra's case, the feds had joined the manhunt for Sinaloa lieutenant, Eduardo Sanchez. McCain also asked for Clark's help with locating that gangster, not sure that the Bureau would be able to find the fugitive on their own. Of course, whatever intel that the CIA provided would not be admissible in court. Chuck and his people would have to verify it on their own.

After a weekend to catch up on their rest and personal lives, it was time to turn their attention back to the Jalisco New Generation and the Sinaloa Cartels. Chuck had already been at work for half an hour on Monday when his phone vibrated with a call from Kevin Clark's assistant, Ricardo Gonzalez. Gonzalez also served as Clark's driver and one of his three bodyguards.

"Hey, Gonz. How you doing? You keeping the colonel out of trouble?"

"Man, he tells me every day he'd rather be out kicking in doors with you guys than sitting at his desk, answering emails and phone calls."

McCain chuckled. "The price we pay for saying 'yes.'"

"This is true. I just sent you an email with some information that I think you'll find interesting. First, let's talk about the Sinaloas. The reason that the Bureau jumped into that case with the young lady you guys rescued is they were already working the intel the Spartan provided. They're watching a couple of locations, waiting for Eduardo Sanchez to show up. Of course, I'm not sure what they'll do with him if they find him, but they're trying.

"For the New Generation pricks," Gonzalez continued, "I put Stephen Chan to work on it."

Chan was one of the Agency's premier IT experts. He and Gabby had worked together for a while and it was a toss-up as to which one of them was better at breaking into secure databases or finding obscure intel on the dark web. Stephen was assigned to the operations directorate at the CIA, supporting Clark's clandestine activities.

"Good deal. What'd he find?"

"Contreras seems to be feeling the heat. I sent you three possible addresses in Southeast DC. If he hasn't run back to Mexico, he's probably at one of those locations, maybe even bouncing back and forth."

"He doesn't strike me as the runaway type," Chuck commented.

"I had an analyst do a profile on him and they agree with you," Ricardo said. "He's much more likely to be laying low, regrouping, and waiting for an opportunity to go on the attack again. With his amigo Chilo Barajas in jail and a bunch of their soldiers dead or in custody, the NGs are struggling a bit at the moment. They don't seem to have the structure that the Sinaloas do. For the moment, what I sent you is the most up-to-date intel we could find."

"Sounds good, Gonz. We'll take a look at this and see what we can do. Since we're working this case in our status as reserve deputies, we don't have any jurisdiction in DC. Thanks for the help and let Kevin know that I'll keep him in the loop."

After disconnecting, McCain reviewed the intel that Gonzalez had forwarded him and printed it out. He opened a Google map to check the addresses, not surprised that the locations were in some of the worst areas of Washington, D.C. That makes sense, he thought. The cartel had selected high-crime neighborhoods where it was unlikely that anyone would call the police on them.

The big man went around to everyone's office or cubicle and requested that they join him in the conference room. It was time to get back to work. He passed around copies of the intel, along with printouts of the possible NG safe houses on Google maps. Chuck summarized what Ricardo had provided.

"Obviously, we don't have any jurisdiction in DC, but...

"We only need jurisdiction if we're going to arrest him, right?' Scotty asked. "What about if we just handle it our way?"

This elicited several grunts of agreement around the table.

"Guys, you know that one of my guiding philosophies is that some people just need killing," McCain replied. "At the same time, I really don't want to spend the next twenty years in prison and neither do you. We're going to have to play this one out as Loudon County deputies, whether we like it or not. Andy, didn't you, Scotty, and Eric work with the Metropolitan Police Department at the end of the zombie crisis while we were on loan from the Agency to Homeland Security?"

"That's right. We spent almost two weeks going door-to-door in some of their nastier neighborhoods, cleaning out the last of the Zs in the city."

"Zs and gang bangers," Scotty added. "The bangers were kind of like Crips and Blood wannabes and had taken over some areas in their 'hood. That was back when things were still crazy and we didn't have to worry about trying to arrest the bad guys."

Chuck pointed to Andy. "Can you see if you can track down any of those officers y'all worked with? Maybe they can help us with some surveillance and maybe a takedown of Ramon Contreras. I don't know anyone with DC-Metro and I'm not sure how much help we would get going through normal channels. Gonz gave us the location of three possible NG operations in Southeast DC. There's a good chance that Contreras is at one of them."

"Good idea," Fleming responded. "I think I've still got those DC cops' numbers."

McCain gave out several other assignments before standing, signaling an end to the meeting.

"Let's meet back here at 1500 and see where we're at. I'd like to be in action by tomorrow, if possible."

With the Agency's help, the team now had clear direction. The warriors spent the morning and early afternoon digging into the intel that Chuck had given out. Now, it was time to regroup and find out what the rest of the week was going to look like. The big man was in the conference room at 1455 hours sipping from a fresh mug of coffee. When everyone was seated around the table, he nodded at Andy.

"Were you able to track any of those officers down?"

Fleming gave a rare smile and pointed at his yellow legal pad. "I did. We've got a meeting with Lieutenant Alex Bell tomorrow morning. He's the head of their Emergency Response Team, their version of SWAT. They're short-handed so he's also a road LT on day shift."

"Wasn't he a sergeant when we were working with him before?" Smith asked.

"He was but got promoted not long afterwards. Remember Kendra Lockhart, the female who was on my team? She's a sergeant now in their gang unit. Lieutenant Bell was going to ask her to join us. The LT seemed more than willing to help out. He even said he's trying to get an approval to have Century come run his team through a SWAT refresher."

"Good work, Andy," Chuck said. "Where are we meeting?"

"He said that his captain is an idiot and it's better if we meet off-site rather than at their precinct. There's a sub-station on Alabama Avenue in a strip center that he said would work. He wants to hear what we need and then he and Sergeant Lockhart will have a better idea of what resources they're going to need. Scotty and I know them, so I'd recommend me, him, Chuck, Jimmy, and Chloe go meet with them. If they'll play ball, I think we can be sitting on these suspect locations by tomorrow night."

**Metropolitan Police Substation, Alabama Avenue, SE, Washington, D.C., Tuesday, 0905 hours**

"Thanks for meeting with us, LT, Sarge," Chuck said, after the introductions were made.

Alexander Bell nodded as he studied his guests. Bell was a fit, forty-three year old white man with intelligent eyes and a serious expression. Sergeant Kendra Lockhart was an early-thirties black female who smiled easily, but at the same time gave off the vibe that you didn't want to end up on her bad side.

"My pleasure," the lieutenant replied, motioning at Andy and Scotty. "We learned a lot working with these two guys. Where's Eric?"

Eric Gray had led the third team of MPD officers in eliminating some of the last zombies from the city. The former MARSOC Marine once served with Andy Fleming in the Corps. After retiring, he had worked in the operations directorate of the CIA until taking his current job as one of Colonel Clark's bodyguards.

"Eric's doing well, working for another government agency," Andy answered.

"Things are just as screwed up in DC as ever, although, as you can see, Kendra got promoted and went back to the gang unit and I'm doing double-duty: running a shift in District Two and ERT commander. I'm curious to hear what this is all about.

When we worked together, you guys were with Homeland Security. And now you're reserve deputies with a sheriff's department in Virginia?"

"I won't bore you with the whole story," Chuck replied, "but when the opportunity came along to start Century Tactical Solutions, it was too good to pass up. It allows us to train SWAT teams and even some military units all over America. At the same time, it made sense for us to keep our law enforcement certification, so we have an arrangement with the Loudon County SO. In exchange for deputy badges, we oversee their yearly qualifications, SWAT training, and even help out on the occasional investigation, like this one. You probably saw the story a few weeks ago— Sergeant Dwayne Thomas and his wife Shelly were murdered in their home by Ramon Contreras and some of his New Generation sicarios."

"Contreras? El Asesino?" Kendra repeated. "I saw the story about the officer and his wife being murdered but I guess I missed the part where Contreras was involved. We've been looking for him for over a year. He's a suspect in a couple of murders in the city and we've heard he's running a lot of drugs in the District and surrounding states. He's also known for his sex-trafficking operation, but he's like a ghost. We have no idea where he's at."

"Dwayne was a sergeant in the narcotics unit in Loudon County," Chuck answered. "He had overseen an operation that took down two of Contreras' stash houses. We got around a hundred kilos of drugs, a bunch of guns and even managed to snag el Asesino and a few of his men. Unfortunately, a judge let him out on bond and Contreras and some of his people murdered the deputy and his wife. Our intel shows that the NG has some safe houses inside the Beltway. We've got three possible locations to look at. Have any of your informants given you any specifics?"

"No," the sergeant frowned. "They know that if word ever got back to Contreras that they gave the police any information, their lifespan would be very short."

The sound of the front door opening carried into the small office they were using. A moment later, a thuggish looking African-American male, wearing his hair in corn-rows, stuck his head in the door. He was wearing a white wife-beater, baggy jeans, and several gold chains. At the sight of Smith, the man's face broke into a huge grin, a gold grill sparkling inside his mouth.

"Scotty, do you recognize me?"

The bearded man stared at the newcomer for a moment before standing and embracing him in a bear hug.

"Dude, I was getting ready to draw down on you," Scotty laughed, pulling back but keeping his muscular arm around the younger man. "Guys this is Officer Jamal White. He was with us, killing Zs and gang members, even though he kind of looks like one now. What happened to you? You were so clean-cut looking."

The young man smiled again. "It's Detective Jamal White now. I work for Sergeant Lockhart in gangs and I have to look the part."

After Scotty introduced White to the others, the detective glanced shyly at the former sniper.

"I never got to thank you," he said, before looking at Chuck, Jimmy, and Chloe. "Scotty saved my life. I took a round when we were clearing a community center that a group of bangers had taken over. The bullet nicked my femoral, but Scotty had that tourniquet on in a flash. The ER doctor said that it was perfectly placed and was the only thing that kept me alive."

Jimmy nodded and motioned to his teammates. "He's good. I think Scotty's worked on every one of us at some point. He can do it all—make those thousand plus yard shots and then patch up a team member."

Smith waved a hand in front of his face, laughing with embarrassment.

"Bro, you're making me blush!"

"Hey, Jamal, go grab a chair and come join us," Bell said. "Our friends have some hot intel that I think you're going to want to see."

When he returned, Chloe passed folders to everyone. As they studied the satellite maps and other information provided by the CIA, the lieutenant glanced up over the top of his file.

"Can I ask where you got this? This is some pretty detailed intelligence and Loudon County is a long way from Southeast DC."

"We still have a good working relationship with some of the federal agencies, especially Homeland," McCain replied.

The big man hated being deceptive but the CIA wasn't supposed to be working in America and he couldn't admit they had assisted him.

"Fair enough," Bell replied, accepting the answer. "So, are the feds involved in this case?"

"The FBI provided some assistance after the Thomas' were killed. When nothing materialized right away, they moved onto other things."

The Metro-DC officers nodded having seen the federal agents in action before.

"That's when I made a few phone calls," McCain continued. "My source said they believed these three addresses to be current New Generation locations. Of course, we would want to confirm that ourselves before we took any action."

Jimmy spoke up. "Sarge, you said you've been looking for Contreras. Have you guys got warrants on him?"

"No. I'm impressed your department was able to arrest him. I think he likes retreating into DC because it's easy to get lost here. If we do find Contreras, I'd like to interview him about our two open homicide cases. Like I said, he's the prime suspect."

"I don't think he'd have a lot to say," Chloe interjected, "but you can see in your folders the copies of the murder warrants from Loudon County. Plus, like Chuck said, he was already out on bail for weapons and drug trafficking. His bail's been revoked so when we find him, we'll have to overwhelm him. Our psychological profile of Contreras is that he'll never willingly surrender to the police."

"Who did the psyche profile?" Kendra asked.

"I did, along with the director of intelligence and investigations at Century. We both have a background in intelligence analysis."

In reality, the Agency had provided the psyche profile, but Chloe couldn't say that and she had done them before and knew what she was talking about.

"When we arrested Contreras a few weeks ago," Wilkerson continued, "he tried to file a brutality complaint against Chuck but he didn't have a mark on him so the IA investigator just laughed at him. That's a factor in our psychological profile— El Asesino has a massive ego and it must've been severely bruised when Chuck took him down so easily."

"What was the nature of the brutality complaint, Chuck?" Lieutenant Bell asked. "Did you guys have to fight him?"

"Not really..." McCain started to reply.

Fleming laughed, motioning at the big man. "Chuck has some very special skills. Contreras was trying to escape out a window and the boss pulled him back inside. The thug made a grab for Chuck's pistol and Chuck choked him out with a front guillotine. When he woke up, he was already handcuffed. When we were escorting him out for transport, he started screaming that we had beaten him but obviously no one believed him."

"Nice work," the lieutenant smiled.

The sergeant looked over at the young detective who had grown up in inner-city DC.

"Jamal, you know those neighborhoods better than all of us. What do you think?"

"Those are rough areas, Sarge. The cartels are getting smarter. They've taken over the drug and sex trade but they hire some local thugs to work for them. As long as the cartel gets their cut of the money, everybody's happy. Plus, the home boys aren't going to sell out the Mexicans to the cops because they're the ones bringing in the dope and some of the women."

"What's the best way to get eyes on these addresses?" Andy asked.

Detective White leaned back in his chair, blowing out his breath as he stared at the three maps. After a minute, he pointed at one of them.

"Scotty, you were a sniper. This one's right up your alley."

"You want me to pick him off from long distance?"

"No, man," Jamal grinned. "It's just this address has some woods around it. You can put on your, what's it called? A goonie suit?"

This elicited a laugh from everyone.

"Bro, it's a ghillie suit."

"Yeah, but on you it's a goonie suit," Jimmy cracked.

"Anyway," White continued, his finger on a wooded area off of Newcomb Street, "this little forest parallels I-295 and then backs right up to DHS's property. If you still have some pull with them, we could insert you and a partner there. It's only a few hundred yards to that cartel house. You should be able to get eyes on it from the woods.

"We're gonna need to think about the other two addresses, Sarge. They're both in the middle of their blocks, surrounded by other houses. The bangers have gotten wise to us trying to sit on them in a UC car. The bastards have even started calling the police on us, giving a description of our car or van and saying that we're selling drugs. A marked unit shows up to check us out and the op is blown."

They spent the next twenty minutes throwing out ideas before the lieutenant glanced at his phone and stood to leave.

"I hate to rush off but my captain gets nervous if he can't come to my office every couple of hours to get me to do his work for him. He's already blowing my phone up. Sarge, keep me in the loop and if I can pull in any Emergency Response resources, let me know. I'd love to serve search warrants on any of those locations if you can confirm Contreras is there."

After Bell left, Sergeant Lockhart excused herself to make a phone call while Jamal and the others discussed options for getting eyes on the target homes. A few minutes later, Kendra returned.

"Okay, Chuck, I just got approval from my LT in gangs. He's retiring in a few months so he signs off on most everything I ask. What I'd like to do is let my squad finish up what they're working on today and in the morning and then have our two teams meet at the gangs office on Shepherd Street tomorrow afternoon. Will that work? I think we need to move on this intel as quickly as we can."

"Yeah, that would be great," McCain answered. "Let me have an address and a time and we'll be there."

He had hoped to start today, but beggars couldn't be choosy. Chuck was just grateful that he was getting some help inside the beltway. Hopefully, they could corner Ramon Contreras and take him into custody. And, if what Chloe said was true and the thug would not surrender, the big man or one of his friends would not lose any sleep over permanently ending el Asesino's life of crime.

As Sergeant Lockhart and Chuck exchanged business cards, she pointed at the address on hers.

"The gangs unit is off-site from PD headquarters which is great, but we do have to share a building with the Lesbian, Gay, Bisexual and Transgender Liaison Unit."

"Say what?" Jimmy asked.

Kendra and Jamal both laughed.

"When Lieutenant Bell said things were screwed up," the sergeant smiled, "he wasn't kidding. We can't fill all the beats, investigations is understaffed, but we have an LGBTLU."

"What do they do?" Chloe queried, a confused look on her face.

"That's a good question," Jamal replied with a shrug. "From what we can see, they're kind of like a gay version of crime prevention. They do a lot of educational campaigns and community events, waving that rainbow flag."

"I wanted to go ahead and prep you," Lockhart said, making eye contact with Smith, "They're kind of sensitive so please don't say anything tomorrow to set them off."

"Me? How could you think that I would ever make fun of a police unit dedicated to who the members sleep with? Hey Jimmy, you gonna wear your wig?"

"Don't even go there," Jones replied, shaking his head.

"On the plus side," White interjected, "they can all bake and they like to share their cakes and cookies."

"Oh, I bet they like to share," Scotty said with a grin.

**MPD Gangs Office, Shepherd Street NW, Washington, D.C., Wednesday, 1325 hours**

Sergeant Lockhart ushered Chuck, Andy, Scotty, Jimmy, Hollywood, Chloe, Gabby, and Tex past the LGBTLU's offices and into the gang unit's briefing room. Scotty and Jimmy both snickered as they passed but a nasty look from the gang sergeant convinced them to keep their thoughts to themselves.

McCain was impressed when he noticed that the satellite photos he had provided of el Asesino's locations had been blown up to make them easier to study. Investigator White and the other five detectives were already there, looking over the intel that McCain had provided the previous day. After introductions were made, Kendra wasted no time in starting the meeting, pointing to Smith.

"First, let's talk about the townhome on Newcomb Street. Are we still good with Scotty slipping into the woods and setting up a surveillance?"

"We are," Chuck replied. "I spoke with a friend at Homeland and it won't be a problem to park there and make entry from their property."

"Who's the lucky investigator going with me?" Smith asked.

A stocky Latino man wearing a flannel shirt and a Raiders ball cap raised his hand.

"That would be me. I'm Detective Joey Guevara."

Lockhart continued her briefing. "You two will go in after dark so you've got some time to plan this afternoon. There are a number of trails in those woods that some of the residents, and even dopers, use to cut through as a shortcut to the other side of the neighborhood. Just keep that in mind as you're setting up.

"This duplex on Orange Street is less than a quarter of a mile from the Newcomb address and the triplex on S Street is north of there, maybe fifteen minutes away. Those two are going to be more challenging, but that's why we're all here. I'm sure we can figure out a way to get eyes on them to determine if Ramon Contreras is hiding out in one of these three places. And if he's not, we should still get some solid intel that we can use later."

The Loudon County reserve deputies and the Metropolitan police investigators threw out ideas and brainstormed for the next two hours. They eventually came up with a strategy. None of them were sure if it would work with the gangsters having located themselves in the middle of crowded neighborhoods, surrounded by local thugs to bolster the cartel's ranks. At the same time, they were going to give it their best shot to track down the cop-killer.

As the meeting was winding down, Investigator Guevara stood and motioned for Smith to follow him, leading the sniper to his cubicle.

"Sorry, it's kind of small but we can talk about what you're thinking for tonight."

As Scotty seated his large frame in a chair next to Joey's desk, he glanced around noting a framed photo containing a younger version of the detective in desert fatigues, holding a scoped M-14. The backdrop was familiar to Scotty.

"Iraq?"

"Yeah, I was in the Marines. I kept trying to get them to send me to Scout-Sniper School but could never get my captain to sign off on it. He tossed me a bone and made me the designated marksman in my platoon. I just did one tour and got out and took the job with MPD. I'm on ERT here and Lieutenant Bell sent me to SWAT sniper school."

"Nice," Smith nodded appreciatively. "The little white guy with the wire rim glasses on my team was in MARSOC. The black guy was an infantry captain in the Marines."

"Wow, those MARSOC operators are squared away. Jamal said you were an Army sniper?"

"Rangers lead the way. Have you ever been in these woods where we're going?"

"No, but I know the neighborhood. It's a gang paradise."

Scotty was silent for a moment before speaking. "Are you gonna be good with being in the wild for an extended period of time? I mean if the locals are in and out of there and using some of the trails, I don't think we can take a chance on moving around during the day."

"What are you thinking?"

"I'd plan on at least twenty-four hours, maybe forty-eight."

Joey looked surprised. "That makes sense. I guess I just hadn't thought about camping out in there for a day or two."

"I don't think we have a choice. Of course, we could rotate you out if it goes into a second day..."

"No, no, I'm in. I'd love to take down Contreras and some of his bangers."

**Department of Homeland Security, Ash Street SE, Washington, D.C., Wednesday, 2050 hours**

A tall chain link fence, topped with barbed wire and equipped with motion sensors, surrounded the block-plus sized compound containing the DHS, the United States Coast Guard Headquarters, and the Cybersecurity & Infrastructure Security Agency. A uniformed Homeland Security officer opened one of the rear gates that led into the wooded area, allowing Smith and Guevara to disappear into the darkness.

Joey led the way, the NVGs giving everything around them a greenish tint. The Metropolitan detective was armed with his ERT-issued suppressed M-4 rifle and his 9mm Sig Sauer 226 pistol and was wearing his emergency response team BDUs. Scotty was similarly attired in OD BDUs, with his MK 12 Special Purpose Rifle slung over his chest and a 9mm Glock 17 on his hip. Both men wore body armor and ballistic helmets that held their night vision devices. Over the top of their uniforms and weapons, the snipers wore their ghillie suits, designed to make them look like part of the landscape.

Just as they entered the tree line, it started to rain. It wasn't heavy but the late Fall temperatures let them know they were in for a miserable time.

"I don't know about you Marine or SWAT snipers, but us Rangers aren't happy unless it's raining," Smith whispered.

"And I say you're full of shit," Guevara answered with a grin.

"Yep," the bearded man agreed, shaking his head. "This is gonna suck."

It was only three-hundred yards from the back of the DHS compound to where the two men planned to set up their surveillance across from the cartel townhome, but Joey took his time. Scotty was impressed by how the Marine-turned-detective moved through the trees. They didn't expect anyone to be in the forest but they weren't taking any chances. After a slow incursion, they arrived at the spot they had picked out on the map to set up their hides.

They were only fifty feet off of Newcomb Street, near where it curved sharply to the right and continued back to the left in a big loop. Inside that circle were the Washington Overlook Townhomes. Two rows of nine homes faced each other with a parking lot in between. Additional rows of townhomes were scattered around the bend on Newcomb Street. The cartel address was the third one down on the right, inside the parking area.

Scotty laid out a small black tarp to make lying in the rain a little more bearable. They nestled in next to a downed pine tree on their left, blocking anyone from seeing them from that direction. Ahead of them, they could watch the suspect location through the trees and thin vegetation. After they were settled, they adjusted their ghillie suits, and Joey pulled out a red-lensed flashlight to check the satellite map just to be sure. Scotty texted their backup team to let them know they were in place.

"That's it with the front porch light on," he confirmed quietly.

Each of the men had NV binoculars and NV optics on their rifles. Scotty immediately scoped the residence and the area around it. Joey had also brought a camera with a telephoto lens. The front door opened and a mid-thirties black male exited, turning to smile at someone inside. There was a brief conversation before the man walked across the parking lot, got into an older Buick Regal and drove away. Joey snapped several photos of him as he left.

Scotty's watch showed 2137 hours. As the Buick turned onto Newcomb Street, a banged-up white pickup pulled in and parked in front of the target location. A hefty Hispanic looking male knocked on the door and was quickly ushered in. Ten minutes later, an older black male exited, this one looking to be in his fifties. He left in a maroon Chevrolet Malibu.

For the next two hours, this was the pattern. Men came and went, never spending any longer than thirty minutes inside.

"Damn, bro!" Smith whispered to his companion. "It must be like a production line in there."

"Yeah," Guevara answered, continuing to snap photos of everyone going in and out of the gang operation. "I don't think this is a drug house. These guys are coming out with a spring in their step and a smile on their faces like they just got laid."

The cold rain continued to fall. The ghillie suits offered some protection and they had both layered thermals under their uniforms. At midnight, the front porch light finally went out. By 0030 hours, the townhome was dark. The rain slowed to a drizzle as the two snipers kept up their vigil.

"I'll take first watch if you want to get some sleep," Scotty said quietly. "I'll wake you at 0330."

Joey handed the camera to his partner and within a couple of minutes had dropped off to sleep. Scotty texted Andy with a status update and then continued to scan the area.

Andy, Tex, and Jamal sat just a few hundred yards away in a black Century Tactical Suburban, near the back fence of the DHS compound. They were Scotty and Joey's backup team. If something went wrong, they could be with them in a matter of minutes. The snipers had checked in after getting settled, letting the other three officers know they were in position.

"Man, this is a good night to be on the backup team," Tex Davis commented, spitting tobacco juice into an empty plastic bottle.

"No joke," Fleming replied. "Scotty's a Ranger, though. Part of their training is crawling around in a Florida swamp for a couple of weeks. He can handle a little rain."

"I heard that Army Sniper School is pretty tough."

Andy shrugged. "It's not as tough the Marines' course, but it's pretty good and Scotty's one hell of a sniper. I've seen him make some shots that I wouldn't have believed were possible."

"Did you go to Scout Sniper school?" White asked.

"No, MARSOC training was tough enough. I led a tactical element for most of the time I was in. Jamal, you remember Eric?"

"That brother would be hard to forget," the detective laughed. "Wasn't he the one with the frag grenades?"

"That's right. Anyway, he was another tac element leader when he and I served together."

"I learned a lot working with you guys, at least up until I got shot," Jamal chuckled.

"That does tend to put a damper on things," Tex said. "I do like the idea of having some frag grenades, though. That would be a nice addition to our basic load out."

Andy shook his head with a grin. "Yeah, I don't think that's gonna happen. The only reason we got away with it then was because the East Coast was still mostly shut down because of the zombies. We got away with a lot of stuff that would be frowned on now."

**Washington Overlook Townhomes, Newcomb Street, SE, Washington, D.C., Thursday, 0331 hours**

Scotty yawned, glancing at his watch for the hundredth time. 0331 hours. Finally. The rain had stopped an hour earlier. Before waking his partner, Smith texted their back up team, letting them know they were still OK. The sound of traffic from the nearby interstate provided a steady background noise. An occasional car drove down Newcomb Street, either a resident coming home after working second shift or someone looking to buy drugs. The former Ranger gently shook the former Marine. Joey was instantly awake, glancing around him in the darkness.

"Tag, you're it," Smith whispered, handing over the camera. "Nothing stirring. Wake me up if you need me."

With that, the sniper pulled his balaclava around his face and snuggled under the ghillie suit. Guevara stretched as much as he could in his confined position, opened a bottle of water and took a long drink. He wondered about the massive man sleeping next to him. Jamal had worked with Scotty and that MARSOC Marine, along with another of their teammates in cleaning out the last of the zombies in DC a few years before. The biological terror weapon had taken the lives of thousands and had caused billions of dollars in property damage, mostly on the East Coast.

According to Investigator White, Smith had dropped two gang members with head shots from a hundred yards away, before the thugs could even get a shot off. They were the watchmen on the roof of a recreation center that a local gang had made into their headquarters after the zombie virus had been released. The young criminals used the chaos to kill a number of rival group members, as well as rape and murder innocent civilians who had refused to leave their homes after the bio-terror weapon infected so many of their fellow citizens.

Just a few minutes after Smith took out the sentries, the team forced entry, killing a number of zombies on the lower level and then engaging in a fire fight to eliminate the rest of the criminals. During that shootout, Jamal was hit in the leg by a 9mm bullet and Scotty had immediately shifted into medic mode, applying a tourniquet to save the wounded officer's life.

The detective rubbed his eyes as he kept watch, scanning their surroundings with his night vision, but the remainder of the night was quiet. Around 0500 hours, lights started to come on in some of the townhomes and people were leaving for work by 0530, hoping to miss the infamous Washington, D.C., rush hour. Guevara composed a text to Sergeant Lockhart, appraising her of what they had seen so far and of his own sense that this was a cartel house of prostitution.

Around 0620, Smith was awake, stifling a yawn, and rolling onto his side, away from his partner to empty his bladder.

"Ah. That feels better," he whispered, turning back to check on Guevara. "Anything going on?"

"No. The neighborhood started coming alive around 0500, but those folks are heading to work. Our friends in there should be sleeping a while longer."

"If that is a brothel, those girls worked late last night. Let me check in with Andy," Scotty said, sending a message to his friend, letting them know that they had survived the night.

"If you're cooking me breakfast, I like my six eggs scrambled with cheese and bacon, with a few slices of toast on the side," Smith whispered to his partner, digging a meal-ready-to-eat out of his backpack.

Scotty chose an entree of hash browns with bacon, peppers, and onions. Joey smiled at his partner as he pulled out his own MRE with a beef taco entree. The former Ranger added some zest to his breakfast with the small bottle of Tabasco Sauce provided in the MRE, before handing it to the former Marine who did the same. The temperature was chilly, but it wasn't currently raining and the woods slowly started to come alive. Two squirrels chased each other up a tree and then leapt through the air to land on another, following each other back down to the ground.

"Man, I swore that once I got out of the Marines, I'd never eat this shit again," Guevara grumbled quietly, motioning at the pouch he was eating from.

Smith grinned as he finished off the hash browns. "What are you talking about? This is fine dining. At least the hot sauce gives it a little flavor. We'll see how it affects my stomach later."

By 1100 hours, the front porch light was back on and the brothel appeared to be open for business again. The clouds were dark and there had been intermittent showers throughout the morning. Today's customers drove work vans, pickups with ladder racks, or pickups pulling landscaping equipment.

At 1340 hours, a rough looking white van pulled into the parking lot. "Martinez Painting" was plastered on the sides of the vehicle. Four Hispanic men exited and walked up to the front door. Seconds later, a loud voice came from inside, shouting at the men in Spanish.

Joey quietly translated. "He's saying that only two of them can come in at a time. The others have to wait in the van. One of the guys is pissed because they let him sit in the living room and watch TV last time, while he waited his turn."

Finally, two of the men went inside and the other two walked back out into the parking lot where they stood by the van, checking their phones. A few minutes later, the rain returned, forcing them back into the vehicle. Less than a half hour later, the first two customers exited the townhome, smiling broadly. They exchanged places with their friends in the van as they made their way to the townhouse.

When the second pair of Mexicans finished and headed for their work van, Jerry Brewer let them out, sticking his head through the open door to see if they had any other customers waiting to get laid. Rainy days always brought a few more horny men than usual, especially those who couldn't work because of the weather. The painters who had just left were the perfect example. They normally showed up a couple of times a month, always in the evening after they had finished their workday.

The parking lot was mostly empty, the majority of the residents still at work. Sucks for them, Brewer thought, shutting and locking the door. This was the best job he'd had in his forty-six years of life. I get to work from home, someone else pays my rent, I get to screw these whores anytime I want, and my income is all tax-free, he thought with a smile.

He pulled the wad of money from his jeans pocket. The four Mexicans had paid $300.00 each to bang one of the two prostitutes. That was $1,200.00 to go with the other $2,400.00 they had made from the eight earlier customers in the day. There was also the $2,100 that had come in the previous evening after he returned from his money drop at Carlos' duplex on Orange Street, less than a mile away. And there were still a lot of hours left for the girls to make us some more money, he thought. Later, he'd take the day's earnings to Carlos where the Mexican would count it and give Jerry ten percent as his daily salary.

The African-American did the math in his head. He was already at $5,700.00 which meant a cool $570.00 for him. Hell, I might clear $1,000.00 before I turn off the front porch light tonight, he realized. Brewer considered himself fortunate. He had been on the wrong side of the law for most of his life. His own mother had turned tricks in their government subsidized apartment to support her heroin habit.

Even though Jerry had sold drugs on and off over the years, he had never been much of a user, the trauma of finding his mother on the bathroom floor one morning, dead from an overdose seared into his mind. He had been in and out of prison from the time he was thirteen up until just a year ago. He had picked up Spanish in jail and during his infrequent times of working on a landscaping crew.

Jerry's last arrest had been on a probation violation warrant. The original charge was driving under the influence and having a suspended license. Carlos had been serving time, as well, and the men became friends. It helped that the black man spoke Spanish. The Mexican told the American to look him up when he got out of jail. When Jerry did just that, Carlos extended the job offer to be the house pimp for one of the cartel's brothels.

The pay and the perks were great. The only real stipulation that the gangster had given Jerry was a simple one— "Don't ever steal from me or the cartel. We're amigos but if I find out you take money, I kill you myself."

Brewer might be a convicted felon several times over, with a lengthy criminal history, but he had never considered himself a thief. Every evening around 7:00pm, he turned off the front porch light for an hour for the girls to eat and clean up. Jerry would count up their used condoms and make sure that number lined up with the cash in his pocket. He had only been off in his count once over the last year that he had worked for the Mexicans. On that occasion, he wasn't sure what had happened but he put in $300.00 of his own to make everything add up.

Jerry always enjoyed his evening visits with the Mexican gangster. Brewer was impressed by how well the cartel was organized. His small part of the business was just one cog in the organized crime operation. Carlos and Jerry would chat for a little while and drink a couple of beers before Brewer would head back to the townhouse to turn the front porch light back on. There were usually people waiting in their cars for him to return so they could get some action on their way home.

The terrible weather ensured that pedestrian traffic was at a minimum throughout the day. Late in the afternoon, Joey's phone vibrated with an incoming text. After reading it, he leaned close to his partner's ear.

"That was Sergeant Lockhart," he whispered. "She said that the photos I sent her of all the different men going in and out house was enough to get a search warrant. They're going to hit it later tonight. She'll give me more details later."

"What about the other two addresses?" Scotty asked.

"She said they don't have anything yet, but they're still working on them."

**Fort Circle Park, SE, Washington, D.C., Thursday, 1055 hours**

Chloe checked the drone a final time before sending it airborne, heading towards the New Generation location on S Street, less than three blocks away. There were only a few vehicles scattered around the recreation area's small parking lot. Fort Circle was known for its hiking and biking trails but the rain was keeping the exercisers away.

Jimmy and two of the Metropolitan PD gang detectives waited inside the maroon Cadillac Escalade. The undercover car had dark windows, preventing anyone from seeing inside. Satisfied that the UAV was operating normally, Wilkerson climbed into the rear passenger seat, shaking her head in disgust at the water dripping from her rain jacket.

"How's it look?" Investigator Tara Robinson asked.

"We'll be over that address in a couple of minutes and we'll see what we can see."

"Any chance of people on the ground spotting it?" Detective Orlando Costello queried. "Isn't the ceiling for private drones just four-hundred feet?"

Wilkerson was focused on flying the aircraft so Jones answered for her.

"It is but Chloe will be hovering between three and five thousand feet, so no, they're not gonna have a clue they're being watched. It's got a special sensor on it to alert the operator in case any aircraft come within a mile so she can drop down to avoid them."

"But three to five thousand feet is pretty high," Tara commented. "Will we be able to identify Contreras if he's there?"

"Oh, yeah," Jimmy replied. "That bad boy has all the bells and whistles. The camera is top-of-the-line, plus it's got FLIR and night-vision. And, Gabby's using the same model at that location over near where Scotty and Joey are hiding in the woods. If el Asesino shows his ugly face, Chloe or Gabby will capture it."

What Jones couldn't say was that the drones had been worked over by the CIA's Directorate of Science and Technology and had been involved in more than a few clandestine missions.

"How's the battery life?" Costello asked. "I've got one that I love to play with but after about fifteen or twenty minutes, I've got to land and change batteries."

"I'm over the target location," Wilkerson said, manipulating the controls as she watched the display screen. "I'm gonna move around a little bit and get a feel for the area. To answer your question, Orlando, the battery life on our drones is a little over an hour. Gabby and I both have several extras so we can keep them up for a while.

"I've got two vehicles pulling away from the curb near the address," Chloe said, zooming the camera in for a closer look. "I didn't see who got in them and it might not even be related but there's a red pickup and a gray or silver passenger car. Should I follow or maintain the surveillance?"

Jimmy thought quickly before answering. "Stay over the target location. Can one of you provide the others with the vehicle descriptions Gabby just watched leave? If they show up on Orange or Newcomb Street, we'll know they're probably connected."

"I got it," Tara said, putting her walkie-talkie to her lips.

While the detective passed along the lookout, Chloe focused on the area around the New Generations address. The intel indicated that the gang occupied all three apartments in the triplex. It was almost thirty minutes later when Wilkerson picked up a pedestrian making his way down the sidewalk, pausing occasionally to peer behind him. She zoomed in to see a middle-aged black male, wearing a Washington Commanders ball cap and dark shades, stop in front of the NG's apartment building. Scanning the area again, he hurried up to the door on the far right, knocked, and quickly disappeared inside.

"That was weird," Chloe muttered, telling her friends what she had seen.

"I'd be looking around, too, if I was going to buy some drugs," Orlando commented.

"I think he's buying something else," the drone operator said. "Let's see how long he's inside."

## S Street, SE, Washington, D.C., Thursday, 1102 hours

Ramon Contreras was tired of staring at the same four walls, the same prostitutes, and the same NG soldiers. From what his lawyer had told him, though, he understood that the pigs were actively trying to find him. Most of the American cops he'd come across couldn't find their ass with both hands, he laughed to himself. He wouldn't go far and he wouldn't stray from where he had plenty of security, but he needed a change of scenery.

Andres had mostly recovered from the gunshot wound he had suffered during the killing of the narcotics sergeant and his wife. It was embarrassing enough that a woman had shot him. The thug laughed it off now, even though el Asesino saw the occasional grimace of pain if Andres tried to use his left hand. Andres and Miguel were in charge of Ramon's security, in spite of the senior NG lieutenant still believing he was the toughest hombre on the planet.

Contreras told them that he wanted to go visit Carlos and see how his corner of the cartel business was going. Miguel gathered three additional soldiers and they loaded up the Silverado and the Nissan Altima for the fifteen-minute drive to the Orange Street address. Even though Carlos worked for Ramon, he always seemed to have good ideas and suggestions on how to make their various operations more successful.

Case in point was the whorehouse on Newcomb Street. It generated a steady cash flow and the black American Carlos had running it seemed to be doing an excellent job, delivering around $10,000 a day to the house on Orange Street. Carlos, in turn, delivered half of the income to el Asesino as his cut. And that was just from the prostitution side of the business. Carlos' men, including some of the locals, also moved a lot of drugs. They supplied the area with crack, meth, heroin, and pills.

Ramon had been thinking about what Chilo had told him about his operation in Maryland. Providing children to the sick bastards who like them young was an even more lucrative market. What had the fat man told him? Those rich, DC elite paid two-thousand dollars to play doctor with a kid. That was something else to chat with Carlos about. If he could just stay out of jail, he could be one of el Asesino's lieutenants for a long time to come.

Contreras still needed some more soldiers. He was planning on borrowing a couple of Carlos' men until they got a few more from Mexico. Losing those two sicarios the previous week infuriated him. He really wanted to kill some more cops, but realized he needed to be patient until he had replenished his ranks. Contreras had again requested the big dogs in Mexico to send him some more people, explaining how the pigs had killed the two recent arrivals.

Ramon had been diligent to wire the gang leaders their cut of his profits every month so he knew they would honor his request. Maybe I should send another message and ask them to send some little girls, as well? More money for me means more money for the cartel leaders south of the border.

At some point, Contreras still wanted to track down that big son-of-a-bitch who arrested him in Virginia. He'd been arrested many times before, but he had never been handled so easily by a single pig. Ramon knew that he was better than any cop out there. Most American pigs were fat and out of shape. The one who had choked him out at their Sterling stash house had been the exception. I'll put a bullet in his head if we cross paths again, el Asesino thought.

**Department of Homeland Security, Ash Street SE, Washington, D.C., Thursday, 1125 hours**

Gabby, Hollywood, and their two partners from the Metropolitan Police Gang Unit had elected to set up near the rear of the DHS compound, parked next to Scotty and Joey's backup team. Vargas was operating their drone as they all sat in a nondescript white Dodge work van. Investigators Alex Lopez and Marvin Daniels both admitted they were new to the gang unit but seemed sharp and were willing to take suggestions from the two Virginia deputies.

The drone was currently hovering at twenty-five hundred feet, it's camera snapping photos of the two men sitting on the front porch of the duplex. The real-time video showed them passing a joint back and forth while scanning the street and sidewalk, one of the sentries clearly concealing a long gun of some sort in his lap, a jacket covering it. Gabby handed the controller to Hollywood.

"Can you fly it for a minute? I need to send these pics in and see if we can get an ID on them."

Estrada took the controls but was clearly uncomfortable.

"You know I'm not a pilot. What if I crash?"

His partner smiled. "I've got it set on auto-hover so just hold onto the controller and don't push the red button."

"Who are you sending the pictures to?" Investigator Daniels asked. "I don't think we have access to facial recognition software."

"Homeland will do it for us," Gabby answered, her fingers flying over her laptop's keyboard. "Their agents are stretched pretty thin, but they are good about giving us technical support."

In reality, Vargas sent the photos of the two cartel goons to Ricardo Gonzalez at the CIA. Their facial recognition system was much more robust than Homeland's or even the FBI's. After sending the files, Gabby took the controller from Hollywood.

Investigator Lopez sat behind the steering wheel of the undercover van. He held a walkie-talkie up to his ear and listened for about a minute before answering. When he was finished transmitting, he laid the radio down and pulled out a small notebook, writing something down.

"That was the other team over near S Street. Two vehicles left just as they got their drone up— a red pickup and a gray passenger car. They couldn't see who got in. Tara wants us to watch for them, just in case they come for a visit."

Vargas nodded and took the drone on a circle of the area, passing over the location on Newcomb Street. In moments, she had found Smith and Guevara through the UAV's FLIR system, the two snipers lying motionless in their hide. She circled back around to the address on Orange Street, noting that the two sentries were still in place. Her computer beeped, alerting her to an incoming email. She handed the controller to Estrada again and opened the message from Gonzalez.

After reading what Gonz had discovered, she sent him a quick reply and spoke to her teammates. "Nothing is coming back on the soldier on the left. The one on the right is Salvador Rivera. He's wanted for multiple counts of murder out of Mexico. I'm asking for confirmation, but maybe that would get us in the door?"

"Yeah, that would be a good lick," Marvin replied. "That's good stuff, Gabby. Alex, you want to check with the sarge?"

# Chapter Eight

**Orange Street, SE, Washington, D.C., Thursday, 1355 hours**

"Let's do it, Ramon," Carlos said, passing the marijuana pipe back to his boss. "You want me to find us a place? I think we need to put it in a better part of town. The rich people who want to bang kids aren't going to come into a shitty neighborhood like this. It's too dangerous. They'd get robbed or carjacked before they ever got inside to give us their money."

"Yeah, you're right. We definitely need a better area. Why don't you see if our realtor can find us a townhouse or apartment over near the capitol? Chilo told me that some of his best customers work in the government and will drive an hour to play with his kids in Maryland. If we could set up a few blocks away from some of the government buildings, we'll have a steady stream of customers in no time."

El Asesino sucked in the high-grade pot, feeling more relaxed than he'd felt in several days. He and Carlos had talked and made plans for the last two hours. He remembered something else.

"One more thing, Carlos. Before we open another whore house, I want to put hidden cameras in the rooms. We'll make more money blackmailing those sickos than from what they pay to have sex with the kids."

Carlos chuckled as he took another hit off the pipe. He was feeling good, too. His chuckle turned into a full-blown belly laugh. After a minute, he was able to regain control.

"Sí, buena idea, Señor! I know something else that would make us a lot of money."

"¿Qué es?"

"One of my hombres is good with computers. He says there's a special level of the internet where people sell everything. We could sell videos of people having sex with the kids."

"A special level?" Ramon questioned.

"Hey, Santiago!" Carlos called over his shoulder.

A moment later, a small-framed man appeared from down the hallway.

"Sí?"

"If we wanted to sell child porn on the internet, isn't there a secret level that's harder to find and secure from the police?"

"It's called the 'dark web,' Señor. People sell everything on there— illegal porn, weapons, drugs, even sicarios find work there."

"But what about the cops?" Contreras asked.

"Some police departments have special computer detectives that know how to maneuver around in the dark web. I know how to hide from them so anything you want to put on there, we can do it. Those kid sex videos are some of the biggest sellers on the dark web."

"Gracias, Santiago," Carlos said, dismissing the diminutive man.

"So, he's a computer expert, huh?" Ramon queried.

"Oh, yeah. He's small, but he's tough and smart."

"Bueno. I'll get us some kids and then we'll put them to work. I guess anybody can shoot the videos for us. Any dumbass can work the camera on a cell phone."

"Or we can buy a better camera? People will pay more if the movies are better quality."

"Sí. Don't spend too much money, but go ahead and buy whatever you need. I never thought I'd be getting into the porn business, but I think we're going to be very rich men, Carlos. As soon as we finish this pipe, I'll head back to S Street and send a message to Mexico.

"Hey, amigo," Contreras said as he stood, "I need to borrow a couple of your men. The pigs have either killed or arrested some of my best soldiers."

"No problemo. You want them now or can I send them over later?"

"Later is OK," El Asesino nodded.

"I've got two good hombres you can use for a while," Carlos said. "They're out making deliveries to some of our dealers around town. I'll send them over when they get back."

"Bueno. Gracias, amigo."

A few blocks away, inside the DHS compound, the two Virginia reserve deputies and the two Metropolitan gang detectives waited for something to happen. Vargas kept the drone circling the area, only landing momentarily to change out the battery. The pickup and passenger car from S Street had shown up, parking in the narrow alley behind the duplex. An overhanging tree blocked her from getting a visual on any of the six men's faces as they slipped in the back door or the residence.

Now, almost three hours later, sudden movement behind the suspect location caught Gabby's attention. The six men were climbing back into their two vehicles. She moved the controller in an effort to get a better angle on the vehicle occupants, quickly dropping the UAV's altitude. The last man out of the house paused, speaking with someone inside, a grin on his face. She caught a glimpse of him before he turned and climbed into the pickup truck, a sudden jolt of energy shooting through her.

"I think we've got Contreras. Those guys are leaving and I'm pretty sure I saw him," she announced, handing Hollywood the controller while she reviewed the footage on her computer.

Less than a minute later, Gabby had a screen shot of el Asesino staring out from her laptop.

"No question about it, that's him! He's in the front passenger seat of the pickup truck. Call the sarge and find out if we should try and intercept or just watch to see where they go."

The reserve deputies weren't on the same radio frequency as the Metropolitan DC officers. While Estrada managed the drone, Vargas quickly contacted McCain over their own frequency to let him know she had spotted the man wanted for murdering Dwayne and Shelly Thomas.

### S Street, SE, Washington, D.C., Thursday, 1402 hours

Sebastian Hernandez glanced over his shoulder, continuing to scan the area as he made his way up the sidewalk to see his client, Ramon Contreras. After speaking with his police informant an hour earlier, the attorney immediately changed into jeans and a Washington Wizards hoodie. He followed his normal practice of parking three blocks away and then taking a roundabout stroll to el Asesino's lair.

The Metropolitan officer who had called his office had used the code phrase requesting the lawyer to call them back. Hernandez recontacted Officer Hickson immediately, using one of the prepaid cellphones he kept in a desk drawer. Hickson was assigned to the Lesbian, Gay, Bisexual and Transgender Liaison Unit and the lawyer paid her for any information that she gleaned on the Gang Unit's operations, especially concerning the NG Cartel.

Hernandez didn't know what letters Hickson used to describe her own sexuality. All he cared about was that she had a chip on her shoulder because her Mexican girlfriend had been arrested and deported two years earlier by a combined gangs and narcotics unit drug raid. Today, Hickson reached out to the lawyer because she had stopped by the gang office that morning to drop off a batch of homemade cookies. That gave her a couple of minutes to chat with the gang detectives and eavesdrop on whatever conversations she could hear.

What she'd heard had sent a chill down Sebastian's spine. The gang detectives were in the process of obtaining search warrants for some unknown locations but Contreras' name had come up several times. Officer Hickson stayed for as long as she could without arousing suspicions before making her way back to her cubicle in the LGBTLU. Hickson had back-to-back meetings that morning and wasn't able to call the attorney right away.

After finally speaking with the dirty police officer, the attorney contemplated calling or texting Ramon but decided against it in the event the authorities were monitoring his or the gangster's phones. Even using a prepaid device was no guarantee that the communication would be secure. Instead, he opted for a face-to-face conversation, now walking briskly through the light rain, just half a block from Contreras' triplex, hoping he wasn't too late.

When he knocked on the front door of the middle apartment, the soldier who answered told the attorney that the gangster would be back later, but wouldn't divulge where Ramon might be. Sebastian decided to wait inside, hoping his client would return soon. He accepted a bottle of water from the young thug who had let him in.

"You want to bang one of the girls while you wait? They not busy right now."

Hernandez shuddered at the thought. There's no telling what kind of diseases those poor women are carrying.

"No, gracias. I'll just wait for Señor Contreras."

The young man shrugged and grinned, clearly trying to be hospitable. "El Jefe won't mind if you want to make it with one of the women."

"I...I need to check some emails while I wait," Sebastian stammered, having a seat on the worn couch and withdrawing his phone.

A few blocks away at the Fort Circle Park, Chloe and the others stared at the image of the man wearing a Wizards hoodie walking up the sidewalk and then disappearing inside the suspect location. Wilkerson captured a few stills and sent them to Jones' and the two detectives' phones.

"And who are you?" Jimmy asked.

"A customer?" Tara pondered, staring at the man. "We still don't know what they're doing in there. I'm sure they're selling drugs but they might be selling flesh, as well."

"He went in the middle apartment, while the last couple of guys have gone in the one on the end," Chloe added.

"He looks familiar," Orlando said, staring at the photo for several minutes. "I know I've seen him somewhere before."

**Near Newcomb Street, SE, Washington, D.C., Thursday, 1415 hours**

"What does the sarge want us to do?" Scotty whispered. "There's no one moving around so we could be back inside the DHS compound in less than ten and be able to support them wherever they need us."

Smith had heard Vargas' radio traffic to McCain that Contreras had been spotted and Guevara heard Investigator Daniels give the same message to Sergeant Lockhart.

"She said to standby. She's trying to get Lieutenant Bell to send some tactical units our way."

"That'll take too long. Let's pull out."

Joey watched the other sniper quietly gathering his things and putting on his backpack. Even though it was the middle of the day, the inclement weather was keeping pedestrians off the street.

"Are you sure?"

Scotty patted the smaller man on the shoulder. "Look, we've gathered a shitload of intel here. Mission accomplished. Let's get back to the others so we can help when the real shit hits the fan."

In minutes, they were retracing their steps through the woods, back towards the DHS compound.

**Eaton Road, SE, Washington, D.C., Thursday, 1420 hours**

Chuck and Kendra sat in the big man's Century Tactical white GMC Yukon on the deserted side street, roughly halfway between the New Generation's locations on S Street and Orange Street. The vacant lots that surrounded them once held public housing but had been shut down, condemned, and leveled. The city had already started construction on new apartment buildings on the next street over. For now, the secluded location allowed Chuck and the gang sergeant to monitor all the data coming in from their teams.

McCain realized earlier that even with his and Lockhart's combined squads, they were still spread too thin to conduct a proper reconnaissance on the three addresses. Now that Ramon Contreras had been spotted, he wondered how the sergeant was going to handle it. A map app was open on Chuck's phone, their officers' positions highlighted by flashing red dots, while his iPad displayed a split screen, allowing him to watch the footage from both drones. As he watched the pickup and the sedan pulling away from the duplex, Kendra spoke with Lieutenant Bell, trying to get some of his tactical officers to come help in taking down the murderer and his protection detail.

She sighed as she disconnected. "He's activating a team and sending them our way but it's gonna take a while."

"In the meantime, we have eyes on Contreras," McCain replied. "If he gets back to S Street, he's probably got more soldiers there and we'll have to go in and get him. That's a much more dangerous scenario for the tactical team."

Lockhart dialed another number on her phone, glancing over at McCain. "This guy murdered a cop and his wife. We're not losing him on my watch. I'm calling dispatch to send us some marked units. Now that we have him out in the open, I don't want to take a chance on him getting back to that triplex and barricading himself inside."

A minute later, she nodded at McCain. "They're keeping me on the line while they find us a couple of available officers."

"Alpha One to Alpha Two," Chuck called Andy over their frequency.

"Alpha Two, we're clear that Contreras is moving," Fleming answered. "I've been watching on my tablet. Where do you want us?"

"Go ahead and start towards S Street, in case they're heading back there. The sarge is trying to get some uniformed cars so we can do a vehicle takedown."

"Alpha Two's clear."

The two-vehicle, cartel caravan was soon heading north on Martin Luther King Jr Avenue, not far from where McCain and Lockhart sat, he realized. That route was almost a direct shot back to the safe house on S Street. Chuck handed the iPad to Kendra and laid his phone in the console between the seats. He quickly steered the Yukon through the rundown residential area, turning onto Sumner Street and accelerating towards MLK Jr Avenue just ahead.

"Slow down," Kendra ordered, staring at the iPad. "They're coming up on the intersection now."

Chuck had no choice in the matter. The Excel Academy Public School was on their left, the carpool line spilling over into Sumner Street and forcing him to stop fifty yards back from the MLK Jr intersection. For a moment, the road was completely blocked as traffic came from the other direction, the Yukon stuck behind parents waiting to turn into the school. Up ahead, McCain saw the Silverado and the Altima shoot past on MLK Jr Avenue.

As soon as there was a small opening, he jerked the SUV's steering wheel to the left and held the horn down for two seconds, accelerating around the stopped cars. Oncoming traffic swerved to the right on the narrow street, giving the Yukon just enough room to get by. Chuck scanned the intersection as he turned left through a red light, forcing several vehicles to slam on their brakes to avoid a collision. In seconds, though, they were free, attempting to catch up to the suspects.

"Any word on the marked units?"

"There's one close," she answered, still holding the phone to her ear. "He's going to stand by at Talbert Street, less than a mile from here."

"Alpha One to Alpha Two," McCain called Fleming again.

"Alpha Two."

"It sounds like it's going to be somewhere north of Talbert Street. We're three cars behind the suspects now on MLK Jr Avenue. What's your ETA?"

"Alpha Two to Alpha One, ETA is around five."

Kendra clicked over to the uniform division's frequency and contacted the beat car, providing the two-officer unit a detailed description of both vehicles and letting them know that Ramon Contreras was in the Chevrolet pickup. She also gave a description of their car and the other team's so there would be no mix-up. No police officer wants to get dragged into another department's or another division's drama. When the gang sergeant let the uniformed officers know what Contreras was wanted for, though, she knew they would be locked in.

"This is the asshole who broke into that Virginia deputy's house and killed him and his wife? Wow!" Officer Darian Wilson exclaimed.

After receiving the information from dispatch, the twenty-six year old African-American had pulled the marked Ford Police Interceptor Sedan into the parking lot of Sammy's Liquor Store at the corner of MLK Jr and Talbert Street. Wilson's partner, Terry Stafford, nodded in agreement.

"Yeah, this guy is supposedly some big wheel in one of the cartels, trying to get them up and running here," the twenty-eight year old white officer commented.

"Bro, I hate to spoil the surprise but they're already up and running here," Wilson laughed. "You just don't spend enough time in the city on your off days."

The two men had graduated from the police academy together four years earlier and had been partners in the second district ever since. They both had aspirations of becoming detectives but the officer shortage ensured it would be a while before either earned the coveted gold shield.

"Where are we gonna stop them?" Stafford asked, a concerned look on his face. "This could get nasty fast. That gang sergeant said that there are six bangers total in the two vehicles."

"We'll see how it plays out. Did Sergeant Lockhart have any idea when those ERT officers will be here?"

"No, she said they're coming but her concern is that these perps get back to one of their safe houses. She thinks they're enroute to an address on S Street but she'd prefer to take them down in the open before they can barricade themselves inside a house."

"S Street is a good neighborhood for a cartel gang house," Darian replied. "There they are!"

The red Silverado was followed by the gray Altima as they drove by the liquor store, continuing north on MLK Jr Avenue. Darian had to wait for two other cars to go by before he could make the right turn out of the parking lot. A large white SUV came up rapidly on his rear, flashing its headlights.

"I guess that's Sergeant Lockhart and her partner behind us?" Wilson asked, watching the Yukon in his rearview mirror.

Stafford glanced over his shoulder and nodded. "Looks like them. Dispatch gave me her number so I'll give her a call."

As his partner spoke with the detective, Darian concentrated on the two suspect vehicles. One of the cars between the police and the suspects turned onto a side street, leaving just a black sedan between them. After a moment, Terry disconnected.

"They've got another unmarked, a black Suburban, that'll be here in just a couple of minutes. The sarge wants us to try to go around the Nissan and stop the pickup. That's the one Contreras is in. They'll deal with the Altima."

"In a UC car? What are they gonna do?"

"It sounds like they're going to wreck it."

Wilson shook his head. "Bro, this has got cluster written all over it."

Andres spotted the cop car as soon as it turned out of the liquor store parking lot.

"¡Mierda! Es la policia," he exclaimed, instinctively pushing the accelerator to the floor, the Silverado jumping forward.

Ramon was in the front passenger seat with Miguel seated behind him. Pancho was seated behind the driver. Two other soldiers occupied the Altima. At the mention of police, everyone turned to stare out the back window.

"Miguel," Andres said over his shoulder, "call the guys behind us and make sure they saw the pigs. I only saw one car. Maybe they're just looking for a doughnut shop but if they try to stop us, we need to be ready."

Ramon laughed, drawing slain Sergeant Dwayne Thomas' 9mm Sig Sauer P-320 and racking the slide to chamber a round.

"I hope some stupid pig tries to stop us. I'll kill him with another cop's gun!"

Andres focused on driving while the other gangsters checked their weapons. After a short conversation on the phone, Miguel spoke up.

"They saw him, too. They're ready. Andres, maybe you should turn to see if they keep following us?"

Without comment, Andres jerked the steering wheel to the right, turning onto Marion Berry Avenue.

Tex was pushing the Suburban for everything he could get out of it as they rushed to back up the other officers. Andy, Scotty, Jamal and Joey clutched their rifles or pistols as they closed in on an appointment with el Asesino and five of his soldiers. They were just seconds behind the others now when Chuck's voice alerted them that the perps had turned right onto Marion Berry. Almost immediately, the big man transmitted again.

"Alpha One to Alpha Two, hurry it up guys. The shit's about to hit the fan!"

After the sudden right turn by the two suspect vehicles, Officer Wilson managed to stay with them, noticing the Yukon had managed to make the turn, as well. There was no traffic coming from the other direction so Darian activated the cruiser's blue lights and siren, pulling around the Altima and shoving the accelerator to the floor. He hoped to get around the tail car to stop the pickup.

"Here we go!"

The maneuver surprised the driver of the Nissan but he reacted quickly, steering into the police car as it went by on the left.

"Look out!" Officer Stafford yelled from the passenger seat as the Altima slammed into his side, just behind the passenger door.

The violent impact carried both cars into the small convenience store parking lot on the corner of 14th Street and Marion Berry Avenue, the driver's side of the police vehicle slamming into a parked Ford Fiesta. Wilson's head smashed against the side window, knocking the police officer unconscious.

The Silverado continued less than a block on Marion Berry before making a sharp left onto Minnesota Avenue. McCain saw the Nissan sedan ram the police car but made the split-second decision to follow the pickup and Ramon Contreras. Lockhart radioed the police dispatcher, giving her the location of the crash while Chuck also alerted his teammates to check the officers on their way by the scene. The big man felt a momentary pang of guilt for not stopping to help the uniformed cops, but his first priority was to apprehend el Asesino. Hopefully, those officers would be able to take care of themselves.

"If you're gonna take them out, you better do it fast," Sergeant Lockhart said. "We're only about five blocks from that house on S Street and I doubt we'll get a warm reception there."

Using an unmarked vehicle to stop a fleeing felon is always frowned upon in law enforcement circles. Many departments have clear policies forbidding an unmarked vehicle from even getting involved in a vehicle pursuit. Chuck, however, had just witnessed a uniformed police car intentionally wrecked by NG gang members in an effort to protect a senior cartel leader who was wanted for murder, along with a list of other serious charges. The reserve deputy made up his mind that he was ending this pursuit right here.

McCain saw an open lot just ahead on the right, past several rows of brick homes lining both sides of the street. He quickly closed the distance on the pickup, even as the gangsters were also picking up speed. Chuck executed a perfect PIT maneuver, sending the big Chevrolet swerving out of control where Minnesota crossed 16th Street. The right rear of the pickup slammed into one of the hardwood trees that lined the street, jolting it to a jarring stop.

As Chuck skidded to a halt and kicked his door open, gunshots from down the street filled the air.

Terry was momentarily stunned by the crash, but his training quickly clicked in. He glanced at his partner and saw him slumped unmoving against the door. *"Deal with the threat first!" he heard one of their instructors from the academy yelling as the recruits went through active shooter training.* I'll check him later, Stafford thought, releasing his seatbelt, shoving his door open, drawing his 9mm Glock 17 pistol and moving to confront the gangsters in the car that had wrecked them.

The driver of the Nissan had to muscle his damaged door to get it open and he and Terry exited at the same time. He was a short, stocky Mexican with a thick head of greasy hair. He raised a .40 caliber Smith & Wesson M&P pistol as the cop extended his own pistol in a solid two-handed stance. Officer Stafford and the thug fired at the same moment. A sledgehammer blow punched the Metropolitan DC officer in the chest but Stafford kept pulling the trigger of his Glock and was rewarded with hearing the cartel soldier cry out in pain and seeing him crumple into a heap next to his open door.

Terry instinctively grabbed at his chest where the bullet had struck his body armor. That hurts so bad, he thought with a groan, leaning back against the police car, the pain only intensifying as he tried to take a breath. He wondered if he might pass out, the act of breathing bringing an agony like he had never experienced before. Sudden movement in his peripheral caused him to turn to his left. A second cartel soldier advanced from the passenger side of the Altima, shouldering an AK-47.

Even as he tried to bring his Glock around, Stafford knew that he was dead. The guy was already raising the muzzle of the rifle and the officer saw his finger tightening around the trigger. Gunfire suddenly exploded from inside the police car, the gangster with the AK jerking as Darian's bullets punctured the windshield and then punctured the gunman. Terry quickly joined in, firing his pistol until the slide locked open, the gangster finally dropping his weapon and collapsing on top of it.

"You OK?" Wilson's pained voice called out.

"I...I think so. I got shot but I'm pretty sure my vest stopped it. How about you?"

"My head is killing me and I'm kind of trapped in here. Is that all of them?"

Terry quickly dropped his empty magazine and performed a combat reload for the Glock.

"I'll check," he answered, carefully approaching the suspects' car.

A black Suburban skidded to a halt beside the two vehicles, armed men and women pouring out of it. They all held up badges and Stafford gratefully realized that the calvary had arrived. The roar of another firefight up the street let them know that Contreras and his other minions weren't going down without a fight.

"¡Vamos!" Ramon yelled at Andres, seeing the police car's blue lights come on behind them.

Thankfully, the soldier driving the Altima reacted fast enough to wreck the pigs.

"Turn there and let's get back to the house," Contreras pointed at Minnesota Avenue, pulling out his phone, scrolling through his directory, trying to remember who was currently at the triplex on S Street that he could call for help.

The intake of marijuana had slowed his reflexes and before he could push the dial button to request his soldiers to come to their assistance, an unmarked SUV closed quickly and knocked the big pickup out of control. Andres fought with the steering wheel but it was no use. The Silverado crashed into a massive hardwood tree. The rear passenger window shattered, sending shards of glass flying through the air, and jamming the door closed, forcing Miguel and Pancho to both exit on the driver's side.

"Kill them all!" Ramon shouted as the gangsters sprang into action.

Pancho was out first, racking a round into the chamber of his .12 gauge Remington 870 shotgun. The windows on the

Yukon were tinted but both front doors flew open. The thug fired a round of buckshot into the passenger windshield just as a black woman came out shooting.

Miguel held an AR-15 but couldn't get out with Pancho standing in the doorway. Even as Pancho racked the shotgun for a second shot, the black woman pig with a badge around her neck was pumping rounds from her pistol towards them. Miguel heard Pancho grunt as the cop's bullets slammed into him.

More gunfire exploded from the other side of the SUV as the driver engaged Andres. Even as he was taking rounds, Pancho somehow managed to fire the .12 gauge again, the buckshot thudding into the open passenger door. As Pancho finally dropped to his knees with blood pumping out of his torso, Miguel came out firing his AR-15, one of his bullets finding flesh.

"I'm hit!" the woman screamed, even as she was pulling the trigger on her 9mm Glock 19.

The last bullet in her pistol tore into Miguel's right shoulder, his arm immediately going numb. That bitch! I'll kill her if it's the last thing I do, the gangster thought looking down at the blood pouring out of the wound. He used his left arm to keep the rifle locked into his wounded right shoulder, the blood flowing down the front of his white t-shirt. Through the sheer force of his will, he was able to get his right hand back around the AR's pistol grip, the numbness now replaced by a deep, burning pain, as he started towards the bitch, intent on finishing her.

The woman cop stumbled to the rear of the Yukon, fumbling to reload her pistol. Just as Miguel was almost to the open passenger door, a voice called out from the other side of the engine block.

"Hey, asshole!"

As the thug turned, he saw the pig who had been driving, a big white man with a badge around his neck. His pistol was pointed at Miguel's face. The last image the gangster had was a flash before everything went dark.

The Yukon was facing the driver's door of the wrecked pickup, the gangsters' right rear door resting against the large tree. Chuck and Kendra were both moving as soon as they came to a stop. The gang sergeant was quickly engaged by a gunman wielding a shotgun. McCain's H&K 416 was laying uselessly on the seat behind him, but the cartel driver was out of the pickup truck quickly, tugging a 9mm Beretta from his waistband. Chuck forgot about the rifle, drawing his Glock and double-tapping the thug in the face.

The big man caught a glimpse of Ramon Contreras diving out the on the opposite side of the pickup. The cartel lieutenant fired two shots over his shoulder in McCain's direction as he ran unsteadily away from the gunfight. Lockhart dropped the thug with the shotgun but a round from the next gangster's AR-15 evidently connected. Thankfully, the cartel soldier was experiencing tunnel vision and never even glanced in Chuck's direction until he called to get the Mexican's attention. After shooting that soldier between the eyes, McCain retreated to the back of the SUV to check on the sergeant.

Kendra had just slapped a fresh magazine into her Glock but Chuck saw the blood dripping from the area of her left triceps.

"Let me see your arm. Have you got a tourniquet?"

"Did you get Contreras?" she asked, pulling the device from her belt with her uninjured arm.

"No, he ran away when the shooting started."

"You've got to get him! I'll be OK," the sergeant grunted, expertly applying the tourniquet above her gunshot wound.

The bullet appeared to have just grazed her arm, between the elbow and shoulder. Andy's SUV came roaring up the street and Chuck knew they could render aid. He wasn't going to let the murderer get away again. He turned and dove into the driver's seat of the Yukon, transmitting to his team as he did so.

"Alpha One to other units. We've got three perps down, but the sarge has a minor gunshot wound to the arm. Contreras is fleeing on foot and I'm going after him."

"Alpha Two is clear. Alpha Three and one of the detectives is out with the uniforms. Two perps down there along with two wounded officers. We'll check Lockhart and back you up."

It had happened so fast, el Asesino thought as he sprinted away from the fight, his right shoulder throbbing with pain from impacting his door when they hit the tree. That asshole wrecked us! Cops aren't supposed to do shit like that. They're supposed to try and stop us using their blue lights and sirens. He had recognized the cop who was driving as the one who had choked him out in Virginia. Chuck McCain. I need to even the score with this asshole today.

Contreras fired a couple of rounds towards McCain, but the gangster had been running away at the time, trying to reach his safe house. Those bullets had not come anywhere near the pig. After sprinting for almost a hundred yards, the out-of-shape NG lieutenant was gasping for breath. He glanced over his shoulder just in time to see the white unmarked SUV lurch forward, heading straight towards him.

Ramon had run past four sets of duplexes with several more ahead of him. A small alley ran between each set of buildings and Contreras sprinted for the closest one. Just as he darted down the narrow opening, he heard the vehicle skidding to a stop where he had just been. The thug didn't have much left in his gas tank but fresh adrenaline pushed him to the end of the alley.

It opened up into a parking area for the residents, the driveway exiting onto 17$^{th}$ Street. I'm only two blocks from the house, Contreras realized. It might as well be a mile with that pig behind me. Ramon looked back just as McCain entered the alley. The gangster fired two shots, sending the big man scrambling for cover. McCain fired three answering shots just before el Asesino could turn the corner. One of the cop's bullets hit the brick wall and ricocheted into the cartel lieutenant's back.

¡Mierda! That son-of-a-whore shot me! Ramon thought. I've got to kill him. He took cover behind a beat-up Buick LeSabre and waited for McCain to show himself.

Chuck knew he shouldn't be chasing the dangerous criminal by himself, but he also knew that if the gangster managed to get back to his safe house on S Street, he would have access to his other gunmen and there would be a barricaded situation in a crowded neighborhood, which was never a good option, even with a tactical team at their disposal. And, there was no guarantee that was where el Asesino was going. He had proven to be very slippery over the last few weeks and Chuck wanted to end this today.

When Ramon ran down the narrow alley, McCain abandoned the Yukon, taking a moment to grab his H&K 416 from the backseat, and transmitting his location to his team before sprinting after the murderer. As the reserve deputy entered the walkway between the two buildings, Contreras shot at him from the far end, over thirty yards away. Chuck ducked to the right for cover behind an air conditioning unit, returning fire from his rifle. He was rewarded with seeing Ramon flinch as one of the rounds struck him in the back.

Chuck paused momentarily to assess the situation. The problem was that the murderer had turned left around the corner and was now out of sight, probably waiting to ambush me, McCain thought, as he continued down the alley, his rifle locked into his shoulder.

As Chuck neared the far end of the passage, he paused to consider his options. There was no good way to clear the corner, especially if Ramon was waiting with his pistol aimed at where McCain would appear. Or maybe, the gangster had kept running, trying to get back to his safe house. Chuck reached into his side cargo pocket and withdrew a flash bang grenade.

He pulled the pin but kept the safety lever depressed. Chuck slid up to the edge of the wall and, using his right hand, tossed the non-lethal device around the corner. The explosion was loud and designed to be disorienting to anyone in the immediate area. The grenade landed just five feet from Ramon, the roar and concussion of the device causing him to fall to his knees.

McCain followed the explosion, hugging the wall as he turned the corner, looking through the optics for the cop-killer. Contreras was out of sight behind the Buick but stuck his head up just as the reserve deputy was closing in on his location. Chuck saw the surprise in the Mexican's eyes and he fired and moved, every step sending another 5.56mm bullet into the fugitive. Ramon tried to bring the Sig into play but McCain's high-velocity bullets were all on target from close range, round after round slamming into his chest, throat, and face, the gangster finally collapsing onto his back. He still clutched Sergeant Dwayne Thomas' duty pistol in his right hand but didn't have the strength to raise it.

Chuck reached the rear of the Buick LeSabre, staring down at the Jalisco New Generation Cartel lieutenant. There was hatred in the gangster's eyes until the very end. After a few seconds, his heart stopped beating and his eyes stared lifelessly at the sky above. McCain moved in, stepping on the hand with the pistol, pulling it free and sliding it away. He rolled the dead man onto his face and handcuffed him before pushing the transmit button to let his team know that he was OK. Footsteps sounded from the alley as Andy rushed to his friend's aid.

**Police Command Post, Marion Berry Avenue and $14^{th}$ Street SE, Washington, D.C. Thursday, 1635 hours**

The CP was set up in the parking lot adjacent to where the marked police car had been wrecked. Yellow crime scene tape roped off the area around the damaged cruiser and the perps' Altima. The two dead suspects had not been removed yet, their bodies covered with sheets until CSI had finished taking pictures and collecting evidence. Andy Fleming did not envy the CSI teams or the detectives who were already hard at work. There were three different scenes that had to be processed, with dead bad guys at each location.

The Assistant Chief of Police over patrol, the Commander of District Two, assorted captains, lieutenants, and the Public Information Officer huddled together, trying to piece together what happened and discussing what they needed to communicate to the media. The news vans were currently being sequestered at the lot next to the community center on Marion Berry Avenue at $16^{th}$ Street. The PIO was about to go brief them for the first time, allowing the news stations to have something to run for their 5:00pm and 6:00pm broadcasts.

Lieutenant Alexander Bell, the Emergency Response Team commander, stood off to the side speaking with his tactical team leaders. The word was that they would be hitting three cartel addresses with search warrants in the next hour or two. After Bell let his sergeants know what he knew, he noticed Fleming standing off to the side of the CP speaking with Scotty Smith and Tex Davis.

"All your guys OK?" Bell asked joining the reserve deputies.

Andy nodded. "Yeah, good guys six, bad guys nothing."

"Did your boss really kill three of the six?"

Scotty laughed. "Yeah, two with his Glock and Contreras with his rifle. The two uniformed officers dropped the two thugs who wrecked them. Sergeant Lockhart took out one who was shooting at her with a shotgun and wounded the punk who shot her with an AR. Chuck put a round into that guy's head. He'd already capped the driver of the pickup containing Contreras. Then he chased down el Asesino and dumped maybe ten rounds of 5.56 into him. The only thing that pisses me off was that he didn't leave any for the rest of us."

Tex had a wad of tobacco in his mouth and spat off to the side. "I guess he wasn't in the mood to share."

"He's like that," Andy commented. "I'm just glad none of the good guys are seriously hurt. The sarge got grazed on the arm. It took a big chunk of flesh off her triceps but they'll have her patched up in no time. That patrol cop's vest saved him. He'll be sore as hell for a few days and his buddy has a mild concussion from the wreck but everyone's going to be fine.

"I got to Chuck right after he killed Contreras," Fleming continued, shaking his head. "That asshole gangbanger was carrying Sergeant Thomas' issued Sig. He took it off of him the night he murdered him and Shelly."

"Well, the boss punched his ticket," Tex said. "No long, drawn-out trial, no appeals, just a tag on his toe in the city morgue."

"Where's Chuck now?" the lieutenant queried.

"A couple of the detectives are interviewing him and getting his statement over in one of their cars. That tells you how crazy this scene is: they're doing the interview here instead of back at your HQ."

Alex nodded, glancing around before lowering his voice. "I heard the district commander crawled Chuck's ass."

Fleming shrugged. "I was there. He let that carpet cop vent until he ran out of steam. Then Chuck asked him how he would've handled it? The commander stuttered and stammered about following procedures and not turning the city into a war zone. Chuck then, very helpfully, pointed out that the cartels had already turned it into a war zone but it didn't look like the Metropolitan Police had done much to stop it."

Bell laughed. "I'd love to have seen the expression on the commander's face. And, you're right— he is a carpet cop. He got off the road as quickly as he could after getting out of the academy twenty years ago, running from one cush administrative job to the next. How he kept getting promoted is a mystery."

"Every department has them," Davis said, spitting again. "So, what's next?"

"I'm just waiting on someone to hand me some warrants and we're going to go hit those addresses you guys have been staking out."

"You need some help?" Smith asked.

"Sorry, Scotty. I'd love to have you guys go in with us, but with the brass here, they're going to be watching the rest of this very closely. I've already got Gabby and Chloe flying their drones over Orange and S Street. That'll give us real time footage as we prepare to go in."

"We understand," Andy said, "but you know we're available if you run into any problems."

The Emergency Response Team leader smiled. "I appreciate it. Let me go check on the status of those warrants."

Tactical operations aren't normally launched in the middle of the afternoon. They tend to be much more effective in the middle of the night or early morning. At the same time, the detectives wanted to serve the search warrants as soon as possible to prevent the cartel members from escaping or disposing of evidence.

When Bell gave the order to execute, it was 1755 hours and the ERT officers hit all three cartel locations at the same time. A lone sentry on S Street made the mistake of pulling a pistol as the tactical officers approached the triplex. Two of the officers shot him with their M4s. The other four gangsters onsite gave up without a fight after watching their friend get cut down by the police. The two women were both servicing clients when the police showed up. The prostitutes were quickly removed from the house so that the detectives could interview them and their clients were arrested.

On Orange Street, both of the guards in front of the duplex made the mistake of drawing their weapons as the ERT team approached. They were quickly pumped full of 5.56mm soft point rounds before they could fire a shot. Carlos, Santiago, and another cartel soldier inside the residence surrendered quickly as the assault team smashed in their door.

Jerry Brewer had just counted up the day's earnings from the brothel on Newcomb Street and was about to make his daily trek to visit Carlos a few blocks away. Jerry had been so busy counting the money, he never saw the SWAT team approaching the townhouse. Both of the girls were entertaining customers when the tactical team burst in, screaming and waving their weapons around. Jerry knew the drill and dropped to the carpet, placing his hands behind his head. The two customers were secured and the women were escorted outside. Brewer hadn't been to jail in a while and wondered if any of the regulars were still there.

# Chapter Nine

**Century Tactical Solutions, Leesburg, Virginia, Monday, 1002 hours**

Loudon County Sheriff Jerry Schaefer, General Perkins, Chuck, and Andy sat around the general's desk, holding steaming mugs of coffee. The sheriff had called first thing that morning, asking if he could come by and meet with them. That was just one of the things that endeared him to his people. He went out of his way to connect with people on their turf.

"Chuck, Andy, I don't even know what to say," Schaefer said quietly. "You and your team went above and beyond anything we expect from our reserve deputies. Y'all really went the extra mile and made sure that justice was finally served for Dwayne and Shelly."

"A bonus was that one of the other dead perps was also a part of their murder," McCain said. "The driver of the pickup Contreras was riding in had a freshly healed gunshot wound to the arm. His blood was a match for one of the samples they found in the Thomas' house. The blood splatter was recovered in the bedroom so Shelly was probably the one who shot him."

"I got a call from the Metropolitan chief of police Friday morning," the sheriff said, his eyes twinkling. "I know how to play politics and had already issued a press release first thing that morning, praising the Metropolitan-DC Police Department, their leadership, and all their fine officers for their cooperation and support in helping us track down Ramon Contreras and a number of his fellow cartel members.

"When the chief called me, he wasn't very happy but the press release had backed him into a corner. Of course, I pointed out the obvious to him: his department was getting the credit for the arrest by termination of a dangerous cop-killer and eight of his soldiers, they apprehended another eight gang members, they seized quantities of illegal drugs and weapons, and they freed four young women who were being trafficked. The chief didn't have much to say after that but I did thank him for all his help. Chuck, if you'll let me have all the names of the DC investigators and officers that you worked with, I'll send them a nice letter of commendation."

"Thank you, sir. I know they would appreciate that," McCain smiled.

"That's over twenty dead New Generation soldiers, including Contreras, since they declared war on the police," Andy commented. "There's at least another ten or twelve who've been arrested and are looking at long prison sentences. That should put a big dent in the NG's operation, at least for a little while. Any word on that Sinaloa lieutenant, Eduardo Sanchez? He needs to end up in the morgue, too."

Schaefer sighed. "Our detectives have taken warrants out on him for sex and drug trafficking, false imprisonment, rape, child abuse and a number of other serious offenses. Lara

Sagarra is the victim in the rape and child abuse charges. The problem is we have no idea where he's at. This manpower shortage has really hurt our department and our investigators can't keep focusing on cases where the leads have dried up. I certainly don't expect you or your people to keep working on this. I know you have courses to teach and customers to serve."

Perkins cleared his throat. "Chuck, perhaps you could check with some of our friends in the Bureau and see if they could help us locate Sanchez? This is a great opportunity to slow down the cartels' advance in the US."

"Yes, sir. That's a great idea."

"Andy, how far behind are we on our contracts?" Perkins asked.

"We're caught up, sir. I did have to reschedule a couple, but Scotty and Tex are teaching a two-day patrol rifle course tomorrow and Wednesday at a state police academy in Tennessee. Jimmy and Hollywood are conducting a three-day tactical course for narcotics investigators Wednesday through Friday down in Georgia. We've got a week-long Basic SWAT class next week over in Fairfax. That'll be Chuck, Tex, and I."

"We've got a lot going on," the general replied. "Well, Chuck, when you get a chance, why don't you make a few phone calls? I hate the idea of this Sanchez character getting away. He violated that young Lara Sagarra and sent her and her family into hiding. I'd like to see him brought to justice."

"Will do, General. Sheriff, I'll notify Major Kim if I get any useful intelligence. He can pass it on to whoever is working the case."

"That would be fine, Chuck. That was damn good work over in DC. Hopefully, we can take down Eduardo Sanchez with a little less drama."

**Tyson's Corner, Virginia, Monday, 1335 hours**

Sebastian Hernandez sat down at his desk and pulled up two local news websites, reading the latest on the Metropolitan DC Police Department's raids and shootouts against the Jalisco New Generation Cartel. There was still a lot of information that had not been released because it was an active investigation, but the lawyer found it hard to believe the weak, inept administrators of the DC police department had authorized the case. It was even more difficult to believe that the cops had killed Contreras and eight of his soldiers without losing a single officer. The reports indicated a few cops had been wounded during the shootouts, but none of the injuries were life-threatening.

Hernandez was grateful that the tactical team had not hit the house on S Street while he was waiting for Ramon Contreras to return. That would have been difficult to explain, especially when the detectives executed the search warrant and found el Asesino's stash of drugs and weapons, along with the women who were being forced to turn tricks to pay off their debt to the cartel.

He had driven into DC earlier that morning and met with the cartel members who were in custody, representing them in their preliminary hearings. The charges were long and varied—drug trafficking, human trafficking, weapons violations, along with the assorted parole and probation violation warrants. No one had a bond, except the black man. Sebastian suspected that he was cooperating with the authorities and they had allowed him to post bail for running a house of prostitution. The fact that he had not been charged with the more serious sex trafficking charge was another piece of evidence that pointed to him having cut a deal in exchange for reduced charges.

This Jerry Brewer must not know who he's dealing with. If he testifies against the cartel, he will die slowly and painfully, Hernandez thought. Of course, for the moment anyway, the NG gang was in disarray. With Chilo Barajas in custody and Ramon Contreras dead, there was going to be a leadership vacuum for the cartel on the East Coast. It will be interesting to see who steps in to fill that gap. Sebastian hadn't visited Mexico in years, but he suspected that the cartel leadership in the home country was already putting a team together to send to Northern Virginia to rebuild what the police had destroyed.

The attorney had chosen Tyson's Corner as the location for his office for two reasons: it was close to his apartment and it was conveniently located to DC and the rest of NOVA. It was a small practice with just a tiny reception area and his office. He occasionally brought in a temp paralegal if he was working on a big case, but the cartel's stipend was generous enough that he didn't have to go looking for business. With Ramon dead, though, will I still get paid? The cartel lieutenant had one of his men hand deliver the envelope of cash once a month.

Maybe I should pack it up and go set up shop in another city? Sebastian had never met el Guapo, the NG lieutenant who controlled New York City, Boston, and the rest of the

Northeast. Hernandez didn't even know the man's real name. I wonder if he needs a lawyer?

**Fairfax, Virginia, Tuesday, 2325 hours**

After receiving a phone call on one of his burner phones Tuesday morning, Sinaloa Cartel lieutenant Eduardo Sanchez had given orders to abandon their safe house, hurriedly packing his computer, some of his clothes, and a few personal items. He hadn't kept a lot of drugs or weapons there, but his soldiers loaded up the small stash earlier and drove it to their new Northern Virginia location in Falls Church, just twenty minutes away. Several of his soldiers were already living in the single-story home, tucked inside of the older neighborhood. Sanchez and a few more of his men would be joining them until he rented another house or apartment.

After learning that the Loudon County Sheriff's Department had obtained a number of new warrants for his arrest, he decided that it would be good to move across town. It was the call from an informant inside the FBI on Tuesday evening, however, that confirmed he'd made the right decision to abandon the Fairfax location. How had the feds found out about his safe house? There was no paperwork linking the rental to Sanchez and he had one of his men drop off the rent in cash every month to the real estate office that managed the property.

Eduardo had been closely following the story from the previous week in DC where the police had killed the New Generation's Ramon Contreras and a number of his men, arrested several more, and served warrants at three of their safe houses. Good riddance to that piece of shit, Sanchez thought, but what were the gringo cops up to?

Of course, the NG gang wasn't as organized or as well run as the Sinaloa family, Eduardo mused. That idiot el Asesino or one of his goons must have screwed up in a big way to allow the cops track them down and take out a significant part of their operation. The notification from Sanchez's informant, though, indicated that the Sinaloas might be next on the FBI and DEA's hit list.

It had been almost two weeks since he had sent Pancho and his team of sicarios to kill Lara Sagarra and her family. He still wasn't completely sure what had happened but their lawyer had spoken with Alejandro who was being held without bond in the Loudon County Jail. According to the only surviving assassin, the cops were waiting for them inside the house and cut down the other three sicarios.

The police report indicated that Alejandro had dropped his gun and surrendered without a fight. Eduardo couldn't believe that any of his soldiers, especially a sicario, would willingly give up without trying to kill a few cops. He wondered if his man had cut a deal with the gringo police? He's always been dependable, Sanchez knew, hoping the soldier would keep his mouth shut about the inner workings of the Sinaloa Cartel. Either way, Alejandro knows the penalty for betraying his brothers.

Eduardo had not survived this long by taking chances so he was consolidating his operations. After Ernesto's arrest, the Atlantic City Police had shut down two Sinaloa brothels but Eduardo still had the two condos at the Seaside Club

Condominiums near the Boardwalk. Enrique had done well to not get arrested and was quietly working to rebuild their business in the resort town. He had four girls working at the condos and Nayara Palacios was an exceptional escort. Eduardo had told Enrique to treat her a little differently.

After losing Lara and two of his best income producing whore houses, the lieutenant knew he couldn't afford a repeat with Nayara. Enrique was going to take the prostitute shopping and allow her to pick out a few outfits. From here on out, the escort would also be allowed to keep a small percentage of her earnings for her personal use. This was not the normal way to treat a whore, but Sanchez was making a lot of money off Palacios. AC was a convention hub and many of these men loved nothing better than getting away from home for a few days to spend some of their hard-earned cash on a young piece of ass, gambling in the casinos, and enjoying plenty of drugs and booze.

Eduardo had been back and forth between New Jersey and Virginia several times over the last two weeks, helping his team get back on track. Even though they sold a lot of drugs in DC, Sanchez had no desire to live there, the slums reminding him of the slums he grew up in in Mexico City. Falls Church was a nice place to live, even for a cartel lieutenant on the run from the law.

**Fairfax County Criminal Justice Academy, Chantilly, Virginia, Wednesday, the following week, 0845 hours**

The first two days of the basic SWAT course had been spent in the classroom, with Chuck, Andy, and Tex taking turns teaching the various blocks of instruction on the nuts and bolts of police tactical operations. Now, they had moved to the range where students would begin the live-fire portion of the course, warming up with a number of drills to improve their speed and accuracy.

As Andy was giving a safety briefing, Chuck's phone vibrated with an incoming text from FBI Supervisory Special Agent Joe O'Reilly asking McCain to call him. He stepped out of the range to make a call.

"Hey, Joe," the big man greeted his friend.

"McCain, sorry it's taken me so long to get back with you. This guy Eduardo Sanchez is pretty slippery. I had Agent Hernandez working this but he said that Sanchez has no footprint for us to track. Hernandez has been digging through that intel you gave us on that thumb drive and found an address in Fairfax that turned into a dead end. Hernandez and a few agents went by last Wednesday and it was empty. The neighbors said the residents had been Hispanic males, but kept to themselves and no one saw when they packed up and left. That was probably one of their safe houses but we took too long to follow up and missed them.

"We've tried to coordinate with Atlantic City PD but they don't like feds and either they don't have any leads or they just don't want to share. The word on the street is that even after the cops shut down two of his locations, Sanchez and the

Sinaloas are still running brothels and escorts in the city but other than staking out the casinos and resorts, we just don't have much to go on."

"That sucks," Chuck sighed. "This guy needs to be put out of business."

"Well, that's Sanchez and the bad news. The good news is that one of his key guys is not quite as careful. He likes to call Mexico regularly and wires money home to his mother."

"Nice. How'd you find him?"

"Hernandez found his name in that intel dump—Enrique Castro. He's evidently an up-and-comer in Sanchez's pipeline. It looks like he's running things there since your team took down Ernesto Salazar. With all the publicity on human trafficking by the cartels, Agent Hernandez was able to get a warrant for Castro's cell phone history. Like I said, Enrique calls his mom a couple of times a month and sends her money. She thinks he's a construction worker."

"Thanks, Joe. What's next? It sounds like you guys are putting a case together against these Sinaloas thugs?"

"We're trying. In the spirit of inter-agency cooperation, we're also working with that DEA agent you introduced us to, Frank Simpson. They're looking at the drug aspect and we're focusing on the human trafficking and racketeering. With the election coming up, we need to wrap this up ASAP. The rumor is that if Reverend Sampson gets elected, and he's leading in all the polls, he's going to replace Director Pickard and most of the other competent cabinet members. We've already been warned that if Sampson becomes president, our investigations will all have to be run through the race filter."

"The race filter?" Chuck questioned. "What's that?"

"You know exactly what I'm talking about McCain. This guy has been a civil rights activist for years and ran on that platform. If he becomes the man, the Mexican Cartels and black gangs are going to be given a lot of free passes."

Chuck had not been following the presidential campaign very closely. He knew the outgoing, two-term incumbent, President Benjamin Asher, on a personal level. Asher and General Perkins were friends and it was the president who had funded and been the silent partner for Century Tactical. Asher was a straight shooter and had led the nation through the zombie crisis, a war with Iran, and several other terror attacks on American soil.

The Reverend Virgil Sampson was a former four-term congressman from Alabama who seemed to be present at every police shooting where a black suspect was involved. Sampson always found a way to get his face on the news, usually with an incendiary soundbite. His organization, the American Equality Society raised money to support the families of those African-Americans killed by the police and pay legal fees for others who were arrested on "false" charges.

"I've been kind of busy, Joe. You really think Sampson is going to be the next president?"

"The polls and everything I've read points that way. But, if we can track Sanchez down, I'd like to make a move in the next week or two. We're hoping this Enrique Castro will lead us to him. We've pinged Enrique's phone a couple of times but it looks like he shuts it down and removes the battery when he's not using it. If we can get a good ping, we'll move on him as soon as we can."

"Thanks for letting me know, Joe. That's great news. I've got an idea to get Sanchez to come out of his hole if you guys can't find him. It might even speed the process up."

"Oh, yeah? Your ideas always scare me, McCain, but you also usually get results. What are you thinking?"

After Chuck explained his plan to the senior FBI agent, there was a pause.

"I like it," O'Reilly grunted. "That might just work. Let's give it a try. Are you enjoying playing cop again?"

"Joe, I'd forgotten how tough it can be, trying not to violate a criminal's rights."

"Ha! Welcome to my world."

"Three of us are currently teaching a SWAT school in Fairfax. I'm hoping that we're done with supplementing the SO for a while."

"Have fun. Let's keep each other posted. Maybe we'll get lucky and shut these Sinaloa pricks down, at least for a little while."

**Loudoun Adult Detention Center, Leesburg, Virginia, Thursday, 1220 hours**

Alejandro Tapia sat at the stainless steel table on the stainless steel bench, both bolted into the floor so that they couldn't be used as weapons. The sicario ate the shit that passed as food in the jail cafeteria surrounded by several low-level Sinaloa soldiers and even a few wannabes, waiting on their own day in court. His reputation as a hitman for the cartel earned him something like rockstar status among the other inmates. It also ensured that none of the other prisoners would bother him. Instead, they made a wide berth around him and his minions on the exercise yard, in the cafeteria, and other common areas in the detention center.

He knew he wasn't going anywhere. The judge had denied his request for a bond on the long list of charges against him. His case had been bound over to superior court and he would be stuck here until the trial, several months down the road. The attorney that Eduardo had sent to represent him discussed the possibility of a plea-bargain before the case went to trial.

He was still looking at ten years with the plea, but if a jury convicted him, he would probably receive a twenty-five to thirty year sentence. The plea-bargain was probably the way to go, as long as he didn't have to testify against the cartel. He would never say or do anything against his gang family. The lawyer had reminded him that the judge didn't have to accept the negotiated deal and his case still might go to trial.

Tapia was still amazed that he was even alive. After watching his three friends cut down by the pigs, he wondered why the cops hadn't killed him, too. There was a sense of guilt that he had not even raised his pistol. Of course, if he had, he most certainly would not be sitting here in the jail's cafeteria. His bullet riddled body would be wherever they disposed of gang members killed by the pigs.

At least he had some fellow Sinaloa members in jail with him. Alejandro knew that the gang was la familia and they protected each other. There were other cartels represented in the jail but there was an undeclared truce inside the facility.

Still, Tapia felt better knowing he had hombres to watch his back.

The cops had tried to interview him but he had sat silently or told them to go to hell. He had enjoyed that hot puta detective. What was her name? Sergeant Lopez. He had let her talk and talk, trying to get him to become an informant. She had not appreciated his counter-offers.

"Hey, you want information you got to put out, chiquita," he had told her, with a laugh a week earlier. "We can do it right here on table. You know you want it."

That was the last time he had spoken with any of the pigs. They must have finally gotten the message that I'm not telling them shit, he thought.

Tapia tensed as three deputies approached the table where the Sinaloa bangers ate.

"Good news, Alejandro! Your lawyer's motion for a bond just got approved," one of the pigs said in Spanish. "The judge reversed his earlier decision and you can leave."

"Hey, that's great, amigo," one of the younger bangers laughed, patting Tapia on the back.

"Bueno!" another gangster agreed.

"Yeah," the deputy continued, his voice loud enough for everyone at the surrounding tables to hear what he was saying. "I guess the detectives told the judge about that deal you made with them. You're a smart guy, Alejandro. Cooperating is always the right way to go. If you keep giving the investigators good information, it'll probably get your sentence reduced, as well."

The deputy's words sent a cold chill down Tapia's spine.

"You asshole! I haven't told the detectives shit!"

The deputies shrugged. The Spanish speaker motioned for the thug to come with them.

"That's not what we heard, but what are you upset about? You're getting out of here."

"But I'm not a snitch!"

The Sinaloa gangsters around the table now stared at Alejandro with doubt in their eyes, those closest to him even sliding away, further down on the bench. The sicario looked around at his friends, sensing their attitude shift towards him.

"I'm not a snitch!" he repeated.

The sicario stood, glaring at the deputies, considering going after them to prove he wasn't an informant. That would just get him tased, beaten, and tossed into isolation with even more charges and he really did want to get out of jail. He made eye contact with the other cartel members around the table.

"I didn't talk. I didn't tell those pigs anything!"

He saw the suspicion on their faces. What was happening? he wondered. He followed the deputies towards the door, feeling the eyes of everyone in the cafeteria watching as he left.

Within forty-five minutes, Tapia had changed into the clothes he had been arrested in, minus the painter coveralls, signed several pieces of paper, was handed his cell phone, wallet, and ushered out the door. The sicario blinked in the bright sunshine wondering what he should do. He was surprised his attorney wasn't there as he was released. The deputies had not said much but everything seemed official.

Alejandro was still reeling over what the pig had said in the cafeteria. He hadn't made a deal with anyone and had certainly not given the detectives any information on his Sinaloa family. Everyone in the vicinity had heard what the cop had said, though, and that left the sicario feeling queasy. Maybe I can call Eduardo and he can have someone come pick me up?

I need to let el Jefe know what the cops said before he hears it from someone else, he thought. If Eduardo thinks I'm a snitch for the pigs, he'll kill me. I don't even want to think about how he might torture me before he puts me out of my misery. Tapia turned his phone on and texted the cartel lieutenant deciding to tell him everything. If he hears it from me first, it'll be better than him hearing it from one of the other Sinaloa members I was in jail with. Alejandro knew that there was a good chance some of those men would be released from custody in the near future. He texted Eduardo as he started walking, ready to be far away from the detention center.

On the second floor of the facility, Chuck and Gabby sat with Major Joon Kim, and Sergeant Julia Lopez in a conference room. Vargas' fingers were flying over the keyboard of her laptop as she stared intently at the screen.

"We're live and he's moving," she said.

"This is risky," the major commented. "I hope it works."

Sergeant Lopez had been able to persuade a superior court judge to sign a warrant, allowing them to place GPS trackers in Tapia's shoes, clothes, and phone. Chuck had been impressed, not sure if they were going to be able to get the warrant or not. At the same time, Lopez had a beautiful smile and was able to turn on the charm when she needed to. That smile had also led to the judge reversing the no-bond order on Tapia.

The sergeant felt butterflies as well, knowing they couldn't afford to lose Alejandro, but understanding that he was their best hope to lead them to Eduardo Sanchez. She wiped her sweaty palms on her pants and glanced at Chuck. The intensity in his eyes let her know that he was more than ready to go after the cartel lieutenant.

She had heard about the shootout the week before in DC in which McCain and a few others had eliminated an entire cell of the New Generation Cartel, including their lieutenant, Ramon Contreras. Had the big man really killed Contreras and two other NG soldiers by himself? It had only been a couple of weeks earlier when McCain and Scotty Smith had also taken out two NG sicarios on Lieutenant Donaldson's traffic stop.

J-Lo had heard that Chuck and his teams were some genuine bad asses and had no issue with using deadly force. Even the attractive, curly-haired woman working the computer had killed a few sicarios herself when the hit team attacked Andy Fleming's home. McCain and the other reserve deputies were dangerous people.

The detective sergeant, along with the rest of the sheriff's department, had been elated to learn that Dwayne and Shelly Thomas' murderers had been terminated, without the need of a long and drawn-out trial. Maybe, they'd get lucky and Eduardo Sanchez would decide he didn't want to be taken alive, either.

An hour later, Alejandro still had not received a reply from Eduardo or any of the other cartel soldiers he had messaged. He now found himself standing in the parking lot of the Wegman's grocery store a mile from the detention center, wondering what he should do. It was about a half hour drive to Sanchez's Fairfax safe house, where Tapia had been staying. The sicario knew that would translate to many hours of walking and he wasn't sure he could find his way home. Pancho was usually driving and Alejandro wasn't always paying attention to the many roads and towns of Northern Virginia. Using the map app on his phone wasn't an option because he only had ten percent battery life left and no charger.

He pulled his wallet out of his pocket and checked to see if the pigs had stolen his money.

"Gracias, Dios," the thug muttered, seeing the $140 still tucked inside.

Tapia checked the phone again, hoping one of his friends had answered. The only notification was that the device would die soon. A dark blue Toyota Corolla slowed to a stop in front of the store, a sign on the side reading, "Latino Express Taxi." A hefty, older Hispanic woman handed her payment over the seat and climbed out, making her way into the grocery store. The driver took a moment to check his phone to see if he had any other pickups pending.

Alejandro hurried over and tapped on the driver's window.

"How much to take me to Fairfax?" Tapia asked when the glass came down.

The obese, middle-aged Mexican man looked him over before speaking.

"Did you just get out of jail?"

"Sí, how did you know?"

"It's just a guess. The jail is not far and you have that look. Sixty dollars. You pay first."

"That's too much, amigo. I'll give you forty."

The Corolla started to roll forward and the window started to go up.

"No, don't go! No problemo," Alejandro said, pulling the money out of his wallet and handing it to the man.

He climbed into the back and after giving the driver the address, he laid his head back on the seat, finally able to relax, thankful to be rejoining his companions.

Chuck had left Andy and Tex to finish up the SWAT Course after learning that they were going to be able to track Alejandro Tapia. Hollywood and Chloe were paired up, joined by SWAT Sergeant Brandon Cobb. Jimmy, Scotty, and SWAT Corporal Norman Stephens were the second team, both squads positioned near the main intersections in proximity to the jail. They had also been tracking Tapia on their phones or tablets.

"Alpha One to Alpha Two and Three, it looks like he found a ride."

"Alpha Two's clear," Jimmy answered, "we're about a quarter mile behind him."

"Alpha Three to Alpha Two, we're a couple of minutes behind you," Hollywood transmitted.

"Alpha One to units, we'll be leaving HQ in five. Maybe today's the day."

Thankfully, the taxi driver wasn't talkative or maybe it was just the vibe that Alejandro gave off. Either way, it was a quiet thirty-five minute drive to the safe house. Tapia's phone finally died so he just stared out the window, trying to decide how to tell Eduardo why he had been released from custody. The taxi slowed to a stop in front of the address the gangster had provided.

The sicario nodded at the driver as the taxi pulled away. There were no vehicles in the driveway. I wonder where everyone's at? He knocked on the door and waited, not hearing anything from inside. He walked around to the rear of the house and banged on the back door. When he peered through a window, he gasped in surprise. All the furniture was gone and the house appeared vacant.

Alejandro instinctively reached for his phone as walked around to the front of the empty home. The blank screen taunted him, reminding him that it needed to be charged. Now, what do I do? He sat down on the steps leading up to the front door. The soldier had only lived there for a few months since arriving from Mexico. He had heard some of the other guys talk about another house in the area, but he had no idea where it was located. Alejandro also knew that Eduardo had additional operations in New Jersey and other places, but this was the only safe house the sicario had stayed at.

It had been a long time since the gangster felt so exposed. He was normally armed and with a group of his fellow assassins. Tapia was alone in a foreign country in which he didn't speak much of the language, and with no way of getting in touch with his friends.

McCain, Vargas and Lopez followed the beeping red light, moving steadily towards Fairfax. The detective sergeant was driving her issued undercover black Toyota 4Runner. Eventually, the light stopped moving in a neighborhood east of the city, off of Highway 236. Chuck felt the adrenaline start pumping, knowing that they were close to finding Eduardo Sanchez, the man who had forced Lara Sagarra and many other women into a life of prostitution.

Sex trafficking was only one of the gangster's many sins, but it was the reason that McCain and his team had gotten pulled into the investigation. If Chuck had his way, the Sinaloa gangster would meet the same demise as the New Generation's Ramon Contreras. But, if they managed to capture the thug alive, he would probably spend the rest of his life in an American maximum-security prison.

Thankfully, Lara and a few other women had been freed from the clutches of the cartel. Many other women and children, however, were still being sold to whoever wanted to use and abuse them for thirty minutes or an hour. Arresting Sanchez would hurt the Sinaloa crime family, even if it was only until someone else took the gangster's place.

Now that it looked like they were closing in, Chuck dialed FBI Supervisory Special Agent Joe O'Reilly's number. The G-Man answered after the first ring.

"What do you have, McCain?" O'Reilly's gruff voice came over the speaker so that the women could hear the conversation.

"We've got him in a neighborhood in Fairfax," Chuck answered, relating the information to the FBI agent. "We'll be in the area soon and I've got a few of my guys and some Loudon County deputies following, as well."

"OK, but if your guys are following try not to kill anybody if you can help it. Let me get things rolling and I'll talk to you in a few. You gonna call Fairfax County PD?"

"That's my next call. Thanks, Joe," McCain said, as he disconnected.

"He sounds like a ray of sunshine," Lopez commented.

"His bark is worse than his bite," Vargas said, with a smile. "He's actually a good guy, for a fed."

"If you say so," the sergeant responded. "Every single time we've worked with the feds, they moved in, took over the investigation, and then took all the credit."

"I had the same issues when I was a cop in Atlanta," Chuck agreed. "Joe's not like that. We've worked on a lot of cases together and he's not your stereotypical special agent. I just hope Alejandro Tapia is actually leading us to Eduardo Sanchez."

An older model, white Chevrolet Impala rolled slowly down the street, getting Alejandro's attention. It turned into the driveway and stopped, not pulling all the way up to the house. The passenger door opened and an hombre that Tapia recognized climbed out, his hand under his hoodie. The gangster's eyes lit up when he saw Alejandro sitting on the front steps.

"Hey, amigo! They moved out of here. Come on, and we'll take you to the new place."

Relief washed over Tapia. He was back with familia.

"Gracias, amigo. My phone died and I wasn't sure what to do."

"No problemo. Eduardo got your text and asked us to come get you."

A few minutes later, the Impala was heading towards Falls Church.

"Is Eduardo there?" Alejandro asked.

"No," Felix, the passenger answered. "He's traveling a lot."

The driver, Ronaldo, glanced over his shoulder. "The pigs raided a couple of the whorehouses in Atlantic City. We do a lot of business there so the boss is rebuilding the network. He'll be back in a couple of days."

Ronaldo was soon pulling into the garage of the safe house in Falls Church. He had not noticed his tail, the unmarked vehicles keeping their distance, content to follow the GPS signals that Alejandro was unknowingly sending out.

# Chapter Ten

**Atlantic City, New Jersey, Friday, 1035 hours**

"Are you sure about this?" Eduardo Sanchez growled into the pre-paid cell phone, staring out at the Atlantic Ocean from the Boardwalk, near the Hard Rock Casino.

"Sí, Señor," Attorney Arturo Torriente answered. "I was supposed to meet with him this morning but he'd already been released. He told me the last time I spoke with him that he wasn't talking to the detectives, but the deputies at the jail today made it sound like he worked out a deal with the investigators. I don't know how else he could have gotten out of jail. I filed a motion for bond last week but the judge denied it."

Sanchez was silent, seething at the idea that one of his trusted sicarios had betrayed him and the Sinaloa family. Torriente was paid well to represent the cartel. He was no soldier but he served his purpose and always did his best when called upon to defend a Sinaloa gangster who had gotten arrested.

"Gracias, amigo. It was good that you let me know."

After disconnecting, Eduardo continued to stare out at the ocean, the cold, salty breeze chilling him to the bone. After receiving the text asking for him to call Torriente, the lieutenant had Enrique bring him here, two miles from the condos where his sex operation was thriving. He wasn't worried about the pigs tracking his burner phone, but he wasn't taking any chances. Plus, the cops might be tracing the lawyer's device.

Eduardo started to open the phone to take out the battery but stopped. He needed to make another call first. Had Alejandro already been working as an informant before this? Was that why he was the only one to survive the attack at the Sagarra's home? That would explain a lot. Why else would the pigs have been waiting inside unless someone had warned them?

Enrique was standing a respectful distance away, watching their surroundings. Sanchez motioned for him to come closer as he dialed Felix in Falls Church. The soldier answered on the first ring and Eduardo activated speaker mode so Enrique could hear both sides of the conversation.

"Sí, el Jefe? Que pasa?"

"We've got a problemo grande."

The gangster related what the lawyer had told him.

"You and Ronaldo secure him for me. Enrique and I will be leaving soon and will be back there tonight. I want to have a very serious conversation with our hermano."

"Sí, Señor, but if you want, me and Ronaldo can handle it for you."

"Oh, no. If Alejandro has betrayed us, I'm going to make him wish he had never been born."

**Falls Church, Virginia, Friday, 1635 hours**

Alejandro lay face down on the floor of one of the bedrooms, his hands and feet secured with what felt like an entire roll of duct tape. The two soldiers that he knew, and two others he didn't, had approached him a few hours earlier as he ate a burrito he had found in the freezer and microwaved. The sicario had not been given a gun since arriving at the house and when he tried to fight back, the four gangsters beat him until he stopped resisting. The physical pain had subsided a bit, but the emotional hurt went far deeper.

"Por que, Felix?" Tapia had asked as they taped his wrists behind his back.

The sicario felt blood dripping from his nose where one of the men had punched him. Another one had hit him in the mouth, busting his lip open and loosening a couple of teeth. After they had wrapped him up, Felix stood, still breathing hard after the short struggle. He looked down at the assassin, disgust on his face.

"Eduardo told us that you betrayed la familia. He's on his way back to talk with you. I'm guessing it's going to be a short conversation."

This elicited a laugh from the other three gangsters.

"The pigs set me up!" Alejandro yelled, willing them to believe him. "I would never betray familia!"

Felix shrugged, slapping a piece of tape over the prisoner's bloody mouth. "El Jefe thinks different. We'll see if you can convince him."

A little after 5:00pm, Enrique pulled the gray Dodge Durango into the garage of the safe house. Eduardo had brooded during the entire drive, thinking through how he wanted to handle Alejandro. A plan had formed in his mind that snapped him out of his funk. When he shared it with Enrique, the gangster had slapped the steering wheel and laughed.

"Buena idea, Eduardo! That will definitely send a message to the pigs."

After the garage door closed, Sanchez paused for a moment before exiting, glancing over at Enrique.

"I want to take care of this tonight. You can go back to Atlantic City tomorrow and I'll stay down here for a while."

"Sí, Señor. I can't believe Alejandro would sell out to the pigs. I'd rather rot in jail than make a deal with the cops."

Hollywood, Chloe, and Brandon sat in their burgundy Ford Explorer, four houses down from the suspect location. The windows were heavily tinted to keep anyone from seeing inside, but with all the other vehicles parked on the street, they fit in perfectly in the middle-class neighborhood. The deputies had been rotating out every six hours with one of the other teams for the last twenty-four hours, knowing it might take a couple of days before they had definitive evidence of the fugitive's presence.

Wilkerson peered through the binoculars, hoping to get a glimpse of something that would let them know Eduardo Sanchez was at the location.

"You see anything, Chloe?" Estrada asked.

"No," she sighed. "Nothing at all."

A gray SUV suddenly sped by them and turned into the driveway of the safe house, pausing only long enough for the garage to open, allowing them to pull inside before the door closed again.

"Damn!" Chloe exclaimed, lowering the binoculars. "Their windows were as dark as ours. I couldn't see anything or anybody."

Less than half a mile away, Chuck's and Jimmy's squads sat in an empty parking lot on Highway 50. The lot was attached to a vacant warehouse. Gabby had sent their drone up and was watching the screen on the controller as McCain and Lopez continued to monitor the GPS trackers that Tapia was wearing. Hollywood kept Chuck updated as they watched the residence from their UC vehicle. The big man hoped that the drone might allow them to determine if Sanchez was already in the safe house or had arrived in the gray SUV.

McCain sighed in frustration. Even though the cartel lieutenant was wanted on a long list of serious felonies, the law restricted them from raiding the house unless they knew for certain he was inside. They could get a search warrant, listing Eduardo as the subject of the search, but if he wasn't there during the raid, someone would likely tip him off as to how close the authorities were to catching him. That would send him deeper into hiding, possibly even causing him to flee back to Mexico.

No, Chuck realized, we've got to get this right. Sure, we could raid the house with a search warrant and lock up the cartel soldiers who were there. Without nabbing Sanchez, though, it would be a hollow victory. The reserve deputy's phone vibrated with an incoming call from Andy.

"What's the latest?" Fleming asked without preamble.

McCain had notified his friend earlier in the day of what was happening as Andy and Tex were finishing up the SWAT training with Fairfax Police Department. Falls Church was located within the county and Chuck had Andy notify the SWAT commander that they might be needed for a raid later.

"Hollywood's team is currently sitting on the house and we've got the drone up. Tapia is still there but that's all we know."

"Tex and I are getting ready to leave. Where do you want us?"

Chuck gave him their location off of Route 50. "Come join us at the CP and we can put our heads together."

Inside the cartel safe house, Eduardo Sanchez knelt before Alejandro Tapia and ripped the tape off his mouth. Enrique and Felix fanned out around the room, not taking any chances with the sicario, bound or not. Their pistols were visible, tucked into the front of their pants.

"Eduardo! Gracias Dios! Tell these assholes to let me go!"

Sanchez laughed a humorless laugh, pulling a Benchmade automatic knife out of his pocket and flicking open the razor-sharp blade.

"How did you get out of jail, Alejandro? Arturo said that a judge denied the motion for bond. Your own attorney said the only way you could've gotten out was by making a deal with the pigs."

"No, Eduardo! I told the police to go..."

"Shut up, you traitor!" Sanchez commanded, sticking the point of the knife under Tapia's chin, drawing a slight trickle of blood. "What did they promise you? What kind of deal did you make?"

Alejandro's eyes grew wide with fear.

"Eduardo, I swear on my mother's grave, I didn't tell the pigs anything. I don't know why they let me go. I was just eating in the cafeteria when a few of the cops came and got me. They didn't tell me shit— just that I was being released. As soon as I got out, I tried to get in touch with you. I would never betray la familia."

Sanchez pulled the knife away and wiped it on Tapia's clothing. He pointed the blade at the sicario's face.

"I'm having trouble believing you, amigo. The pigs were waiting inside that house for you and the others, yet somehow, miraculously, the other hombres are dead and you're still alive. Then, when your lawyer tried to get you out of jail, the judge said, 'no.' But somehow, you managed to get released."

"You've got to believe me, Eduardo!" Alejandro was starting to sound desperate.

The lieutenant laughed and motioned at the other two men. "So, I guess the pigs just decided to let him go out of the goodness of their hearts, eh? What do you think, Enrique?"

"I think he's full of shit and cut a deal with the pigs, Señor."

"Felix?"

The gangster shrugged. "No sé, Señor, but how else could he get out of jail? You want me to take care of him for you?" Felix asked, patting the 9mm Taurus.

Eduardo sighed and slowly climbed to his feet, staring down at the man he had once trusted. Suddenly, he kicked Alejandro in the stomach, once, twice, three times, before stopping. The bound man groaned in pain, pulling his legs up to shield himself against anymore blows.

The gangster boss glanced over at Felix. "No, amigo, I have an idea for how Alejandro can serve us one more time. Enrique, why don't you take Felix into the living room and tell him our plan?"

"Sí, Señor."

The two men left the room, leaving Eduardo staring down at the assassin.

"I trusted you, Alejandro. I trusted you and you betrayed us. You know the price for betraying la familia."

The sicario was still protesting his innocence as Sanchez taped his mouth shut once again.

**Command Post, Route 50, Falls Church, Virginia, Friday, 2050 hours**

Jimmy's team of him, Scotty, and Corporal Stephens had relieved Hollywood's squad a couple of hours earlier, their white work van not drawing any attention in the middle-class neighborhood. They still had no idea if Eduardo Sanchez was in the safe house or not. Now that it was dark, Jones planned on going for a walk around the block, hoping he might find a reconnaissance location closer to the target house.

The Fairfax County Police SWAT Commander, Lieutenant Dusty Miller, chatted with Chuck and G-Man Joe O'Reilly at the

CP waiting to hear some good news. The large, empty parking lot provided plenty of room for the Fairfax tactical unit, along with one of the local FBI SWAT teams.

"That was a great course you guys ran for our new SWAT members," Miller said. "I'm going to see if I can get it approved for you to come put the entire team through that advanced tactical course you offer."

McCain nodded. "Thanks, LT. Sorry I had to leave early, but they were in capable hands with Andy and Tex. That was nice of you to open up some slots for a few of the smaller departments in the area."

The lieutenant shrugged. "We've all got to help each other. You said we could have twenty students and Fairfax County only had twelve guys that hadn't gone through basic. Those other eight will go back and help train their teams."

Chuck's role at Century had allowed him to meet many of the top tactical officers in the country. He had originally connected with Dusty years earlier while McCain was an assault team leader for his department in the Atlanta area and Miller was the same for his agency in Virginia. They had met at an advanced Special Weapons and Tactics class put on by the FBI.

McCain and Miller had spent some time catching up on each other's careers, Chuck telling his friend as much as he could about what he had done since retiring as a local cop. O'Reilly listened quietly, learning a few new things about the big man.

"Everything gets a little murky after the zombie crisis when you left the CDC," Joe commented.

"We were on loan to Homeland, Joe. You know that."

"Sure, McCain. Sure."

The FBI agent's tone suggested, however, that he knew there was more to the story than what Chuck had shared. In reality, McCain had been an assistant director of operations at the CIA for a short time and even after leaving to work with Century, he and his teammates often took contract jobs for the Agency.

Miller grinned. "One of the things that I've learned about working in the Northern Virginia/Metro-DC area, Agent O'Reilly, is that sometimes things get a little blurry about who works for who in the federal law enforcement arena."

Joe grunted and nodded at the SWAT commander, a new respect in his eyes.

"You're a very perceptive man, Lieutenant."

The senior FBI agent's phone vibrated with an incoming call and he stepped away to answer it.

Dusty motioned at Joe with his head.

"It sounds like you two have a bit of a history."

Chuck smiled. "I think we've actually become friends, although that's probably up for debate. We've helped each other out a few times. And, no matter what he says, he's not your typical fed. He's pretty good at cutting through the red tape that defines the Bureau."

Joe rejoined the two men, snapping his phone angrily back into its belt holder. He sighed before speaking.

"That was my boss, CT Director Valerie Morris. She gave us a deadline. We've got to make entry on that search warrant in the next six hours."

"We don't even know if Sanchez is in there, Joe," Chuck said. "What's the rush?"

"Politics," O'Reilly answered, spitting the word out. "The AG is evidently worried about getting replaced by the next president so he wants to ride the momentum from all the recent cartel violence that's been in the news to maybe save his job. He's already got a press conference scheduled for ten in the morning, to announce another blow against the Sinaloa Cartel."

"Unbelievable," McCain said, shaking his head. "What's the point if we don't get Sanchez?"

O'Reilly chuckled. "To add a little more spice for the media, the attorney general added Eduardo to our Top Ten this afternoon. But either way, it's a win-win for the AG. We know that's a Sinaloa safe house and we know there are people inside. If we get Sanchez, it's a big victory for the attorney general. If he's not there, but we arrest several other cartel soldiers, he still wins."

"Damn!" Dusty muttered. "Politics at the federal level are much worse than some of the crap I have to put up with."

"And that's why I need to retire," Joe grumbled. "Anyway, I'm going to go get my SWAT leader and let you and him figure out who's going to do what. Why don't you guys plan on hitting it at 0200?"

Chuck gathered his people around him and let them know of the change in plans. He felt their disgust with an order that might very well send the senior cartel leader deeper into hiding.

"It's not our show anymore," he shrugged. "It's a Bureau and Fairfax County show now."

"At least O'Reilly's here to bring some sense of order to the feds," Andy commented, "and Lieutenant Miller's guys are squared away."

"Yeah, but if we miss that son-of-a-bitch, it'll be a long time before we get another shot," Hollywood added. "He's too slippery!"

McCain shrugged. "If we get lucky and he's inside, though, O'Reilly told me that he'll be tried in a federal court. With all the charges pending against him, he'll die in prison."

Tex spat off to the side. "I'd just as soon take care of that now."

"If only it was that easy," Chloe spoke up.

By 0100 hours the two tactical teams were getting their equipment ready. The FBI SWAT Team would be the one making entry into the house. The Fairfax County tactical unit would provide perimeter security, sniper coverage, and would be available as backup if things went bad. At 0130 hours, the heavily-armed officers performed a final weapons check and started to load into the two armored vehicles.

Jimmy had provided regular updates, but there had been no news to report. The former Marine had just returned to the van after a walk around the block. He told the others that all the drapes were pulled closed and he couldn't see anything or anyone inside. Gabby and Chloe had taken turns flying the drone over the target location but it had also revealed nothing. The tactical team would be going in dark.

"Alpha Two to Alpha One," Jimmy's excited voice came through Chuck's earpiece at 0140 hours.

"Go ahead, Alpha Two."

"We've got activity. Two vehicles just pulled out of the garage, a gray SUV and a white passenger car. Looks like they're turning left out of the neighborhood. We'll be following them."

"Alpha One is clear. I'm gonna send Alpha Three and Four your way and I'll be enroute after I brief O'Reilly and Lieutenant Miller."

Hollywood's people were quickly in their SUV and rolling that way, followed by Andy and Tex in their Suburban. Lopez was staring at Gabby's computer, set up on the hood of her vehicle, watching the GPS transmitters from Alejandro Tapia. After hearing Jones' radio traffic, J-Lo noticed that the red dots still appeared to be inside the house. She hurried over to McCain.

Vargas had just brought the drone in to change the batteries and McCain was speaking with her.

"Pack it up, Gabby. They've got two full SWAT teams here. They can manage on their own. We need to follow those cars."

"Chuck," Sergeant Lopez said, "come look at this. I think Tapia's still inside the house."

After confirming what the sergeant had said, he quickly alerted O'Reilly and Miller of the activity at the suspect location.

"I've got a team on the two cars that just left, but it looks like the guy we followed there, Alejandro Tapia, stayed behind. We're all going to head out in case one of those vehicles turns out to contain Sanchez."

"Call me if you need some uniform support," Lieutenant Miller said.

Agent O'Reilly motioned at McCain, speaking to Miller.

"If I was a betting man, LT, I'd put money on the fact that Eduardo is inside one of those vehicles and McCain here is going to end up being the one to take him down."

"That'd be OK with me, Joe," Chuck smiled, "but I figure you guys have this covered. Y'all have to help the AG keep his job. I'll keep you posted."

The two target vehicles made their way west, utilizing Highway 267. They kept to the speed limit and used their turn signals, Jimmy noticed.

"So, maybe we'll get to see some action after all," Scotty commented, anticipation in his voice, as he kept the Dodge van a safe distance behind the gangsters.

"Maybe, although I hate the idea of getting into a shootout outside of our jurisdiction," Jimmy replied.

"Yeah, maybe we'll get lucky and they'll keep going west, right back into Loudon County," Corporal Norm Stephens interjected.

"Whatever," Smith said. "These guys need to be taken out, no matter which side of the county line they're on."

"You'll have to pardon my friend, Corporal," Jones grinned. "While you and I are Marines and are trained to be much more sophisticated killers, this Ranger is a bit rough around the edges. He's a killing machine, mind you, but he sometimes forgets little things like jurisdiction."

"Jurisdiction didn't matter a whole lot over in the desert," Stephens replied. "The judges and lawyers seem to take it pretty seriously over here."

"If they can't take a joke..." Smith started.

"Alpha One to Alpha Two, location?" Chuck's voice came over their earpieces.

"Alpha Two to Alpha One," Jimmy answered, "we're between Tyson's Corner and Reston. I don't think they're going to Dulles, so my guess is that they've got some business in Loudon County."

"Alpha One's clear. If that's the case, at least we don't have to worry about jurisdictional issues."

"We were just talking about that."

"One other thing, Alpha Two. It looks like Alejandro Tapia stayed behind at the house in Falls Church. The GPS signals haven't moved. I don't know what that means but it definitely seems strange. We're all enroute to you."

"10-4. Thanks for the update, Alpha One."

"See, even Chuck knows that jurisdiction is important," Jimmy said.

Scotty laughed. "Bro, the boss popped three bad guys in DC a couple of weeks ago. The last thing on his mind was which municipality he was standing in. He just took care of business."

"I can't argue with you, buddy. Chuck certainly took care of business, that's for sure."

Enrique piloted the gray Durango with Eduardo in the passenger seat and Felix seated behind the driver. A newer soldier named Juan was in the back with Felix. Ronaldo drove the Impala accompanied by three additional heavily armed gangsters. Ronaldo also had another passenger, this one riding in the trunk of the large passenger car. Alejandro's clothes had been cut off of him and extra duct tape added to his bonds before he was unceremoniously tossed into the storage compartment of the vehicle.

"When we get there," Sanchez had told his companions, "we need to be quick. Normally, I'd drag it out and make him suffer but we're going to be right across from the cops' headquarters. Plus, as much as I want to punish Alejandro, I really want to send a message to the pigs. We'll make them think twice before recruiting a Sinaloa soldier to be a snitch."

As they cruised west on Highway 267, Eduardo pulled out a glass vial of white powder. He used a small spoon to place some of the cocaine inside of each nostril, pinching the other side shut as he snorted the powerful drug. After repeating the process, he passed the vial over his shoulder to Felix. Sanchez closed his eyes, savoring the intense pleasure the drug always gave him. The Sinaloa lieutenant didn't use their product very often, not wanting to become an addict. Whenever he was about to deal out cartel justice to a traitor or a rival gangster, though, he loved how the white powder made him feel.

"Bueno, that hits so good. Sorry, Enrique. You've got to drive. I don't want the pigs to give you a DUI."

This elicited a laugh from everyone. As he savored the cocaine high, Sanchez drew a nasty looking, Rambo-style survival knife from the sheath on his belt. He carried the blade on his left side, opposite of his holstered 9mm Beretta pistol. While many of his colleagues carried Glocks, Eduardo held onto the Italian pistol for sentimental reasons. He had taken it off a rival gangster, his first assassination. He'd killed the Tijuana soldier with a blade but kept his pistol.

This knife had been purchased at a gun show in Arlington. Gun shows were just one of the many reasons Eduardo loved los Estados. Although, contrary to the narrative that said anyone could buy anything at a gun show, the gangster had never purchased a firearm at one of the events since he was in the country illegally and was a wanted felon. There was no background check for knives, though, and he had used this one to maim, kill, and inflict pain on more than one rival gangster or unfaithful Sinaloa soldiers.

Sanchez liked the way this one looked, but he especially enjoyed the look of terror that it produced before he carved up a deserving victim. Sanchez wouldn't have time to inflict as much pain on Tapia as he deserved. At the same time, he intended to keep the traitorous sicario alive long enough for the punk to feel the blade slicing through his throat, neck, and spine.

Eduardo's soldiers would drag the piece of shit out of the trunk and drop him to the asphalt. They would hold him still while Sanchez removed Tapia's head from his body. It's too bad that we have to rush off. In Mexico, the Sinaloa lieutenant had watched his soldiers play soccer with the severed head of a disloyal member. They even have several nice futbol fields at this park. No, I'll just leave Alejandro's head laying nearby as a message to the pigs.

The gangster grinned, imagining a couple of young American soccer moms getting to the park early the next morning for a walk after dropping their kids off at school. He'd love to see the shock and horror on their faces. They might even throw up before they could compose themselves enough to dial 911.

With four vehicles, McCain's squads were able to alternate their tail every few miles. Five minutes after they left Fairfax County for Loudon, Chuck's phone vibrated with a call from Agent O'Reilly.

"Hey, Joe."

"It's your show now, McCain. The house was empty."

"Empty? What about Tapia?"

"There's some blood in one of the bedrooms and a pile of clothes that have been sliced with a blade. It's not a lot of blood but somebody's leaking, probably your boy, Alejandro."

"Thanks, Joe. We just passed Dulles. They're heading towards Leesburg but I'll let you know where we end up. I thought they might be heading back to try again at the Sagarra's house, but they've already gone past the turnoff."

"The last I heard was that the Sagarras are getting settled with new identities in Florida," the FBI agent said.

"That's good. What's the AG going to say in his press conference now that the FBI SWAT raid has come up empty?"

The G-Man laughed. "I could care less. I really am serious about retiring this time, McCain. If Sampson becomes president, I'm turning my papers in and coming to work for you."

"That's probably a good idea. We'll have you and your buddy, Thomas Burns, working corporate espionage cases and teaching courses at Quantico. Let me know when you're actually doing it and we'll talk."

A few minutes after disconnecting, Chuck got an update from Andy. He and Tex were now the vehicle tailing the suspects.

"They just got off the highway south of Leesburg. This is getting weird, Boss. They're actually heading back towards the jail."

"Alpha One's clear."

"What are those guys up to?" McCain asked, his mind racing.

"I'll notify the watch supervisor," Sergeant Lopez said, steering with her left hand, grabbing for her walkie talkie with her right. "I think it's Lieutenant Donaldson."

Chuck grunted. "That's good. I feel better knowing Jake will be organizing the calvary if we need it."

The car ride seemed to go on forever. Where are they taking me? Alejandro didn't know how Eduardo planned on killing him but the sicario wasn't planning on making it easy. Even with his hands restrained behind his back, in a pitch-black environment, he managed to explore most of the Impala's trunk. His Sinaloa "brothers" had tossed him on top of a throw rug. They probably plan on wrapping me up inside before disposing of my body, he thought. They may kill me, but they're going to have to work for it.

He managed to tug the rug aside, exploring the area underneath. His hands grasped a long, metal object that curved on one end. After a moment, he realized it was a tire iron, used on older-model vehicles to operate the jack and remove the lug nuts. The flat end wasn't sharp but after a few minutes of work, he felt the duct tape beginning to tear. His forearms and wrists were bleeding where the crow bar had cut into his flesh but he kept working on the layers of tape.

Finally! Alejandro felt his bonds weakening. He strained, feeling like he was going to rip his shoulders out of joint. Suddenly, his hands were free. He tore the tape off of his mouth and went to work on his ankles.

It didn't feel like they were on the highway anymore. The car had slowed and stopped a couple of times now, making several turns. He hurried, using the flat end of the tire tool to rip the tape open. Tapia inadvertently sliced open his shins, but it would be worth it if he could just get free.

The car slowed and turned again, finally coming to a stop. The engine shut down and he heard the car doors opening.

When the two-vehicle cartel caravan left the Dulles-Greenway Toll Road, Tex took his foot off of the accelerator, allowing a little more space between them and the gangsters. After a couple of turns, the Sinaloa vehicles were moving North on Crosstrail Boulevard. That route would take them right by the sheriff's department HQ and the Loudon County Detention Center.

While Davis drove, Fleming kept his teammates apprised of their location. The other units were closing fast, to be in position whenever the gang members reached their destination.

"What are they doing?" Andy muttered.

The Philip A. Bolen Memorial Regional Park was on the opposite side of the street from the detention center. The park contained soccer fields, baseball and softball diamonds, lacrosse fields and a cricket oval. Eduardo directed Enrique into the first entrance, allowing them to enter the recreation area before they were in sight of the jail. The gangster led the way into the first parking lot, stopping in a remote, dark corner. There were no other vehicles there at this late hour.

The Sinaloa lieutenant could see the lights of the sheriff's department HQ shining brightly through the trees, the location no more than a few hundred yards away. The ambient light and a couple of flashlights would be just enough for Eduardo to see to perform his grizzly task.

"Vamos!" Sanchez ordered as soon as they stopped, quickly exiting the Durango and walking over to the Impala, drawing his knife. "Pull this asshole out and drop him on the pavement."

The older-model passenger car required a key to get into the trunk. As Ronaldo opened the storage compartment, Eduardo flicked on his flashlight, aiming the light into the trunk. Ronaldo suddenly flew backwards as Alejandro launched a powerful kick, catching the gangster in the chest. The soldiers weren't expecting any resistance and stared in surprise as the nude sicario nimbly sprung out of the trunk, swinging a tire iron. The first blow caught Felix on the side of the head with a sickening thud, sending the thug to the ground.

By now, the cartel soldiers had shaken off the lethargy and were all moving away from the naked man, a few of them attempting to draw pistols. All of their rifles and shotguns had been left inside the vehicles, none of them expecting any problems from the restrained traitor. Juan didn't carry a handgun and turned towards the truck to grab his AK-47. Instead, the tire tool crashed into the back of his skull, sending him facedown on the asphalt.

Eduardo was not surprised by much, but when Alejandro came out swinging that piece of metal, he involuntarily took a step backwards, trying to keep the beam of light on him. The big knife was already in his right hand. Eduardo instinctively grabbed Ronaldo with his left to help him up but dropped the flashlight in the process. The nude sicario kept moving and swinging, taking out Felix and Juan. A sudden fury replaced Sanchez's surprise as he raised the survival knife and went after the assassin-turned-police-informant.

Tapia glanced over his shoulder to see where Sanchez was. The blade glinted in the ambient light and the sicario knew it was time to make his escape. Thankfully, the gangsters had parked at the far edge of the parking lot, a copse of trees rising up in front of him. One of the soldiers jumped in front of the fleeing man, a pistol in his hand. The gun roared and the fire from the muzzle flash singed Alejandro as he brought the tire iron down the man's right wrist. Bones cracked and the Mexican screamed in pain as the gun went clattering across the pavement.

The bullet missed but that interaction slowed Alejandro just long enough for Eduardo to reach him, thrusting with the blade, and stabbing the traitor in the back. Tapia gasped in pain as he sprinted for the cover of the trees, just a few yards away. Gunfire erupted from the cartel soldiers, angry bullets whizzing by Alejandro. Almost there, he told himself, the adrenaline masking the pain from where he'd been stabbed.

Just as his feet left the asphalt for a short strip of grass, something slammed into his back, the searing agony taking his breath away. The trees were right in front of him now, but just as he reached them, he felt the ground give way and he was suddenly tumbling head over heels down a steep embankment. At the bottom of the hill was a retention pond and the wounded gangster splashed face first into the green water.

Back in the parking lot, Eduardo and the others noticed multiple sets of headlights roaring towards them.

"Vamos! It's the pigs!"

At 0215 hours, Tex parked on the shoulder of Crosstrail Boulevard, a hundred feet south of the entrance to the recreation area. As the other vehicles arrived, they stopped behind him with their lights off. Now that they were back in Loudon County, Sergeant Lopez took charge.

"Sergeant Cobb, can you take Corporal Stephens into the park on foot and see if you can see them? We should have some marked units here soon, as well."

After a fast equipment check, the two men were quickly moving through a patch of woods adjacent to the recreation area. Just fifty feet later, a soccer field appeared to their right with a road in front of them. A large parking lot was on the opposite side of the street with Spanish-speaking voices coming from that area. Cobb led the way, the officers hurrying to where they could get a view of the suspects.

Their NVGs allowed them to see the two vehicles parked several hundred feet away, a single flashlight moving between them. Stephens turned to speak quietly into his radio, updating the others. Yelling and cursing suddenly erupted from the rear of the white passenger car. The deputies were too far away to see what was happening, but it sounded like a struggle. Seconds later, the darkness was lit up by muzzle flashes and the roar of indiscriminate gunfire.

Eduardo hated to leave Felix and Juan behind, but they were probably dead anyway. There just had not been time to drag them into one of the vehicles. The soldier with the broken arm was screaming in pain as he was pulled into the Impala, the bones sticking out of the skin in the compound fracture. Ronaldo led the way out of the parking lot, turning left and heading deeper into the park before turning left again, now speeding towards the other entrance. They would exit directly across from the jail, but a right turn would put them back on the main road and a short drive to the highway.

Sanchez looked to their rear, the headlights continuing to follow them. Just as they got to the park exit, though, a police car roared towards them from their left on Crosstrail Boulevard, it's blue strobe lights and siren activated.

"¡Vamos!"

Enrique shoved the accelerator to the floor, following the Impala as the two vehicles squealed out of the park.

Lieutenant Jake Donaldson was in his office at the SO finishing up his nightly administrative duties. All of his deputies were tied up on 911 calls in different parts of the county. He only had one sergeant and a corporal working tonight, the other supervisor out on annual leave. Sergeant Bradley was assisting one of his deputies in investigating an alcohol-related crash on the far side of the district.

After Detective Sergeant Lopez alerted him to the presence of the gangsters in the nearby recreation area, Jake logged off the computer and hurried out to his patrol car. The brand new Ford Interceptor SUV had been issued to him after his other cruiser had been shot up a few weeks earlier. Jake still savored the new car smell with less than a thousand miles showing on the odometer.

Sergeant Cobb's excited voice came over the police radio. "SWAT 405 to dispatch, we've got shots fired inside the Bolen Memorial Park near HQ. Unknown victims, the suspects are fleeing in a gray SUV and white passenger car. They're heading out of the park on Claudia Drive."

Donaldson activated his lights and siren, approaching the park entrance within seconds. A white Impala and a gray Durango turned right onto Crosstrail Boulevard a few hundred feet in front of him, accelerating to a high rate of speed, clearly not planning on stopping for his blue lights. The lieutenant had a tough decision to make. Like most law enforcement agencies, Loudon County had adopted a very strict vehicle pursuit policy.

The deputies were only allowed chase for the most serious felonies and even though shots had been fired in the park, Jake didn't know the entire situation. The last thing that he wanted was to get involved in or to get one of his deputies involved in an unauthorized chase. While car chases always got an officer's adrenaline pumping and looked great in movies, they were incredibly dangerous. Municipalities paid out millions of dollars each year in settlements as a result of innocent motorists being injured in car crashes caused by police pursuits.

All across the country, law enforcement officers had been suspended, fired, sued, and in some cases, even arrested for chasing criminals for minor offenses. For the moment, Jake continued after the suspects but didn't advise the dispatcher. There wouldn't be much traffic on Crosstrail this time of night. State Route 7, Leesburg Pike, was just two miles up the road and Donaldson decided to let the pursuit play out until then, hoping Sergeants Lopez or Cobb would update him and the other responding deputies with more details about the situation in the park.

Less than a minute later, the SWAT sergeant transmitted again. "SWAT 405 to dispatch, we need an ambulance and investigators enroute to the park. I've got two Hispanic males with serious head wounds. No pulse from one and the other is critical."

That's what I needed to hear, thought Donaldson, flipping his siren off before hitting transmit. "101 to Dispatch, I'm clear on that radio traffic— a possible double-homicide at the park. I'm following the two suspect vehicles northbound on Crosstrail Boulevard, a half mile from Leesburg Pike. Have every available unit start this way."

"10-4, 101," the dispatcher's calm voice replied. "Any unit that can assist 101?"

Two other deputies had just cleared a domestic call and advised they were heading towards the lieutenant, but were at least five minutes away.

"101 to dispatch, they're not stopping," he transmitted, this time leaving his siren on for everyone to hear. "I'm 10-80."

A 10-80 in most jurisdictions is a chase. With the strict policies in place, an actual 10-80 was a rare thing and other deputies immediately rushed to finish up their calls so that they could respond as backup. If the lieutenant was in a car chase, these must be bona fide bad guys.

"What do we do, Señor?" Enrique asked, a hint of panic in his voice.

The Sinaloa gangsters understood how well the police in America were organized. They might outrun one officer, but they would never outrun the pigs' radios. The cartel members relished the idea of killing an American cop or two, but the idea of getting arrested or killed themselves had no appeal at all.

Before Sanchez could answer, the Impala driven by Ronaldo, made a sudden right turn onto the Leesburg Pike, heading east.

"Keep going straight!" Eduardo ordered. "We'll split up."

Enrique nodded and pushed the Dodge Durango even faster as they went under the interchange. The lone deputy stayed on their tail rather than following the other vehicle. An intersection was coming up quickly, the light turning yellow and then red just before the Durango arrived.

An older black pickup on the cross street got a green light and started across the intersection, the suspects' SUV just barely missing the front of the civilian's car. Donaldson tapped the brakes and the Loudon County cruiser slowed enough to avoid an accident as the lieutenant steered around the pickup. Enrique tried to put some distance between them and the deputy as they approached the next intersection, but the Ford Interceptor quickly closed the gap.

Eduardo couldn't remember the name of the soldier who had jumped in the car with them. Ronaldo also had two gunmen in his car, their other two left behind after the traitor had smashed their skulls in. I hope a few of our bullets found Alejandro, he thought. I stuck him pretty good in the back with my blade, too. Maybe that'll be enough to send the punk straight to Hell.

The Sinaloa lieutenant knew it was just a matter of time before the entire area would be swarming with police cars. If they could eliminate the asshole chasing them, they might have a chance to escape.

"Stop before that next intersection," he ordered Enrique.

He pointed to the soldier seated behind the driver. "Get ready to take out that pig!"

The man gave him a nod, clutching a chrome-plated .40 caliber Taurus pistol. Sanchez pulled his Beretta and looked back over his shoulder. The blue strobe lights were blinding but it didn't matter, Sanchez thought, feeling the Durango slowing. This cop was a dead man.

Jake Donaldson was grateful that they had avoided a collision with the black pickup and hoped those backup units got to him quickly so they could end this chase before an innocent person got hurt. He and his sergeants had stop-sticks but since he was the primary chase car, there was no way to deploy them. Jake had alerted everyone that the white passenger car turned east onto Leesburg Pike, directing some of the responding units to go after them. The Durango's brake lights suddenly came on and the suspect vehicle came to an abrupt stop in the middle of the road, two hundred feet from the intersection with Riverside Parkway.

"101 to dispatch, the suspects are stopping just before Riverside," the lieutenant transmitted.

The deputy slammed on his brakes, skidding to a halt three car lengths behind the gang members. He turned the steering wheel to the left, angling the engine block between him and the Sinaloa soldiers. The doors of the suspect vehicle flew open, but Jake was already moving, quickly exiting the cruiser and drawing his 9mm Glock, wishing he had time to retrieve the AR-15 from the cargo compartment of the SUV. A slim man with shoulder length hair bailed out of the door behind the driver and immediately started shooting at the sheriff's deputy. The thug was blasting away, "gangster style," the pistol turned sideways with the ejection port pointing up.

Donaldson brought up his Glock in a two-handed stance, crouching behind the door frame, and firing at the Mexican. One of the cartel soldier's bullets smashed into the windshield, while a second slammed into the light bar on top of the cruiser. The deputy's first 9mm hollow point found the gangster's abdomen and a second round caught him high on the right leg.

The gunman staggered backwards after being hit but continued shooting, most of his unaimed rounds going high. Another of Jake's bullets sent the man to his knees just as additional gunfire erupted from the right side of the Durango, the incoming rounds thudding into the side of the cruiser. Instinctively, the lieutenant retreated to the rear of the police car, putting more metal between him and the new threat. Chuck McCain's voice echoed inside his brain from one of the in-service training sessions conducted by Century Tactical,

*"Fire and move! Get off the X! Don't get attached to that piece of real estate!"*

From his new cover position, the lieutenant chanced a peek around the right corner of the cruiser, seeing Eduardo Sanchez firing round after round towards the police car. The deputy raised his pistol, placed the front site over the wanted man's torso and squeezed the trigger just as the gangster took a step to the left. Jake's 9mm bullet missed the fugitive, shattering the right taillight. Sanchez saw the muzzle flash and shifted his aim to where Donaldson was crouching. The cop dropped back behind his cover as the cartel lieutenant's gunfire thudded into the police vehicle.

Sirens sounded from behind Jake alerting him that the calvary was almost there. Eduardo fired a few more shots at the Ford Interceptor before turning to rush back to the open passenger door. The driver of the Durango was now out and also shooting at Jake, with even more bullets slamming into his new police vehicle.

The deputy wasn't about to let Sanchez escape and raised up, squeezing off three rounds before the gangster managed to dive inside the Durango. The driver also retreated into the SUV and sped away, turning South onto Riverside Parkway. Donaldson fired at the fleeing vehicle until his slide locked open.

Enrique had been halfway out of the vehicle when he heard the soldier behind him grunt in pain. A bullet tore into the door frame next to the driver's face and he fell back inside the Durango. The rear gangster cursed loudly as he was hit again. Eduardo was now blasting away from the passenger side of the SUV. Enrique gripped his own pistol and raised his head over the seat, peering through the rear window.

The wounded soldier was attempting to pull himself back into the Dodge. Enrique hurried out and shoved the man into the backseat, blood pumping out of several bullet holes. The exchange of gunfire between Eduardo and the pig had not let up. Enrique squeezed off two shots from his Colt Government Model .45 ACP pistol, even though he couldn't see the cop behind the wall of light thrown off by the police car.

Sanchez was back in their vehicle and yelled, "¡Vamos!"

Enrique threw himself inside and accelerated away.

"Estás bien, Señor?"

Eduardo fumbled with his Beretta, trying to shove a fresh magazine into it but his left arm wasn't working, a burning pain coursing through the appendage, blood pumping out of a hole on the back side of his arm, just below his shoulder.

"That asshole pig shot me!"

Enrique turned right onto Riverside Parkway before chancing a look over at the cartel lieutenant. He could see the agony on el jefe's face as he finally managed to get his gun reloaded.

"What about him?" Sanchez asked, nodding at the motionless man on the backseat.

"He got hit bad, maybe two or three times. There was a lot of blood."

Eduardo grimaced in pain as he turned to look behind him. The street lights let him see that the soldier still wasn't moving. The gangster was thankful for a momentary reprieve, not seeing any blue lights behind them.

"Where does this road go?" Enrique asked.

"I think it reconnects with the highway. Stay on it as long as you can. I don't see any more cops."

"Did you kill him, Señor?"

"I think so," Sanchez grunted, hoping one of his many rounds had found the pig.

Two Loudon County cruisers pulled in behind Donaldson as he radioed in the shooting and gave the last location for the gray Durango.

"LT, are you OK?" a young female deputy asked, rushing up to her shift commander as he reloaded his pistol and holstered it.

Jake pointed to the next intersection as a male officer joined them. "They just turned right. I counted at least three in the vehicle, including Eduardo Sanchez. I know I hit the one in the backseat and might've gotten lucky and hit Sanchez, too. Go find them!"

The two deputies sprinted back to their cars and tore off after the gangsters. Jake took a moment to catch his breath and check his new cruiser. Damn! He shook his head. The windshield was shattered, the strobe bar was only working on one side, and the right rear tire was flat. The beautiful new Ford Interceptor had been punctured multiple times from the gangsters' bullets. He was officially out of the fight, he realized, shaking his head.

A pair of unmarked vehicles slid to a stop behind him. Sergeant Lopez, Chuck, and Gabby emerged from the first one and Hollywood and Chloe exited the second.

"I'm fine but my cruiser is shot to hell!" Donaldson exclaimed. "They just turned right at the light. I'm almost positive Eduardo Sanchez is in that Durango. Go back up those two deputies!"

In seconds the two unmarked vehicles were rushing to catch up with the marked units.

**Eastbound Leesburg Pike, Leesburg, Virginia, Saturday, 0228 hours**

Lieutenant Donaldson's earlier radio traffic had alerted everyone that the white Impala had turned east onto the highway. Chuck ordered two of his squads to follow that suspect vehicle until they could get a marked unit there to try and stop the fleeing gangsters. Jimmy and Scotty acknowledged the radio transmission and were followed by Tex and Andy. Smith pushed the work van for everything it was worth, finally catching sight of the Chevrolet passenger car near the Ashburn exit. With no police cars around, the suspect vehicle slowed to sixty-five miles-per-hour, not wanting to attract attention to themselves.

"That looks like them," the former Ranger said, maintaining several car lengths between the suspects and moving into the adjacent lane. "Time to go to work."

"Damn! Where's a cop when you need one?" Jones asked, glancing into the rearview mirror again.

Jimmy alerted the dispatcher to their location, requesting marked units join them to attempt a traffic stop.

"Want me to PIT him? We can end this right here."

"No, bro. You heard what Chuck said. We have to act like cops. We don't have any blue lights or a siren."

Scotty sighed loudly. They had heard the radio traffic from Lieutenant Donaldson about his shootout. It sounded like he had hit one or two of the Sinaloa soldiers while avoiding injury himself. He said that his car was a casualty, but that was a good trade any day of the week.

Finally, blue lights appeared in their rearview mirror, rapidly closing the distance. Three Loudon County cruisers passed them, sirens blaring. The suspect vehicle accelerated again and the chase was on. Thankfully, the traffic was light on the highway and the sheriff's deputies were content to follow until an opportunity presented itself to end the pursuit. The state police had also been requested but dispatch did not have an ETA for the troopers.

The Impala suddenly veered to the right, taking the south ramp onto Sully Road. As the suspect vehicle swerved onto the ramp, the lead deputy decided to attempt to take the perps out. The PIT maneuver is designed to be performed at speeds of less than forty miles an hour. The danger level increases for the police officer and the suspect at higher speeds.

At almost fifty miles an hour, the deputy decided to chance it, closing in on the Impala and skillfully turning into the right rear corner panel, sending the Chevrolet into a spin. The deputy then slowed his Ford Interceptor SUV as the suspect driver lost control, left the roadway, climbed the embankment and flipped over, landing in the middle of the exit ramp. The Impala slid on its roof for a hundred feet, sparks, smoke, and dust filling the air.

The three deputies blocked the road with their cruisers, all of their lights focused on the overturned vehicle. Jimmy, Scotty, Andy, and Tex parked on the shoulder grabbed their rifles and moved up to support their uniformed colleagues. Andy had alerted the deputies over the radio that they were approaching and their badges hung around their neck. The officers were going to be keyed up after the chase and Fleming didn't want to take a chance on them not recognizing the reserve deputies.

A fortyish looking corporal took charge of the scene, not letting anyone approach the wrecked Impala. They knew that the cartel members were armed and dangerous and the corporal wasn't taking any chances. After making sure the deputies were all safely behind cover, he reached inside his Interceptor and activated the PA system, issuing commands to the perps.

"You in the vehicle, come out with your hands up!"

A loud groan came from the overturned vehicle and Corporal Barrett repeated the command.

"What if they don't understand English, Corporal?"

The question came from a pudgy female deputy.

"They're in America," he shrugged. "They should've taken time to learn the language."

"Damn straight!" the third deputy, a mid-thirties African-American male commented.

"We could try to get a translator here," the female replied.

"Stay focused on the car, Robinson!" Corporal Barrett ordered the woman. "The LT was just in a shootout with these ass wipes' friends."

After a third command over the PA system, a voice spoke up in Spanish and a pair of hands extended out the passenger window, followed by a bloodied and banged up male. He glanced around him, unable to see the cops because of the bright lights shining in his face.

"Estan heridos," he said, pointing back at the vehicle. *They're hurt.*

"Vamos aqui," the corporal ordered, in one of his few Spanish phrases.

It wasn't correct grammatically, but the cartel soldier understood and slowly climbed to his feet, making sure he kept his hands up. He walked unsteadily towards the closest police car where Tex and Jimmy grabbed and took him back to the ground. Davis applied the handcuffs and Jones searched the man. They then pulled him back to his feet and secured him in the police Interceptor.

The Loudon County deputies all knew the reserve deputies and had been through various firearms and tactical courses put on by the Century employees. The corporal glanced over at Fleming.

"What do you think, Andy?"

"My Spanish isn't very good, either, but I think the one who came out said the others are hurt. Why don't you challenge them again and then we'll make an approach?"

The uniformed supervisor called out again on the PA system for the suspects to come out. After waiting a couple of minutes, Andy motioned to Scotty, Jimmy, and Tex to follow him.

"Robinson, can you request an ambulance?" Corporal Barrett asked the female deputy.

As she turned to speak with dispatch, the other full-time and reserve deputies focused their weapons on the suspect vehicle, careful to make sure their muzzles never covered the four men who slowly approached the overturned Impala. Sirens sounded in the distance as additional backup units responded. Smith and Jones took a wide turn and approached from the driver's side, while Fleming and Davis paused on the passenger side.

Scotty dropped to his knees, his rifle pointing inside the passenger compartment. Andy did the same thing on the other side, but a few yards further back to prevent the possibility of a cross-fire. Smith activated the flashlight on his rifle and remembering that the uniformed officers were wearing body cams, he did not say the first thing that came to mind.

"The driver is possibly deceased," he called out instead. "From here it looks like his neck is broken."

On the other side, Fleming crawled close enough to reach through the smashed out rear passenger window and grabbed the foot that was visible. A strong tug pulled an unconscious Mexican out of the vehicle. The man's right arm was clearly busted, with bones protruding and his face was a mask of blood. The former MARSOC operator searched the man, not finding any weapons and pressed two fingers against the gangster's neck.

"He's breathing and has a strong pulse."

By this time, Scotty and Jimmy had carefully pulled the driver out, his head lolling at an odd angle. Smith, the team's medic, confirmed that there was no pulse, and left Jones to handcuff and search him as he moved to Fleming's perp to provide aid until the paramedics arrived.

Sergeant Lopez's voice suddenly came over the air.

"Gangs 605 to Dispatch, shots fired! Shots fired from the Durango!"

One of the uniformed officers yelled over the radio that he had been wounded and ordered all the other deputies to back off.

It took the two unmarked vehicles a couple of minutes to catch up with the marked units pursuing the Durango on Riverside Parkway. McCain would've preferred to be behind the steering wheel but this was Sergeant J-Lo's issued vehicle so the big man focused on where they were going. The suspects blew through several intersections, narrowly missing other vehicles.

After the perps started shooting through the back window of the Durango, they had watched the lead deputy peel off to the right, advising that he was hit in the shoulder and requesting an ambulance. The second officer dropped back, but continued the pursuit. A minute later, however, several rounds smashed into his Ford Interceptor, one in the radiator, another in the windshield, with the third destroying the cruiser's left front tire, forcing that deputy to pull over, as well.

"It's just us, with Hollywood and Chloe behind us," the sergeant said, glancing over at Chuck.

"We can't let them get away," Gabby said, from the rear seat.

"I know, but we're not supposed to chase in an unmarked car."

"I think these are extenuating circumstances," McCain replied. "They tried to kill the LT. Another deputy is wounded, they shot up the other guy's cruiser, and they've got at least one dead in the park. There's a sharp curve coming up in about a mile, right before Ashburn Village Boulevard. I think that if you can close the distance and get in their blind spot, Gabby and I'll be able to take them out."

The sergeant took a deep breath, knowing Chuck was right. If these dangerous cartel members got away, she wouldn't be able to forgive herself. She knew she was in uncharted waters as far as their departmental policy and even state law were concerned, but she trusted the big man and his team. Lopez also trusted the sheriff and knew he would do everything he could to take care of his people after the dust settled.

"Okay," she said, depressing the accelerator to close the distance with the suspects.

McCain alerted the dispatcher and his teammates as to what they were doing and readied his H&K 416 rifle. Vargas had her own rifle up, the muzzle sticking out the open window, behind Chuck's.

"Gabby, I'm gonna take out the driver. I need you to engage any other threats."

"Got it."

The Durango was in the inside lane, the sharp bend now less than a quarter of a mile ahead. J-Lo was in the outside lane, expecting cartel bullets to start slamming into her Toyota 4Runner at any moment. The road suddenly curved sharply to the right, forcing the driver of the suspect vehicle to tap the breaks. Lopez closed the remaining distance, watching McCain out of her peripheral vision raising his rifle.

Chuck was naturally left-handed but had no choice but to shoot right-handed out the passenger window. Thankfully, Andy and their former SEAL Team Six friend, Jay Walker, had drilled them all repeatedly on shooting both ways, just in case they ever ran into a situation like this. The film industry makes shooting out of a moving car look simple, while in fact, it is a very difficult skill to master, especially when attempting to fire into another moving vehicle. Just a little further and they would be in position.

A sudden flash came from inside the Durango as one of the gangsters shot at them. Gabby squeezed off two rounds at the flash, the noise deafening inside the SUV, even with a suppressed rifle.

Time to stop fooling around, Chuck thought, sighting in on the rear of the driver's headrest and depressing the trigger, feeling the recoil of the German rifle. He was prepared for a second shot, but the Durango suddenly swerved to the right and jumped the curb. Both passenger side tires were destroyed by the impact and the Dodge continued for fifty feet into an open dirt field, coming to stop in the soft soil.

Sergeant Lopez skidded to a halt with Hollywood right behind her. The deputies took cover behind their vehicles as Estrada shouted in Spanish for the occupants to exit with their hands up. After a moment, the passenger door opened but no one came out. The officers clutched their weapons a little tighter, waiting for a cartel soldier to come out blasting.

Hollywood yelled again for them to surrender as sirens drew closer. A leg, and then another, came out of the open door, followed by the rest of a man's body, sliding out of the SUV onto the ground. As two more Loudon County deputies and a Virginia State trooper arrived, they turned their headlights and spotlights onto the suspect vehicle, illuminating the scene.

Sergeant Lopez was the ranking deputy, but she had no problem with accepting McCain's suggestion to allow him, Gabby, Hollywood, and Chloe to clear the vehicle. As McCain and Vargas moved slowly towards the driver's side, they had their rifles locked into their shoulders. A figure lay in the floorboard behind the driver's seat.

"Manos alto!" Chuck yelled, but there was no response.

"Cover him, Gabby, and I'll check the driver."

Vargas kept her rifle trained on the suspect as McCain moved up slowly. Chuck's earlier shot had done its job as the 64 grain soft-point bullet had punctured the head rest and entered the back of the gangster's skull, killing him instantly. Blood and brains were splattered all over the dashboard, windshield and seats.

"Hollywood and Chloe," he called over the top of the vehicle, "the driver is dead and the guy in back is not responding. What's the story on the perp on the ground?"

"I think this is Sanchez," Estrada answered. "He's been hit a couple of times, but is alive, for the moment, at least."

"Okay, Gabby and I are going check the perp in the backseat."

He carefully pulled the rear door open as she kept the muzzle of her rifle pointed at the non-responsive suspect. With the door open, Chuck saw the blood pooled under the gangster. He carefully pulled the man out onto the ground and felt for a pulse.

"He's dead," McCain announced, handcuffing him and searching him just to be safe.

Chloe's voice went over the radio requesting an ambulance for their suspect as Chuck and Gabby walked around to join them, the other deputies and state trooper all moving up to check the scene. Hollywood had a knee in the gangster's back, handcuffing him in spite of his injuries. He had taken a bullet high on the back of his left arm near the shoulder and a second had torn through the bend in his right arm, almost severing it. McCain knelt down and shone his flashlight on the unconscious suspect. It certainly looked like the cartel lieutenant, even wearing some of the driver's blood and brain matter on his face.

Chuck stood, took a deep breath and smiled at his teammates.

"I'd say that this mission is accomplished."

**Century Tactical Solutions, Leesburg, Virginia, Thursday, 1135 hours**

Chuck placed the phone back in its cradle on his desk and breathed a sigh of relief. Major Kim had just called to let him know that the investigation of the officer-involved-shootings was complete. Normally, an incident like this might take weeks before the detectives managed to conduct all the interviews and take statements from everyone involved, including the witnesses, examine the evidence, study the autopsy results, and review the ballistic reports.

Sheriff Jerry Schaefer, had made it clear that he wanted this investigation expedited. The Virginia State Police worked the incident with the help of the Loudon County detectives, and had submitted their report late the previous evening. The sheriff and his staff had reviewed it that morning before having Kim call McCain to give him a summary of the investigator's report.

Starting in the Philip A. Bolen Memorial Regional Park, one cartel soldier was killed, with another severely injured by blunt force trauma to their heads. A tire tool was found at the scene and was consistent as the murder and assault weapon. The gangster who survived was in such critical shape that he was going to need full-time care for the rest of his life. A number of empty shell casings were also located in the parking lot.

As CSI scoured the area for every available piece of evidence, they found the nude corpse of Alejandro Tapia floating in a retention pond near the parking lot. The sicario had been stabbed and shot in the back. Neither of those wounds were fatal, however. The cause of death was drowning, probably after being weakened by the other injuries and his tumble down the steep embankment.

The FBI forensics team had recovered Tapia's clothes and phone at the Sinaloa safe house in Falls Church. When they compared notes with the CSI reports from Loudon County, it was believed that Alejandro was transported to the park in the back of the Chevrolet Impala. They discovered where the gangster had freed himself from the duct tape which had bound him. Investigators speculated that it was Tapia who had wielded the tire iron against his former colleagues before being shot, stabbed, and eventually drowned in the retention pond.

The report determined that the deputy who pitted the Chevrolet Impala had acted within departmental policy. The dead driver had several outstanding felony warrants so those would be recalled. The thug who had crawled out of the overturned vehicle had refused to talk, but the investigators had found gunpowder residue on his right hand and his pistol, complete with fingerprints and was found inside the Impala. The cartel soldier that Andy pulled out had a serious compound fracture of his right forearm, along several injuries incurred when the vehicle flipped over. Both of the surviving gangsters faced a laundry list of charges and were looking at long prison sentences.

For the part of the scenario involving the Dodge Durango, it was found that three of Lieutenant Donaldson's 9mm hollow point rounds had terminated the gangster in the backseat. One of the lieutenant's bullets had also scored on Eduardo Sanchez. The gunshot wound to the gangster's right arm was from Gabby's H&K rifle, the 5.56mm bullet doing so much damage, the doctors were forced to amputate at the elbow. Ballistics had indicated that Sanchez's pistol fired into the marked units during the chases and one of his 9mm bullets had wounded one of the deputies involved. The Commonwealth Attorney anticipated that Eduardo Sanchez would spend the rest of his life inside an American maximum-security prison.

Chuck's fatal shot of the Durango's driver was deemed in line with state law and departmental policy, commanding law enforcement officers to do everything in their power to prevent the escape of a fleeing, violent felon. McCain had done just that, ensuring that no innocents were ever in the line of fire. Enrique Salazar had been a career criminal, having spent time in prison in both Mexico and the United States for rape and many other aggravated sexual assaults.

The big man glanced at the yellow legal pad where he had taken notes as Major Kim had briefed him. Now, it was time to pass the good news on to his teammates. He went around the office and asked everyone to join him in the conference room.

A half hour later, the reserve deputies and General Perkins were all sporting relieved smiles. Having the investigation behind them was a big relief. They were professional warriors and would lose no sleep over the dead or wounded cartel members. Their only concern was that everything had been done properly within the context of state law and departmental policy.

Scotty held a fist up for Gabby to bump.

"It's good to see that my superior coaching has paid off. Great work putting a round into Sanchez."

"Yeah, but I only hit him in the arm," she chuckled self-consciously.

"The arm that he doesn't have anymore. That was as tough as it gets, shooting and hitting your target in a car chase."

"Of course, Chuck has to be the overachiever of the group," Jimmy laughed, pointing at McCain. "Are you sure you weren't a Marine at some point in your life? Maybe in a past life? Making a head shot shooting backwards is pretty impressive."

"Plus, he took out Ramon Contreras and his minions not long ago," Andy added.

"All I know," Chuck shrugged, "is that everything we do is a team effort and this is a team of some extreme badasses."

Hollywood smiled. "We've killed a lot of cartel soldiers over the last few weeks."

"Like the boss always says," Chloe interjected, "some people just need killing."

McCain asked Tex to join him in his office after they wrapped up the group meeting.

"I just wanted to check in with you and see how you're doing? You came to work for Century as an instructor and we've had you doing some crazy stuff over the last couple of months."

The rangy former SWAT officer gave Chuck a slight smile.

"I'm good, Boss. I wasn't sure how I was going to like it, moving into a purely teaching mode. In Atlanta, I was a full-time SWAT cop and got to teach firearms in the police academy on the side. This has been a pleasant surprise."

"I'm glad to hear it. We're sure happy to have you— both as an instructor and as a reserve deputy. Andy told me you did a great job at that shootout when those thugs attacked his home."

Davis laughed. "I appreciate that. I managed to drop a couple of the bangers, but Andy and Gabby are serious operators. They killed the other six."

Chuck nodded. "They're good. Gabby, especially, has come a long way fast. She's probably one of the best computer hackers in the world but she's become very dangerous on a tactical level, as well. We're due to train with my friend, Jay, in a couple of weeks. He's a retired SEAL and has made us all better. You'll enjoy it."

Tex's eyes lit up. "That's what I'm talking about! Is he a contract instructor?"

"No, he works for another government agency. I first got to know him when he was working for CDC Enforcement out of DC during the zombie crisis. He trains us a few times a year because we're friends and who doesn't need a little extra money?"

"Thanks, Chuck. It'll be nice to meet him. I'm really glad to be here at Century and just know that you can depend on me. For anything."

After Tex headed back to his cubicle, Chuck got the sense that when the former SWAT officer said that McCain could depend on him for anything, Davis might just suspect that Century Tactical Solutions was involved in more than training, private investigations, or helping out the local sheriff's department. Maybe I need to have a chat with Kevin at the Agency about reading Tex in as another contractor. The past couple of months had been intense, but Chuck knew better than to relax completely. With all that was going on in the world, the big man knew that it was just a matter of time before Colonel Clark had another mission for him and his team.

**One month later, Reston, Virginia, Thursday, 1935 hours**

"Any idea what this is about?" Elizabeth McCain asked her husband, picking up Ray for Chuck to kiss goodnight.

"See you tomorrow, buddy," Chuck told his son, kissing him on the cheek.

"He told me he had some information about a case that he knew I'd want to hear and he wanted to give me something. I forget—have you been around Joe that much?"

"Maybe once or twice," Beth answered, "but he always comes across as gruff and unpleasant."

"That's Joe," Chuck smiled, "but he's really just a big teddy bear, at least that's what Gabby thinks."

FBI Supervisory Special Agent Joe O'Reilly had called Chuck earlier in the day, asking if he could drop by the big man's home that evening. A knock at the door alerted them that their guest had arrived. The burly man accepted Chuck's hand and invitation to come in, clearly out of his element.

"Joe, you remember my wife, Elizabeth, and our son, Ray?"

The G-Man nodded at her and the toddler. "I apologize for the intrusion, Mrs. McCain. I won't be long."

"Please come in, Agent O'Reilly, and have a seat. Can I get you something to drink?"

O'Reilly hesitated, but McCain spoke up. "I was just about to pour myself a bourbon. Can I fix you one?"

"Well, if you insist," Joe answered, a smile creeping onto his face as he looked around the room.

Boxes were stacked around the living room as the McCain's prepared to move. Everyone's house in Haymarket was completed and Chuck and Beth, along with their friends, had already started moving things into their new homes.

"I forgot that you were moving. Didn't you tell me you were building a house out in the country?"

"That's right. Us, the Smiths, Flemings, Donaldsons, and Eric Gray got a deal on a piece of land near Haymarket and decided to build close to each other. After we get settled, I'll invite you for a cookout."

"Good for you," Joe said quietly. "And I'd enjoy that."

A few minutes later, they were seated in the living room, each holding a tumbler of Buffalo Trace Kentucky Straight Bourbon.

"That's good stuff," O'Reilly said appreciatively. "Very smooth."

"Yes, it is."

After another sip, Joe set the glass down. "Thanks for letting me drop by. First, I wanted to give you some good news. Early this morning, we raided two New Generation sex operations in Frederick, Maryland. We rescued eight children and four teenagers that those animals were pimping out. This was Chilo Barajas' operation. Evidently, they didn't miss a beat with him being in jail. We arrested five bad guys, including a woman who evidently helps run the houses."

"That's great news, Joe! Congratulations! Thank God you were able to get those kids out of there. How'd y'all develop that information?"

Joe picked his bourbon up and took another swallow before giving a slight smile.

"Every now and then, we get it right, McCain. That intel dump you provided actually helped us locate the two brothels."

"I thought everything on that flash drive was connected to the Sinaloas?"

"It is. One of the Sinaloa bangers we arrested on an outstanding federal parole warrant was actually pretty smart. When we interviewed him, he told us straight up that he wasn't telling us anything about the Sinaloas but that he did know some of the NG's deep, dark secrets. He worked out a deal with the AG's office. Since it turned out to be good information, he'll probably get a reduced sentence."

Chuck nodded, sipping his whiskey. "That's pretty slick. Again, thank God you freed those kids."

"I thought you'd want to know after all the time and energy you put into taking down Ramon Contreras and Eduardo Sanchez. I can't even imagine the hell those children have been through but at least now, we can get them some help and give them a chance at having a normal life."

They sipped their bourbon in silence for a couple of minutes before O'Reilly slid a manila folder across the coffee table towards McCain. Chuck set his tumbler down and picked it up, flipping it open.

"This looks a lot like a resume, Joe."

"It is. I put my retirement papers in this morning, after the raid. I figure it's good to go out on top and it would be hard to beat shutting down two cartel brothels and rescuing a bunch of children who were being trafficked. If you were serious about having something for me at Century, I'll be available in a couple of weeks."

"Sandra and I were talking earlier in the week about needing someone with your background in her section. Let me have a chat with her and the general in the morning and I'll call you to set up an interview. Your buddy, Thomas Burns, is getting a lot of frequent flyer miles teaching interviews and interrogations at police academies around the country.

"We're also getting more and more inquiries from big companies, asking us to take on some corporate espionage cases. The Chinese, especially, are doing a lot of bad things but, as you know, the Bureau doesn't have the manpower to look into every one of them. How does that sound?"

Joe shrugged. "Why not? I'm done with the politics and bureaucracy. I guess I've just reached the age where I don't have the patience for it anymore."

"You know most everyone at Century. General Perkins is as good as they come and we work hard but have a good time. Burns is sure loving it."

"I think he's loving being around Ms. Dunning."

"That may be but he does great work. I think having you on board would really solidify the intelligence and investigations section."

O'Reilly finished his bourbon and stood, extending his hand. "I'll get out of your hair, Chuck, but thanks for the opportunity. And no matter how much shit I talk, I look forward to working with you guys."

After McCain let the FBI agent out, he realized that was the first time O'Reilly had ever used his first name. Maybe we really are becoming friends, he thought with a smile.

## Free Excerpt from *When the Future Ended- Volume One of the Zombie Terror War Series*

### Outside of Commerce, Georgia, Wednesday, 1700 hours

Mostafa Alamouti taped shut the last cardboard box from his laboratory. Today was the day that he would leave and start over in another city. He had infected almost one hundred different packages of medicine over the last three weeks. His wife, Fatemeh, smuggled the drugs out and then back into the distribution center of PharmaSource, a leading pharmaceutical manufacturer.

Fatemeh's job in their warehouse had made it easy for her to get her hands on what her husband had requested. She slipped a few different medicines into her purse each afternoon. Mostafa treated them by opening the package and using a dropper to add a small amount of the virus to the pills and then drying them under a heat lamp. If the medicine was a liquid, he just opened it and added a few drops to the bottle, put a small amount of glue on the plastic safety ring, and then closed it up.

Fatemeh then took the drugs back to work with her. They had been shipped out to customers all over the country. There had not been any news reports of anyone infected yet but that would change soon.

This was the first step in a much bigger terror attack on America. The same process was being repeated in other cities throughout the United States. Drugs that had been infected with the virus had been mailed out to their victims for the last three weeks. This was Phase One of the Jihad against America. As people began to get sick and as the virus began to work, it would take the government a while to figure out what was going on as people began to die, with some of them turning into monsters. Then it would be time for Phase Two.

An hour earlier, Mostafa had received a text from Amir that said in Farsi, "It would be good if you could leave as soon as possible. Alone." The message was clear. Something had gone wrong. The FBI or the police knew something and were coming to get him. But he could not leave without packing up his lab. There was too much evidence and too much of the virus that he could not leave behind.

The message was also clear that he was to leave alone. His wife would have to become a martyr. They had been assigned to work together on this mission by Amir al-Razi. Their marriage had been more of convenience than of love but he had grown to enjoy her company. No matter. Mostafa had his orders.

His first allegiance was to Allah and to the Jihad that was about to be unleashed on American soil. Al-Razi was his boss and if he said that Fatemeh needed to be eliminated, there must be a reason for it. After he left, Mostafa and Amir would meet at a predetermined location and he would receive his new orders.

The boxes from his lab just needed to be loaded into his car and he would be ready to leave. Mostafa had one last thing that he needed to take care of. Fatemeh did not suspect anything. She just assumed her husband had been in the lab working.

He came back into the house and asked her to prepare them a cup of tea. When she stepped over to the cabinet to get the sugar, he poured a small vial of liquid into her tea. His plan was to finish his drink and then leave. By then, the virus would have done its work and the responding police or FBI agents would have a special surprise waiting for them.

Fatemeh drank her tea but made a face. "Something is wrong with this tea. It tastes bitter."

"I don't know," Mostafa shrugged. "Mine tastes ok."

"So, what's next? You said we'd be wrapping up our work here pretty soon."

"As a matter of fact, I'm going to meet with Amir later tonight," he told her. "He wants to give us our next assignment. I'll let you know what he says," he lied.

She nodded. "It'll be good to leave here, maybe go to another state. Amir scares me. He seems like a very dangerous man."

If you only knew, he thought.

The sounds of the front gate opening and a vehicle pulling in startled them. Mostafa felt a moment of panic. He touched the Makarov pistol he had pushed into his waistline. Who was he fooling? He was a scientist. He had been given some weapons familiarization from the Iranian Ministry of Intelligence and Security when he went through his training but he knew that he did not stand a chance against the American police.

He glanced at Fatemeh. She was looking into her cup of tea, her eyes not focusing. There were beads of sweat on her forehead.

Alamouti rushed into the front room and looked out the window. The panic gave way to relief. He saw the big pickup truck and trailer of the lawn maintenance crew.

The fat one, Jose, the owner of the company, came to the front door. He always knocked to let them know that they were there before they started working on the yard. Mostafa needed to get rid of them quickly. He opened the door about a foot.

"Hola, Señor. How are you today?" said Jose.

"I'm fine. Listen, I really don't need you today. Can you come back tomorrow?" His English was flawless, with just a hint of a British accent.

Mostafa heard a sound from the kitchen that sounded like an animal growling.

"But Señor, today is the normal day for your yard. We're already booked up for tomorrow."

"I'm sorry but I have a lot going on and..." Something grabbed at his left arm and bit down. Fatemeh had his forearm in her mouth. Her teeth were digging deep.

Mostafa gasped in pain and stepped backwards. The front door swung open and Jose saw Mrs. Alamouti biting her husband's arm. A growl was coming from deep in her throat. Blood was dripping onto the floor and Mostafa was trying to pull his arm free.

"Señor, Señora, que esta pasando?"

Jose stepped into the house but he didn't know what to do. He reached out his hand to try and pull Fatemeh off of her husband. She quickly released her grip on him and bit down on Jose's right hand. He managed to jerk it free, ripping the flesh. The pain was intense. Then she grabbed his right arm and bit down on his forearm.

"Señor, please make her stop!"

"Help me get her into a bedroom. Come on, grab her," Mostafa said, "and let's take her down the hall."

He grabbed his wife by the collar and the back of her belt and started pulling her towards the hallway. She turned and bit Mostafa's other arm.

"Come on. Help me get her down the hall."

Jose did not want to do anything but leave, but he grabbed the crazy woman's right arm and helped the man drag her. She turned and bit Jose again, this time on the other arm. He promptly let go.

Mostafa was able to drag his wife down the hallway and propel her into the last bedroom on the right. He quickly shut the door.

He looked at the injured lawn man. "I'm so sorry about that, but thanks for your help. She's not been feeling well today."

"Señor, she bit me bad. I'm bleeding. Look at my arms!"

"I'm very sorry. Of course, I'll pay for your doctor bills. Just send them to me."

Jose turned and went back outside. Mostafa knew that he was as good as dead. The fat man would be an extra surprise for the police.

He also knew that he was in trouble. The infection was, no doubt, already coursing through his own veins. She had broken the skin on both of his forearms and it was definitely enough to have infected him. Her teeth had dug deep.

For now, he would leave Fatemeh in the bedroom. He was starting to feel dizzy and he felt the sweat on his forehead. Alamouti knew that the virus was unpredictable but he also knew that his time was short. There was no way he was going to allow himself to turn into one of those things.

By the time he got outside, Jose was not feeling well. That crazy woman had really chewed him up. His young employee, Juan, had started to unload their equipment.

"Hey, Juan, look at this. That woman who lives here bit me."

The young man walked over to see what his boss was talking about. He saw the blood on Jose's arms and his eyes got big.

"A woman did that to you? It looks like you got attacked by a lion."

"She bit me, she bit her husband. She was growling like a dog or something. I'm not feeling so good. I need to sit down for a minute."

He opened the passenger door of his truck and grabbed a roll of paper towels from the floor to staunch the flow of blood. Jose was hot and it wasn't because of the weather. He was sweating profusely. He tried to apply pressure to his wounds but was having trouble holding onto the paper towels.

Juan walked around to the back of the house to look at the yard. He wanted to make sure that there was nothing lying in the grass that might damage their big mower. As he walked back towards the truck, Jose was walking towards him.

"Hey, Jose. You don't look so good, man. Are you sure you're OK?"

Jose did not answer but kept coming closer.

"Man, why don't you just sit in the truck and rest. I'll do this."

Juan heard a sound like a growling dog. He looked behind him to see where it was coming from. He didn't think these people had a dog. Then he felt hands. He turned back and saw Jose was right in front of him. He had hold of Juan's head and was pulling him towards his mouth.

"No, Jose, stop!" He tried to push his boss away but the fat man was too strong. He felt teeth biting into his neck.

Mostafa was unsure what to do. What was Allah's will? His car wasn't packed yet but by now it probably didn't matter. He could turn into one of those things at any time.

He walked back to the living room and looked out the window. He felt hot and feverish. Both of his arms had been bitten and he didn't even try to stop the bleeding. What was the point? He had heard nothing more from the lawn guys.

He saw movement on the street. Someone was in front of his house. Four men wearing black shirts, two of them carrying rifles. It has to be the FBI, he thought. They were almost to his gate. Alamouti drew his pistol. He thought about waiting until they approached the house and then shooting as many of them as he could before they got him. He thought that he could kill at least one, maybe even two of them, before they shot him.

The problem with shooting at the police, though, was that they would shoot back and they might only wound him. Then, he would be arrested and interrogated by the authorities. They would eventually break him. He knew he was not strong enough to resist for very long. He knew that he would eventually talk.

The other, much more likely, possibility, however, was that he would turn into a monster. He was a loyal servant of Allah, but he had decided early on in this mission that he would not allow himself to turn into one of those creatures. Mostafa made his decision and ran towards the rear of the house.

**END OF PREVIEW**

# Additional Books by David Spell

## The Zombie Terror War Series

*When the Future Ended*
*The Darkest Part of the Night*
*When the Stars Fell from the Sky*
*Running Towards the Abyss*
*Climbing Out of the Ruins*
*Where the Vultures Gather*

## The Chuck McCain Series

*Storm Clouds Rising*
*Between Destiny and Duty*
*Actionable Intelligence*
*A Violation of Conscience*
*Diablo's Dust*

Made in the USA
Columbia, SC
06 June 2024